SHIT SHOW

More Books by Arthur Nersesian
The Fuck-Up
Dogrun
Manhattan Loverboy
Suicide Casanova
Chinese Takeout
Unlubricated
East Village Tetralogy (4 Plays)
Mesopotamia
Gladyss of the Hunt

The Five Books of
Robert Moses`(series)
The Swing Voter of Staten Island
The Sacrificial Circumcision of the Bronx
The Terrible Beauty of Brooklyn
The Postmorphogenesis of Manhattan
The Cognitive Contagion of Queens

SHIT SHOW

Arthur Nersesian

EPONYMOUS
BOOKS

ISBN-9798991509114

Eponymous Books

www.eponymousbooks.com

Cover Art: Kim Kowalski

Copyright 2024 Arthur Nersesian

Printed in the USA

EPONYMOUS
BOOKS

Thank you, dear friends

Mary Forsell

Michael Granville

Luciano Guerriero

Kurt Hollander

Donald Kennison

Earl Wallace

Acknowledgements

Coree Spencer, Anne Spencer, Paul Lembo, Shannon Spencer, David Malaxos, J.C. Hopkins, Agnes Field, Grace Higgins, Lisa Najavits, Linda DeBruyn, Jeff Vari, Jennifer Belle, Claire DeBrunner, Kim Kowalski, Johnny Temple & to the memories of Patricia A. Burke and Faina Koss.

Also special thanks to members of my writing workshop:

Francis Levy, Heidi Boghosian, Joseph Silver, Michael Avery, Tommaso Fiacchino, and Henry Alcalay

1

Eric Stein, New York City, March 1999

A weathered, slightly warped paperback entitled Kasabian's Tales: The Selected Stories of Haig Kasabian, published by Progress Publishers, Moscow ©1969 was the only prose on Eric Stein's small shelf, otherwise packed with heavy hardcover financial books. Its slimness caught the old man's eye and pulled David Lande to the book.

The ninety-five-year-old real estate tycoon, David Sr., and his sixty-four-year-old son, David Jr., had an appointment at the Midtown investment firm of Kaye & Oden. Founding partner Samuel Kaye greeted them in the reception area. The old man was in a wheelchair, pushed by an attendant. Kaye led the three to Stein's office to hastily retrieve a file. That was when the old man glanced at Stein's tiny book-shelf and grabbed the book from his wheelchair.

"Dad, we should get going," the son said as the old man kept flipping through the pages of the paperback. Samuel Kaye was trying to lead them to his sumptuous corner suite a few doors down.

"I briefly met him years ago," Eric volunteered. It had been a long day and, without intending it, Stein had erred – he had actually met the writer's assistant.

Lande opened the paperback and gasped when he read the inscription written in Cyrillic, Сыну, о котором я всегда мечтал and signed by the late Haig Morozov Kasabian.

"Oh my god!" the old man gasped and mumbled something that could've been in Russian. Lande's son, who leaned on a cane, was impressed when he saw tears instantly come to his father's dull eyes as he stared at the young VP seated before him. For some reason, the inscription scribbled in Stein's ragged book had instantly moved the old man – something the son very rarely saw.

"You okay, Dad?"

"We were childhood friends back in the old country," Lande slowly whispered.

1

"Wow! You were with him when you were young," Stein said.
"I was actually with him when he died."

"So," Lande paused. "You were in Russia?"

"In fact I was, yes," said Stein tiredly. He had visited there in '88, just after Gorbachev's appointment. Again, he didn't intend to deceive the old man, but had reinforced his original error. It didn't even occur to Lande that Stein had actually been born a year after the writer, Kasabian, had died.

"How's your mother?" Lande asked, reaching out to Stein, who offered his hand.

"My mother?" asked Stein.

"Yes."

He squeezed Stein's hand as he stared deep into the younger man's bewildered eyes.

Eric saw the small memorial plaque on the edge of his desk due to the money he had donated to the cancer research foundation and assumed he was responding to that.

"Oh! She passed on a few years ago from ovarian cancer." Both Lande Jr. and Samuel Kaye looked on perplexed.

"I'm so, so sorry," the old man said, wiping his tears. Before Stein could add that his father was still going strong, Lande nudged the attendant who pushed his father's wheelchair out of the room.

A week later, Samuel Kaye came into Stein's office. Pointing at the single book of fiction, he said, "That commie writer you met might've done you a big capitalist favor."

"What are you talking about?"

"You made a real impression on old Diamond Dave. The old man keeps asking me about you."

"Who's Diamond Dave?" Stein asked.

"David Lande – the "e" is silent. That's what they used to call the old man."

"Diamond Dave? I didn't see any diamonds."

"Rumor was, early on, he used to buy properties with diamonds."

"Diamonds?"

"You know Cartier on Fifth Avenue was supposedly purchased with a string of pearls."

"Sounds unlikely."

"Forty years ago you couldn't give away real estate in this city. If someone offered you a diamond, even a small one for a brownstone in the ghetto, you took it quick."

"Well, he never gave me no diamond," Eric kidded.

"He might eventually. His son is coming over soon. Should be here in an hour. When my secretary buzzes, I'd like you to join us for a martini."

"I'd be honored," he said.

Sure enough, within an hour he got a call from the secretary. Eric went to the boss' lavish corner office which had a large balcony and a million-dollar view. Twenty minutes later, the three men were sitting outside, overlooking the southeastern corner of Central Park.

David Lande, Jr. told Eric about how his father had escaped Communist Russia back in the mid-1920s. He settled in New York City, changed his name, and took an Italian wife. They lived in the grimy Lower East Side where he worked hard as a street merchant, just learning the language and absorbing the culture.

"Wow! That's the long road up!"

"It wasn't easy."

David Junior described how by the end of World War Two, second-generation immigrant families, like his, finally earned their way out of the rat-infested tenements. They began flooding into the newly burgeoning suburbs. As they evacuated out into western Jersey, eastern Long Island and southern Connecticut, his old man began buying up their vacant buildings and rundown brownstones and staking claims on abandoned properties in the expanding ghettos of the city.

"Where exactly did he buy?" Eric asked.

"You name it. Entire city blocks were being abandoned overnight. It was like people fleeing a sinking ship—the city was going under," Lande Junior replied.

"It must've been like picking up gold," Kaye said.

3

"At the time, it was actually a big gamble. People nowadays don't remember when it looked like New York was going the way of Detroit. It was all going back to the weeds."

"Where'd he get the capital?" Eric asked.

"He never really talked about it," his son replied, "but frankly I think he got it from the street. He had a lot of rough friends back then."

"I hope your father isn't mobbed up," Kaye said jokingly.

"No, if you do business with the mob, you end up dead or get absorbed by them and Dad was never mob." Eric was going to ask about the diamond rumors, but one look in Kaye's twitchy eyes and he knew better.

The son explained how his dad soon drew up his own map and made his own red lines: Outer Borough Park, Outer Bensonhurst, the Polish and Hasidic edges of Williamsburg, while avoiding the more entrenched areas, like Bed-Stuy, Fort Greene, Bushwick, East Flatbush. Neighborhoods that were too far gone.

"Sounds like Black neighborhoods were in the red, and gray neighborhoods were in the black," Eric kidded.

"Back in the 1950s, he'd take me on buying sprees through the city," said Lande. "I'd watch him inspect the abandoned buildings, checking how sound the structures were. Electricity and plumbing were usually gone. When I turned sixteen, he put me in charge of all the legal filings."

"Wow."

He'd send in his mothball crew. First, they would drop arsenic for the rats. They'd nail the roof and basement doors shut. They'd put up signs warning about the penalties of trespassing. The windows of the bottom two floors were always shattered. The crew would knock out the glass frames and cover them in sheet metal. They'd cinderblock the front and back doors. But it never mattered. Within weeks, the junkies or gangs would break in.

He went on to say that when he joined the family business back in 1958, they owned one hundred fifty-three parcels scattered throughout Brooklyn, Queens, and the Bronx. Those that weren't completely empty were rarely half full.

4

"But by the 1980s," Eric declared, "you guys were rich."

"We were old-fashioned slumlords. During the '60s and '70s, Lande Inc. barely broke even. We were mortgaged to the hilt. Dad did everything from legal work to major repairs just trying to keep expenses down and hold his little empire together."

"So he knew the city would eventually come back."

"Hell no, it was a big gamble. And we got an awful reputation in LT Court. By the early '80s, I sold off some of the more desirable parcels and used the money to improve property management. Almost a hundred years old and he still monitors every cent that goes out."

"That sounds like my wife," Eric replied.

After Lande Junior finally left, Sam Kaye said, "For some mysterious reason they've taken a real shine to you."

"I can't imagine why."

"Eric, what I'm about to tell you is highly confidential. Oden is looking to make some deep cuts in the next quarter. Lots of people are going to be let go. If you can develop this friendship with Lande, give Oden some reason to hope that you can be our liaison with Lande Properties, I think I can protect you for a while."

Stein smiled. The old partner was his guardian angel. Eric had been noticeably dragging lately. His best years were clearly behind him, but he couldn't afford to retire.

Lande Jr. stayed in touch with Stein, and in May he invited Eric to a fundraiser at the Museum of Modern Art, which Eric attended, knowing the relationship could someday prove to be valuable.

Shortly after, on June 9, 2000, Eric Stein was surprised to read about the passing of Lande's father in *The Wall Street Journal*. It said there would be a private service. Over the next few days he was a bit concerned that neither he nor his boss, Sam Kaye, were invited to the funeral. He sent a dozen long-stem roses and a condolence card, and wondered if he had done or said something wrong at the museum event.

5

2

Nearly thirty years earlier, on Monday, August 11,1969, just after dinner-time, a firmly seated sixteen-year-old Eric Stein confessed to his older brother Josh that he had an erection for over an hour, and it was showing no sign of abating.

"You're kidding!"

He explained that he had just run into a classmate in Washington Square Park. "Anna O'Brien is, by far, the hottest, hippest chick in my entire class." Both were attending Stuyvesant High School. He was near the top of his class and she was near the bottom, but both were scheduled to graduate in June 1971. He went on to say that Anna told him that she just celebrated her sixteenth birthday and her big gift to herself was finally seeing "the great Jimi Hendrix," so she was desperately looking for a ride to the Woodstock Music Festival upstate this coming weekend.

"I tell you, dude," Eric said, "If I had a car, I'd be in fucking paradise."

"They actually moved the concert from the town of Woodstock to Bethel," Josh said. "They lost their original permit."

"So what?"

"So, I'm going near there in a big empty car," he half-kidded. "If you like, I can take her with me."

"No way!"

Josh was obliged to take a volunteer camp counselor job for the month of August working at nearby Ten Mile River Boy Scout Camp, which was only about ten miles away from the concert site. Although he didn't say another word about it, that night while lying in bed, Josh had a revelation—he decided he was going to try to help his younger brother pop his cherry.

The next day, when the two brothers were alone at the breakfast table, he asked Eric, "So how would you like to spend the weekend with this hot chick?"

"I could never pull it off," said young Eric, refilling his bowl with Wheaties.

"Why not? What would you need?" Josh asked.

"Well, money for starters. I just bought my Hi-fi! I'm freaking broke."

"I can lend you some cash."

"Cut it out! Mom and Dad would never go for it."

"We just tell them you're going upstate with me for my first weekend in a Boy Scout camp. And I'll drive you guys up to the concert. You spend the weekend there and take the bus back Sunday."

"You don't think they'll figure out that there's a big music festival up there?"

"They're clueless," Josh said, lowering his voice.

"You're making me nervous, man!" Eric said.

"If you don't want to do this, that's fine. But if you do *want* to do this, I'm willing to help you."

"I can't think of anything in the whole universe that I'd rather do than spend the weekend balling Anna O'Brien, but..."

"Why don't you call her and ask her what the situation is?" Josh added. "Maybe she already found a ride. Or maybe she's got a girlfriend who has a country house up there and you guys can sleep in some cottage out back."

Josh had a point. It was worth checking out. They had sat side by side in the same writing class for their sophomore year, reading their heartfelt poems aloud. In the back of his poetry notebook, he found her phone number. Later that afternoon, after Josh left, Eric got up the courage to bring the phone into the bathroom and call her. An older female voice picked up.

"Hi, is Anna O'Brien there?"

"This is Anna's mother, and who might you be?" She had a noticeable brogue.

"My name is Eric, Eric Stein—'m in her writing class at Stuyvesant taught by Mr. Blaustein."

7

"Anna! It's your classmate Eric Stein!" she hollered. Apparently, he said the right words.

A moment passed before Anna picked up and asked, "How'd you get my number?"

"You gave it to me last year, when I told you I might be able to get you tickets for..."

"Oh yeah! What's up?"

"Are you still looking for a ride up to Woodstock this weekend?"

"Hell yeah! Do you know someone who's going?" Her voice grew quieter.

"Sorta, my brother works a few miles from the festival, so I was thinking of hitching a ride with him. But I'm just wondering what it will entail."

"Entail?"

"Yeah, do we need to bring sleeping bags and money and stuff, 'cause I'm not sure I have all that stuff."

"Well, frankly I was just looking for a ride alone. Not a partnership."

"Oh, I might've misunderstood."

"Actually there's going to be a zillion people up there, so if you want to go up there with me, I guess we can pool our resources," she said.

"So what resources would we need to pool?"

"I have about a dozen friends with cars and vans all going up. They're going to have, like a three-day party. They have everything but car space or I would go with them."

"But would they have extra food or sleeping bags?" Eric asked.

"Just the opposite, they've got more than they can handle. They were going to give food out at the festival. And I know they've got blankets and tents. I'm telling you all we got to do is get our butts up there and we're fine."

"Where exactly would we meet them?"

"I can't tell you, but I can show you if you get me there." The remark sounded suspicious.

"Well I can get us up there, but I can't get us back."

"If we can get up there," she said assuredly, "my friends'll probably have enough space to give us a ride back."

"So, your parents are cool with you going up there all alone?" he asked. "'Cause the only chance I have of going up there is by lying to my parents."

"Oh, my mom and I have a very adult relationship," she assured him.

"Well, let me speak to my brother and make sure he's on board," Eric said. The thought of going off alone with someone who had little money and hazy plans began to concern him.

By dinner-time that evening, he started having doubts about the prospect of going up to Woodstock with Anna O'Brien, and he confessed it to Josh.

"Listen," his brother replied. "Most older people I know are depressed, and you want to know why? 'Cause they were afraid to do what they really wanted with their lives."

"Maybe 'cause it's risky."

"Everything is a risk, but very few things are really dangerous. This is 1969 and we're in the greatest country in the world. You're not going to starve or die. This could be the best weekend of your whole life. I mean, this young babe asked *you* to go up there with her. I mean, you are going to be alone with her for three fucking days! And the music will be out of sight!"

"But she's a little ditsy," Eric began softly. "I don't know her that well. And I have no clue who we'll be staying with, or what I'm going to be eating. I mean, it sounds like some big love-in."

"Worst comes to worst, you grab the next bus back. What's the big deal?"

"Money, for one thing."

"I told you, I'll loan you a twenty."

"Can you loan me forty dollars just in case?"

"Twenty is all I can spare."

"Suppose I go all the way up there with her and nothing happens?"

"All we can really do is put ourselves in a position where the opportunity for joy might occur."

"That sounds pretty remote."

"Maybe. But you don't want to look back at the summer of 1969 every day of your life as you grow fat and old and say, *I had a chance to nail the hottest chick in my high school class and I passed it up.*"

"Unless of course I look back and say, remember the most excruciating weekend of my life when I almost starved and died of blue balls," Eric kidded.

"At least you won't regret not trying. And most people really do! It's the *what ifs* in life that kill you," Josh said. "And for the record, if nothing else, you'll be going to one great rock show."

Eric didn't have the courage to say that, although he liked rock music, he simply didn't share the enthusiasm of Josh or most kids of his generation. When he awoke the next morning, he was overwhelmed with a very precise vision, which he suspected was prophetic—going all the way up there, getting into a massive fight with Anna, then being separated and robbed and beaten in some hillbilly town, then getting sick and dying in the woods. At the very least, even if they made it back alive, she'd probably spread rumors about what a wimp he was to all his classmates at school.

3

Alexei Novikov, NYC, Friday, August 15, 1969

Lying in bed in his Midtown Manhattan hotel room, experiencing intermittent chest pains, Alexei Romanovich Novikov wondered if he was having a heart attack. When his hotel phone rang, he picked it up and held it to his ear without saying a word.

"Alexei!" said a voice in Russian. "How would you like to see Charles Parker singing? I got good tickets to see him and the others." It was his old buddy Sergei Hagopian whom he had last seen over a decade earlier in Moscow.

"Charlie Parker died fourteen years ago and he actually played the saxophone. He didn't sing," Novikov corrected him, also

10

speaking in Russian. Sergei knew that his old friend loved American jazz, but he knew little else about the music.

"Okay, not Parker, but all the others."

"What others?"

"Come on! You're finally in America! You won't have this opportunity ever again!"

"Perhaps, but..."

"First we'll have a nice steak dinner," the Armenian pushed, "then we'll go see this jazz festival, yes?"

"I didn't think you even liked jazz," Alexei replied.

Alexei had called his old friend a week ago just before leaving Moscow. Sergei Hagopian, who was an attaché at the Armenian consulate in New York, knew that he was going to be in the city to write his big post-moon landing story.

No one had expected the moon landing to be such a big hit for the Americans. Most in Moscow believed it was all faked. How could the Americans have come up with all the technological advances to travel to another planet in only ten years!

The few who thought their extraordinary effort was real were equally sure it'd be a fiery disaster, that the rocket would blow up right on the launch pad, incinerating all three astronauts on international TV. Instead, the lunar landing was a spectacular success and every country was now ecstatic about American democracy. So, Tass and every other Communist news outlet was currently scrambling for propaganda to show that the bloated capitalist giant cared more about extravagant, impractical outer space projects than feeding their own sadly neglected citizens.

Additionally, Alexei's divorce had just gone through. So, instead of sulking at his editor's desk and assigning the story to one of his energetic young foreign correspondents, he took the piece for himself and left his overeager assistant in charge—a mini-vacation. Over the years, he had become quite proficient in English and wanted to see America once before he died. This was the perfect opportunity. As his wife moved out, he could roam around on foreign soil, practice his English, and study his adversaries up close.

After three days of tramping the filthy streets of New York City and interviewing drunken bums on the Bowery, trying to transcribe their scrambled English while not smelling their horrible breath, Alexei noticed a nondescript black car always parked about a block away. It had to be CIA, which was fair as Russian correspondents had to report to the KGB when they returned. By the fourth day however, while being mugged by a dusky youth with a small pocket knife for twenty-four U.S. dollars, the black car was nowhere to be seen. Alexei decided he had as much Western imperialism as he could handle. He was eager to get back to his emptied-out Moscow apartment and begin his bachelor life anew. All that stood between him and his return Aeroflot flight was this one steamy August weekend.

"It's a big outdoor jazz festival," his friend repeated comically. "All the big Negroes will be blowing their horns and banging their tom-toms. You can't see this anywhere but here!"

"My flight is for Monday evening," Novikov tiredly relented.

"Perfect! We'll leave later this afternoon and be back tomorrow night – a bachelors' weekend!"

"Be back? Where are we going?"

"Just outside the city, it's the *Woodstock* Jazz Festival," Hagopian replied.

"Where's that?"

"Brothel, New York."

"Doesn't 'brothel' mean whorehouse?"

Sergei checked his notebook. "Bethel! A sleepy hamlet just north of here. We can sit at a table, sip vodka, eat caviar, listen to live jazz, and meet all these fast American women in their miniskirts and white go-go boots!"

Admittedly, it sounded a lot better than sleeping with whatever diseased hooker happened to be passing by the Summit Hotel on 51st and Lexington Avenue at 1 a.m.

"What time do you want to...." Alexei asked.

"I'll pick you up at three," the Armenian replied.

"See you then!"

It was only 11 a.m. when he hung up the phone and he was hungry. Alexei showered, dressed, and walked west to the towering

12

Art Deco emporium—Rockefeller Center. Pushing through the tourists, he found a subterranean diner that looked out over the sunken skating rink, which held a giant golden statue of Prometheus. There he had eggs and coffee. Afterward, he walked past the grand movie theater Radio City Music Hall, then east, across the big street to the crowded department store Saks Fifth Avenue—where all of New York's fascist elite shopped. The entire time he had an ever-growing smirk on his face. This was the bastion of the notorious Rockefeller family. The grandson of the scion who started the oil dynasty was the current governor of the state. This was the land where money and power went hand in hand. After leaving Saks, he paused before St. Patrick's Cathedral, the giant voodoo factory where superstition was spun to manipulate the brainless masses. This was the final piece of their troika—what further proof was needed of this perverted democracy?

By the time Morozov finally got back to his hotel room, he was experiencing vertigo. He flipped on the television. A movie had just begun, *It's a Wonderful Life*, which he had seen once before in Russian. While packing his bags, he watched it again. Poor George Bailey, portrayed by the actor Jimmy Stewart, was steadily crushed by capitalist deceit until only divine intervention could save him.

He lay down and closed his eyes until he regained his equilibrium. Looking at the far wall, he remembered when he could still see his toes instead of his rising belly. Excessive eating, drinking, and smoking had taken their toll. Once he returned to Moscow, he vowed to start an all-juice diet. This was going to mark a new chapter in his life. He was going to lose weight, dress smartly, and find some young woman who would help return him to his former joys. As he turned off the TV, the hotel room phone rang. The desk clerk announced that his friend "Serge" was out front waiting for him.

"His name is Sergei," Alexei corrected and then dressed. Then he grabbed his suitcases and his portable typewriter. He took the elevator down to the lobby, paid his bill, and joined Sergei who was parked out front in a shiny black Cadillac, the official car from the Armenian Consulate, where a traffic cop was writing him a ticket.

13

When he handed it to Sergei, he immediately tore it up, citing diplomatic immunity, and put his friend's bags in the trunk. As soon as Alexei got inside, he saw the new paperback copy of *Kasabian's Tales, The Selected Stories of Haig Kasabian*, with its bright red cover.

"He beat me here!" Alexei said, grinning at the title.

"What's so funny?"

"They Armenianized him," Alexei said. "Morozov—that was his sole name when I knew him."

"That's right. You worked for him, didn't you?"

"Just long enough to realize fiction was a bad career choice and stay with journalism."

4

Haig Morozov, Moscow, February 1943

Twenty-six years earlier, six thousand miles away in Moscow, a young, slim Alexei Novikov had picked up the esteemed older Armenian writer Haig Morozov Kasabian from the Kurskaya Train Station. A porter followed him with a cart loaded with half a dozen boxes and suitcases. No sooner did Alexei greet him outside the terminal than the writer got in the back seat of his car. Alexei alone loaded his luggage into the trunk of the university's car. As they drove through the city, Morozov was surprised by all the giant zeppelin-shaped barrage balloons that were floating above. Each balloon went up roughly two thousand kilometers, fastened to steel cables, forcing German bombers around them, protecting sacred sites and landmarks.

Morozov's young driver drove circuitously, circumventing countless anti-tank obstacles that had been placed along many of the main streets. As the writer stared up at the passing windows, he noticed all the thick masking tape outlining the panes, clearly taped down to reduce the risk of falling glass due to the bombing.

After twenty minutes, Alexei drove the older writer to Moscow State University.

"Why are we at the University?" the older writer asked.

"They're having a brief meet and greet for you, sir," said his young driver. "Just quick introductions. We can leave your things in the trunk."

Morozov gave a low groan and got out of the car. Due to the cold, few students were outside the sprawling campus.

Alexei escorted Morozov up the long stone steps through the spacious, vaulted entranceway and down into a sunken marble-lined reception hall where a small crowd of academics applauded as he entered.

"It's an honor to meet you," said the chair of the philology department, Alexandrovich. He introduced the writer to some of the senior faculty. For Morozov, it was a rapid succession of handshakes and names he wouldn't ever remember.

When Alexei Novikov glanced up, his eyes touched on two men huddled near the doorway. He knew only one, Ivan Ivanovich Lemokh, his friend and immediate superior. He was a short, thin youth with a long beak and a hawk-like stare. An older, stockier man was behind him.

Ivan Lemokh discreetly waved down at his subordinate just as the heavy man asked, "Ever read Morozov?"

He turned to his pudgy superior, Arkady Davidovich Petrov, and said, "Yes, years ago, back in grade school. Don't remember a word." Then he asked his boss, "Why'd the Morozov get this fellowship anyway?"

"Supposedly, the writer needed to return to Moscow to finish his memoir about growing up here, but Zhdanov is clearly using the opportunity to rub Malenkov's face in it."

"Is that why we're doing all this? Intra-office politics?"

"The great leader is not in great shape," Petrov replied.

"So?"

"You're leading one of the first skirmishes in the next great war."

"A great war for what?"

"Succession of the next great leader," the pudgy man replied, "Six months ago, Andrei Alexandrovich Zhdanov had a bureau chief arrested in Saint Petersburg during the last party purge—he happened to be Malenkov's brother-in-law. Now Malenkov is obliged to take one of Zhdanov's pawns." Petrov paused and said, "Only Morozov is more of a rook or bishop."

"How is this over-the-hill Armenian one of Zhdanov's back pieces?" Ivan Lemokh asked.

"He's one of his theoreticians. Zhdanov gave a famous speech at the Eighth Congress a few years ago. It was based on Morozov's essay lauding the new social realism. Something like that."

"What did the essay say?"

"The language of the proletariat, or some such crap. The essay fleshed out one of Zhdanov's key directives."

"Maybe I can use it to interrogate him," Ivan Lemokh replied.

"Let me warn you again," Petrov said to Alexei's young boss. "This is 1943 not 1938. The old shortcuts no longer work. Beria is tight with Zhdanov. We bring this Armenian in on some flimsy accusation, he's going to take *us* out. Understand? We need solid evidence."

They watched as Alexandrovich, the balding, older chair with sad turtle eyes stepped behind the large oak podium. At the same time, the head of the Adjutant Subcommittee of Literary Fellowships from the Cultural Ministry ushered Morozov to the seat of honor front and center. The rest of the guests and faculty grew silent as old Alexandrovich spoke: "For twenty years Haig Morozov, known here for his wonderful stories, was in self-exile on the edge of the world in the ancient city of Yerevan, Armenia. There, he helped launch the nation's fledgling writer's union, and unified the unions of the neighboring Caucasus countries of Georgia and Azerbaijan." Lowering his voice, smiling, he turned and asked him, "And I believe you're coming to my little symposium next week to give us a talk about your work?"

All chuckled as Morozov smiled and nodded.

"Now he is working on his memoirs, specifically on his formative years here in Moscow where he grew up."

"A very savage place under the Tzar," Morozov interjected.

"Haig Morozov Kasabian is our very first writer to be honored with a hiatus at the newly refurbished Ulanov House. He's back here to edit his chapters about being raised in our great city before the Revolution—a book I personally can't wait to read. Join me in welcoming a great writer back to the city of his birth—Comrade Morozov!" All applauded as he rose to take a bow, then patiently waited for the applause to stop.

"Thanks for this warm reception," the Armenian said, rising to his feet. "For all your kindness, I'd like to toast you!" Morozov lifted his glass. The faculty members did likewise, snatching up half-filled wineglasses that subdivided the tabletop. Morozov stepped into the crowd and all broke into conversational circles. Slowly, the visiting writer made the rounds. The chair of the subcommittee of the Ulanov Fellowship, a tall, thin man, was the first to introduce himself as Professor Slotkin. He said that he routinely taught at least one of Morozov's stories in his classes every semester. The Armenian writer thanked him and shuffled off before a conversation could ensue.

"I'm famished," Morozov confided to Alexei when he spotted a nearly empty platter of lumpfish caviar.

"We can check the school cafeteria."

"Excuse me," said the tall, thin youth who had been lingering in the doorway, "I just wanted to shake your hand, sir."

Morozov gulped down his fourth glass of wine before obliging.

"I've been fascinated by your generation of writers, those who lived through the Revolution, particularly the poets. Frankly, though, there don't seem to be that many left."

Not listening, Morozov turned to Alexei and asked, "Did the cafeteria stop serving lunch?"

"Why do you suppose that Mayakovsky, Yesenin, and so many other fine poets of your generation had such a difficult time of it?"

"No clue. I write short stories."

"Did you have any difficulty... adapting to the new way?"

As Alexei kept looking away, Morozov narrowed his eyes on the young man. "The new way! Who are you again?"

"Ivan Ivanovich Lemokh," he introduced himself. Alexandrovich, the acting chair, edged closer to better hear the two.

"'Did I have trouble adapting to the new way?'" Morozov repeated the phrase.

"I couldn't help but wonder."

"For starters it's not new," he smirked.

"I just meant..."

"We're trying to eliminate the cancer of capitalism that has turned mankind into a slave auction for the rich..."

"I know. I just meant..."

"Apparently you don't, so listen and learn!" He raised his voice angrily. People around him grew silent. Ivan Lemokh politely smiled not wanting to create a scene. "Our great motherland is under attack for this very reason..." Morozov pointed to the black bunting around the podium that he assumed was for the mounting war dead.

"Professor Morozov just arrived from a long train trip," Alexei Novikov intervened. "I'm sure he's tired and hungry."

"We just won in Stalingrad," Morozov resumed, "but the war is far from over. And as far as the difficult time with my generation of writers, I think our best writers are still going strong."

"I think Ivan just meant to ask if there are any poets you like today," the chairman Alexandrovich said, hoping to smooth things over.

"That's precisely what I meant," said the youth.

"Okay, poets," Morozov took a breath and tried to regain his composure. "One of my old favorites who wrote about my native Armenia was Osip Mandelstam. He hasn't published anything in a few years."

"Professor, the cafeteria's closing," Alexei said under his breath. "If you're hungry we should go at once."

"Mandelstam?" asked Ivan Lemokh, surprised. "Osip Mandelstam?"

"It was a pleasure meeting you all," Morozov concluded in a loud voice.

All applauded and Alexei led him out of the large hall.

"So where is this cafeteria?" the older writer asked once they were in the hallway.

18

"It's actually in the neighboring building about five minutes away, and I'll have to enter through the kitchen. Why don't you wait in your office over here, and I'll get some food for you?"

"My office?"

Alexei escorted the writer down a wide polished corridor filled with students and lined with doors, until he came to one, which was unlocked. Alexei led him through a small outer office lined with empty bookshelves to a large inner room with a big desk and a hard, wooden chair. Morozov looked around the spacious room, which was completely bare. "This is my office?"

"Yes, sir." Alexei pointed to the smaller office, "And I think I should be sitting out there."

Morozov collapsed in the chair. In need of a paint job with only a single window, the room had an official chill to it.

"Do you like borscht?" Andrei asked. "I know they make a fresh pot every afternoon."

"Some black tea, please!" Morozov said tiredly as the young man exited. "The thicker the better."

Alone, the writer considered the inquisitive bastard in the reception hall. Only someone from the dreaded NKVD, the secret police, would be so bold as to taunt him with such a leading question of how he was adapting. He had gone through all this before. When he said he needed to return one last time to Moscow before he died, Zhdanov, his old friend and patron, had warned him that the trip would probably prove perilous. He said that due to his growing tension with rivals, his allies would be vulnerable to traps and attacks. Still, Morozov was surprised by such a brazen move so soon.

Five minutes later, Alexei returned with a large bowl of steaming hot soup, a basket of challah and a pot of leafy tea crowded on a small cafeteria tray.

Alexei left the visiting writer with his food, but before he could return to his own desk, the writer said, "I need a favor."

"Of course."

"That empty bookshelf out there, mind if I use it?"

"This is your office, sir."

19

"Good," Morozov said, "In the trunk of your car are six boxes containing my library. I'd like to have some of my books here with me. I find them inspiring. Each box is numbered. Can you bring up the boxes numbered 4, 5, and 6? I'll stock the shelf myself."

"I can bring them all if you like."

"No, the rest are my journals. They're coming home with me."

Minutes later, as the Armenian began slurping the borscht and tea, Alexei returned with the first box. By the time he had carried in the second box, huffing and sweating, the writer had finished the soup and had alphabetically shelved his first box. Fifteen minutes later, Alexei brought in the final box. When Alexei took his seat and caught his breath, Morozov had shelved the last of them.

Other than appearing that Morozov was up on the latest authors of the Writers Union, no one knew what the books actually represented. In the same way that some pagans once hid the identity of their savage gods in the images of Christian saints, Morozov had carefully selected these bland party scribblers to remind him of the wild and supportive authors who he had truly admired during his formative years. Now, nearly all were officially banned. The two poets, who he didn't have to disguise as they were still in print, were Sergei Yesenin and Vladimir Mayakovsky. Both these popular poets were mentioned by the slimy young agent he met in the reception hall. Thirty years ago, he remembered when his best friend Lunz, had introduced him to Yesenin late at a bar one night. This was shortly before the poet had married that crazy Western dancer, Isadora Duncan.

A couple years later he remembered meeting the great iconoclast poet Vladimir Mayakovsky. He was the one who boldly declared that all poetry must serve the Revolution. Both were truly inspiring and had a wonderful sense of humor. Both men killed themselves five years apart. And though officially they were both suicides, rumors circulated that they might've been secretly assassinated.

Seeing another party-line writer on his shelf, Peter Kleibenov, he flipped through the pages of his book. It was typical party tripe, not even trying to tell an honest or original story as to offer an affirmation

20

of political identity to those living in a dream in which they alone are wide awake. The only reason he selected the Kleibenov book was because it reminded him of another unsanctioned writer, also partly Armenian, who he had liked immensely, Viktor Khlebnikov. He called his outlandish work "Futurism," but he couldn't be further from the truth. The future as it turned out was far more bland and conformist than the scant, liberating works Khlebnikov had left behind. He remembered the poet suddenly taking sick and dying at the age of 37. Times were tough and poets usually didn't live long anyway.

Morozov gradually became aware of a muted yet repetitive ringing. When he looked around, he realized it was the phone in the outer office. As he was about to answer the extension on his desk, he heard Alexei's muffled voice.

"No, no! I'm sorry," he heard, "but I must get your name."

Morozov snatched up the extension next to him and asked, "Who is this?"

"Haig! It's me." He heard a gruff voice. "How've you been?"

"I'm sorry, who?"

"Aleksandr Konstantinovich Voronksy."

"Voronsky the critic?" Morozov responded. He had assumed the old Marxist was dead.

"You're probably the last person in all of Russia who still remembers Voronsky the critic. Closest I've come to manuscripts in the past decade is sweeping them up in the Gosizidat offices, where I'm Voronsky the janitor." Alexei hung up his extension.

"I'm hanging up the phone before I get arrested," Morozov said, unamused.

"Wait! I wrote a crucial review of your work early on! Don't deny it, Haig!" he said in an almost playful voice. "It got you noticed by everyone! I just need one small favor in return."

"There are no favors small enough."

"I need to know the whereabouts of someone, then you'll never hear from me again, I promise."

"Who!"

"A children's book writer in Leningrad—Yuvachyov. He writes under the name Kharms."

"How'd you find me?" Morozov asked and growing panicky, he said, "What's that clicking! Who's listening to us?"

"No one, I swear. I read in the *Gazette* that you were selected as the first writer in Moscow University's new writer's residency," Voronsky replied.

"This Kharms character, he's from Leningrad?"

"Yes, and since you're friends with the big commissar up there..."

"If Kharms is up there, I would hardly worry about arrests. The Germans have probably killed him by now." Since September of 1941, the Nazi army had been holding the entire city in a stranglehold and was slowly starving hundreds of thousands to death.

"I think he was arrested just before the invasion," Voronsky pushed. "His wife is worried sick so I thought that maybe you could help."

"The only person I could ask is Commissar Zhdanov and he wouldn't like it."

"It's just a quick question. Only take a minute."

"If he was arrested before the invasion, he's probably been exiled to Siberia, which means he's safer than any of us." No sooner did he complete this remark than the line went dead. Morozov chose to believe that the old critic was satisfied and abruptly hung up.

As he dashed off to the bathroom, he recalled that the irritating critic kept getting into trouble. First he was arrested by the tsar's police, then afterwards, by the Cheka. He hadn't heard from him in years and assumed he had finally been packed off into exile somewhere with so many others.

Presumably, due to old debts owed by countless other writers he had helped—others who knew how to play by the rules—upon returning to Moscow, they must've helped Voronsky get his present custodial position.

Fortunately, Morozov had lost touch with so many writers like Voronsky, an entire community who were lucky enough to escape the arrests, but could never publish again. He knew that for many of them, their need to write still persisted, so they'd quietly circulated hand-copied poems, stories, and essays and would exchange them with others in their silenced community. Morozov also knew that they kept tabs and tried to help each other—writers who somehow managed to survive below the radar. Though he respected them, Morozov also knew that to help any of them would certainly put himself at risk.

When he returned to the little anteroom of his office, he saw someone inside, a woman was sitting with her back toward him at Alexei's desk. When she turned, he saw that it was a beautiful girl in tortoiseshell glasses wearing an out-of-style blouse that was too tight for winter clothes. She was drinking tea and eating apple slices.

"Who are you?" he asked walking up behind her.

She sprang to her feet, spilling her tea.

"Where's my bathroom attendant?" Morozov asked dryly.

"Alexei Romanovich Novikov is no bathroom attendant!" she said through a mouthful of fruit. She swallowed it, rose and said, "He's in class. I'm Darya Lebedova Kotova."

"How can I help you, Miss Kotova?"

"Alexei asked me to take telephone messages for you until he returned."

She stared at him so relentlessly, he finally asked, "Do I know you?"

"Why would you say that?"

"You look familiar," he replied.

"What would you say if I told you..."

Suddenly a messenger from the Philology Department stopped in his office to drop off an intra-office envelope.

"If you told me what?" he asked while twirling open the little red string on the envelope. Inside was an announcement of some upcoming facility meeting.

"Just that I read all your books. I've always been a big fan of your work."

"Then I'm sorry I haven't written more." After a moment, he asked, "Did you get any telephone calls for me?"

23

"Two. The first call had very bad reception. And before I could get a message, the line went dead. The second call was from your assigned housekeeper." Darya picked up a note and paraphrased it. "She said she is making dinner for you at six."

"You really do look familiar," he said.

"You probably saw me at your reception."

"That boy makes me nervous," Morozov confided. "All the young people today are Cheka."

"The police are now called the NKVD," she corrected.

"In my day they were Okhrana," he replied. "Annoying by any name."

"That was the tzarist police, wasn't it?"

"Same people, different name. You're probably one too, aren't you?" he asked blithely.

"'It's a foolish man who doesn't know his own friends,'" she said. It was the title of one of his more popular stories. "Alexei is your best friend. He was protecting you!"

"When did he ever protect me?"

"He hustled you out of the reception hall when you mentioned that Hebrew poet."

"Mandelstam?"

"You said he was great."

"So?

"Alexei said he *disappeared* a few years back."

"Oh!" Morozov said, then muttered in Armenian, "I hadn't heard!"

"If Alexei hated you, he would've let you dig yourself deeper into trouble," she replied. "Not everyone at the reception was friendly."

"I know."

"Can I ask you a question?" Before he could answer, she asked, "Why did you give up your paternal name?"

"Long story. I'm actually hoping to explain it in my memoir," he replied. "Your accent sounds Ukrainian."

"Actually, I was conceived right here in Moscow just like you," she said. "My mother birthed me down there afterward."

24

"I visited Kiev briefly about ten years ago."

"Really? Why?" She seemed surprised.

"A writers' conference," he said.

"Oh."

"It was during the, uh, the famine," he said softly. "A very rough time."

"My country is cursed," she said simply.

"Cursed?"

"My mother died ten years ago during the famine. Now, when we finally recover, we get two giant armies from other countries using our little nation as their battlefield." The girl looked off and nodded dismally.

"I imagine it's tough."

"The constant stench of death and just the exhaust from all the tanks, jeeps, and planes makes the air almost unbreathable. Endless streams of soldiers marching to and fro, taking whatever they want, destroying our homes and buildings, crushing up against each other and leaving only bodies and shit in their wake—what would you call it?"

"What are you talking about?" Alexei asked, suddenly entering.

"Say goodnight to your beautiful friend," Morozov replied, ignoring his question.

"Are you leaving?" Alexei asked Darya.

"No, you're finally driving me home," Morozov said as he marched out the door. "You said we were going to be here for ten minutes and now it's two hours later. Let's go!"

Alexei gave Darya a dry peck on the cheek and caught up with his boss.

5

Eric, NYC, 1969

The day after he decided not to go to the Woodstock Music Festival, Eric Stein heard the phone ringing in the living room. His mom answered it. A moment later, he heard her call out, "Eric, it's your classmate Anna!"

As soon as he brought the phone to his ear, Anna said, "Ask your brother if he can drive us on Friday instead of Thursday."

"No way," Eric replied, seeing this as an opportunity. "He can't do it. He has to report for work on Thursday—so I guess it's off."

"Hell no! We'll just go there a day early is all."

"Oh, okay," he said, completely unable to stand up to her.

"Can you guys come down here and get me?" she said in a little girl voice. "I'm in Chelsea."

"There's no way he'll go into Midtown traffic," he said gaining courage. "You'll have to come up to the Upper West Side." He held his breath again, hoping this would break her resolve.

"Okey dokey," she replied.

"The northwest corner of Ninety-sixth and Amsterdam at three o'clock?" he pushed. "He wants to get a jump on the traffic." They lived on Ninety-fourth and Amsterdam and Josh had already told him that that was when he was planning on ramping onto the Henry Hudson Parkway.

"See you then," she said blithely and hung up.

When Josh returned home about an hour later, Eric said, "So I guess I'm gonna do it."

"Really! You're going upstate with that hippie chick?" Josh asked. Throughout the day he had sensed that his brother was backing out.

"Looks that way," Eric said. Even the remotest possibility of just cupping one of her firm, big breasts was too much to resist. "But I still have one big hurdle—Mom and Dad."

"Let me handle them," Josh said. "We'll wait til dinner. Just let me do all the talking."

"Okay," Eric said nervously.

Over the next few hours, Eric's imagination went wild with the images of all the unholy sex acts until his mother opened his door to put some clothes away.

"How are you doing?" she asked.

"Fine," Eric said, desperately keeping a math textbook on his lap.

Finally at seven p.m., his mother called the boys for dinner. Over meatloaf, mashed potatoes, and steamed broccoli, they touched on the issues of the day. Eric retold some corny jokes that he heard on last night's episode of *Laugh-In*.

"Verrry interesting," his mother joked back.

"Sock it to me," Josh added. All burst out laughing.

Eric's father recapped the latest advances of the Yankees and their chances of winning the playoffs that year. Then he turned on the TV in the middle of the news, and they silently watched some footage of a battle in Vietnam and got that week's casualty count of American troops.

None mentioned, but all dreaded the notion that Eric and Josh might someday be drafted and sent to the fight. The boys cleaned off the dishes and put them in the sink as their mother brought out mugs filled with scoops of Sealtest chocolate ice cream.

"So tomorrow afternoon I'm leaving," Josh said, spooning it into his mouth.

"Don't wait too late," said his father. "You don't want to get caught in the rush."

"A month in the woods," their mother uttered. "Aren't you the lucky one."

"Actually, that's what I was thinking," Josh said, glancing at Eric. "During the first weekend there I'm just getting things ready, and I have the entire bunkroom to myself 'til Monday."

"Afraid of ghosts?" his father teased him.

"Funny you should say that," he replied, "cause I was telling Eric about how it creeped me out a little and he asked if he could join me. And I could actually use his help."

"Out of the question!" their mother said automatically.

"It just seems like a wasted opportunity," he said softly.

"There's no way I'm letting you two alone in the woods for a week," she said.

"Yeah, the deer won't sleep a wink," their dad kidded.

"Not a week, just the weekend. And we wouldn't really be alone," Josh spoke up. "The Boy Scout camp has hundreds of campers including many adult camp counselors."

"And a trained nurse nearby," Eric chimed in.

"Right!" Josh remembered. "Nurse Bridges."

"What exactly would you guys do up there for four days?" their father asked.

"The usual stuff," Josh said. "Hiking, swimming, hanging out with some of the other campers."

"And you say there are other Boy Scout counselors up there?" Their father asked for their mother's benefit. Josh sensed he already won him over.

"Absolutely. There are like a dozen different troops up there at any given time," Josh said. "We could join them around a campfire, roast marshmallows, tell horror stories, fun stuff like that."

"I don't like the sound of this at all," their mother muttered, clearly distressed.

"Jessica," their father appealed, "when I was only a little older than Eric, I was fighting the Japs in the South Pacific..."

"Spare us the war stories!" she shot back angrily.

"They're both young men. They want to spend a hot August weekend with other Boy Scouts in the woods. It's probably safer than Eric being alone in the city. What could go wrong?"

"They could shoot each other!" she said.

"We don't have guns," Josh said.

"You told me you did target practice at some shooting range when you went there."

"Yeah, one of the camp counselors brought his own rifles for his troop, but he took them with him when he left. They don't keep guns up there."

"How would you get back?" Eric Senior asked Eric Junior, knowing that Josh was going to stay for the entire month.

"I can put him on a Trailways Bus on Sunday night," Josh said. "It'd take him right to Port Authority. He can take the train from there."

28

"What if he chooses on a whim to stay longer?" Their mother asked.

"What!" Eric exclaimed.

"He couldn't if he wanted to," Josh retorted. "A new troop is occupying his cabin on Monday, there will be nowhere for him to stay."

As their mother brought the empty ice cream mugs back into the kitchen, Eric Sr followed her out. The boys could hear their parents talking softly in there.

"Congrats, dude," Josh whispered with a smile. "You're gonna pop your cherry."

"You're sure this is the right thing?" Eric asked nervously.

"Without a single solitary doubt," Josh said emphatically.

Suddenly the kitchen door swung open and their father said, "Okay, so against our better judgment your mom and I are going to give you the benefit of our many doubts, but we want you guys to call us every night, understood?"

"No problem," Josh said for Eric, who was too paralyzed with fear to respond.

"I want you guys to be as careful as you can. No unnecessary risks, no trusting strangers, no crazy acts, understand?"

"Yes sir," Eric replied.

"Anything happens 'cause of some dumb stunt on your part..."

"Nothing will," Eric cut in.

"Yeah and no crazy stunts from you guys while *we're* away," Josh kidded back.

The next day, after breakfast, both brothers began preparing. Josh packed his duffle bag for an almost one-month stay, Eric packed his smaller knapsack for the weekend. As Josh looked over and saw him finishing up, slipping the canvas strap through the buckle at the top, he asked Eric, "Aren't you forgetting your sleeping bag?"

"Anna said we won't need one. All we got to do is get up there and they got everything."

"No one brings a spare sleeping bag," Josh said and, reaching into the top shelf of his closet, he took out his light sleeping bag and an air mattress. "This unzips so you can use it as a blanket if you need to and it's really light. You can strap it to the top of your knapsack. The air mattress will make it comfy."

"If I bring it," Eric said, "it'll be like I don't trust her."

"Just say you misheard," he replied. "'Cause if she's wrong, and they don't have a sleeping bag, you're going to be seriously screwed."

"Shit," Eric muttered.

"I think it's supposed to rain this weekend, I'd bring a tent myself."

"No way."

Eric strapped the sleeping bag to the top of his knapsack but left the air mattress. In a few short hours it was time to go. Both boys kissed their parents goodbye and headed out the door to Josh's ten-year-old Chevy Impala parked on Ninety-third and Amsterdam.

6

Kasabian, Moscow, 1943

It was pitch black when Alexei finally drove Morozov to the guest residence at the Ulanov House, several streets away from the university. While passing through the neighborhood, the Armenian writer silently noted the various business establishments along the route. A grocery store was two blocks away as was an old movie theater. A rundown bathhouse was just around the corner. Also, there was a new pharmacy where he could get some snuff for his constantly blocked sinuses. Though there were definite changes to Moscow, the city of his youth was subtly breaking through.

During his teenage years, the final gasps of the Romanovs' reign, young Morozov found himself more and more intrigued by the concepts of Russian communism and all the shadow committees that the Bolsheviks would swiftly organize. Like a band of sorcerers, they were nearly metaphysical and highly alluring, with remedies for all the ills of the great nation, committees for food, housing, even for the weather. If there was any problem, they would start a committee. Though it did nothing to relieve the suffering, it allowed people to believe that once in power these issues would at least be addressed. His street-bitten friend, Dimitri Lunz, was not so easily won over. He kept making comments like, "Better the devil you know than the one you don't."

"But Marx is absolutely right," Morozov argued. "Capitalism is little more than the rich slowly devouring the poor."

"I suspect you only feel this way 'cause of what the Turks did to your people, you see everything in terms of bullies and victims. But that's not the way life really is," Lunz argued back. "Consider the plight of the entrepreneur. When he invests in a business, the odds of his success are far less than his failure. I know men who have lost entire fortunes trying to make their businesses work."

Morozov said he thought Lunz's sympathies were misplaced considering the fact that his family was wealthy whereas Lunz was always poor.

"If I ever had a chance to be a millionaire, just one tiny chance," Lunz replied, "I'd take it to the exclusion of all else."

"Good luck," Haig replied. "And if you ever need any help or assistance from me or my family, just let me know."

Lunz smiled graciously. In hindsight, Haig knew that Lunz found his sense of compassion patronizing. He wondered if it didn't eventually compel his friend to test his limits.

Still, political discourse remained in the abstract until one of their dear friends, Vadim, a young Maldivian in Saint Petersburg, was arrested in the dead of the night.

He must've given up names. Others from their circle of friends were soon rounded up as well. One day, while smoking cigarettes outside the school, a paddy wagon pulled up and both he and Lunz were snatched off the street by the members of the Okhrana. Hoods were pulled over their heads. They were bustled into two different prison cells. Haig still remembered the chill he felt when being shoved into a small interrogation chamber and asked by the officer for the names of his fellow revolutionaries. Trembling with fear, he swore he knew no one.

"Liar!" shouted the rail-thin interrogator who smacked him across the face with the back of his bony hand.

"With all due respect, are all your suspects wealthy?" Haig played his one ace. "Have they all met the royal family?"

"I don't care who you've met!"

"All I'm saying is if a revolution occurred, I'd have far more to lose than most."

"Why's that?"

"My mother is from aristocracy. My father is a very successful entrepreneur." Haig listed some of his father's more influential clients, statesmen, generals, and industrialists. Although the interrogator was hardly contrite, within a matter of hours he was released.

For Lunz it was an entirely different matter. He was held for a week and a half, mainly in isolation, during which time he was periodically interrogated, beaten, and starved. Although he told them every name he knew, under threat of death, he refused to sign a confession.

When he was finally released, black and blue with bruises, he was utterly converted to the new religion of the street. Intent on getting even, Lunz joined a rudimentary Bolshevik spy ring who focused on sniffing out informers among their ranks.

Overnight he fully embraced the Bolshevik dream, a world in which each worked according to his ability, and received each according to his needs, where every man was given a fair shake and wasn't at the mercy of some brutal dictator.

"We've arrived, sir," said his young assistant, coming to a graceful stop in front of the old Ulanov House.

Most of the pre-revolutionary homes around the campus had been torn down to make room for the ever-expanding university complexes. Stopping in front of this lone, single-family house with its old mansard roof, Morozov knew enough about architectural style to realize that the building was over a century old. Next to the door was a brass plate engraved with the year 1799.

"Wow," Morozov said aloud. "Not many places around here survived the Great Fire." Napoleon had burned the city down in 1812. Alexei turned off the ignition of the university sedan.

"Oh! I almost forgot, here." Alexei gave Morozov a set of keys to his new abode.

"I enjoyed chatting with your girlfriend," Haig said as Alexei lifted Morozov's remaining boxes of books out of the trunk.

"She's a big fan of yours," Alexei said, following him with full arms.

"A fan?" he asked.

"Darya said she wants to be a writer just like you." Alexei placed the boxes on the top step.

"Shame, I thought she was smarter than that," Haig muttered.

"I can bring them inside," Alexei offered, hoping to get a glimpse of the interior of the old building.

"Not necessary, thanks," Morozov said, and simply stood on the top stoop until Alexei returned to the car and drove off.

Haig entered the old family dwelling. A middle-aged woman in a babushka was busy in the kitchen, stirring pots and washing dishes. She finally glanced up at Morozov and blurted out, "Hello, sir. I'm making some plov, but it won't be ready for a little while."

"That's fine," he replied, inspecting the spacious rooms with their fine workmanship and beautiful antique furniture that only decadent aristocrats from an inequitable age could ever afford.

He made a big show of carrying his own boxes, one at a time as though he had lugged them all the way from Armenia. Upstairs, he discovered a glorious room with a high-vaulted ceiling and large bay windows looking out over a small, snowy field. The bed had four tall, hand-carved posts like little minarets. The wainscoted walls were freshly shellacked, which made him feel acutely self-conscious of his elevated position. Investigating the next flight up, Morozov found a cramped, unpainted bedroom with a low ceiling, a former servant's quarters.

"So, what's your name?" Morozov asked, entering the dining room after washing himself.

"Katerina Kuznetsova Petrova," she replied.

"Kata. You called me 'sir' instead of *tovariesh*," he observed grinning. "And we fought a bloody revolution to make it so."

"Sorry, comrade."

"Or you can call me Haig. I'm sleeping in the bedroom on the top floor," he announced, upon returning to the dining room, where Kata had put a single place setting at the head of a long oak table.

"Isn't the one upstairs less of a walk?"

"Yeah, but that master's bedroom is like the Sistine Chapel. I'd be too self-conscious to fall asleep in there."

"Suit yourself," she said, bringing out a small metal platter filled with the rice, carrots, and beef that made up *plov*. Next, she carried out a second dish with string beans in tomato sauce and a third smaller bowl with cucumber salad covered in freshly minced dill and a cream sauce. Then she returned to the kitchen.

"Have you eaten? Why don't you join me?" he ordered more than asked when she finally came out with a basket of black bread.

"I feel more comfortable in the kitchen, thanks."

"Then I'll eat with you," he said, lifting his plate and rising.

"But here it's a lot prettier!" She pointed to the large dining room windows.

"Prettier! That's the poison of the *bourgeois*! Ever read Chekhov? Do you know how many people suffered for prettiness!" he asked, following her into the kitchen.

He set his plate down on the counter, then proceeded to scoop his food onto a bowl for her, scattering cooked rice and string beans along the counter top that she had just cleaned.

"I actually ate earlier," she confessed.

"Eat a little now, if only to prove that you're not poisoning me."

She sighed, sat down, picked up a fork, then pushed the food around feeling too frazzled to eat. At the very least he did all the talking. He rambled on about returning to Moscow after decades away.

"Back then this city was just a big gypsy village compared to what it is now."

34

When he finally finished eating and put his fork down, she rose and began putting away the leftovers. When she wasn't looking, he snatched a bottle of vodka from the shelf that she had intended for special occasions. He uncorked it, grabbed a porcelain tea cup, filled it and replaced the bottle. Soon after Kata left for the day, Morozov brought the teacup into the study. There he opened one of his boxes and took out the first volume of his diaries, the raw material for his intended memoirs.

He was instantly amused by the naïve spirit that permeated the pages of his childhood— the expectation of great things that were yet to come. It was as if life were some kind of magic genie that was obliged to eventually fulfill all his wishes.

As he read on over the ensuing day, he didn't find the juvenile volumes of his diary particularly intriguing, usually just a record of childhood events, until he finally reached a section that detailed his first major rupture with his parents. It occurred when he declared his great desire to be a cadet at the prestigious Mikhailovskaya Military Academy up in Saint Petersburg. The country's shameful naval defeat to Japan filled every school boy's fantasy with vengeance. A friend and older classman, Peter Sokov, had just been accepted at the academy. When Sokov wore his cadet uniform to school, every boy was feverish with envy.

As tensions with the Austria-Hungarian Empire heated up, Haig kept bringing his ambitions to his parents. Although he didn't write it in his journal, he remembered the final discussion he had with them.

"I'd make a great officer!"

"No doubt," his father replied absently.

"I'd be stern, but fair to my men."

"As well you should," his mother replied.

"Can I register this spring? I don't even need to finish my final semester. The school is allowing recruits to graduate early."

His parents only smiled and said they would think about it, but months later, when war was finally declared with Germany, Haig was still attending school with children half his height.

"We have to hurry," he warned. "The war could end, then it'll be too late!"

They politely conveyed that they had made other more important plans for him, but refused to disclose them. When he learned that his father had managed to purchase an exemption to get him out of military service, he was livid. How could he deprive him the glory of a lifetime! He didn't speak to either of them for days afterwards. He finally forgave them a few months later when he learned that Peter Sokov and most of his brigade had been mowed down by German machine-gun fire during an ill-planned charge outside Smolensk.

One night after his housekeeper, Kata, left but before he could finish his customary teacup of vodka, an air raid siren shattered the silence. He froze. This must be a mistake, the old writer thought nervously. He had been assured that Moscow was no longer within Luftwaffe range, yet the siren outside blared. He looked out the window and could see search lights combing the sky, but no planes. No sounds of anti-aircraft guns. After knocking back his drink, it was all he could do to jump back into bed and pull the blanket over his head. Suddenly, he awoke to a subtle vibration, accompanied by muted thunder.

Bombs had to be falling to the northeast of the city. Soon he heard the air raid warden outside, blowing his whistle and knocking on doors to make sure all his neighbors had complied. Tiredly, Haig rose out of bed, pulled a coat over his underwear, and yanked on his slippers. As he started down the stairs, he decided that he was too drunk to make it all the way to the freezing subway station half a mile away.

Instead, he shuffled down another flight, to the chilly basement. There he found an old stool under the steps. The tight corner reminded him of Dimitri Lunz's first hovel as it too was little more than a broom closet under a flight of stairs in some dilapidated embankment house, just big enough to hold his worn-out cot. Though he was regularly bitten by bed bugs and scratching from lice, how his young friend missed contracting tuberculosis was a mystery. In another moment the writer fell asleep. A few moments later, he slid backwards off the stool and whacked his head against the basement wall.

"Shit!" He rose just as the second siren sounded twenty minutes later. The air raid was officially over.

He struggled back up the stairs. As he passed the master bedroom he thought that it was a crime to let such an exquisite chamber go unused. Too tired to climb the last flight to the servant's quarters, he plunked down on the giant mattress—it was like sleeping on a cloud. He pulled off the quilt that was more like a drop cloth and slept in the former aristocrat's boudoir.

The next evening, while in the new bed, he opened his next journal and read about Moscow during the last war:

"I've never seen the city so crowded, or quite so agitated. You can feel the electricity when you go outside, like the air just before a great storm. Spontaneous marches, protests against the government are ongoing. We all feel that it's just a matter of time before the crowds explode. As my parents both keep saying, the only question is what will follow. Since his arrest by the Okhrana, poor Dimitri has joined the riffraff. On the one hand, I envy his freedom. Yet he is steadily getting pulled deeper into this dark whirlpool. Though I don't fully trust him, I still worry about him. Unlike me, he doesn't have protective parents to look after him.

Morozov remembered how Dimitri had finally confessed to him that he had joined with one renegade cell who were part of "an expropriation team." He was one of a carousel of men who robbed a number of large businesses to fund the growing upheaval. But throughout those years, all wanted to believe that Tzar Nicholas would stabilize things. England and other European countries had peacefully transitioned from crown rule to democracy. As his father said, "It's a race to see what comes first—parliamentary monarchy or revolution, whatever that is."

When Nicholas finally permitted the Duma to represent the people, it was a big step forward, but he had given them little power.

It wasn't until the third year of the war that the Revolution started to boil, as ever more soldiers either came home wounded or had deserted. Either way, they seemed to draw in even more malcontents from the ranks of the impoverished. Lines popped up everywhere as things grew scarce, but the only lines that lasted, regardless of the weather, were the bread lines. Morozov remembered as basic city services were gradually overwhelmed. Garbage piled up, trolleys slowed down. The scarcity of jobs, housing, and other necessities kept things in a constant state of crisis. Slowly they heard reports of mass defection at the front. Then finally they learned that the tzar's most loyal troops were beginning to turn against him.

7

Alexei, NYC, August 15, 1969

Instead of going up through The Bronx, Sergei Hagaopian drove his friend Alexei Novikov over George Washington Bridge. It had been nearly a decade since they last spent an evening together back in Moscow so the two men talked about their current lives.

"The idea of returning home as a bachelor for the first time in twenty-three years worries me," Alexei confessed.

"Nonsense," Sergei replied. "You've always been a Romeo."

Sergei refrained from saying anything regarding Alexei's bloated appearance. His old friend had gained at least a hundred pounds. His puffed-out face was exacerbated by alcohol and he had a smoker's hack. Alexei had just sworn off tobacco, Sergei refrained from smoking as well.

For his part, Alexei noticed that instead of decreasing, the traffic seemed to only increase the further they got from New York City. But at least it kept moving.

The shiny, black Cadillac from the embassy was supposed to be getting a tune-up that weekend, but Sergei also discovered it had barely been used in months. The mechanic was only happy to get paid to validate it without even having to pop the hood. It stood out among the VW microbuses and other old jalopies filled with young people. As they headed further north, clouds began rolling in over the mountains.

"Are they *all* going to this jazz festival?" Alexei asked dryly.

"Who knows?" Sergei replied, flipping on his windshield wipers to clear away the thickening mist.

"They don't look like jazz types," Alexei said, staring at the long hair of parallel passengers in other cars.

"What type of people listen to jazz?"

"Alcoholics and intelligentsia."

When Sergei finally exited the New York State Thruway, Alexei said, "Pull over if you see any nice restaurants, will you? I'm famished."

"And I can use a drink," Sergei added. After reaching the Teutonic-sounding town of New Paltz, they located a nondescript diner with a gaudy orange bar. Both men ordered twelve-ounce bloody rare strip steaks and multiple drinks as the rain finally began to come down. They decided to remain seated until it passed. Two hours later when it tapered, they were both intoxicated as they staggered back to the car. To their horror, they discovered that although the rain had subsided, the traffic had only increased. As the sun dimmed over the Catskills, Alexei, who drank far too much, nodded off in the passenger seat.

Sergei drove over endless hills, weaving around a lengthy valley in the Catskill Mountain Range. Only by slowly following the steady flow of cars around him did he not get lost or go off a cliff. As the traffic started slowing down, he noticed more and more cars parked along the shoulders. Soon foot traffic also appeared. Long-haired kids moved along the narrow walkway between the traffic and the parked cars. As it grew darker, the distant echo of primitive music grew steadily louder as though they were heading toward some great tribal powwow. Using the headlights of passing cars, Sergei spotted cardboard signs announcing the festival and finally he saw a grassy field packed with vehicles. A teenager guarded the entrance. Still intoxicated, Sergei swerved his American car inside, nearly hitting the lanky youth.

"Hey, I'm holding a spot for some friends," said the skinny kid shining a flashlight.

39

"International press!" Sergei's intoxicated calm made him sound solidly authoritative. Seeing the unusual diplomatic plates, the kid jumped out of the way. He drove through the tight cemetery of motionless vehicles. Slowly he found what appeared to be the last narrow slot. The bordering cars were so close, Sergei was afraid he wouldn't be able to open the doors.

It was raining again but in the last rays of sunlight, he could scan the sprawling concert area, which sloped downward. Kids were everywhere. At the bottom, along the eastern edge of the property, was a big illuminated wooden stage. It was framed by two towers made up of crisscrossed piping, which supported the massive row of lights and amps. Music echoed everywhere. Looking behind him, above the top of the slope where he had parked, were the designated campgrounds. Yet people seemed to camp wherever the hell they wanted. Along the north side he could see various large tents and latrines. Near the northwestern tip was a shallow lake. Intermittent trees and bushes dotted the area, but most of the woods bordered the rear and sides of the rolling grounds.

Instead of waking up his old companion, Sergei took out a flashlight, clicked it on, opened his trunk and grabbed two new drawstring bags containing both a tent and a sleeping bag that he had purchased at the Army Navy Surplus Store earlier that day. Careful not to get lost in the dark, he followed the trail of kids westward about fifteen minutes away. Although it was dark and wet, a series of small campfires illuminated the area. Loose rows of tents, tarps and lean-tos were divided by a constant flow of skinny kids zipping back and forth like feral cats. The sprawling encampments bobbed with flashlights, buzzed with chatter and boomed with laughter. Finally Sergei spotted an empty stretch on the wet grass. He opened the drawstring bag and pulled out the pup tent. A booklet dropped out. Carefully using the flashlight, he read the instructions in the rain. It took him about twenty minutes to figure out how to lay out the tent, insert the poles, and hammer the spikes into the wet mud with a big rock before pulling the enclosure up from the four corners. Next, he unrolled the sleeping bag inside the floor of the little tent and slipped it to one side.

He then hiked back to the car where Alexei was still snoring away like an old bear. The rain subsided to a drizzle, Sergei popped open his trunk and located a large suitcase containing two large comforters and pillows that he had snatched off his own bed. He also tore open the small cardboard box in the very back of the trunk and took out the first of six new quart-size bottles of Stolichnaya vodka.

It had been twenty-four years since they had been roommates together at Moscow University, two trim, young men, just after the Great Patriotic War, ready to take on the world. Now staring at Alexei passed out, Sergei saw that his sad friend was a wreck and he himself wasn't in great shape either.

"Hey," Sergei said, gently smacking the Russian's loose jowls.

"Huh?" Alexei began to stir.

It took Sergei a whole twenty minutes before he finally got Alexei to his feet and out of the car.

"Where's the hotel?" he asked in the steamy darkness. Rock music continuously throbbed in the background.

"This way," Sergei said, leading the older man up the muddy path, only shining the flashlight before his feet. If Alexei was any less intoxicated, he would've noticed that there weren't any hotels in the woods. Instead, he trustingly plodded down the wet path like a groggy child.

"Hold on, hold on!" Alexei finally said. He stopped, leaned against a tree, took out his pecker and peed like a horse.

A few minutes later they resumed, with Sergei leading and Alexei following until they finally reached the little pup tent.

"Here we are—home!" Sergei said, dropping his suitcase. He snapped open his bag, took out the comforters and unraveled them inside the empty tent, then tossed the two pillows at the far end.

Too drunk and fuzzed out to argue, Alexei dropped to his hands and knees, crawled inside and collapsed onto the blanket. In another moment, he was snoring away as Sergei unlaced and removed his old friend's wet shoes.

8

Although Haig was born in Moscow, the sole child of older parents, during the first ten years of his life his family would spend most of the year in the Ottoman capital down south, which once was the seat of the great Byzantine Empire. Throughout his early childhood, he and his mother would go north only in the summer and spend the rest of the year in his father's land to the south. His two uncles kept up the huge and palatial mansion in Constantinople, right on the Dardanelles. The Great Kasabian Estate had been in their family for over a century.

With colorful Middle Eastern music, a strange-sounding language, the smoky scents, and spicy flavors, Haig always found Turkey mysteriously exotic. Yet his life growing up in Constantinople was not without challenges. As a child, he couldn't fully comprehend the problem of the Armenian people. If his people occupied the area before the Turks had arrived, why were they regarded as outsiders? Indeed, why had *they* ever allowed the Turks into *their* country in the first place?

The millet system, as it was called, gave the Armenian community some autonomy, just as it did with the Greeks and Jews, many of whom had resided there before the Turkish conquest, but they were all clearly second-class citizens. They were excluded from the political system. Non-Muslims in Turkey were denied basic civil rights and required to pay extra taxes. Despite this fact, Armenians had done well there. They had filled key positions in the arts, commerce and science. And for the most part, they were loyal to the Sultanate. In fact, Morozov's father once confessed to him that, without his mother's knowledge, he had once passed sensitive military information that he had learned about the Tzar's forces in the Caucuses to a military attaché in the Turkish embassy.

Unfortunately by the late nineteenth century, the four-hundred-and-fifty-year-old Ottoman Empire began to sway and crumble. Outlying Christian provinces started to break away and the treatment of the Armenians grew increasingly harsh. Under the rule of the final sultan—Hamid the Damned as he was called—state-sanctioned massacres increased. Because it was unseemly to slaughter one's own subjects, Hamid created an unofficial militia largely made up of Kurds known as "the Hamidiye" who did his dirty work for him.

Gradually, as conditions worsened in Turkey, Morozov's family spent more and more time north of the border in his mother's homeland "under the protection of Father Tzar."

By the time Haig graduated from primary school, just after the turn of the century, hostility toward Armenians in Turkey became so open that his family would only winter in Istanbul. They would board the train to Sebastopol, where they would transfer by steamer along the Black Sea up to Moscow.

They continued commuting between the two empires for the next decade. By August of 1912, his father, who usually had a morose disposition, was surprisingly elated one day. He had just heard that a group of young Turkish military officers finally removed old Hamid from power. Haig remembered the fleeting hope that his fellow countrymen might finally gain a modicum of civil rights in their ancient homeland.

By the end of the year though, as the Ottomans lost nearly ninety percent of their European territory to the ever-expanding Austria-Hungarian Empire, Muslim refugees from these newly Christianized territories started fleeing into Turkey, flooding onto the Anatolian Plains. Dispossessed, exposed to the elements, they saw attractive homes and properties built up over generations by the Christian subjects who lived in the Islamic state. Seeing the wealth of these infidels fueled the newly repatriated Muslims with outrage and bigotry.

"Tolerance and decency are great luxuries," his father tried to explain. "When times get hard, those are the first things to go."

Over the next few years, as tensions between the Tzar and the sultan increased, it grew harder to pass from Moscow to

Constantinople. Soon his father would make the passage alone, and whenever he came back, he looked noticeably older and sadder.

When World War One finally broke out, the border was completely shut down and fortified. The ambitious young Turkish Minister of War, Enver Pasha, launched a major offensive up north, in the Battle of Sarikamish against the weaker Russian forces. At first, the outnumbered Russian soldiers retreated, and it appeared to be a Turkish victory. Then a vicious winter storm swooped down from nowhere. In a matter of weeks, tens of thousands of unprepared Turkish soldiers froze to death. When the Russians finally counterattacked, the firing pins of the old Turkish rifles froze. Widespread panic led to soldiers abandoning their posts and running en masse, with the Russians giving chase. The great Turkish military expedition into the Caucasus had turned into a bloody route.

Immediately, Pasha blamed the Armenian communities in northern Turkey for their unexpected loss. Haig didn't know until much later that this was a moment many Turks had been waiting for—to turn their minor foreign defeat into a major domestic victory. First, loyal Armenian soldiers, who were in the Turkish Army, were stripped of their ranks and arms and transferred into the labor battalions. Shortly thereafter, they were ambushed altogether and slaughtered. Over the next eight years, roving gangs of the Turkish soldiers went from town to town throughout eastern Turkey where they enlisted the local constables and villagers. They rounded up the Armenian men, marched them into the village squares where, with the help of Turkish villagers, they were murdered. Photographs of their mass beheadings appeared in newspapers all over the world. In one photograph that Haig never forgot, he saw a tall bookshelf in the center of the town: each cubicle was filled with a different Armenian man's head. He could never forget the haunting image of their mouths loosely gaping, their eyes half-open and unfocused. It stayed with him all his life. Inasmuch as the men were slaughtered quickly, this turned out to be the most merciful part of the slaughter.

A far more drawn out and barbaric outcome awaited the women, the elderly, and their children. They were "deported," or sent on excruciating marches, mainly south into the desert, allegedly for their own protection from foreign armies that would never come. Along the way marauding gangs of Kurds and others were allowed to swoop in and have their pick of the young ladies and girls to be kept or auctioned off to the sex trade. Those seniors who didn't quickly collapse away were savagely beaten to death. Their rotting corpses soon littered the countryside.

Many of their Armenian children were snatched up for slave labor. The lucky ones were adopted by foreigners and renamed; the remainders were dumped into already crowded orphanages throughout the Middle East. In Constantinople, where the international spotlight was brighter, the genocide was still concealed, so Haig's uncles were able to sell off their holdings for pennies before they could be seized by the State. Their beloved family manor was taken over by a chubby Turkish statesman who renovated it into his private palace.

Despite losing everything, they were the fortunate ones. Hard-earned properties belonging to deported Armenians were officially deemed as abandoned. In villages throughout Turkey, jealous neighbors fought over the possessions of their murdered neighbors, sleeping in their beds, wearing their clothes and shoes. Overnight, they turned their ancient churches into new mosques and claimed the buildings had always been Turkish, instantly erasing centuries of Armenian history before the Turkic tribes had ever invaded the region.

Fortunately, after decades of running a profitable business, Morozov's father had built up a tidy savings, but obsessed with the ongoing slaughter of his people, his life essentially became a steady decline into alcoholism.

During those years, Haig clearly remembered what his mother would refer to as "the circle of woe." Twice a week, influential Armenians living in Moscow would meet in their large living room. Together, they would bring international newspapers and magazine clippings as well as share anecdotal news heard from the lucky few Armenians who escaped through the northern provinces. Together they would pool the latest news on the massacres—they heard of the most recent villages that were being cleared out and prominent citizens who had been publicly butchered. After outrage, the group would grow silently somber and misty eyes would gradually turn to inconsolable weeping.

Haig soon became the youngest member to sit in the circle.

"The Allied powers will intervene," Haig would repeatedly say to his dad. "The Turks are losing the war."

"Enough!" his father said one day. "This isn't for you."

"What do you mean?"

He lowered his voice and pointed to the living room, from which both could already hear fellow expatriates crying. "That is a bottomless pit of suffering. And you're my only son. I want you to have a happy life."

"But I'm Armenian too!"

"You were born here and your mother's from Russian royalty. Don't ever forget that!" She was the youngest daughter of some obscure duke.

"But I'm also Armenian..."

"No, you were born in Russia! You're Russian!"

"Why are you saying this?!" It felt as if his own father was disowning him.

"It's true!"

"The Turks aren't invading Moscow. We're safe here!" Haig appealed.

"Trust me they're already here." His father pointed to his own head. "They're the first thing I see when I wake up in the morning and the last thing I see when I go to sleep at night. I'm hoping I can still save you from these monsters."

Though still a teenager, Haig decided this was where he had to put his foot down. During dinner, he told his father that he was born Armenian and he couldn't simply unhook his ethnicity. His mom also spoke up, "Actually, Haig, you *were* born here. It sort of hurts me to hear that you're denying Mother Russia."

"I'm not denying anything, I'm simply saying..."

"You have a duty to us," his father finally said, "to do everything you can to be a happy, successful person. You owe us that."

"But I can't just ignore what's happening!" he replied.

"Ancient Armenia is being slowly eradicated from the earth. The whole world is just letting it happen and there's nothing we can do about that," declared his father. Looking into his boy's eyes, he added, "If you don't let it go, your heart and soul will die with it."

After that night, the circle of woe vanished. Its members were never invited into their house again. Additionally, no more newspapers or mention of the ongoing tragedy were allowed to be brought up. Soon after his eighteenth birthday his parents approached Haig with a painful request: They wanted him to legally change his last name from Kasabian to Morozov—his mother's maiden name.

"Out of the question!"

"This isn't just a symbolic request," his father appealed. "You're never going back to Turkey and your mother's name will grant you much greater privilege here. An Armenian last name will forever make you a second-class citizen in Russia."

"I won't do it!"

For his father, the psychological burden of his loss manifested itself physically. Rapidly his father shuffled around with a stoop. He seemed to talk with a slur. Even his facial muscles seemed to go limp as though he suffered from some palsy. Haig could see his mother's heart break as she watched her husband shrink away from life. Finally reaching a point where he was willing to do anything to lift his dad's dying spirit, Haig announced that he had decided to accept the name change. Other Armenians were doing it the world over to blend into their host countries.

Not wasting any time, they contacted their solicitor who immediately did all the legal paperwork. Upon signing a single document, his name was officially transformed to Haig Morozov.

9

Eric Stein's older brother, Josh, stopped his car at the light on Ninety-sixth Street and spotted her standing across the street on the northwest corner of Ninety-sixth and Broadway. The voluptuous teenager in frayed denim cutoffs and a tight white tee shirt was turning every head and catching every catcall within a half block radius.

"Holy shit!"

"Told you, dude!" Eric said, seated next to him.

Josh pulled up just long enough for her to toss her bag in the backseat and hop into the spacious front seat next to the two brothers. Eric quickly introduced them as Josh drove up the ramp onto the West Side Highway.

Over the rock music glowing from his radio with the wind whistling through the window on the hot August afternoon, the three chatted with a great view of the Hudson to their left. Josh did his utmost to be a good wing man and make his younger brother look sharp, but it wasn't easy as Eric kept making wimpy comments, like how nervous he felt about leaving the city.

Half an hour later, as they approached the Tappan Zee Bridge, Josh finally said, "Anna O'Brien, I have to say you don't look at all Irish."

"My father was Italian," she said with the utmost sensitivity. "He died a few years ago."

"I'm so sorry," said Eric. "That must've been..."

"What happened?" Josh asked, almost amused.

"He died during an aerial accident," she said.

"An airplane accident?" Eric asked.

"No, he was a trapeze artist."

"I don't suppose his last name was Wallenda?" Josh asked, restraining a smile.

"Oh, you know about that?!"

"Sure, the famous pyramid fall. Seven family members all fell at the same time – the biggest family reunion ever," he kidded.

"Wow!" Eric said, not knowing exactly what they were talking about.

As Josh sped north and the miles flew by, they chatted through a flurry of topics until they finally touched on Nixon and the war in Vietnam. Josh had just gotten his first draft deferment. Anna made a derogatory comment about "the commies."

"You're opposed to the war, aren't you?" Josh asked Anna softly.

"Well, I don't like the draft, but we were able to stop the commies in Korea. Why not give the Vietnamese a fighting chance?" she said, compelling both brothers to look at her in disbelief. No one they knew supported the imperialist war in the Far East.

"We already gave them five years and twenty-five thousand American lives," Josh shot back. "The Korean War was only one-year long, hon."

"Good for you!" Anna said to Josh, grinning. "Most guys just shut up."

"What?"

"'Course I'm against the war." She said, "What do I look like, an asshole?"

"Wow!" Josh laughed and said to Eric, "Your girlfriend's a wild card!"

Eric nervously shoved his knee against Josh's. She was far from a girlfriend.

"This is a great song!" Eric cut in and turned up the radio. It was Credence's *"Born on the Bayou."*

Eric fidgeted with the dial as the reception started failing.

"They're performing this weekend. So we'll probably hear them sing it live," Anna said.

"That'll be so cool," Eric added.

"So what's this job you got?" Anna asked Josh.

"Basically I'm a lifeguard."

"Sounds like fun. They don't need any female lifeguards, do they?"

"If they saw you, they'd all start drowning," Josh joked.

"How much does it pay?" she asked.

"Actually, not a cent. It's all volunteer," he said.

"Really!" She was impressed by his altruism.

"Yep," he replied. Eric smirked as he knew it was part of a sweetheart deal. Josh was going to get a summer internship at a major corporate law firm in exchange for three weeks of lifeguarding at the camp, so one of the law partners could earn points with his son's Boy Scout troop. But all that was strictly hush-hush.

As they drove past a diner in the town of Middleton, Josh commented that he could sure use a bite. Both Eric and Anna concurred, so he circled back and pulled into the parking lot. Upon grabbing a booth, all three ordered the Burger Deluxe Special, two dollars and fifty cents, which came with a free soft drink.

Anna excused herself to use the ladies' room and, stopping at the payphone first, she took out her change purse and dialed her number. When the operator asked for eighty-five cents, she inserted the coins.

Her mother answered on the first ring.

"Hi Mom, I'm calling like you asked," she said, cupping the mouthpiece, trying to shield off the background noise.

"Glad to hear you're still in the land of the living," her mother spoke with a brogue. "How was your day?"

"Hum drum. We hung out with Denise's mother."

"How's Doris doing?"

"Fine, we're about to sit down and eat some grilled cheese sandwiches."

"Sounds nice."

"We might catch a movie afterwards."

"What movie?"

"*Charly*, about the retard who becomes a genius."

"That doesn't sound like the kind of film you usually see."

"It's Denise's mom's choice."

"Oh, I'm jealous. I long for the day when I get to pick the movie. Put Doris on a moment, I want to say hi."

"That'll have to wait. Denise is waving to me, I gotta run."

"Call me before you go to sleep."

"I'll try, but we might be going to a later show, so if we return too late, I can't."

"Just try," she said. "And I'll see you tomorrow."

"It's going to be a scorcher tomorrow," Anna said, paving the way for lie number two.

"I can't control the temperature, hon."

"You could buy an AC," Anna said.

"If I could, I would. I don't want to go through this again."

"Goodnight, ma."

"Nighty night."

She hung up with seconds to spare before all the coins would drop and reveal to her mother through a series of loud clicks that she was no longer in the city.

When she returned to the booth where the fellas were finishing their burgers, Anna asked exactly how far the Boy Scout camp was from the rock concert.

"About ten miles," Josh replied.

"Any chance you could drop us off there?" Eric asked, knowing that that was what Anna was hinting at.

"I could drop you off there tonight but not tomorrow," he replied.

"Isn't it only about a ten-minute drive?" she pushed.

"Tomorrow's crunch day: I have to check all the canoes, rowboats, and life preservers, and make sure all the buoys are out on the lake. Then that the oars, oar locks, and paddles are all up to snuff. It's all the time I got to be ready."

Eric shrugged. After they finished their food and paid the bill, they tiredly returned to the Impala. Since there was no reception in the mountains Josh resumed his drive in silence, just enjoying the scenic valley below. Anna was beginning to nod off while Eric was fantasizing about having sex with her.

10

A banging sound downstairs awoke Morozov. It turned out that Kata had arrived early and was doing housework. He dressed, then grabbed the last journal he had read and went downstairs where he and Kata exchanged greetings. He took a seat in front of the big window, opened his journal arbitrarily, and began reading:

"I noticed that Dimitri had scratch marks on his arms and face. I jokingly asked him if he had been taming Siberian tigers."

"If you really care about someone, you'll make sacrifices to help them."

"I thought he was kidding, then I realized he was serious. When I asked what he was talking about, he said young women have been trained to fight for their virtue and trade it as a dowry for marriage. He felt that one duty of the Revolution was to help women shed their bourgeois sense of inhibition. Before I could ask what he was talking about, Lunz changed the subject and said he had just finished a new poem about the Revolution and insisted on reading it at that very moment."

"I just put on a fresh samovar," Kata interrupted him.

"This beautiful view of Sparrow Hill is quenching enough," Morozov replied, not even looking out the window.

"It's now called Lenin Hill," she corrected him. He didn't respond, reading on, thinking about how much he hated Lunz's latest poem. Though Lunz was fairly productive, his work lacked growth. He was hitting the same boring nail over and over.

When Morozov heard a knocking at the front door and answered it, he found Alexei standing outside.

"What are you doing here?" he asked.

"I'm supposed to drive you to school."

"Why would you think that?"

"Because you're supposed to give a lecture to Professor Alexandrovich's class on literature of the Caucasus in forty minutes."

"Of course," he said, instead of acknowledging that he had forgotten about the event and was in the youth's debt. He told Alexei to wait for him in the car, then quickly dressed and grabbed his index cards on the subject and joined him.

"I hope you slept well," Alexei asked as Morozov reviewed his index cards.

"How well do you know Professor Alexandrovich?" he asked, ignoring the pleasantries.

"Well enough, a good man."

"How much sway does he carry?" asked Morozov, a skillful practitioner in any political system he found himself.

"Well, he's no Kostanovich. That was the former chair, a powerhouse."

During the rest of the drive, Morozov's political instincts got the better of him and he pressed Alexei about the political workings of the Philology Department, specifically the senior faculty members who might be possible allies and possible foes. After mentioning some of the key professors, Alexei added, "The executive committee is convening for its spring meeting later today. If you're really interested, as a visiting writer you have the right to attend the meeting."

Soon they parked and went to his office. On his desk, he saw a couple pieces of mail including a large parcel that had been forwarded from his office in Armenia. Morozov opened it up and found an unedited galley manuscript by the great Konstantin Fedin.

Inside was a note:

Dear Comrade Morozov,

Just read about your honored posting in the University. Congratulations. As I'm sure you remember, a couple of years ago, we published one of your essays. You said that you'd be happy to return the favor, so I'm hoping you might be able to have a six-hundred-word review of the enclosed book ready for publication in the next thirty days.
Sincerely,
Fyodor Tallen,

Suddenly, a bell in the corridor echoed.

"Sir, Alexandrovich's class is beginning and it's a bit of a walk across campus," Alexei said from the doorway. Without thinking, Morozov clenched the Fedin manuscript in his hand as his aide escorted him down a flight of stairs, out the door, across the partially shoveled grounds of the campus, past a handful of buildings and statues, then back into a large dome-shaped building, through semi-crowded hallways to Professor Alexandrovich's contemporary literature class in a multi-tiered lecture hall. As soon as he entered the chapel-size room, the old professor smiled at him and rose before his class. Alexandrovich took out a sheet of paper and read:

"Today, we are honored to have the great Haig Morozov, a man who was the first president of the Armenian Writers Union, the second president of the Caucasus Writers Union, Winner of the Guggeneya Banner, Order of the Migarchov-Genyez Award, and Winner of the illustrious Pulachov Prize..." All were amazed as the professor went down a long roster of honors bestowed upon Morozov over the years. He considered how each of the awards or titles was acquired through old-fashioned politicking and vote swaps, but he knew it was important that the introduction be read in its entirety. Like the cocktail of medals pinned onto a general's chest, they established his unquestioned authority. Finally, when both the introduction and applause ended, Morozov rose to his feet and realized that instead of taking his index cards with his lecture points, he had brought the galleys of the Fedin manuscript.

"Oh, Comrade Morozov, we were all hoping you might read to us from one of your wonderful stories," asked the old professor.

"I'd love to," he replied, tensing his face into a smile, "but alas, I brought nothing with me."

A half dozen copies of his latest short story collections were thrust in the air by the students seated before him. Morozov grudgingly snatched up one and mumbled, "I had actually prepared notes on the literature of the Caucasus..."

As more students arrived late, Morozov considered reading a story he wrote twenty years earlier, entitled *Empty as the Steppes.*

It was about a wealthy man who loses his factory after the Revolution and refuses to accept the new ways. He harbors dreams that the White Army will liberate Moscow, quell the uprising, and return his former life and business to him. But with time, the communists firmly consolidated their power. His wife and daughter came to accept and soon embrace the new ways, but he is unable. Eventually, the story ends in his suicide.

Initially, when Morozov wrote the first draft, the story started out about his father's growing isolation and eventual demise in the years of the genocide. It detailed much of what he learned about the Ottoman massacre. But with each rewrite, the Turkish atrocity was steadily replaced with the new ways of communist life—this conformed to party-line themes until it turned into its completely revised incarnation.

"Have you found a story?" Professor Alexandrovich asked.

Morozov flipped through the pages of the book to a piece half the length, entitled *The Misspent Seed.*

"I wrote this after I spent time with some of the members of the Serapion Brothers who came down to Moscow in the mid-1920s." Morozov switched on his narrative tractor: "The year froze up, making the earth pale as death, Mother Nature covered it with a blanket of frost. And instead of the sun, a beautiful young woman appeared in the village with hair as long and shimmering as the sun's golden rays. Her heart lit up the forgotten village and warmed the hard cold ground, quickly melting away the snow. Though none knew her name, every male, from boy to old man, immediately fell in love with her…"

Line after line, Morozov's eyes touched the words and his mouth rattled them out without changing pace or intonation.

Reading the work in front of students who were his age when he wrote it, Morozov confirmed that he hated this piece as much as the last one. The sentimental phrases and dandified syntax were clearly constructed to inflate the sappy story. Another clichéd tale about a saintly beauty who turns ugly when she falls in love and has implied sex with a simple-minded farm boy.

Lacking any of the usual Party parables, it wasn't even good as propaganda. It was basically a cannibalized version of some other writer's story, who he now forgot. Of all the great themes to write about, why did only the most mediocre ones get published? Morozov knew that the only reason he was still in print was because of his political capital.

Of course, he had drawn on his love for Masha to write the piece. That was the most powerful aspect of the story, which kept him engaged. Masha Rodchenko was the most beautiful girl he ever knew. He wrote it soon after meeting her at college.

After the Bolsheviks took control, they opened Moscow State University to the proletariat. It wasn't simply another place for the privileged. Now, even a farmer's daughter from the Ukraine had an opportunity to be a somebody. They set up an accelerated preparatory program for the children of peasants from all the new Soviet states to ready them for the rigors of the university. Young Morozov, who had a solid private school education, was enlisted as a Russian-language tutor. Masha Rodchenko, a blonde girl from Kiev, distinguished herself in primary school excelling in the sciences. Her great dream in life was to become the first female doctor in her district. She explained that her mother and grandmother had been midwives; it was high time for women to study obstetrics.

"You're old enough to join the Party," Morozov said, looking away from her. She was so beautiful he was unable to make eye contact without blushing.

"I'm not political," she replied, simply.

"That's foolish. In fact, I really don't think they'll let you into medical school unless you're a member of the Party. And even if they do," he explained, "a strong communist background would give you access to much better opportunities."

She didn't reply and it wasn't his place to argue with her. It was a month into their tutoring that she commented that she had learned he was Armenian.

"Who told you that?" he asked. He had been careful not to disclose his birthday.

"Some handsome guy who loves himself...Dimitri?" she replied.

"Where'd you meet Lunz?" he asked.

"I was waiting for you in the lounge last week and he came up and started talking to me. When I told him I didn't speak to strange men, he said that you were his best friend."

Damn Lunz! Morozov had made the mistake of telling him about this shy, beautiful Ukrainian girl he was assigned to tutor on Tuesday mornings. Lunz had obviously come into the school lounge and targeted her.

When he saw Lunz later that day and began scolding him for being a cad, Lunz interrupted him and said, "Just calm down! I did it for your sake!"

"My sake!"

"You're inexperienced with girls," Lunz replied. "I just wanted to check and see if you were wasting your time."

"And am I?" he asked.

"No, she's smart, beautiful. And she *likes you*. But you're taking much too long. You should've pounced by now."

"Pounced?"

"It might sound harsh, but I guarantee there are at least a dozen other guys hot on her trail. And she's even more naive than you. So whoever grabs her first will win her. That's how it is when they're young."

"She's not a stray kitten!"

"They are! Young girls commit themselves to whoever plucks them first," he said as if reciting a law. "It's as simple as that."

"That's insane."

"It's true. 'Cause they don't realize that guys will have sex with anything and everything."

"So why don't women have sex with everything and anything?" he asked, amused by Lunz's savage notions.

"'Cause it's not the same for them as it is for us. There's a tremendous shame for girls to reveal so much of themselves. When

57

they finally are forced into it, they mistake it for love, and they love you back."

"This is ridiculous!"

"It's god's own truth! It's how he made us!" Dimitri declared. "They're so gullible they mistake aggression for love and what starts as shame soon becomes loyalty. That's why the pushiest guys, not the best ones, end up getting the pick of the litter."

"Hogwash."

"When she walks away with Vasily, tell me it's hogwash!" Vasily was a heavily scented fop who dressed like a peacock but hunted like a hyena.

Suddenly, a wave of applause pulled Morozov back to Alexandrovich's packed lecture hall. He appeared to be the last to know that his own story had ended. When the clapping finally subsided, the old professor rose and stood alongside him. Without asking his permission, he said, "Mr. Morozov can only entertain a few questions." Hands shot up.

"Actually, I regret to say that this ran much longer than I anticipated." Morozov-Kasabian confessed. He snatched up the unbound manuscript pages that he had accidentally brought with him and held them in the air. "I have roughly thirty minutes to write a review of the great Konstantin Fedin's latest masterpiece, so unfortunately I'm all out of time."

"But..."

"Thank you for this privilege! Let's all serve the Revolution honorably." Morozov bowed slightly toward the portrait of the mustached idiot.

As he and Alexei walked to his office, he asked Alexei to fetch him a pot of tea. Silently the assistant veered off to the school cafeteria.

When he arrived alone back in his office, Morozov angrily tossed the Fedin manuscript in his assistant's waste-paper basket. Being forced to read the thick manuscript of a successful contemporary, the length of which he could never produce, was an exquisite form of torture. But what choice did he have? A moment later, he fished the pages out of the can and, to his surprise, he located another parcel at the bottom—a small heavy box wrapped in butcher paper with twine. Also in the garbage can he found a torn fragment of a handwritten note:

"Purportedly you were raised here in Moscow, so I think you'll find that it really hasn't changed too much. As you know, the University was closed during the last quarter, but now that the Huns have been repelled, they've put Lenin's body back in his mausoleum so the city is as it should be. I'm always happy to do the good Commissar Zhdanov a favor. Due to the war shortages not to mention the endless red tape, I was glad to help secure the new Ulanov grant for him, but his list of special needs (the off-campus house, the extra ration cards) were a little harder, so I'm hoping he can..."

The ripped page ended there.

"What the hell?" The message was clearly addressed to him, but he never requested for any special needs or added ration cards. As Alexei entered with a tray holding a hard roll and hot pot of tea, the assistant saw the package on top of his desk.

"I found this letter to me in the trash," Morozov said, waving the torn page in the air.

"That must've been from Dr. Konstanovich. He was killed in an air raid shortly before you arrived. We had a memorial for him hours before you arrived last week."

"I didn't know Moscow was still getting bombed."

"Very rare now. During the initial invasion, planes covered the sky."

"Did they hit the university?" he asked.

"Oh yeah, they also bombed the Bolshoi Theatre. They even hit the Central Committee Headquarters."

"Oh my god!"

"If you just obey the warnings, you'll be fine. Konstanovich would pretend it wasn't happening, ignore the sirens and sure enough, he got killed."

"That's no reason to throw away his gift and tear up his letter to me," Morozov replied.

"I didn't throw anything out. I didn't even know it was there."
Alexei wondered if his superior and friend, Ivan, had put it down
there, setting some kind of trap.

Morozov unwrapped the package and found a box of Georgian
brandy.

"I'll honor his memory by savoring this," Morozov replied
somberly.

"Yes sir."

When Alexei exited, Morozov uncorked the brandy and poured
some into the tea that Alexei had just brought him. Morozov then put
the remainder of the bottle into his bottom desk drawer. Hoping to
find the rest of the letter, he looked through the bottom of his waste-
basket. Hearing a sharp snap, he turned to see Alexei standing there
watching him.

"You must be Stalin's favorite nephew," Morozov sat upright.
"How else could you evade service to the motherland?"

"I did serve," the young man corrected him. "I was in the 32nd
Division, wounded on the Moscow-Minsk highway."

"Wounded?"

"I forgot to mention earlier that somebody who wouldn't
identify himself called yesterday and said he mailed you a book of
poetry..."

"Where on your body did the bullet strike you, your fingernail?"
Morozov asked, ignoring Alexei's message.

Alexei delicately pulled up his shirt revealing a large ugly scar
the color of tomato paste. It had only just healed. But Morozov let out
a loud yawn, too tired to even glance at it. The phone rang, Alexei
returned to his desk to answer it.

Morozov sat at his desk and opened the newspaper. He tore
open the roll and buttered it as he read the paper. As his eyes scanned
the page, he gobbled down the bread. Then he gulped down his
brandied tea and said, "Whoever called you will call back. They
always do."

He lifted the paper and Alexei left. Everything in the news was
on the damned war or the war effort. Though there were

deprivations, compared to poor little Armenia, he was living in Moscow like Kubla Khan.

Rapidly flipping to the last page, Morozov's eyes caught the latest casualty count:

750,347—killed

478,982—missing

1,812,982—wounded

Because no official prisoner of war counts were listed, Morozov knew they weren't even pretending the statistics were real. Even on a good day, figures were played with. The only question was which way. Were they trying to impress the people by the great sacrifice of so many loyal soldiers or were they trying to hide the gross incompetence of inexperienced generals? Morozov tossed the crust of the roll into the waste-basket, then, after wiping off his slick hands on the newspaper, he shoved that in as well.

Suddenly Alexei heard a series of shrill screams from outside. Racing over to the window, opening it and looking outside, Morozov saw an attractive, young co-ed dashing and a filthy man in rags with a large tangle of dirty, black hair limping wildly behind her. Despite his handicap, he caught up and thrust his right hand up her skirt. She shrieked again.

"Leave her alone!" Morozov shouted.

Alexei dashed to the window, looked out, and ran out the door. Morozov watched as some tall youth raced up to the scoundrel, who turned and slugged him with his left hand. It was then that Morozov realized the man's right hand was a stump, missing clean up to the elbow. He could only fight with his one hand. Moments later, half a dozen other male students had knocked the bastard down, revealing that his left leg was missing as well. A splintered crutch was in its place. Morozov watched as the men proceeded to kick and pummel the madman until Alexei finally arrived. Surprisingly, he dragged the semi-conscious cripple away from them. Then he gave the scoundrel his own handkerchief to compress his head wound and squatted over him. Morozov watched them talk.

Although the police were called, they saw that the instigator was already bloody and punished enough. And he wasn't drunk. Alexei chatted with them a moment and they soon left as well.

11

Eric, Woodstock Festival, August 14, 1969

A burnt orange sun broke through the clouds and appeared at eye level, compelling Josh to drop the sun visor of his Impala and ask, "So where exactly are you kids sleeping tonight?"

Eric looked to Anna who whispered, "My friends don't arrive 'til tomorrow."

"Oh shit," Eric muttered.

"Well, at least it's warm out," Josh said, noticing small drops of rain hitting the windshield.

"Can you put us up overnight in your camp?" Eric asked his older brother.

"It's a Boy Scout camp. Scouts are all over the place. Anna will stand out."

"I guess we'll have to rent a motel room somewhere," she said.

"I barely have enough to cover the bus ride back," Eric revealed.

"We've arrived," Josh said as he turned his car in the weeded parking lot and into a nearby space. There were about half a dozen other cars parked throughout the large field. In the distance, they could make out log cabins, groups of tents, and packs of boys and men all mulling about in their regulation green uniforms.

"So there's no way you could put us up for just one night?" Eric asked, suddenly aware that he and Anna had no accommodations for the next twenty-four hours.

Josh sighed, turned the engine back on, and drove the Impala to the most remote part of the parking lot, under an overhanging apple tree.

"Lucky you happened to bring a sleeping bag," he snickered. "You can spend the night here. Then head out at first light before anyone sees you."

"Are there any grocery stores nearby?" Anna asked.

"I have a canteen of water and a big bag of potato chips in my trunk," Josh said as he got out of the car.

"What'll we do in the morning?" Eric asked. "How will we get to the concert?"

"Walk to the main road, put your thumb out and hitch that way," Josh replied, pointing left. "It's only about ten miles away. Everyone here does it. That was your plan, wasn't it?"

"I suppose."

"Let me be clear," Josh added as he pulled his duffel bag out of the trunk and placed it on his scratched-up fender. "You guys are not supposed to be here, so you got to keep it quiet and stay low 'til tomorrow because if you get pinched, you're screwed, understand? They'll toss you out and there's nothing I can do about it."

"Okay," Eric said.

Josh pulled a couple items out that he thought they might be able to use, including the canteen and a small shovel.

"What's the shovel for?" Eric asked.

"I don't know, protection." Josh said.

"Protection from what?" Anna asked.

"Whatever goes bump in the night," he said, smiling at Eric. "Help me with some of my stuff, will ya?"

Eric carried his duffel bag about halfway across the vast unweeded lot, leaving Anna alone in the car. After about a hundred feet out, Josh finally grabbed the duffel away and said, "I just wanted to give you my secret weapon. If all else fails, try this." He handed Eric a small corncob pipe filled with something dark and brown in the tiny bowl, as well as a ball of aluminum.

"Oh shit! This is your opium stash!"

"And it'll knock you on your ass, so be very careful."

"Does it make you hallucinate?"

"No, you just feel very numb and happy for about twenty minutes. Oh, and here," Josh opened his wallet and gave his brother two Trojan condoms. "Please try not to get any bodily fluids on my new upholstery."

"Thanks."

It was only seven o'clock when his brother went off to report for duty. The sun was still in the sky. Since Josh took the car keys, Eric and Anna couldn't even softly play the radio. Almost immediately, it resumed raining and the car grew steadily colder. Initially, the two passed the time awkwardly, talking about different students in their common high school classes. That led to discussion about some of the poetry they and others had read in their writing workshop over the past year. It wasn't 'til the sun began to go down and it stopped raining that they could see their breath and Eric nervously said, "I'm not trying to be fresh, but if we move to the backseat we can use our body heat to stay warm."

"I'm fine," she replied, "but you can go back there." He did so, if only to prove he wasn't pursuing sex.

In the backseat, rustling through his knapsack, he was unable to find the deck of cards he was hoping for, but he found something else. "Hey, I brought my notebook with some of the latest poetry that I wrote over the summer." He took it out.

"What is that sound?" Anna asked nervously, staring into the darkness.

"What?"

"It kinda' sounds like a rattlesnake!" she said, now fearful.

"Oh!" He realized what she was talking about. "Those are cicada. They're these big bugs like giant grasshoppers. They don't bite or anything. Nothing to worry about, I swear."

"Okay," she said relieved. Then, instead of opening the door, she squeezed over the top of the seat joining him in the back. "Go ahead and read your poems if you want to."

But it was now too dark to read. He was worried that others might see the flashlight inside the car, so he undid his sleeping bag and pulled it over his head before turning it on.

"I'm actually working on an epic poem called EPOCH," he said in a muffled barely audible tone. "It has a lot of references that allude to Spengler's *The Decline of the West*."

"The West declined?" she asked earnestly. She didn't know Spengler and didn't ask.

"It's been declining," he said. "It's all in my poem."

"Let's hear it."

He pulled the sleeping bag over his head and read his poem so softly, she couldn't decipher a word he said, but she was too tense to listen anyway. After five minutes of his mumbling, she abruptly dug her fingernails into his neck and said, "Shush!"

Eric pulled his head from out of the sleeping bag and saw Anna staring at a pair of bouncy flashlights about twenty yards away walking directly toward them. They could hear voices talking loudly as two youths walked right past their car and out toward the main road. A few minutes later, another flashlight also passed. A couple more Boy Scouts passed soon after. Anna and Eric talked in whispers for a while about how many Scouts had passed and where they might be going. Seeing her shivering, Eric took the liberty of rubbing Anna's shoulder. She didn't say a word. At one point, when they could see the outline of a couple more Scouts pausing near a tree, Eric softly whispered the word "urinating." When Anna let out a chuckle, Eric's hand instantly went up to cover her mouth, but accidentally brushed against her left breast. Either she didn't notice or didn't care.

In another moment, the Scouts began returning to their campsite.

"So, do you have any poetry?" Eric asked, remembering that whenever Anna read her poetry, she always acted more sensitive afterwards.

"I just feel a little odd is all."

"Hey, I won't tell anyone," he said, thinking the poetry might be sexual in nature.

"For starters it rhymes and I'm usually not a big rhymer."

"Now I definitely want to hear it," he said, trying to keep his voice down while sounding enthusiastic.

"Also it's not something I'd ever share in class."

"It'll be our secret."

"You keep watch if you see anyone approaching, all right?" she said.

65

"Absolutely," he said, trying to stay vigilant of what was going on outside.

Anna took her notebook from her knapsack, flipped through the pages to the poem she mentioned, then flipped on the flashlight, stuck her head under the sleeping bag, and began reading aloud:

> "When we met, I thought it was you,
> that whoever ordains had ordained,
> With flights and fits and private rights,
> In a stream of babbling names,
> And you thought I, a surveyor of limits,
> uptight, pretty but bored,
> Who constantly weighed the ways of others,
> Enriched by what they mourned,
> And there you were,
> strong yet gentle,
> never having second doubts:
> Funny, spontaneous, penniless and loud,
> a series of drunken bouts,
> Our lives other-locked from when we first met
> On the corner of Avenue C,
> But when you did that bitch on Avenue A,
> I thought, why ain't he doing me?"

"Doing what to you?" he asked uncertainly.

She didn't respond from under the sleeping bag but by her gentle trembling he realized that Anna was crying. He figured the poem had to be about her father, the dead trapeze artist. Over the sleeping bag, he gave her a hug. She immediately hugged him back.

12

When Alexei returned, he escorted Morozov to the afternoon faculty meeting room.

"I thought you were running down to help that young woman," the writer said to his young assistant.

"She was safe when I arrived."

"You should've let them beat the scoundrel to death," Morozov clarified.

"He's missing an arm and leg."

"Then maybe he shouldn't be attacking girls on the street, should he?"

"Daniel wasn't really attacking her. What he actually does is provoke guys into beating him up."

"Then you should indulge him."

"I met him at the veterans hospital when I was recuperating," Alexei explained. "Two years ago, during the invasion where I got wounded, they wiped out most of his unit. Almost single-handedly, he held the Germans off with a machine gun as the rest of his men retreated. He was found the next day, riddled with bullets, barely alive. Instead of giving him a medal, they gave him a dishonorable discharge because it was a retreat. They released him crippled and half-crazed."

Morozov didn't have a chance to respond as they suddenly entered the conference room, which was packed with professors. Each one with their stiff collars and pruned or puffy faces looked older than the next.

"Who are these decomposing clowns?" Morozov whispered, scanning the long conference table of esteemed men.

"The guy with the funny hat and crazy beard is the head of the Curriculum Committee," Alexei pointed out under his breath. "The one with the droopy left eye is the attaché of Political Affairs..." Morozov quietly sized up the key figures around the table until

67

Alexandrovich, the Chair who he recognized, called the meeting to order.

The Chair then greeted Morozov and commended his participation, but because there was limited space at the long table, he was relegated to a hard-backed chair toward the rear. He tried not to act indignant. For Alexei, though, there wasn't even standing room, so he nodded farewell.

Morozov didn't see a single faculty member that he had met at his reception. The session was soon called to order. As issues came up, the Chair recognized different speakers on a host of boring topics that meant absolutely nothing to Morozov. As the meeting pressed on, Haig's mind began to wander.

Prompted by the violent incident he had just seen outside his window, he soon lapsed into an awful childhood memory that he could never shake: He was fifteen years old, wearing his new school uniform heading to school when a group of ragged street toughs suddenly encircled him. First, they shoved the books out of his hands. When he fought back, they knocked him to the ground, kicking and punching him, eventually tearing his uniform right off his back. Out of nowhere, some taller kid raced over. He slugged a couple of the bigger bullies and the others scurried off.

He then helped Haig to his feet and said, "Those guys are just bad for business." He kept an eye on young Morozov as he staggered down the block and up the steps to school with a bloody nose and split lip.

That was how he first met Dimitri Lunz. Haig would see him chatting with other smartly dressed lads, upperclassmen. It turned out Lunz was a con man in training, popular with all the kids. A natural-born wheeler-dealer. He had a reputation of catering to the thrills of semi-privileged youths: fireworks, jagged daggers, small, dark bottles of alleged absinthe; there was even talk that he had access to a house of ill repute. From the day he was rescued by him, Haig was in awe. But Lunz didn't really notice the Armenian until he saw him carrying the book entitled *Verse About a Beautiful Lady* by Alexander Blok.

"You're reading that?" Lunz asked, surprised.

"Yeah, why?" Haig actually was doing his mother a favor, dropping the volume off at a local lending library.

"Blok is great," he said, opening the book. "I saw him read at the Peacock Eye a few years ago." This was a loud, smoky coffee shop frequented by scholarly vagabonds and raggedy poets.

Lunz recited several lines of Blok's poetry. Although Morozov enjoyed hearing the rhythmic, singsong cadence, the words had little meaning to him.

Perhaps registering Morozov's uncertainty, Lunz asked, "Do you know symbolism?"

"Symbolism?"

"It's kind of like writing in a secret code."

"A secret code, like spies use?"

"Sort of. You know the Okhrana reads everything, right?"

"Yeah."

"So if a symbolist wanted to write a poem about the corruption of the Tzar, without getting into trouble, he would make all the ministers different animals in the forest. That way if the police read it, they won't have a clue."

"Clever," young Morozov said. For the first time, poetry seemed intriguing. He liked the notion that one could hide meaning in it.

"My poetry isn't particularly symbolic," Lunz explained. "It's more prose, like Gorki, not a lot of room for interpretation. How about you?"

"Me?" Haig asked.

"Yeah, you write poetry, don't you? Everyone in your class does."

"Of course," Morozov replied, wanting to fit in, "but I'm not really ready to show it."

"Well, let me know when you get up the courage."

Instead of dropping the Blok book off at the library that afternoon, Haig read the slim volume. When he returned it to the lending library the next afternoon, he withdrew another book on his mother's account. Over the next month, he read as much symbolist poetry as he could stomach; only then did he try his hand at writing a symbolic poem:

"The birds are forced south in the winter due to the freezing cold, but they only return in the spring with their wings on fire."

The poem was meant to convey his frustration at being from two countries, Russia, where he felt second class and Turkey, where he was despised just for being Armenian. He read his new poem a few times, making slight alterations before he finally gave up. It just sounded silly.

A few days later, as he was on his way out, he heard shouting from his father's study. He dashed over, thinking he was wrestling with an intruder, but he didn't hear a second voice.

"How can you do this to us?! How can you kill your own people?!" he slurred. Haig could tell his father was drunk.

Although he had promised to avoid reading about the Armenian slaughter, he knew that his defenseless people, the giant womb of earth his ancestors had originated from, were being steadily annihilated each day by the thousands. Though he frantically prayed the allied armies would eventually stop them, time was running out. The Turks would continue their bloodthirst until every single Armenian living on their native soil was extinguished.

He could hear his drunken father howling:

"Where are you? WHERE THE HELL ARE YOU?!" he shrieked through the door. At first Haig thought his father might be addressing the civilized nations of the world who all had hoped would intervene. Soon though, he realized he was addressing God himself. "We honored our pact! Weren't we your most faithful tribe! How could you send us these monsters who are marching us to our death! At least kill your servants quickly!" Haig listened further, but only heard him weeping.

Haig went to his room and quickly wrote down what he heard.

A couple days later, he gave up on symbolism and just began writing and rewriting his father's words until he completed his first poem. The next day he modestly handed it to Lunz adding that it wasn't really symbolic. Lunz read it aloud softly:

God honored his pact not to allow his most faithful tribe to die.
The butchers made them march, god would not lie.
Though starved until their stomachs dropped, they walked.
Sunbaked until they shed their skin, they marched half-insane.
Their skeletons crossing the arid terrain.
They marched through the rapid bone-snatching rivers and streams.
And still keeping his holy word, god refrained to shorten their pain, they
hiked just the same.
Just the same, just the same.
God's folks pressed on, though their arteries were sliced open,
he refused to let them bleed.
"Their faith, their agony, that's what I want, he laughed, that's all I need!"
Eventually, unable to squeeze out anymore suffering,
Since there was no sign of a heaven, god dropped them on the Syrian
Plains to let his vultures feed.
They were the bread unleavened, his hateful creed.

"Interesting!" Lunz said upon finishing it. "I know a magazine editor who's looking for stuff. He's with an insurgent journal though so you really should put in a few more particulars."

"Like what?" Haig asked, wondering if he should mention the Turks by name.

"For starters, we're in Russia," Lunz said, not fully aware of Morozov's heritage. "You have really powerful feelings, but if you want to get this published here you need to change this to describe the horrors under the Tzar."

"The Tzar?" Morozov felt too embarrassed to mention that these were his people. "Let's see," Lunz said and, picking up a dull pencil, he made some quick edits but steadily added more and more. "You know what. Give me the night to fix this up for you."

"Okay," said the youth holding back his feelings.

The next day, Lunz said his poem was ready for submission as he proudly handed him the newly rewritten page. Morozov read:

At the Winter Palace they had their feet and legs shot off, but Nicholas
refused to let them drop,

*Some he imprisoned them in the bone-chilling cold of the Kolyma
riverlands,*

*Others he marched into the Kaiser's machine guns who mowed them
down.*

*Even dead they leapt up again and again until they realized that heaven
was as empty as the steppes,*

*Thankfully, the closest thing to god is Communism which will
eventually free us of our sins…*

"It's much more succinct. I think it really comes to life now,
right?" Lunz said proudly.

"I guess," Haig replied. Initially, Morozov wrote the poem to
impress the older youth, but along the way found joy in the process
itself.

"Would you mind if I put my name down as the coauthor?"
Lunz asked.

"I guess not," Morozov said, since he didn't even recognize the
work.

"I guarantee it'll help get you published."

Lunz gave the piece to the editor of a tiny underground
revolutionary journal called *Seize!* It was the first published work for
both of them.

13

Alexei, Woodstock Festival, August 15, 1969

The Russian journalist opened his bloodshot eyes and
wondered where the hell he was. Still dressed in last night's
suit and tie, he was hot, sweaty, and painfully hungover. His
old pal Sergei was snoring loudly next to him. Entombed in
the thick canvas of a surplus army pup tent, hearing the strange
pulsating strings and booming lyrics of nonsensical music, Alexei
wondered how the hell he had wound up there. Although
emphysema had compelled him to stop smoking, he craved a
cigarette more than life itself and even more desperately he needed
to piss. Rolling onto his big belly and lifting to his hands and knees,
he tiredly crawled backwards like an old alligator out the little flap.

It took him a long moment to slowly rise to his feet. Longhaired draft dodgers and poorly raised girls who he figured were probably pregnant ran past barefoot. They all had to be on drugs, he thought. What else would they be doing here in the middle of nowhere? This strange seductive blend of Western hell only fortified his belief in the virtues of communism and made him grateful that his sons were safely in Moscow. He took several steps toward a muddy trail before reaching the first tree, which he leaned against as he unzipped and began urinating. Looking forward, he suddenly realized at least a hundred kids were standing on some line staring at him.

"Looks like someone missed his morning commute," said one hippie, referring to Alexei's formal dress. Others burst out laughing.

"The urinals are up the hilltop, pop," said the hippie's companion.

"It's okay," Alexei said, holding up his hand, "I have a medical condition." He continued peeing as though he were invisible, then zipped up. He started coughing and spitting a while, then he yawned, thirsty, squinting at the clouds coming up over the hills. He started roaming around looking to serve his needs.

Alexei waddled across other tents and encampments divided by steady streams of kids trickling down toward the distant noisy stage. Along the high ground, there were various large wooden food stands; but they all had lines, long, long lines.

At one small camp, he spotted a hand-scrawled sign, "Good Coffee! 25 cents!" Under a broken umbrella, a hairy youth had put a large percolator on a wire mesh that was over a delicate flame.

"A little expensive, no?" he greeted the junior proprietor.

"We also provide milk and sugar," said the kid.

"How about tea?"

"No."

"Do you have any real food?" Alexei asked.

"I got donuts, fifteen cents!" Price gouging in desperate circumstances was universal.

Alexei ordered a cup of coffee and two small crumb donuts from a large brown paper bag.

"Let me ask you," Alexei said, pointing down at the big stage in the distance packed with a rather primitive group of long-haired youths who were playfully banging pieces of wood like overgrown children. "Who are these people?"

"Quill."

"Quit?"

"No, the thing Shakespeare wrote with—Quill!" The coffee seller wiggled his hand as if writing with a pencil.

"Okay, then who's after them?"

"Santana."

"Satchmo?"

"No, Carlos Santana and his band. I'm going down to the stage when he starts playing."

Another unknown.

"Who else?"

The young entrepreneur handed him a wrinkled piece of paper listing all the bands scheduled to perform.

Instead of seeing Coltrane, Mingus or Monk, Alexei was horrified to see silly cartoonish names like Incredible String Band, Canned Heat, and The Grateful Dead.

"What the hell is this?!" he said in Russia, turning the page over. The youth snatched back his list and gave the Russian his cup of coffee. Alexei counted out forty cents, downed his watery coffee in a single gulp and stormed back to the tent to confront the crazy Armenian about being shanghaied to this juvenile freak show. It was empty.

As he trudged up to the car, he spotted the shag of gray hair in the ridge and headed toward him. As he grew closer, he saw that he was holding something up and smiling.

"What's that?"

"A pork sandwich for you, my friend!" He handed him something tightly folded, which Alexei unwrapped. Inside was a thin slice of hard ham slipped between two stale pieces of white bread.

"Where'd you get this?"

"From the enemy—someone from the military was handing them out."

"What the hell did you get us into?" Alexei began yelling. "This isn't a jazz festival. It's a disaster zone!"

"Come on, Alexei. Music is music."

"Are you kidding me!" the journalist replied. "Never has silence been so gravely insulted!"

"Alexei, you were going to spend the weekend in some overpriced flophouse in Manhattan. Look around! Look what I got for you! Tell me this isn't the best story you'll ever file when you get back to Moscow! Tell me this won't get into Tass! You're the only foreign correspondent here—an exclusive! Once they see this back in Moscow, all these crazy kids, they'll forget all about the moon landing. Don't you see! The Demimonde of Decadent Democracy!"

"Actually," Alexei softened his tone, "I thought the same thing, but I don't like being lied to."

"You've got to see this place, Alexei. It's a big, wet world of toddlers! No one is older than 20."

"This whole thing makes me nervous."

"Why?"

"Suppose we needed to evacuate suddenly? We'd never get out of here alive," Alexei said tensely.

"Why the hell would we be forced to evacuate suddenly?" the Armenian asked, slightly amused.

"I was in Rzhev. You weren't there when the Germans rolled in. Tens of thousands of kids the same age as these just hid there in their foxholes petrified." He recalled the horror, the shame of his youth. "The Germans had cut us off, so we waited as they came in and finished us off." Looking downhill at the lawn before the stage, it was most densely packed in front of the rostrum. Alexei vividly remembered the slaughter: tight formations of dive bombers that came out of nowhere, maneuvering into a steep screaming dive, first being bombed then being strafed with machine-gun fire. Watching the planes circle and repeat, methodically raking the area over and over, killing hundreds and thousands of terrified Russian kids like himself.

"Some memories you can never escape," Alexei said.

75

"This is America, Alexei. There are no invading armies."

"I know, but...."

Alexei took a deep breath, bringing himself back into the moment.

"If you want to see something you'll never forget, but in a good way, come with me up to the pond near those woods." Sergei pointed to the tree line behind their tent.

"Look, I need a hot shower and a change of clothes," Alexei said. "Let's go find a nice lodge nearby, sleep, eat, and come back refreshed tomorrow. I can bill it to my expense account."

"There are no lodges around here, Alex. There are showers, but you have to be willing to wait. Like in Russia, there are long lines here."

Alexei sighed, looking up at the increasing clouds piling up. The music had stopped and some bearded man on the distant stage was yammering lyrics over the loudspeaker as the sky grew darker. Both men felt the growing apprehension of the rolling and rising sea of chattering kids swirling around them.

"I think we might be getting a shower without waiting on a line," kidded Sergei, looking at the dramatic increase of cumulonimbus clouds.

"I can really use a cigarette."

Sergei took the pack from his pocket. Though there were only three left, he gave him the driest one.

"Let's go back to the car so I can change at least," Alexei said, upon lighting up.

The men headed up to the grassy field where they were parked. No sooner did they reach the Cadillac than the sky burst like a giant damn and everyone started racing. The two men casually each got in their sides of the car, slammed the doors shut and locked them. Notwithstanding the general mayhem, they felt warm and comfortable as a thick rain fell and a powerful wind whipped around. Soon the rain showers were so dense, the drumming on the roof was exhilarating.

"It sounds like the fists of all the American kids beating to get in," Sergei said, staring at the concert-goers outside dashing around.

14

After the Philology Department faculty meeting, all of the influential professors quickly left before Morozov could engage, which was his primary purpose for going there. When he went to his office and realized that young Alexei Novikov had left for the day, he realized he wouldn't be getting his customary drive home. Just as well, Morozov thought, a brisk walk would clear his head.

On his recent train trip up from Yerevan, he had carefully inspected an updated map of the capital city showing its latest expansion. The surrounding farmland had been absorbed into Moscow. Since his arrival, he noticed that many of the city's major thoroughfares had recently been widened. Morozov was still living in the capital when they undertook the extensive construction of the subway system, which, as of yet, they still hadn't completed.

The next day, he took the new tube and visited his old family house. As he inspected the front windows from when he last resided there, he felt this acute ache, not just from memories of growing up, when his family had the run of the entire building, but during the brief time when he was living on the ground floor with his beloved Masha Rodchenko.

When it grew too painful, he turned and walked away. Countless new government buildings had sprung up in place of the many old landmarks from the former empire.

Reaching one large excavation project near Khitrov, where a tattered gang of construction laborers were gathered, Morozov stopped one of them, an old-timer. He pointed to the empty windows that resembled hollow eyes and asked, "Was this due to the bombing?"

"No, this was 'cause of a burst gas pipe last month." The laborer smelled of booze. He asked, "What bombing are you talking about?"

"Sorry," he said. "I thought this was..."

"I know what you're wondering," said another worker, a Siberian with furry sideburns. "You're wondering if we're from the civilian battalion why we are doing this."

"Actually I was wondering..."

"Answer is, we shouldn't be here at all! It should be the Department of Demolition and Clearance, but our boss owes someone a big favor..."

"So there weren't any air raids?" Morozov asked, nervous about getting bombed in his sleep.

"About a year ago some bombs fell a few blocks away," said the workman with the sideburns. "Maybe you're thinking about that."

"How many were killed then?" Morozov inquired.

"None, thank god. Sirens went off, all were safely evacuated," replied Sideburns. "The bombs just hit the street."

"Hey, you bums!" the commander of the civilian battalion shouted. "Back to work now!"

As Morozov resumed walking, he checked out the street signs and tried to recall some of the former names of the streets when he was last here. Street names that had changed after the Revolution were changed again as the Revolution transformed. He reached one small square and recalled an event that had never officially occurred, Nikolai Bukharin, the Revolution's most valued economic theorist and full member of the politburo, standing on a milk crate, more than twenty years ago passionately trying to explain to a mob of people how the short-term sacrifices of the new economic plan would lead to long-term benefits, trying to win them over instead of bully them.

Once Morozov arrived back at the Ulanov house, he ate dinner without uttering a word to Kata. Afterwards, he skimmed passages from his journal:

"The more dependent one is upon niceties, the more clouded one's judgment becomes. Privilege has distorted my parents from the greater reality. If one hopes to be a serious writer, one should never lose that vital grounding..."

Morozov ran his forefinger across the journal page. He could still feel the drops of wax that had fallen from the candle he had been using when he wrote the entry almost thirty years earlier. The piece

78

read as if his younger self was admonishing his current self. His elevated position had moved him far away from the masses.

Just as he was beginning to doze off, his doorbell rang. He laid perfectly still, hoping Kata would answer it, but then, as the ringing continued he realized she must've left a while ago. After a few more rings, he hoped they'd just go away. But as it kept ringing for exactly the same interval, he realized it wasn't the door at all, but a phone! If he knew there was a telephone in the house, he would've disconnected it immediately—the secret police had turned them all into reverse listening devices. He tracked the ringing to a phone in the kitchen pantry and snapped it up to stop it, but then he was too terrified to say a word.

"Are you there, Haig!" a very distant male voice arose from the crackling silence.

"Yes?" He yelled into it as though down a deep well.

"I tried calling you at work. Did they tell you?"

Although he still didn't know who was speaking, the voice sounded familiar. He knew if the man continued talking he'd recognize him.

"No," he replied tensely. "They didn't."

"I need you to help me with some poetry," he heard. Only one person in his entire life ever asked him that question. It had to be his old friend Lunz!

"Where are you Dimitri!" he shouted. "Are you okay?"

The static suddenly grew so loud it nearly deafened him, then the line went dead.

He quickly hung up. The Cheka had to be toying with him. He went to the silverware drawer and found a small kitchen knife, and for the next forty minutes he carefully unscrewed the metal plate and unwound the copper wires connecting the telephone to the rest of the world.

15

peeding through several day-old messages on his voicemail, Eric Stein found one call that took priority. David Lande Junior— the new head of Lande Properties LLC—asked him if he could call him at his earliest convenience. His father's death was still fresh. Eric could tell by the severity of Lande's tone that it was important. Eric showered, shaved, dressed, and had his morning coffee, all while trying to guess what the mogul could possibly want. When he finally called back, Lande's secretary immediately put him through.

"Hi, Mr. Lande. It's Eric Stein, I'm returning your call."

"Please call me David."

"My profound condolences on your father's passing, David."

"Thanks. I don't suppose you know why I'm calling," Lande said cryptically.

"All I can think of is our last conversation about monetizing your holdings to build equity for a future project."

"I actually am very curious about that, but that's not why I called. Something unusual has occurred and well... this is probably easier to explain in person."

"You want to see me?" Eric could hardly believe his luck.

"If you can spare me thirty minutes of your time. I promise I'll make it worth your while."

"Sure," Eric replied mystified. "You're at the World Trade Center?"

"My office is in the South Tower," Lande said.

"I should be in your neck of the woods later this week," Eric said, looking at his appointment book. "How is Thursday afternoon?"

"Perfect. I should be available all afternoon and this shouldn't take long," Lande replied. "Frankly, it's not easy for me to get around anymore."

"Sorry to hear it."

"My doctor said I'm his first patient who might need both a double hip and double knee replacement."

"Oh god!"

"Yeah, and I'm terrified of surgery. I'm not in the best shape and I'm not sure I'll make it off the table."

"Nonsense, you'll live to be a hundred—you've got your father's genes."

"God, I hope not!"

16

Kasabian, Moscow, 1943

When Morozov arrived at school the next day, he headed straight to the cafeteria for a hot cup of tea. There, he spotted Alexei talking to a curious-looking older gentleman and wondered if he was NKVD. His assistant saw him and must've sensed this as he waved him over and introduced him to the stranger. He turned out to be a science professor named Cohen.

"I remember reading your stories years ago. Enjoying them immensely," said the over-eager Semite. Haig thanked him and explained that he needed some tea.

"I'll fetch you a cup," Alexei rose and said. "I'm refilling my own."

"So how do you like Yosiff's old house?" the older academic asked.

"Who?"

Cohen explained that the former tenants of Ulanov House until five years ago were a brilliant history professor named Yosiff Lucashevski and his family of six, a wife and five small daughters. They had moved into the house in 1933 and lived there until one night in 1938. It turned out they had all been agents of Zinoviev and were involved in some complex espionage scheme involving the French government. Abruptly Lucashevski and his wife and kids vanished without a trace.

"Working for the French, eh?" Morozov said matter-of-factly.

"A lot of Russian capitalists fled there, you know," the old professor said earnestly.

After the family was arrested, Cohen continued, the old house was mothballed. Only late last year had it been redesignated as a new Visitors Quarters by the Ministry of Culture. Accordingly, its original pre-Revolutionary furniture was returned and basic repairs were made.

"As luck would have it, you're the first distinguished visitor in the newly initiated fellowship," the old professor said.

"Why are you telling me this?" Morozov asked suspiciously. Just talking about the arrests was taboo.

"I'm sorry," Cohen lowered his voice and drew closer. "Yoss was a dear friend. Our children used to play together. If they say he was a French spy, then I'm sure he was and I hope they shot him," he said wisely, assuming that Morozov would inform on him. "But I'm a biologist so I can't just ignore the fact that his body never even existed, which unofficially seems to be the case."

Morozov felt embarrassed for the man and nervous for himself.

"It's rude of me, I know, but I need to express that to someone. Even if it puts me and my family in jeopardy." An awkward silence followed.

"Some weather we're having," said Morozov, who assumed he was being set up. Alexei returned with a pot of hot tea, which he set down.

Looking at his wristwatch, the assistant said he had to run for a class. The young halfwit dashed off, so now he was alone again with Cohen, who was clearly ashamed of the risk he had taken and now refused to make a peep. Morozov just sipped his tea and silently cursed his lackey's name.

Young Alexei Novikov headed down a side staircase through a lengthy corridor to his superior's tiny office in the basement. He took a seat and waited for his boss, who was in the middle of typing up a report with his two index fingers. Ivan Lemokh was only a few months older than him.

"So what have you got for me?" Ivan Lemokh asked, pulling the report from out of his typewriter spool.

"Nothing yet," Alexei replied.

"Don't tell me that! That's why I'm paying for that little kulak of yours."

"I'm constantly with him."

"But she's not! And she should be spending more time with him–alone."

"We talked about this, Ivan. She's not going to sleep with him! She's not a tramp!"

"Not while she's your tramp," he replied and lit a cigarette.

"She was hired for her intelligence on him and maybe a little sensuality, but that's all."

"We specifically hired her for *his* entertainment not *yours*."

"But she was *my* girlfriend first," he replied.

"Which is the only reason I'm not cutting you loose!"

"He openly refers to both of us as Cheka," Alexei said, taking out a cigarette. "I don't think he even shits without believing someone's looking up his asshole."

"I have to tell you, Alexei, your performance honestly troubles me."

"What are you saying?" he asked, not lighting up.

"The only time I spoke to him at that reception hall, he boldly informed me that he liked that deposed Jew poet. Do you know what Osip Mandelstam got arrested for? He wrote a poem in which he referred to Stalin as a cockroach. Even saying that aloud gives me a chill! A few years ago, that alone would've been enough—consorting with the enemy. But you whisked him out of there, didn't you?"

"I was trying to gain his trust! I wanted him to think I'm on his side."

"You certainly convinced me," said Lemokh who snubbed his cigarette.

"You specifically told me this had to be a legitimate investigation, not some amateur set-up.

83

"He's not going to be in Moscow for very long," Ivan replied. "We need to land this fish quickly."

"Fine. Call your thug, Lazy Eye, and arrest him tonight! I won't get in trouble."

"You're not my only agent on this case," Ivan replied. "I'm giving you a week, just seven days, to close this case. Then I'll handle it myself and you're going back to the war."

17

Eric, NYC, December 7, 2000

Eric Stein got out at the Cortlandt Street stop, bought a hot cup of coffee to warm himself, and headed to the South Tower of the World Trade Center. Much like the Empire State Building, these iconic buildings, which always looked colossal from the outside were usually cramped and unimpressive when you entered the offices. Up the express bank of elevators, he then transferred to a second elevator at the 78th floor Sky Lobby. Finally, he got out at the 96th floor and entered the suite of offices lining the south side of the building.

In Lande Properties LLC, he was greeted by a crew-cutted receptionist who looked like she had stepped out of an advertisement in *Vogue*. For the past two days, he had used all his self-restraint not to reveal to Sam Kaye, his boss, anything about his appointment with Diamond Dave's son. He didn't want to build up any false expectations that Lande Junior could be asking him to helm a mega public offer. But what else could it be?

"You can go in now, Mr. Stein," said the *Vogue* model five minutes later.

As he walked into the large sunny office, he watched as Lande Jr. slowly rose to his feet.

"Not necessary, please!" Stein said, knowing the poor guy had loose legs. Lande leaned across the desk. Eric shook his hand and took the seat across from him.

"What a view!" Eric said, looking south over the tail end of Manhattan into the greenish-gray expanse of New York Harbor. "Birds must envy you!"

"Eric, I want to ask you a couple of quick questions."

"Sure," he said, expecting them to be about bringing his highly lucrative company public.

"My memory is not great," Lande said, smiling. "Would you mind if I taped this?"

"Be my guest," Eric said, flattered that the older man valued his wisdom. Lande took out a Sony microcassette audio recorder, pressed the REC button and set it on the table between them.

"What's the name of your father and mother?" Lande asked.

"My parents?" Eric asked, not seeing that coming.

"If you don't mind?"

"My father was also Eric Stein—Senior. He's the first. And my son is Eric the third, but he spells it with a *q*." He laughed.

"How about your mom then?"

"My mom's maiden name was Greenberg, Lydia Greenberg from East Tremont, why?"

"I just wanted to know where you're from."

"They're both native New Yorkers," he said. "As am I."

"Any siblings?" Lande asked.

"An older brother," Eric said softly. "Joshua."

"Does your older brother live in the city?"

"Josh died of AIDS a few years back," Eric said, intent on not acting ashamed. He didn't add that no one in the family even knew his brother was gay until he disclosed that he was dying.

"I'm so sorry," Lande said. "I don't mean to be prying."

"May I ask why you're asking about my family?" Eric said, giving the man the benefit of the doubt before growing testy.

Lande picked up the micro tape recorder and pushed the STOP button. "As you might remember, my father passed a little while ago."

"Yeah, I sent you a card and a flower arrangement."

85

"Yes, you did," Lande said, looking down. "I'm sorry if I'm taking a little time here. See, you're at the center of a rather puzzling mystery, and I'm hoping you can solve it."

"Me?"

"We just probated my father's will and he scribbled in a clause at the last moment." He looked directly into Eric's eyes as he said, "In it, he left half of his estate to you, claiming that you are his illegitimate son."

"ME!"

"That is correct. But you just said you were not."

"That's right, I'm not," Eric said, bewildered and amused.

"So here's what we're prepared to do," Lande took a mammoth file from his top drawer. He opened it and took out a typed letter, with a personal check attached by a large paperclip. He spun it around, and slid it across his beautiful, long walnut desk, stopping directly in front of Eric.

"That is called a disclaimer of interest, which is a standard form. If you sign it, you get to keep that check."

Staring at the check, Eric initially thought it was for $500 but looking again, he realized it was for half a million bucks!

"Wow!" he said.

"Wow is right," said Lande.

"I have to confess, Eric replied. "I was hoping that you had asked me here to handle your IPO."

"Coincidentally, I've been giving that a lot of serious thought, but first things first. And the first thing is I have to probate my father's will. Now, if you'd rather not sign the disclaimer, we can go to court and do a blood test and you'll see nothing, or you can take that nice chunk of change and..."

Realizing Lande was sweating bullets over the disclaimer, Eric picked up the pen and signed the two marked fields. Then, without pause, he tore up the check. He carefully placed the pieces back on his desk.

"I don't take money I haven't earned, David."

"Well that's very honorable of you, sir," Lande said, adjusting his glasses. Clearly the real estate tycoon didn't see that coming.

"I don't know why your father thought I was his son. I don't remember doing or saying anything to give him that impression."

"I believe you."

"I don't want to be curt, but if that's all, I really should be on my way." Eric didn't want to waste any more of the man's time.

"Hold on." Lande struggled to get back to his feet. "Can you come to our office New Year's party toward the end of the month? Maybe we can talk then."

"I'd be honored."

"We're having it around four p.m. on December twenty-ninth, we're just sending out a few invitations. It's really just a party for the employees in the office."

"I look forward to it."

The older man insisted on walking Eric to the office door. There they shook hands and Eric left. On his lengthy ride down the express elevator, he figured this was why he hadn't been invited to Lande's father's funeral.

18

Kasabian, Moscow, 1943

Morozov was twice woken up two blaring air raid siren echoing through the cold and silent streets. The Luftwaffe is on its way again, he thought. Staring out the bedroom window, over the clear dark skies of Moscow, he only saw stars. He tiredly headed back down to the basement of the Ulanov House, a rock-solid shell below the old building–his own private air raid shelter. No sooner did he get down there than he heard the second siren. Apparently it was only a false alarm.

He thought of the poor professor's family who had lived here before they were arrested, the Lucaschevskis and their daughters. He imagined the girls playing around on this basement floor during snowy days. He was still angry that his goddamned assistant had put him in that predicament with Professor Cohen.

As he was about to head back up to bed, he noticed where he had hit his head on the some of the boards under the staircase. They were painted a slightly different shade of gray. He also realized that these boards were broader than others. The head of the nails were smaller than the surrounding ones as well. He tapped the wall with his knuckles. It sounded hollow. He had this sudden premonition: Something was hidden behind them.

Feeling wide awake, he looked around for tools, but found nothing. He went up to the kitchen and grabbed an old meat clever. Back downstairs, he started working it between two of the suspicious planks. Once one board was loose, he wedged his index finger in and yanked it free. Morozov shone his flashlight into the space. Something was stuffed back there. Carefully he pulled out the three boards above it.

In the dark, along the narrow framed section of the wall, he made out what appeared to be an old crate. For a moment, he assumed that it must've belonged to the unfortunate family who had been arrested a few years earlier. But as he shined a flashlight on it, he saw by the layers of dust and cobwebs, it must've been stashed here before the Revolution.

Morozov slowly pulled and angled out a worn trunk. Opening it, he discovered that it was customized for an antique saddle. Holding the horn of the cracked saddle with one hand and the cantle with his other, he gently lifted it out of the case. Holes had been cut into the sides. Perhaps gems had been gouged out of the front pads. Although the leather was desiccated and cracked, Morozov could tell that it was once costly–a Moroccan grain. The seat pad was fashioned for a big-bottomed man. The length of the straps suggested it had been on a proportionately large horse. Morozov was about to lower the piece back into the trunk, but he noticed something odd. There was a small hole knocked through the bottom of the trunk, yet below, he didn't see the cement floor. Placing the saddle delicately to the ground, he tapped the thin wooden base. It had a collapsible bottom. Feeling along the edge, he was able to lift out a concealing tray.

Hidden underneath was a lower compartment. Several items were wrapped in yellowing linen. Undoing the first parcel, he found a small saber that was dented and tarnished. Upon close inspection he made out the tiny maker's mark, and next to it "1807 Warsaw."

Wrapping his fingers around the brass handle of the saber and swishing it through the air, it was no longer an artifact. Morozov was able to imagine the fierce Battle of Borodino, not far from here. Seeing the nicks and dents in the blade, he thought, this very sword might've been used against Napoleon's Grand Army.

He unwrapped a tiny second roll of cloth. Inside was a gold signet ring with a mysterious insignia. The owner, probably Ulanov, was a nobleman—a count or a duke. Maybe it signified membership to one of those secret officers' fraternities that attempted the Decembrist overthrow against Tzar Alexander. So the original owner, Ulanov might've actually been a revolutionary in his day.

Another bundle was a "gambler's companion," a small-caliber pistol with a single cylinder that discreetly fit into one's palm. Opening the chamber, Morozov saw a single bullet still inside. He took it out and looked at it. No visible rust or erosion. By its mother-of-pearl inlay and the meticulous fretwork along the snub-nosed barrel, Morozov knew that these types of pistols were commonplace jewelry in Wiesbaden, the gambling capital of its day. He placed the weapon in his robe pocket.

Finally, in a small brown envelope that crumbled to his touch, Morozov discovered an illustrious Saint George Cross. This had once been the highest military award given by the Tzar himself. Engraved on the back was the name Captain Fydor Ulanov. All this belonged to the building's original owner, an aristocratic revolutionary war hero. What a man!

Over the next twenty minutes, Morozov carefully placed the saddle and other objects back in the trunk and slid it all back into the opened wall.

Using the flat side of the meat cleaver, he painstakingly hammered the thin nails as best as he could back into the wooden slats, so that at a glimpse, the wall appeared untouched. Climbing the stairs, feeling something heavy swaying in his pocket, he realized that he had forgotten to put the old gambler's pistol back in the trunk. Too tired to go back down and pull everything out again, he hid it in his bedroom behind his books on a shelf. Then, he washed and readied himself again for sleep.

That morning Kata went to the basement where she saw all the dust and dirt on the floor. Looking up at the ceiling, she couldn't fathom where it had come from. She spent an hour scrubbing the basement floor. When she asked Morozov if he had any knowledge of the mess, he shrugged. Twenty minutes later, when she tried to use the phone, she discovered it wasn't working and saw the loose wires.

"I saw this last night," he said, nervous about being discovered. "I tried fixing it."

"No problem, I'll notify Housekeeping."

"I don't know why it stopped working, but I'd rather not have a phone."

"Don't you find it odd, these things happening at the same time?"

"What are you suggesting?" he asked, suspiciously.

"Maybe we have a ghost," she said earnestly.

"Spare me your peasant's superstitions!"

That afternoon she stormed into the Housekeeping Office at the university and applied for a transfer. In a space on the form marked: "Reasons for requesting the transfer," she wrote, "My charge's erratic temperament."

19

Eric, Woodstock Festival, August 14, 1969

Still in the car alone with Anna after she finished reading her poem, Eric softly asked, "Is that about your dad?"

"My Dad?" she said blankly.

"I figured Rooster was your dad." Instead of adding that she had mentioned his unusual demise, he hugged her sympathetically and without thinking, he gave her a peck on the cheek. Then he thought, *That's too much! And now we're going to be stuck in this car together all night.*

To his utter bewilderment, she kissed him on the lips, something he had never done before with a girl. In a moment, she sliced her tongue through his lips and into his mouth, utterly paralyzing him. He remained perfectly still as Anna ran the tip of her soft, moist tongue along his terrified lips again. It was all he could do to simply remain still. *Where did she learn all this?* he half-wondered. As she continued, he felt goose pimply and could feel his heart beating wildly. When she finally stopped, he very gently cupped her right breast over her shirt. When she didn't smack him, he leaned forward and French-kissed her back. His cock felt hard as a rock. He could hardly believe that he was alone for the night in Josh's car with the hottest chick ever, touching her breast.

"So what do you want to do?" she asked.

He wasn't sure what she meant. They couldn't go to a movie or grab a bite. They were stuck in this car in the middle of woods for the next twelve hours.

"Uh, I don't know," he said. "This is cool."

"No, I mean, you wanna try to get more comfortable?" She seemed amused by his confusion.

"Sure. How?"

Without a word, she reached down and slowly rubbed her fingers along the front of his pants.

"Oh shit!" he moaned and bit his bottom lip.

"Take it out," she whispered. She seemed more curious than aroused. Nevertheless, he could hardly believe his luck. He unzipped his jeans and no sooner did he angle it out, than she spat into her right palm and rubbed it rapidly up and down as if doing a magic trick.

"Easy," he said as she clenched it too tight.

She loosened her grip, compelling him to sigh. He closed his eyes and tried to savor the experience.

She lowered her head to his pelvis and kissed the side, compelling him to groan, which enticed her to wrap her lips around its bulging head. Holding it in her lips, she rubbed his shaft for less than a minute before he shot into her mouth. Although a lot came out, she was very careful about holding it in her mouth and not spilling it onto the blue carpet of Josh's Impala.

In another moment, she quietly popped open the door and spat his spunk to the ground.

"Oh my god!" he replied. "I can't believe we just did it! Where did you learn to do that? You're so amazing!"

"Shush," she said, and took a swig from the water jug, then spat it outside as well.

"I'm so impressed," he whispered earnestly. "It's like you've been doing it your whole life!"

"Actually I've never done it before," she countered.

"Really!" he said, amazed and flattered that he was her first. "You're my first."

"Don't tell anyone," she said.

"I won't! By the way, if I didn't say it earlier, the rhyme scheme of your poem is wonderful," he said, trying to find something else to compliment.

"Thanks."

"When you wrote, 'you did her, but didn't do me,' were you talking about your father's death?"

"Yep," she said, pulling away to her side of the car as though it were a distant island.

"Would you like me to give you... head?" he offered nervously.

"No, I'm fine," she replied. "I kind of owed it to you for the long drive up here and all."

"Oh, okay," he replied awkwardly and, since he couldn't exactly leave, he just sat there looking dead ahead, feeling foolish.

20

Barely noticing Kata's absence that first night, Morozov pulled some leftovers from the fridge and, as he no longer felt he was being watched, he grabbed a bottle of sherry from the pantry. Since he didn't have to eat in the dining room, he piled it all on a tray, carried it into the den, and began eating while flipping through his journals. In addition to reading entries about his old friend Dimitri, the names of other pals kept popping up: Johan, Ivan, Yuri, Hans, Critter, and so many names of supposed friends whose faces he could no longer envision. As he got older, the friends dropped off like leaves in autumn.

Finally turning ahead to his second year at the University of Moscow, he returned to Masha, specifically their brief honeymoon period. He could visibly see his feelings for her solidify on the pages of his journal: His cursive handwriting grew crisper, more figurative. The increased use of exclamation marks showed his excitement and urgency. His crystallized selection of words, all reflected his deepening attraction for her—and for life itself. He finally found one particular testimonial that actually made him blush:

I love the way you reluctantly laugh, my Masha!
I love the way you stare off deep in thought!
I love the way you suddenly frown clownishly then smile brightly!
I love watching you not hiding your unmitigated disgust!
I love seeing you talk softly and delicately to the elderly and infirm.
I love the way you intimately relate with children as though they were your very own.
I love watching your eyes light up when you're amused or excited!
I love the way you effortlessly release yourself into a deep sleep by merely tilting back your head!
I love it when you subtly shake your head barely noticeable in quiet dismay at something unacceptable!

Though his list of affection tirelessly continued, it hurt too much to read. Those pages appeared to have been written by someone else. Only bitterness was left.

He could hardly believe he was capable of even observing such fine subtleties, let alone finding them endearing.

Flipping ahead through the journal, he located a two-page entry where he detailed his brief encounter with the great Vladimir Lenin during a big literary event that he somehow had gotten invited to attend. It was little more than a few forgettable words in passing. But no one witnessed the encounter, so he knew he'd be able to embellish it. He decided to state in his upcoming memoir that he thanked the great leader for ending centuries of tzarist tyranny. Who would be able to contradict him? And he knew that this fictional exchange would get great attention when his memoirs were published. Unfortunately, as he flipped through the pages, he noted all the lengthy pleasurable chats he had with others who turned out to be counter-revolutionaries and therefore couldn't be included in his recollections.

Thinking back at his youth, he remembered the glorious Revolution as it first rolled out like a shiny chariot of hope. Almost immediately, though, it mowed down its own drivers. Soon it was brought to a halt by growing divisiveness and infighting. Haig could hardly believe it. Intellectual debates fueled by cheap vodka or thick teas—the types of which were forgotten the next morning—were culminating in violent accusations and actual arrests. Old friends were soon splitting into cliques and factions. People who spent decades fighting against the established hierarchy were unable to simply stop fighting. Conflict was all they knew. Dimitri Lunz kept saying that when these warriors finally understood that the Revolution was over, they'd eventually calm down. But it only seemed to grow worse.

As he flipped through the thick pages of his yellowing journal, notations became sketchier and less elaborate.

He finally spotted a vague entry—*"July 27, 1922—BITTER TEA!"*

This was when he began to realize for the first time that these scribbled recollections could be used against him, so he went back and tore out certain sensitive pages. And when other difficult events arose, he would simply jot down cryptic phrases that only he would know. It was the first ugly taste of things to come.

He vividly remembered, late one night, getting a hard volley of knocks on his door from two leather-jacketed Cheka thugs, who insisted he join them at once in their car. They drove him to Lubyanka Prison where he was brought into a cramped windowless interrogation room, no bigger than a custodian's closet. He was left alone to stew for hours, drenched in sweat. Eventually he felt as though he were suffocating. He started banging at the door, begging to be released. The two men eventually returned. They led him to a slightly larger interrogation room and asked if yesterday afternoon he went for a cup of tea at the Rising Tide Café.

He said he had—he and his girlfriend, Masha, had stopped in for a drink after classes.

"Did you hear anything unusual, comrade?"

Swimming in perspiration, he immediately feared that Masha, who wasn't politically savvy, might've spoken out of turn.

"Masha is a farm girl from the country, so if she said..."

"No, you fool! Did you hear someone sitting at a table behind you?"

"May I ask who told you I was there?"

"We ask the questions, you answer them!"

"You're putting me through all this to ask me about a conversation *I might have overheard* at a bistro yesterday?" There had to be more to what they were asking.

"Two men were sitting right behind you!" the quiet one said with a penetrating glare.

"With all due respect," Morozov said, "do *you* remember a conversation from a day ago that might've occurred behind you? Do you think anyone would?"

"If you don't want to be helpful..."

"I'd be happy to help. I simply have no recollection of any..."

95

"Do you think you might've heard one man state that he was going to murder Comrade Lenin?"

"Murder Lenin! 'Course not! I would've reported it immediately!"

"So you don't think you might have heard it?" asked the lead investigator glaring at him, then lighting a cigarette.

"I suppose I *might have* heard it. If I knew they were talking about an assassination, I mean, I would've listened more carefully."

"Would you sign a document to that effect?" asked the other interrogator, yet it sounded more like a command.

"That I *might* have heard this?" he confirmed.

They didn't say a word. Seeing the severity of their expressions, he knew that if he wanted to leave tonight in one piece, he could only say one word: "Okay."

They laid out an already typed document and handed him a pen. He tried skimming it, but the room was barely lit.

"Are you signing it or do you need more time alone?" barked the second interrogator as Morozov held the statement up to the dull bulb. The burning tip of the interrogator's cigarette was less than an inch from his face. He saw a name at the top of the pre-written statement. It must've been the accused. He didn't recognize him. Morozov hastily signed the statement and they let him leave. Things were clearly getting worse. He had just condemned some poor son of a bitch to death and didn't even know who he was.

"If they can pressure me to falsely testify against someone who I don't even know, they can easily get someone else to testify against me," Morozov said to Lunz later that night.

"Have a little faith in those in charge," Lunz responded flatly. "You helped round up your first counterrevolutionary. Congratulations, comrade. Hopefully you'll root out many more to come."

21

Eric, Narrowsburg, NY, 1969

In the darkness, Eric wondered if he could legitimately tell his brother, Josh, that he had lost his virginity from a blowjob. An orgasm performed by a woman seemed to be the basic definition of devirgination. No, technically he had to disqualify himself. The term intrinsically implied the involvement of a vagina. He was still a virgin. And he always wanted to see a live vagina without paying for it. It was such a mystery. Even in the few pictures he had seen of vaginas, almost nothing was visible beyond the thick triangle of pubic hair.

Quietly, Anna stared out of the car window into the darkness, nervously listening to the loud chorus of bugs. Finally, she quietly opened the door. Eric watched as she stepped outside, unbuckled her pants, pulled them down a bit, squatted and peed. A moment later, she was back in the car with the door locked, buckling up. Eric went out, stepped behind a tree and peed as well. While hearing the insects around him, he thought, *Grasshoppers, gnats, maybe even a cicada saw her vagina and I have not.*

For a while, the two talked some more about their turn-ons and turn-offs. Then, without asking, he closed his eyes, leaned in and began kissing her again, just her neck and cheek. First, she appeared startled, then she seemed to tolerate it. He felt like he had safely won this new border of intimacy. Pressing his luck, his hand slipped up her shirt and she let him touch the bottom of her right breast. Finally he gently pinched its nipple. After conquering this foreign land, he slowly, boldly turned his fingers southward toward her belt buckle.

"Just the upper," she said, as if reading from a rule book.

"See, it's just that, you know, I've never done that before and I'm really curious."

"You'll get there when you find the right girl," she assured him.

"I was kind of hoping you were the right girl."

"No, I've gone as far as I plan to go. You'll have to continue your voyage with another."

"Can I just see it?"

"It's just a bunch of uncombed hair," she said, and dropping her head forward she shook her hair in front of her face and said, "Just like this."

"Really? Is your vagina Cousin Itt?" he kidded.

"All I'm saying is there's a reason God covered it with hair."

"'Cause something so beautiful should be hidden," he said earnestly.

"That's sweet, but we got a big day tomorrow. Let's try to grab some shut-eye, shall we?" she said. She lifted her knees up, forming a protective barrier, and curled into a ball on her side of the backseat. For a moment, with eyes closed, she could only hear her own breath. He wasn't even exhaling.

"It's just that I can't stop thinking about it," he said softly after a few minutes.

"Too bad."

"You know it was so hard getting my brother to take us up here," he whined.

"Nice try, he was coming here anyway."

"Can't I just see it quickly?"

"Oh god! I thought I was nice getting you off."

"You were and I really don't want to be a nag, but we didn't really have sex and I was just hoping to see it once..."

"Well, that's too bad. And I'm not going to be nagged into doing something I don't want to do."

"I'm not trying to nag you, I mean, call it intellectual curiosity. I just want..."

"Okay, I get it. All right, I'll show you my vagina, but I want you to do something for me first."

"What?"

"I want you to ask me romantically. Can you do that?"

"Romantically?"

"Yeah, you know, romance? Women like romance."

"Oh, okay," he thought about it a minute. "Romantically, let's see. My dear, may I just ponder the beauty of thy..."

"What! Are you trying to romance me poetically?"

"Well, I don't have a box of chocolates," he said. Looking outside, in the moonlight he spotted the white pedals of a daisy a few feet from the car and was inspired. "Hold on!"

He softly pulled up the button unlocking the car and delicately opened the door. He crept on the grass three feet, not wanting to make a sound to startle any of the distant campers. Searching about, he began collecting a handful of the daisies until he heard the click of the car door softly shut behind him. He dropped the daisies and dashed back to find that Anna had pushed the button down, locking him out of the car in the darkness.

22

Kasabian, Moscow, 1943

A few days after his housekeeper, Kata, had transferred out of Morozov's residence, a small, chubby, grimy older man showed up at his door. When Haig asked what he wanted, he introduced himself as Mikhail Antonovich Kamenev and said he had just been assigned by University Housekeeping as a servant in the Ulanov Fellowship House.

"You don't look like a servant," Haig said. The man had a musky body odor, wore raggedy clothes, and badly needed a shave and shower.

"Sorry if I don't fit your expectations, comrade, but we're all on the same level now," the man replied. "I'm not going to dress as a powder puff just to please you."

The raggedy man walked through the hallway as though he was the owner of the premises.

Morozov suddenly realized he was staring at the genuine article—an old-fashioned pre-Revolution Russian. Most of the new Soviet citizens were groomed and so overly cautious, he was afraid to even talk to them. This guy spoke from the heart, devil may care about the consequences.

"I hope you like beef, cabbage, and horse radish 'cause every dish I know has them in it."

"Fine."

"I should say red meat. Because I also use venison and horse 'cause those food lines are usually shorter."

"Long as it's not too gamey," Haig replied, not wanting to smell him any longer.

"Just 'cause you're distinguished," he muttered, "doesn't mean I can cut food lines."

At that point, it was evident that whatever Kata had reported, they had sent this man as a form of punishment. But they had miscalculated. Despite his unpolished qualities, Haig still found him refreshing and at the very least he knew the man wasn't going to rat him out.

"So, you just arrived from Armenia, huh?" the servant asked, looking at the kitchen.

"Yerevan, yes."

"You might have heard, the Luftwaffe launched a major surprise attack."

"What?" Morozov asked, fearing that he meant they had attacked Armenia.

"Here! Two years ago," said Kamenev.

"Oh, yes, I heard..."

"Three massive armies, like giant snakes, slithered into our beloved land! Five million Vikings. One army going north, gulping down the Baltics and coiling around St. Petersburg."

Morozov nodded his head—he knew. Armenia was not on the moon.

"A second army going south into the Ukraine..."

"Yes, I know."

"And a third coming here," Morozov cut him off.

"Yes! A third strike coming right at us to the heart of our beloved capital. They brushed aside all resistance, destroyed all our airplanes, and consumed everything in their path."

Morozov saw no reason for trying to explain to the chatty drunk that everyone in the world from toddler to ancient knew what the Wehrmacht had done and the millions of lives destroyed in the process. "It was Mother Nature that slowed them down long enough for Comrade Stalin to get his troops from Siberia to push them back."

"Thank god," Morozov said tiredly.

"They came within spitting distance of us here in Moscow," the servant said, eyeing the cabinets, checking the stock. "We were days away from being slaughtered."

"I read."

"We were all so relieved a few years ago when Hitler signed that damned peace treaty, weren't we? Next thing we know his army is killing everything in sight and we're all running east with our tails between our legs."

"I'll let you get settled in," Morozov said, retreating out of the living room and into the bathroom, where he closed the door.

Morozov heard the drunk continue to mumble through the door, so he pulled the chain on the toilet. The servant kept ranting as it flushed, so Morozov spun open the bathtub faucets to drown him out further. Eventually, silence. Ten minutes later, he heard the front door slam shut. The servant had left.

Quietly, over the next few days, his relationship with the man turned into a game of cat and mouse. Morozov stayed out when the drunken servant was around, instructing him to leave whatever meals he made on the stove. He could help himself when he got home. For the first four days, despite the same stringy overcooked stews, this strategy seemed to be working.

On the fifth day, due to a cold front, Morozov decided to try to work on his memoir at home. As he was heading into the dining room, he heard Kamenev rattling around in the kitchen and froze in the hallway. That was when he first noticed a small picture hiding in the shadow there. It was a portrait he had always walked past but never really noticed. The subject looked like the poet Lermontov. Under it, a tiny brass plate read, "Count Fydor Danielovich Ulanov, 1795 -1839." It was the illustrious owner of the short sword and the Saint George's Medal, probably the patriarch who first built the house. He had lived forty-four years. *The same age as me!* Morozov thought.

"So that's where you're hiding!" said the manservant, unaware Morozov was staring at a picture. He was holding a plate of pastry. "You like strudel? They got a big shipment of it at the commissary."

"No thanks, I'm fine."

"You sure?" He shoved the plate in his face. "I'm having some."

"Suit yourself," he grunted. The servant returned to the kitchen, where he began singing some old folk song at the top of his lungs.

Morozov realized that he couldn't write at home any longer, not while this obnoxious ogre was around. At least Cheka agents had tact. Morozov shoved four of his journals and his notebook into his satchel, grabbed his coat, and stormed out into the freezing cold.

"Don't overeat! We're having fresh horse tonight!" Mikhail called out as Morozov exited. "With lots of horse radish!"

23

Alexei, Woodstock Festival, Saturday, August 16, 1969

As the rain poured, the two middle-aged Russians sat encapsulated in the smoke-filled luxury car enjoying the silent respite and watched hundreds, maybe thousands, of young wet Americanskis bouncing around like popcorn kernels. As the storm increased so did the kids, and the two couldn't stop laughing.

Sergei asked about Alexei's wife and kids. Over the past decade, during most of the Khrushchev years, the journalist had sent his friend letters painfully chronicling the rise and fall of his marriage. His wife had been the daughter of a big-time party official who had greatly helped him early in his career. Alexei explained that when his second son Vladimir left home to join the Officers Training Corp, there was simply no longer any reason for the couple to remain together. He didn't care for his wife and she silently found him pathetic. Still they remained tensely civil.

"You've been with her for how long?"

"Twenty-two years."

"My marriage only lasted two years," Sergei replied. "After that only girlfriends. I won't ever make that mistake again."

"You never had kids," Alexei explained. "If you did, you'd understand marriage."

"You don't think one can have kids and still be in love?"

"It's just that marriage without kids makes no sense. It's like going to war with no enemies."

Sergei laughed.

"After the sex ends it's all about the kids—there's nothing else. You do things for your sons that you won't do for anyone else."

"Or your daughters, I guess," Sergei added softly.

A break of clear skies led all to believe that the storm was over. But then another battalion of clouds rolled in from the west hitting everyone with another sprinkle, and it started warming up again. The grass was like a giant green Slip'N Slide. Puddles were everywhere. Despite all this, more kids kept arriving, coming down from the highway like water pouring into a clogged rain gutter, trickling over and down to the stage.

"What exactly is it they're all drawn to?" Alexei asked, finally getting out of the Cadillac.

Sergei pointed over the endless beads of wet heads between the two metallic amp towers that framed the slick yellow stage. "They're drawn to that army boy over there." He pointed down at Country Joe McDonald who was covering for Santana while his band was still setting up.

"That said, I still think it's all fake," Sergei said, "like the moon landing."

"An elaborate conspiracy might've created the moon landing," Alexei replied, "but nothing can be cheaper here than tossing some long-haired crybaby in front of a microphone."

"I don't mean he's fake, I mean all these kids pouring out here, jumping around, burning up all this energy," he said. "This is the same bravado that created the Revolution, the same gusto that pushed the German hordes out of Russia when we were up against overwhelming odds. These kids will burn off all their best years on this loud, juvenile crap. Then they'll get fat and old, have kids, and wonder why nothing ever changed in their materialistic country."

"Maybe it's better that way," Alexei said.

Sergei shrugged.

24

Kasabian, Moscow, 1943

No sooner did Morozov arrive in his office at the university than young Alexei jumped to attention and said he just received a call for him.

"From whom?"

"Some man who refused to leave his name and sounded very odd."

"That's my new house servant," Morozov surmised. "I was short tempered with the good one, so now they saddled me with this drunken bore."

Morozov paused at his secret memorial book shelf in the outer room and noticed a novel by one Serge Kuchov, whose book was picked only because the name reminded him of the peasant poet Sergei Kychokov. The man was executed back in '38. Morozov went into his office and took his journals out of his satchel. He sat at his desk and began skimming the pages and making notes until he was interrupted by the phone ringing outside.

A moment later, Alexei answered, then peaked in to say, "It's your drunken servant again, sir!"

Snatching up the extension, Morozov yelled, "Cook whatever horse you want, just leave me alone!"

"If Kharms was in exile, he would've telegraphed by now!" It was the old critic Voronsky.

"I never said he was in exile."

"No, but that's what some official told his wife," he explained. "I thought perhaps you could find out precisely where he is."

"I said I would've called you if I heard anything," Morozov replied in a whisper.

"But you cleverly hung up before I could give my telephone number."

"You're a menace!" Morozov said softly. "Just speaking with you can put me in hot water." Still considering the influence the older man once had on him, he couldn't just hang up.

"All I was hoping was that you could make a quick call to your boss."

"You don't make quick calls to the Commissar," Morozov replied. "He makes the quick calls."

"Call someone else then. You're well connected."

"Making queries such as these usually hurts the party you're inquiring about," Morozov replied. "Ever consider that?"

"Please, Haig, you're all I have."

"Kharms' wife was notified that he was shipped East?"

"Yes," Voronsky replied, "and they always allow the prisoners to telegraph their family upon arrival. But almost a year has passed and still no telegraph."

"She should be grateful they told her that he's been taken out of Leningrad."

"If your wife heard that you were arrested, wouldn't you want her to know you were safe?"

Morozov remembered the last time he had bumped into Voronsky in person. It was about twenty years ago. He was strolling through a park with Masha. They were still young and in love.

Even then, Voronsky seemed old and crotchety. He remembered hearing that a few years before Tolstoy had died, Voronsky savagely attacked the great writer for his latest religious tract "designed to dupe uneducated serfs."

"I'm not married," Morozov replied abruptly. "I don't have a wife."

"I see."

"Give me your number and I'll call you if I learn anything about Kharms, but you can't call me ever again," Morozov said. Voronsky promised he would not and that ended the call.

25

Alexei, Woodstock Festival, 1969

A s some tropical Caribbean street band performed on the big stage, Alexei and Sergei saw that the only way they could get away from the ubiquitous hippies was by crossing over a long, low stone wall. Once achieved, they meandered through a grassy field occupied only by a couple of tired cows.

"Excuse me!" Some hippie in a leather vest was waving at them. "Please come back!"

"Who are you?" Sergei asked the vested hippie.

"I'm with the Hog Farm," he said. "When you climbed over the stone wall you left Yeager's Farm..."

"What is Yeager's Farm?" asked Alexei.

"The rock concert."

"We'll just walk around awhile and come back," Sergei replied.

"No, you're on private property. You must come back now," said the hippie. "I'm the please man."

"The policeman?" asked Alexei.

"No, the *please*, man. As in 'please come back.'" He flashed a peace sign. The two men realized that the only way to stop this pesky youth was to do as he asked, so they climbed back over the stone wall to the parking lot. When they reached their car, Sergei unlocked the trunk, as Alexei opened the rear door and took a seat. Sergei reached behind the spare tire and located the second of the six quart-size bottles of Stolichnaya. When he returned he found that Alexei had removed his filthy, damp suit, and just stood in his shoes, underwear, and undershirt. He then popped open his suitcase and changed into his Bermuda shorts and polo shirt, his most fitting leisurewear for the usual occasion. His expensive dress shoes were soaked so he changed into his flip flops. Afterwards, he patted some talcum powder around his armpits and his privates, sending up a fragrant white plume, then slapped some aftershave on his stubbly face. As Sergei took a gulp of vodka, Alexei grabbed his notebook and located his Minox "spy" camera. Finally he took out an umbrella, which he popped open.

"Okay, let's get that headline story," he announced to Sergei.

They avoided the crowds who were dashing down toward the stage. Instead, they circled back over to the bushes and trees. There, they followed the children who were shifting along the muddy paths created from thousands of sandals, sneakers and bare feet. Alexei would intermittently pause before the more colorful hippies. He'd show his press card and explain he was writing an article on the event. All were happy to talk. He'd ask their names then: Where were they from? What did they want from life? What was their favorite band?

"John Sebastian," one kid replied to the final question.

"You mean Bach?" Alexei asked, surprised to hear one of the classics.

"No, Sebastian," he replied and, pointing toward the stage, he said, "the guy now performing." They hadn't even noticed that the tropical band Santana had finished.

"What exactly do you get from this rock and roll music?" Alexei asked.

"You're kidding!" the kid replied, astonished. "It's so groovy."

"Do you feel groovy that your country spent so much money on the moon launch while the poverty level is so high?" Sergei asked severely.

"Hey, I just try to accentuate the positive," the youth replied.

"The positive what?" Alexei asked, waiting for the next word, but it never came.

One group of kids told Alexei that they drove all night from Winnipeg, Canada. When asked how they felt about the inequities of their great nation, one replied, "Our government never allowed slavery, so we don't have the same racist poverty that they have down here."

An attractive pair of underage girls explained that they had snuck off without their parents' permission and thumbed down from Brookline, Massachusetts. They thought the moon landing was cool, but poverty was a bummer.

One added, "It really is just a laziness. Anyone can find work if they really look for it."

A couple of lean crew cuts explained that this was their "last hurrah." They had signed up and were heading out to Vietnam in a week.

"And how do you feel about the war?" Alexei asked.

"We need to stop the reds the same way we stopped the Germans," the taller one replied.

"The same way you did what?" Alexei asked.

"Same way we stopped the Nazis," the kid said as he began walking away.

"You stopped the Nazis!"

"Yeah, during the Great War."

"America fought the Germans for eleven months costing less than half a million lives," Alexei yelled back angrily. "Russia fought the Germans for four years, costing twenty million lives. You didn't stop anything!"

"Let it go," Sergei replied as Alexei cursed at them.

To free him up so Alexei could take notes for his interviews, Sergei took his long narrow camera and shot photos of the free-spirited youths.

In addition to the interviewed subjects, he would snap away when he saw topless girls. Fortunately Alexei brought a lot of film. He said some of the hippies reminded him of the simple-minded villagers when he traveled through Siberia one summer.

"What the hell do you think you're doing?!" shouted one kid who suddenly stopped balling his girlfriend as Sergei began snapping shot after shot of them from only several feet away.

"It's okay. He's with Tass," Alexei calmly explained, showing his press badge.

"Ass?" the girl asked, pulling down her skirt.

"Tass—The Soviet News Agency," Sergei said.

"Why do you need to..."

With a straight face, Alexei said, "We're showing the world to make love, not war."

"Well, here in America we usually ask permission before we photograph people doing it," the kid shot back. At that point, though, Alexei ran out of film, which was fine as he had gathered enough material to publish a nudist magazine.

26

Kasabian, Moscow, 1943

Whan the former critic Voronsky said he thought Haig was married, it was like ripping open an old wound. Morozov found himself thinking about Masha Rodchenko, who he had never really gotten over. That night, when he arrived home, he flipped through one of his journals to some dog-eared pages that he had deliberately avoided.

"December 21st, 1921 – Newly organized Yerevan State University has sent a recruiter who has been interviewing promising young Armenian educators. If he likes them they get a free trip to the homeland where they are trying to attract some of their native sons back to teach.

Yesterday I was interviewed here and today they offered me a four-day tour of their campus down in Armenia. I explained to the recruiter that I expected to be marrying soon, and any relocation would only be done with the consent of my fianceé. So he agreed to provide a spare rail ticket and accommodations for Masha as well.

Masha has been complaining how she was exhausted by all the political intrigue here in Moscow and would love to get out of the city, so she was happy to accept my offer. I had always wanted to make a pilgrimage to the ancient city that was once Armenia's capital. Masha had read how Tzar Nicholas the First had liberated it from Persian rule and made it part of Russia a little less than a century ago. This was fortunate as it now provides a vital sanctuary for all those who escaped the barbaric savagery of the new Ottomans."

Morozov skimmed through his log recounting the only vacation he and his girlfriend ever went on.

Due to the inclement weather, the train started out relatively empty. Although the recruiter only paid for two third-class tickets that first night, they had the train car entirely to themselves. As the old engine steamed along the scenic banks of the sensual Don, it was as though the car was their private honeymoon suite. They moved from seat to seat enjoying the solitude. The sun came out when they reached Voronezh Station. They awoke to a flood of people rushing inside, snatching up every available seat. Although they lacked the intimacy of that first blissful night, they still had fun, making great plans for their wonderful future together. They lingered in the gated area outside between the cars where they kissed and fondled under the silver light of the moon.

When they reached the busy market city of Rostov, they changed trains to a coastal line along the azure Sea of Azov and then southeast along the Black Sea, over the dramatic outline of the Caucasus Mountains into Georgia.

They got off at the capital city of Tbilisi. Six hours later they were under the awe-inspiring view of Mount Ararat in the ancient city of Yerevan. They arrived late at night and stayed at the state pension. It was two large rooms packed with double and triple bunks; fortunately, there were only a few snoring sojourners.

By the stiff manner in which he was walking to his bunk, Masha could see Haig was stifled in agony. As a student doctor, she had read about the testicular sensitivity that occurs from chronic yearning, the result of lengthy glandular excitation.

They found their assigned beds and put their bags upon them. Silently, Masha followed Haig into the W.C.

"Do you want to use it first?" he asked, bewildered as she followed him inside.

She silently locked the door behind them. As people slept outside, she kissed him on the mouth as she massaged his swollen gland. He hiked up her skirt and fondled her as well. It lasted for all of two minutes before he gasped and ejaculated. She was impressed by the volume of his emission, enough to populate all the girls at the university. Examining the hot fluid, she thought how odd this sticky solution should possess the very essence of life itself. When she looked up, still seeing him with his eyes closed and shuddering, it seemed misplaced how much significance nature had balanced on this trite spasmodic act. It was little more than a repetitive procedure,

110

monotonous in another context. Washing her hands off, she indulged him further, allowing him to continue touching her vagina under her dress. Soon, to her surprise, she found herself stimulated and panting as well. She shoved a towel in her mouth to keep from waking anyone up. When she regained herself, she felt slightly embarrassed by her vulnerability.

After the first day, sitting with Masha at an outdoor café, looking up at beautiful Mountain where Noah supposedly landed his great Ark, Morozov was as happy as he ever remembered being. He knew he was right where he should be–in his ancient homeland with the girl of his dreams. In the faces of the locals, their dark eyes, bold noses and, most of all, the thick heads of hair, Morozov could clearly identify the features of his father's bloodline.

During their hiatus, instead of visiting the campus as he was supposed to, whenever alone, the two stole every moment to kiss, vow their love, and discreetly fondle each other. If they could permanently fuse their faces and groins together, they gladly would have. Looking back at that brief hiatus to Armenia, he came to associate his homeland with love itself and it sealed his decision a few years later to eventually leave Moscow and settle down there forever.

27

Alexei, Woodstock Festival, 1969

The aroma of patchouli and marijuana smoke comingled in the hot August air as the two older men meandered in the woods along the eastern edge of the dairy farm. Greeting kids with victory finger signs, they'd pass various dealers hustling pot or acid. On occasion they'd see amateur jewelry for sale, laid out on blankets or logs or rocks. As Alexei inspected the handcrafted items, Sergei quickly purchased a bag of tightly rolled joints from some very tall, bearded hippie for four bucks. A moment later as a cloud of marijuana smoke wafted into Alexei's face, he saw Sergei toking a bent joint.

"What the hell are you doing?" Alexei asked taken by surprise.

111

"All those jazz recitals and you've never smoked pot?" Sergei asked, apparently experienced.

"Don't lie! You've never done it either. And for all you know it'll kill you."

"I've seen you guzzle down a thousand gallons of cheap vodka over the past twenty years. Whatever this is, it isn't going to kill us any faster."

Alexei took the joint from Sergei's lips and smoked it like a cigarette.

"You have to hold it in," said some curly-haired loafer.

Sergei took the joint back and demonstrated.

"Feel anything?" Alexei asked, referring to his state of mind.

"No, not really."

"Let me try again."

They resumed walking, passing the joint back and forth, sucking the smoke in as deep as they could until they were unable to hold the burning roach in their fingertips any longer. Sergei took out the next long, pointy marijuana cigarette and lit it as well.

"Are you drunk yet?" asked Alexei.

"They call it stoned," Sergei corrected and, looking at the joint, he said, "It's probably black tea."

"Maybe we should stir it in water and drink it," kidded Alexei.

"You know what I find absolutely amazing?" Sergei asked after several long minutes of silence. "The idea, the very concept, that a single solitary human, just another ant, like you or I, some young businessman did *a-a-a-all* this." He waved his hand along the vast panorama packed with kids. "I mean, the notion that one man in this country can affect all this: rent this farmland, find these awful musical acts, put them up on that noisy stage, and attract all these hairy little children here—That's absolutely magical, no?"

"Magic, no, but can you imagine how much red tape this would take, how many committees, the various under-commissars, all the bureaucratic channels they'd have to go through back home?" Alexei replied.

"The bribes alone would be astronomical. In fact, what I can't figure out," said Sergei, who knew that they were both stoned, "is how anyone is even making any money here."

"What are you talking about?" Alexei said. "This place is packed!"

"Very true. Yet I was prepared to buy tickets," Sergei said. "But it's free, as is the parking. Also I'm hungry but there's nowhere to buy any food. They're giving it away!"

"Yes, I saw a long food line over there," Alexei pointed up the hill.

"That's the point! This is American capitalism! There should be competition. We should be buying it at an incredible markup!" Sergei continued. "And if there was a hotel, I'd be happy to rent accommodations, but no hotels. Even these awful musicians, if they were selling their records, I'd probably buy one, just to try to understand what they're yelling..."

"Oh, I have to put all this in my article," Alexei replied.

"This really is pure communism."

"Good point!"

"And I can't figure out what they even regard as a song."

"It's as if this whole fiasco was pulled together by some incompetent assistant under-commissar from Vladivostok, no?"

"Oh! That goes into the article!" Alexei countered, inspired. "A capitalist catastrophe!"

"I'll still say this," Sergei added. "I could never imagine anything like this ever happening in Russia."

"Thank god!" Alexei agreed.

At a distance, Sergei spotted a group of naked blonde women prancing around in the pond like wood nymphs, so they decided to have a closer look. As they circled around the vast crowd of spectators, it began sprinkling again. A group of teens dashed by like a herd of hairless upright deer wearing Levi's jeans.

"Isn't it interesting how all these kids are wearing the pants of railroad mechanics?" Alexei observed, regarding the dungarees and making more notes for his article.

"Blue jeans are actually made from an awful fabric," Sergei said. His father who had escaped the Armenian massacres had settled in Moscow where he became a tailor. "Denim doesn't really breathe. It's too hot in the summer. And they have no real insulation, so they're cold in the winter."

"They're durable though," Alexei pointed out.

"Okay, they're durable," Sergei conceded.

As they reached the bottom outer edge of the stage, the Keef Hartley Band blared.

"This music!" Alexei shouted, amused. "It's far more repetitive than either classical or jazz. It's like they're selling the same six notes over and over."

"At least the lyrics are still old-fashioned love poems," Sergei defended.

"How do you know? I can only understand every tenth word," he continued.

Alexei continued ranting, but Sergei was no longer listening. The effects of the pot allowed the Armenian to drift off in his own head. Soon, both were quietly listening. But they were grateful when the band finally ended its noisy cycle. As the next band began to load in, Sergei spotted a worker in a green tee shirt with an image of a small bird perched on the end of a balalaika. Sergei realized the worker was an official associated with the event.

"Are you one of the pig farmers?" he asked.

"I work here, but I'm not with the hog farm," replied the kid.

"How exactly do you people make money?" Alexei asked.

"What?"

"Where's the food and bathrooms please?" Sergei modified the question.

"Food stands and toilets are up there somewhere," he replied. "Just follow the lines, man."

28

Whent Eric Stein showed up at David Lande's pre-New Year's Day party at the World Trade Center, the mogul had already gone through his stated quota of three thimble-size glasses of champagne. He was sitting alone in his office gazing out over Ellis Island and the Statue of Liberty. The door was open and when Eric asked the short-haired Vogue model if he could say hi, Lande heard him and waved him in.

"Wow, you can see the Verrazano Bridge from here," he said, staring at the magnificent view.

"I personally prefer the Goethals," Lande replied.

Eric noticed a large photograph on his wall. It was of a young man who resembled David only he was wearing fashionable clothes from sixty years ago. It took him a moment to realize it had to be his old man, Diamond Dave, when he was still young.

"Good-looking fella," Eric complimented his dad.

"He was a real cad," his son replied, "an unrepentant lady's man."

"You must miss him."

"'Course, but he wasn't always easy to deal with."

"What parent or child is?" Stein said, thinking of his own son.

"Would you believe me if I told you that my dad started out in Russia as a poet?"

"Your father was a poet?!" Eric repeated, unable to digest it.

"Yep. And I'd love to read the poems, but they were all in Russian."

"I never met a poet worth over a billion dollars."

"Apparently the Bolsheviks assigned him to work in some small warehouse outside Moscow making furniture but he had no appetite for it."

"With his business sense, I'm sure the productivity must have been extraordinary."

"Actually he was so bad he got demoted."

Eric chuckled at the thought.

"He confessed that he was never much good at poetry either," Lande added.

"Did he have anything published?"

"He said he did. And I wanted to locate and buy a journal to give it to him as a birthday gift, but he said he wrote under a different name and he refused to ever talk about it."

"So he changed his name?"

"Yep, he took Lande when he came to America." David added. "He said our original name was something like Zemlya, which means land, but I couldn't find anyone with that name."

"Maybe your father had something to hide."

"He was a quirky guy, with more than his share of secrets, but it's not for me to judge him."

"Judging by his real estate holdings, he was a big success."

"You know, money is nice, but money is just money," David said. "I actually always admired the fact that Dad tried his hand at poetry."

"I don't know any poets, but I do know a few real estate tycoons."

"We're given a handful of years to leave our mark, then we return to the earth," Lande said.

Eric had heard from various sources that over the last few years, the younger Lande had taken meetings with various top architects, offering specs and asking for prospective blueprints on what could be done with one of his larger pieces of property, but he couldn't find out where. He assumed it was one of his sizable parcels in the more up-and-coming neighborhoods of Brooklyn, either Greenpoint or Sunset Park.

"It sounds like you're also ready to leave your mark in the world of developments," Eric said, taking a chance.

"You heard about my pet project."

"Everyone has."

"It was just a lark," he revealed.

"Sounds more like a condor," Eric kidded. "Maybe it's time to let your condor take flight."

116

"No, Dad wouldn't approve. This business was all his."

"But in fairness, he didn't live long enough to see New York transform into the city it's becoming. This is the Golden Age for real estate development."

"I'm not going to gamble his holdings on..."

"You don't have to gamble a cent. That's the whole point of the IPO."

"Jamaica Bay Estates," Lande said.

"Jamaica Bay?" Stein asked. He was unaware that Lande had any property in Jamaica Bay.

"It's been a secret fantasy. I've had it for years."

"But Broad Channel is so blue collar," Eric replied. It was filled with firefighters and policemen.

"Not Broad Channel," Lande said, chuckling. "East New York."

"East New York?!"

"I have five-by-seven square blocks out there right on the water, just sitting empty. It has a spectacular uninterrupted view of the bay. Jamaica Bay Estates can be both a city home and a beach house for those who can afford it. We can turn the shoreline into slips for private yachts. It'll be spectacular."

"It sounds wonderful," Eric paused, not wanting to burst his bubble. "But you have spacious parcels in several neighborhoods that are clearly turning around right now. That's a much better place to start. Isn't it?"

"No, Eric, the zoning and the politics in those areas are really tough. Starting something out there, I still have the freedom to do things."

"You sure?"

"I'm not going to live forever. I only have one big project in me. If I'm going to leave my mark, it's going to be on Jamaica Bay."

"That part of town is still pretty rough. Maybe in twenty years it'll be the right time, but..."

"I'm not going to be around in twenty years," Lande replied. "I mean, if you're not interested, I understand, but..."

"No! No, if this is the project in your heart, so be it. Let's do it."

117

Eric's career had been steadily flagging and though he was one of the oldest VPs at Kaye & Oden, Sammy Kaye, the president of the firm, reminded him that the position as Managing Director of Real Estate Investments was going to be up for grabs this winter. A major public offering managed by the Lande Properties LLC would make him a shoo-in. In addition to a promotion, he'd automatically be made a junior partner. Even if he thought the project was a long shot, it would still be a solid win for him.

29

Kasabian, Moscow, 1943

Morozov fell into a sweet, warm sleep remembering his brief romantic vacation with beloved Masha to his homeland.

It only seemed like a wink later when he was rattled awake by a rude stream of profanities that was bubbling up from below. He pulled on a robe and slippers and staggered down the stairs to see his punitive servant cursing at the morning newspaper.

"What the hell!" he called down. Dawn was just breaking outside.

"Awful news, my friend, just awful news!"

"I don't care!"

"The Vikings have counterattacked!" The drunk held up the paper. "You might see some action after all."

"What?"

The manservant explained that after the German Ninth had been encircled, a Russian advance force had raced ahead to try to cut them off near Kharkov, but Manstein outflanked the Soviet spearhead, effectively capturing the entire army group.

"Ninety thousand men, gone, just like that!" He snapped his fingers. "Now there's nothing between us and the Nazis. They could be here tomorrow!"

He kept ranting on, so Haig retreated back to the bathroom where he spun on the faucets as he had done earlier. He could hear the drunken lout as he washed. His rant continued as he finally returned upstairs. He knew there was no way he'd be able to eat, sleep, or work with this miserable mammal groaning on and on, so he grabbed his valise and crammed it with four old journals. Morozov came back downstairs to find the old bastard mumbling to himself lyrically. His eyes were closed. Studying him, the inebriated servant seemed to be singing in his sleep. Morozov grabbed his coat and walked right past him, out the door.

The slow walk to the school in the brisk cold helped wake him up. Morozov arrived early in the faculty cafeteria, and without even asking, he was given a bowl of warm oatmeal and a weak cup of tea. Holding the tray, he fumbled for his wallet. One pocket, then another. He must've left it at home.

"Allow me," he heard. It was the dapper, young literature professor he had met only briefly at his reception. The man handed rubles to the cashier.

"You're the head of that committee," Morozov responded.

"Theodore Slotkin. Yes, head of the Ulanov Residency Sub-Committee," the young man reintroduced himself. "So glad to have run into you again. I was hoping to make a request."

Even overcooked, oatmeal came with a price, he thought.

"Would you consider coming to my honors literature class and giving a brief talk? We never get living writers. By the time their works arrive at the university, they're usually dead," he kidded.

Morozov began to explain that much as he'd love to, he was overburdened with tremendous obligation. Before he could begin his eloquent rejection though, he spotted Acting Chair Alexandrovich approaching within earshot.

"I'd be honored to talk to your class," Morozov announced loudly.

"Great!" The two men agreed on a time—in one week.

What the hell, he thought, I can still make use of the Trans-Caucus Literature index cards that I had prepared and never used for Alexandrovich's class.

"We read one of your stories last semester, The Loyal Pet, and the students all loved it. When you were picked for the fellowship, all my students requested you." Alexandrovich left the cafeteria so Morozov nodded blankly, took his tray of food and, without any farewell, headed up to his office.

Sitting alone at his desk, after a couple spoonfuls of oatmeal, he put the tray on the floor and opened his bag. He located a specific volume of his diary and flipped to a page dated, November 29, 1917, just after Revolution:

"*Shortages are widespread. The lines are so insane, they are getting tangled up with other lines. People literally live on the lines. And riots are breaking out. I can only wonder how all the people relieve themselves. And another big snowstorm is coming tomorrow!*"

He remembered Dimitri making money, selling supplies to those stuck on line. During those years, his friend volunteered for dangerous, top-secret, high-risk jobs for the cause. Yet after the Revolution, when things began to normalize, he simply had no marketable skills. Unlike Masha and Morozov, his vocational and academic qualifications were severely limited. To his good fortune though, some members of his old gang, thugs from his covert expropriation committee who had risen through the ranks of the Moscow Soviet remembered the daring youth who repeatedly risked life and limb for the cause.

Over many more experienced tradesmen, Dimitri was soon offered a foreman's post at Auxiliary Furniture-making Company #4 just outside of town. It was the best he could hope for.

With the job went new lodgings, and he was assigned a nice room in a workers' dormitory near his factory. The only problem was his newly appointed dwelling was miles away from the center of Moscow, far from all his beloved watering holes. Additionally, he had to routinely rise in the early mornings. He now managed shifts of men, all of whom were older and more experienced than him—and therefore resentful. They privately nicknamed him "the commissar's son."

Though the job started well, soon Lunz began to sneak out early. He'd travel back to his old haunts in downtown Moscow, get tanked, read his bad poetry aloud, get into scrapes with buddies, and occasionally pick up equally soused girls. Frequently afterwards he'd pass out in bars, or in the rear of the trolleys. Once he even got arrested and missed an entire day of work.

Focusing on those early days of the Revolution, just after his father's death, Morozov was informed that with the housing re-allotments, he and his mother were allowed to remain in their family's home. But their spacious townhouse was subdivided for four other families. Their new dwelling was now their former sitting room, which was still a bigger space than most apartments. A fold-out partition ran down the middle of the room. After four weeks of living together and getting on each other's nerves, his mother announced that she was "done with the Revolution." She had decided to join her sister in her small country house outside Saint Petersburg—a space they'd have all to themselves.

The recollection brought tears to Morozov's eyes. Grabbing another diary, years ahead, Morozov flipped through it searching for happier times. He found the entry when Masha first announced that she had gotten accepted into the university's prestigious medical college, one of only three women in a class of two hundred and fifty-two men. In addition to the fact that she liked Morozov, his apartment—the old parlor—was much quieter and more spacious than her cramped dormitory.

Fortunately, the Revolution had ushered in a new wave of liberalization—a relaxation in everything from divorce laws to homosexuality as well as the legalization of extra-marital cohabitation, but neither wanted to have children at that point in their life. So, aroused as Haig was, neither wanted to go all the way.

Still, late at night, between work and study, much as he'd restrain himself, Haig would keep pushing and she kept pushing back. One day he brought home a bottle of vodka. After they both got thoroughly drunk and insanely passionate, with Masha's defenses down, the young writer charged forward. Finally they consummated their love and fell into a blissful sleep.

"Oh, shit!" Haig awoke with a start, both naked and hungover. "I'm so sorry!"

"Relax," she said groggily.

"But suppose you get pregnant?!" he asked in a panic.

"We'll just get married," she replied, still more asleep than awake. Opening one eye, she could see the terror in his face. She knew his mother would never permit the union and despite all his revolutionary rhetoric, he was just another big mama's boy.

"I'm not stupid," she said, and pulling the sheet aside she revealed a small bloody stain on a towel she had laid on the bed. "My flow began yesterday."

"What does that mean?" he asked, not familiar with the mysteries of the female body.

"The likelihood of getting pregnant is greatly reduced," she tiredly explained.

Haig let out a relieved sigh.

"But it can happen," she added. "So we shouldn't do this again."

Not wanting to open a can of worms about marriage, he kept silent.

In addition to constantly writing and getting published in increasingly more prestigious journals, Haig recognized that he needed a more reliable form of income, particularly if he was going to ever support a family. He enrolled in a new educational college program and volunteered at the local Party headquarters.

"You really should join the Party," he warned Masha one day. "They're desperately looking for new members from the outer republics with professional credentials. As a doctor you'd be a shoo-in."

"Communism isn't popular with my people," she said.

"They're going to make the requirements to join steadily harder over time."

"If you keep pushing the Party on me," she said tiredly, "I'm going to push marriage on you."

Although he loved her, that silenced him.

Problems didn't start until the night Dimitri popped in. Although Lunz was drunk and wouldn't stop singing, Haig couldn't refuse his old pal. It was freezing outside that night with a howling wind. Too far away from home and too late to toss him out, Haig let him curl up on his father's valuable Armenian carpet.

Dimitri apologized profusely the next morning saying that it would never happen again. Then two weeks later, it did. In the middle of another freezing night, Haig awoke to banging on his front door, rousing him and Masha from a deep sleep. Haig opened and found Dimitri sleeping against his doorway. He shook him and pointed to the carpet in front of the fireplace. Lunz curled up like an old dog on it and slept as the flames tapered. Soon the visits became weekly, always ending with an apology and a promise that it'd never happen again.

But it was too late. Lunz discovered that no matter how drunk he got, he could stagger the few blocks to his old pal's house. And if he banged on the old oak door long enough, Morozov would angrily open up. Then without permission he'd stagger in and pass out in his spot in front of the fireplace. He'd awaken a few hours later to find his Armenian friend had kindly pulled off his shoes. He'd dash into the bathroom, needing to pee and frequently puke. The sun would just be coming up, so he'd splash some cold water on his face and quietly leave without a word. He'd nearly sleepwalk to the trolley and just make it to work, shout out some basic orders, then slam his office door, lock it, and feign paperwork. There, he'd lean his chair back so his head was up against the wall and slip back into his detoxifying sleep.

30

Eric, NYC, February, 2001

The thought of selling shares of a shiny, luxury high-rise complex on the edge of one of the city's most entrenched ghettos sounded nearly impossible. So for his very first lunch with David Lande, Eric brought charts, graphs, and documents and tried his best once again to politely persuade the real estate tycoon that if they instead located this development on his smaller Greenpoint or even his modest Long Island City properties this would be a much more feasible enterprise.

"But the properties there aren't even half the size—I don't want to spend a lot of time on another silly sixteen-unit condo," Lande dismissed.

"But it would be a great place to start, to learn from. You'd make a ton of money, an easy win."

"Look," Lande said, "I'm not even sure I want to do this whole IPO thing, but if I am going to do it, I only plan to do it once and I want it to be my masterpiece. I want something that will shake up the real estate world. This project will be a foothold for turning that entire part of town around."

"But it's still a large gamble."

"According to you, the money is free."

"But if we don't attract investors..."

"Eric, let's get something straight," David yelled emphatically. "Your job is to work for me or this isn't going to work at all."

"Of course," Stein said, contritely.

"Let me rephrase that..."

"No, you are right."

"Not if I'm wrong," he replied. "Do you really believe that it's too soon to build in that part of town?"

"People are flooding into this city. And they're all heading eastward," Eric said. "They're building in neighborhoods that you and I would never have set foot in five years ago Fort Greene, Bed-Stuy, Brownsville, Bushwick are all steadily being rented and they're all heading toward East New York, so I'm not holding anything back. I just figured that if you wanted to play it safe, we can first build this in an area that is already profitable."

"This project is going to be years in the making. I might not even be around when it's done. So I don't mind overextending myself a bit. Like I said, it's going to be my one big creation. But if you really don't think the IPO will go through."

"There are other big projects being built even further east," Eric said. "Those are risky, but they do come with big rewards."

"Tell me one big project that is further east than mine," Lande said, sensing that Stein was just blowing smoke up his ass.

"The Dunes—Arverne by the Sea out in the Rockaways," he replied. "It's an even bigger tract of land further east than you. And frankly that area is about as dead as your neighborhood. Even more so. It's basically a ghetto."

"Hmm," Lande was suspicious.

"Look, what you said was right. My job is to listen to you. And to try to make your vision work."

"But I don't just want you to placate me. If it flops, and I lose my company..."

"No way, they're two separate entities. No chance of that even happening. The success or failure of Jamaica Bay shouldn't affect your company at all."

"Hold on now, how much control will I have?"

"We'd sell shares of that Jamaica Bay company, but you'd keep controlling interest."

"And you think we could raise hundreds of millions from this?"

"If we do it right, yes. I mean, it's not a company that's earning money, which is a challenge, but you're starting from a highly valued, long-established company that has a lot of equity, so it's definitely doable."

"What do you need from me?"

"First and foremost, I need to have a full understanding of what you want to do."

"Why don't I show you at the location?"

A week later, Lande took Stein out to the site—a sprawling string of properties beginning at a dilapidated paper mill and ending with an obsolete sewage treatment plant, potentially big enough to be its own little community surrounded by marsh. As they slowly walked through the rusted and corroded landscape under the watchful eyes of Lande's security guard, the tycoon pointed out details and explained exactly what he was hoping to do with the property. Eric periodically took pictures. It was truly an impressive vision. The old man had done plenty of homework. But still, the idea of attracting moneyed people this far away from the city seemed remote. Eric kept that to himself.

125

He delicately pointed out the pros and cons of Lande's plan, touching on everything from the amount and pricing of the many different units to the sizes, ending on how much the local infrastructure could support.

"We're going to have to get the city to increase the sewage and electrical capacity out here," Lande replied.

"You're probably going to go the extra mile and make this a self-sustaining mini-city."

"Mini-city how?"

"You know, like Roosevelt Island or Battery Park City."

"Why do you say that?"

"Because the neighborhood... it's..."

He didn't feel comfortable mentioning that it was primarily a low-income Black neighborhood, while the residents buying into his complex would have to be well off and probably non-Black.

"This neighborhood simply doesn't have the resources to support this comfort level."

"What are you saying?"

"You've got solid plans for underground parking, which is good 'cause they'd be worried about their cars. Instead of just turning the ground floor into commercial space, well, you have more than enough space to create a medium-size mall. You could even attract people down from Long Island and other middle-class neighborhoods."

"Maybe a multiplex Loew's Theater or a Costco," Lande added.

"If you build it, they will come," Eric said optimistically.

Lande loved the idea of bringing in mixed incomes, with a decided edge toward upper middle class. He continued going back and forth with him, making his Jamaica Bay Estate Project into a commercial bastion for the middle-class that Stein felt would greatly increase the chances of attracting upper- and middle-class tenants and thereby IPO investors.

31

Periodically, the assigned tenants in Morozov's childhood home, now a housing collective, would stop Haig in the hallway and complain about the drunken lout who was periodically banging on the front door at all hours of the night. According to the Soviet communal housing bylaws, a guest wasn't permitted to spend more than two nights per month, but all knew that Haig's family had owned the building and he had always been helpful to his fellow cohabitants while most former owners were not, so no one reported him. Still, patience was wearing thin.

Finally, after two more midnight visits, a kindly middle-aged harpist on the top floor— which used to be his father's home office— told Haig that one of the grumpier tenants was about to put him on report with the housing committee. Unable to reject his old friend, Haig instructed Lunz that in the future, when he stumbled over at night, he should bypass the door and just climb right through the ground-floor window.

"I might not remember that," Dimitri said. "Can't I just keep banging?"

"If you do that I'm going to be forced to call the police, understand?"

"All right," Dimitri replied and thanked him profusely.

From then on, Haig would leave the window unlocked. Although Masha never liked Dimitri and was equally exhausted by his midnight drop-ins, she knew that Haig regarded Lunz as a kind of needy brother. So, instead of the entire building, soon only they would be awakened as Lunz tumbled into his apartment.

He tumbled in a couple more times. Then one day, the unwelcome visits abruptly stopped.

For several weeks no appearance, no calls, nothing. Haig hoped that maybe Lunz found a pub he liked near his own home.

It was over a month later when an old friend, Eduard, stopped Haig and Masha on the street and gave them his condolences.

"Condolences for what?" Haig grinned, thinking he was kidding.

"Dimitri," he said softly. "His execution."

"His WHAT!"

"Well I assume he was," Eduard replied. "I mean I know they executed most of the others, so I just assumed they shot him too."

"For what?"

"Niki told me he heard he got rounded up with a group of others. And then someone said that they all got shot."

"Niki who?"

"I don't know his last name. One of the guys who Dimitri hung out with at the Drunken Owl." That was a popular bar Dimitri frequented. "You know Lunz was never good at following rules."

"What exactly are you saying?" Masha interrupted.

"Just that if anyone was going to get executed in our new Russia, it would be Lunz," Eduard said. "Am I wrong?"

"Dimitri might've been a bad communist and a drunk, but if that was punishable by death," Masha said, "they'd have to execute half of Russia."

"What exactly did you hear?" Haig asked, still dumbstruck. "Why the hell would anyone shoot him?"

"Nowadays everyone gets shot for the same thing, don't they?" Eduard said. "For treason?"

"Why the hell would a bunch of furniture makers commit treason?" Haig wondered aloud. He had heard that they were finding large-scale conspiracies working within a single trade union or workplace, but furniture construction seemed so apolitical. He also knew that the NKVD was so paranoid that if he even went to the authorities to ask about his friend, he'd expose himself to a possible arrest.

"I don't think they were furniture makers," Eduard replied, but added that he knew nothing else about it and had to run. It was clear that he was nervous just talking about it.

Haig went into a deep depression over his friend's sudden death. Masha kept her thoughts to herself, but silently she thought he was better off. Lunz always seemed to be reckless and selfish.

128

While he was alive Haig would constantly complain about him. Now that he was gone, it was as if all these sour qualities made him all the more valuable.

She lit a votive candle above the fireplace to help Haig with his grief but he wept even more. Together they kept checking the newspapers, trying to find any official statement on poor Dimitri's arrest and execution, but nothing was printed and no one heard a word. Going through his own files, Haig was distressed that he could find only a single photo of his old friend. He placed the picture on his mantelpiece before the candle. Lunz was barely twenty-five years old.

Roughly a month later, Masha and Haig were awakened early one morning by a steady tapping on their window pane. Masha opened the curtain. To her surprise, she saw an emaciated Lunz standing outside.

"It's Dimitri!" Masha called out.

Haig raced outside, opened the door, and helped his old friend in. He was covered in bruises and contusions. Masha sat him down and attended to his wounds with iodine and gauze.

"We heard you were shot," Haig stated.

"Who told you that?"

"Eduard came by about a month ago. He said you and your co-workers were executed for treason."

"Let him talk!" Masha said and asked Lunz, "What happened?"

"The NKVD held me in an isolation cell in Lubyanka for over a month and kept interrogating me, I had no idea that they had grabbed the whole team."

"What were the charges?" Masha asked.

"Anti-Bolshevik acts."

"What acts?" Haig asked. "What team were you a part of?"

"If I tell either of you, you could be dragged into it as well," he said.

"Tell us something!" Masha demanded, looking at him savagely.

"One night you join a bunch of friends at a bar. Soon you're all drunk off your ass. One of the group who you barely even know starts mouthing off about food shortages and someone else starts saying how good things were in the old days. A few days later, you're dragged into a paddy wagon and forced into signing a confession you can't even read."

"This same exact thing happened to me!" Haig said to Masha.

"I remember," she replied. Turning back to Dimitri she said, "So the charges were fake?"

"This isn't a government! It's a gang of thugs!" Haig complained.

"Apparently," Dimitri said. Then in a low tone, he added, "But we really shouldn't be talking any further."

"He's right," Haig said nervously. "Let's end this conversation."

"In fact, I should probably leave here now," Dimitri said, looking at Masha. "I don't want to involve either of you in any of this."

"Where will you go?" she asked, clearly concerned. For the first time, she actually seemed to be worried about the derelict furniture worker.

"I'm staying with friends. I was released yesterday."

"Do you need any money?" Haig asked him.

"No thanks. I just wanted to let you know that I was okay," he said to Haig and smiled at Masha.

"We'll keep the window unlocked for you just in case," she replied sympathetically.

"Thank you," he said meekly.

After he left, Masha commented how Dimitri seemed far more grown up than she remembered him.

"Imprisonment and torture will do that to you," Haig replied.

32

Eric, NYC, February 2001

In January David Lande consulted the firm of Granville Michaels Associates, architects and engineers who specialized in urban malls. After a dozen meetings and site inspections, they had drawn up preliminary blueprints. Once Eric's firm of Kaye & Oden signed the contract to be the lead underwriter, he began approaching several big Wall Street houses pitching the Jamaica Bay Estate Development—or the JBED IPO, as it was known—to half a dozen possible underwriters. He also worked through a big-time wheeler-dealer to look into possible tax breaks and other benefits he could get from the city, state, and federal governments. Upon his advice, Lande opened up the building to mixed salaries which included "a servant's entrance," designed for some token lower-income residents from the neighborhood. This would dramatically cut their property tax bill.

By the first week in February Eric had three choices for a co-underwriter, Goldman Sachs, Bear Stearns and Merrill Lynch. By March, Eric picked Tom Rhondra at Merrill Lynch. The guy had an excellent reputation and he knew he'd do a great job.

"This deal is going to be neither simple nor easy," the mogul said. "We'll also need a really good law firm."

Lande was still having difficulty finding a reputable construction firm to deliver what he thought would be a fair bid. Slowly as the vision grew more elaborate, cost estimates steadily rose. Stein and his team at Kaye & Oden—or K&O—sat with Lande's people and went into details of how to diversify his equity base to get cheaper access to capital.

"First things first," Oden said. He explained that Lande could greatly benefit by a tasteful publicity campaign to increase the company's public exposure.

Soon, early boilerplate drafts of the IPO began to appear. Accountants had finally crunched the numbers and penciled them in. They were hoping to raise three hundred million dollars at $29.58 per share. All told, they hoped to sell 11,563,000 shares, which would make up seventy-eight percent of the new company. David Lande would retain fifty-one percent of the company. As payment, Kay & Oden would be able to issue ten percent of the shares to top customers, which was expected to instantly earn at least three million dollars for K&O. Eric calculated that his bonus for the deal would be at least three hundred thousand dollars. Merrill Lynch would handle the rest of the shares. But by the end of April, Lande was still haggling with different construction firms who he thought could undertake the massive construction project.

33

Kasabian, Moscow, 1921

After Haig discovered that Dimitri Lunz was back in the land of the living, the poet returned the following Saturday in the middle of the day. He was clean, well dressed, and understandably calmer. He brought a bag of apples. Haig was home alone but wished Masha was around if only to show her that his friend wasn't always a boorish drunk.

"So what exactly happened?" the young Armenian writer asked. "What were the repercussions of your arrest?"

"For starters I lost my cushy job," he said, grinning, embarrassed.

"I mean regarding the investigation."

"Apparently they shot six of the sixteen people in my group, so I guess the rest of us were exonerated."

"How do you know they won't arrest you again and shoot you later?"

"Believe me, I live in constant fear of that."

"Do you need money or..."

"No, I still have a job. They reassigned me. Instead of being the boss, I'm now the lowest man on the totem pole. And I'm already getting all my lumps for it."

"Here," Haig said, taking out his wallet. "Masha would want me to give you some rubles."

"No, I'm good."

"Nonsense! How are you going to get vodka?" he teased.

"My drinking days are over," he said resolutely. "I'm turning over a new leaf."

Morozov had heard him say this before. "Turn over your leaf tomorrow." He put the rubles on the table.

Dimitri slipped the money into his pocket. "You're always so good to me. Some day, when I get on my feet, I'm going to pay you back, I promise."

Later that night when Haig explained Dimitri's resolution to Masha, she said, "You should encourage him to stop drinking. That's probably how he got into trouble in the first place."

In the ensuing weeks, on the three occasions when Lunz appeared, it was always midday, he was always sober and well groomed, always bringing some bruised or unripened fruit.

One evening a few months into his sobriety, Lunz showed up with a soft apple. Masha and Haig shared a big pot of watery borscht with him. Haig thoughtlessly poured them all a glass of wine.

"I know you and Masha think I'm kidding." He pushed the glass away. "But I've given up the drink."

"This is all because of your arrest?" Masha asked.

"It's a little bigger than that."

"Bigger how?" she asked, restraining a smirk.

"Six of my comrades were shot and the rest of us had our sentences commuted."

"Now you know how Dostoyevsky felt," Morozov replied. "He almost got executed as well."

"Exactly, and after finishing his sentence in Siberia, his life was changed forever," Lunz replied.

"How exactly has your life changed, Dimitri?" she asked delicately.

"Now I have to live for those others. It's as though they died for me."

"Maybe they were guilty," Haig replied.

"No guiltier than I."

"I think you're assuming too much of a burden," Masha said. Staring into his sad eyes she whispered, "This wasn't your fault."

"He's being melodramatic," Haig said, sipping his wine.

"My friends were shot," Dimitri said angrily.

"So what could you do?" Haig asked. "Confess and get shot as well for something you didn't do?"

"I can get out of this awful town," he said. "And use whatever time I have left wisely."

"Find a nice woman, marry her, and have many children," Masha replied almost sisterly.

"The only reason I'd have children would be in hope that one of them might be a poet," he said, "so I might as well do it myself."

Haig snickered, because Lunz was a lousy poet, but Masha saw him.

"Haig!" Masha shouted. "Can't you see Dimitri is serious?"

"No, Haig is right. It sounds ridiculous," Lunz said. "I don't have the talent, but I'm going to learn. I'm going to try my best to be as great as I can!"

"Just try not to be awful," Haig uttered softly.

Lunz explained that he had almost saved up enough money and was nearly finished making travel plans.

"You're going abroad?" Masha asked.

"Nope, I'm staying right here," he declared. "I intend to travel deep into the unexplored heart of Mother Russia."

"You sound like Oedipus," Haig teased.

"And you make Russia sound like deepest, darkest Africa," Masha added.

"Seriously, I've been making arrangements getting train schedules from all over the country..."

"When are you planning on leaving?" Masha asked.

"Maybe now. This could very well be the last time you'll ever see me," he said, staring intently into Masha's eyes. "Either of you!"

"Quit joking," Haig snickered.

"Moscow's become far too dangerous," Dimitri said, pulling on his jacket. "This whole communist thing. Well it's no more communist than the church is Christian."

"You can get into trouble for talking like that," Masha said as he rose to leave.

"I'm sorry, but it's true. If Marx were still alive, he wouldn't recognize this mess," Dimitri said, and gave Haig a parting embrace. He was even more surprised when Masha leaned forward and hugged him as well. Apparently for her, all his malarkey really hit home. Although Morozov knew Dimitri would most probably turn up inebriated puking on his carpet within the next week, he said farewell as though he would never see his friend again. He never would've guessed that Lunz wasn't kidding.

34

Eric, NYC, March 2001

Over the next month, as the K&O marketing team pitched a thousand shares of JBED, Stein continued working on the IPO all the while adding new members to his team of consultants, many of whom were referred to him through either Merrill Lynch or Davis Polk. They included architects, accountants, appraisers, zoning specialists, engineers, local expediters, and a variety of lawyers and bankers.

At a meeting with Kaye & Oden, Eric proudly announced that real estate speculation was at an all-time high and he sincerely believed the IPO could be launched as early as June.

"That would just be perfect," said Oden, "it has been a slow year."

"Smaller developers have already bought up some adjacent properties!" he replied.

After a series of radio ads proudly publicized Lande Properties and word of the Jamaica Bay project began to appear in print journals, a local East New York activist, Reggie Godfrey started pasting up flyers. He soon organized a rally outside the gates of Lande's property giving a lengthy speech about "outside interlopers pimping out the soul of the community."

Lande Properties immediately issued a press release announcing a list of benefits that the project would have for the neighborhood, including a variety of affordable units and the promise of over a hundred permanent jobs for people from the area.

A second, larger community rally was held in the center of the neighborhood in which activist Godfrey demanded that the Lande site be taken over by eminent domain and turned into a much-needed park for the locals.

"Eric, I'm sorry to say this," Lande said, "but I think we're going to have to delay the IPO 'til this mess dies down."

"Nonsense," Stein said. "These pesky problems are typical for all large-scale projects."

"This guy is more than just pesky. He's a news magnet. This is going to be a dark cloud over the IPO and the project until he goes away."

"I know a guy who took care of something just like this a few years ago."

"Don't tell me about it, but if you can make it go away, we'll keep going."

It took a lot of asking around and cost Eric more cash than he wanted to spend, but after two weeks he was referred to someone who had handled something like this before.

Dwayne Reynolds, a swarthy, intimidating man, who talked like a minister, rented a shiny red Lincoln Town Car and drove out to the edge of Brooklyn, East New York, early the following week. He parked in front of Godfrey's storefront apartment, which now had its window painted: JAMAICA BAY NEIGHBORHOOD ACTION COMMITTEE. Dwayne sipped a cup of coffee until the activist stepped outside. Before he could register anything, Reynolds asked if he could talk for a moment.

"You work for Lande?" Godfrey said without missing a beat.

"Union rep." He handed him his business card, which read:

Amalgamated Construction Workers
& Builders Union Local 49B
Dwayne Reynolds
Organizer

"What you're doing is tying up a lot of important hires from eastern Brooklyn."

"The jobs will come, but first the neighborhood needs to get taken care of."

"Look," Reynolds said, stepping into Godfrey's personal space. "Lande put together a nice little honey pot for this neighborhood and you know that's the best you're gonna get. But I don't blame you, I know how this works and so do you."

"I do?"

"Sure, you want to get something for yourself, and you earned it with all the work and attention you got."

"What's this now?" Godfrey asked.

"Here's the way it goes down. My union gets a big bonus when this job goes through, so we're gonna step in and make sure you're happy."

"Sounds like a bribe."

"You're a community activist, I feel you. And this community needs one. Cause if it didn't, I wouldn't be talking to you."

"Who would be?" Godfrey asked.

"You would've gotten a message, but not with words."

"Is that a threat?"

"State Senator Sidney Rush from this district is vulnerable and some of us think you'd do well in his seat." Godfrey grew silent. "I did my homework, I read the interview you gave last month, trash talking him. You're gunning for him, but you got no bullets in your gun."

"Sounds like another threat."

"We can use someone in Albany who knows the people's needs."

"So you're saying..."

"I can get you some nice union endorsements from around town and speak to people about getting you an exploratory budget. It's a great opportunity to launch a political career."

"Would Lande be willing to..."

"Lande is in the Alps skiing. He's not a part of this."

"That's why I don't want his project here," Godfrey said. "Now what are you going to do, break my legs?"

"Reject my offer and two things happen. First, we're going to make sure that this neighborhood knows all the things it could've gotten if it wasn't for you, And second, he'll stall this another year or two or ten, 'til this dies down and you're gone. Then he'll just build it anyway, because at the end of the day all we're talking about is a little bad press. But your fifteen minutes of fame will be over, you'll get nothing. And my union will lose a bunch of much needed jobs."

"I need to think about it."

"Think quickly, 'cause I'm not guaranteeing how long my offer will be on the table."

Dwayne wished him a good day, got in his car, and drove off. Two hours later, he got a call back.

"Tell me about this exploratory budget," Godfrey said.

"Ten grand, that's enough to get the ball rolling for a state senate campaign. Signs, flyers, robocalls. You already got a storefront to get volunteers for signatures. And enough interest to attract other donors for a run at Rush's seat."

"Twenty," he demanded.

"Twelve-five," Reynolds countered.

"Fifteen."

"I'll have to check," Reynolds said firmly.

"And I want a publicized meeting in which Lande shakes my hand saying we worked things out. It'll give me gravitas in the community."

"Maybe I can ask one of his people, but no way is Lande coming down for this."

"Okay," Godfrey said.

"Fifteen grand and a well-publicized news conference with a representative of Lande Properties at the site," Reynolds informed Eric Stein once he returned to his office.

"And your fee brings that to twenty-five," Stein said, a small price to extinguish the little fire and put the IPO back on track. Lande was pleased with the outcome.

Both Tom Rondra at Merrill Lynch and Eric Stein chose Richard Edel, a senior partner at Davis Polk, as legal counsel to the IPO. The man had a lengthy resume of real estate deals and knew the legal landscape like the back of his hand.

A few days later Lande found a reputable national builder, Cahill Construction Inc., who sent a field supervisor to look over the plans and inspect the site. A week later they began to negotiate the terms, deadlines, and finally the overall costs. Upon hearing this news, Stein broached the topic of a release date for the Jamaica Estates IPO.

"Let me mull this over," Lande replied. A week later, Lande's office forwarded him an email they just got from "Green Bay," an ecological not-for-profit who "expressed genuine concern" with how the project would affect the wetlands of Jamaica Bay, asking details about the overall building project as well as the various building materials. It concluded with a veiled threat to contact the EPA unless they got to see the requested data.

Lande referred Green Bay to Cahill Construction, who in turn put them in touch with their green consultants, who started a lengthy dialogue about various building materials, construction techniques, and designs to make the project eco-friendly.

By late spring, since this too seemed to be resolving itself, Lande Jr. invited Eric over to his office in the Twin Towers hoping to find a suitable date for the IPO launch. But as soon as Stein arrived, Lande gave him a letter he had received that morning. It was from one officer Daniel Keats at the FAA who also had gotten wind of the prospective Jamaica Bay project. They were asking for an immediate injunction against the construction firm due to the site's proximity to JFK Airport—all surrounding properties had strict codes.

"Oh shit!" Eric said. This sort of stuff was supposed to go through Davis Polk, where Eric would first be notified, so he could find some delicate way to spin it.

"As soon as we clear one hurdle," Lande said, "we're hit with another and we haven't even launched the IPO yet."

"David, you've been around long enough to know that this is the nature of the beast. If you push back the launch every time you hit a bump, you're never going to get this off the ground."

"But they're all threatening legal action prior to construction. If I got the IPO..."

"Let them threaten all they want. Let them file the injunctions and suits, let them sign petitions, have rallies. They got their people and we've got ours."

"I suppose so. It just worries me that we're getting this much heat this early on."

"Money is like fresh shit, it draws all the flies," Eric said, trying to nurse him along. "Everyone wants a piece of it."

"It seems like the gods are giving me a sign."

"God is giving us two big thumbs up."

"You know what really worries me?"

"What?"

"I just keep thinking that once this thing goes through," Lande said, "it concerns me that I alone won't be able to steer a ship this big. I mean, the thought that I'll be at the mercy of some board makes me tremble."

"But you'll still have controlling interest."

"I know, and I'll get all this development money without having to risk a cent of my own. I get it. But frankly I'm just a very private person."

"I understand."

"And I know that once we're done, this new company will require much greater transparency."

"Everything comes with a price," Eric said, nervous about where the conversation was heading. He held his breath for a minute, just waiting to see at this late date if Lande was about to pull the plug.

"I'm having a hard time wrapping my head around all this," Lande said. "I just don't know what my life will be like in a year."

"I won't lie. You'll have to adapt, but you're going to be earning a lot more money."

"I don't need more money. I'm not a kid anymore, Eric. I just don't know where I'm going to find all the hours."

"It's really just business as usual. You delegate. You hire the people you need to do whatever job you don't want to do," Eric said firmly.

"How far away are you from having the IPO ready?" Lande asked.

"Actually I think late June would be the perfect time to launch it," Stein said, knowing full well that there was no way he'd have it ready by that time.

"I'll pencil it in, we'll see where it goes," Lande replied. "The lawyers and builders are going to need at least that much time to work out this mess with the FAA."

Eric wanted to ask him who at Davis Polk had directly informed him of the FAA notice, but he knew Lande would sense that Stein was keeping other problems from him, so he didn't say a word.

35

Eric, Woodstock Festival, August 14, 1969

"What the hell! Open the goddamn door!" Eric said softly but firmly, pulling on the handle.

"Shush!" Anna replied, holding a finger over her lips and whispering just loud enough for him to hear. "You're going to get your brother in trouble if anyone hears you!"

"Let me in the fucking car," he said in a tense whisper, then looked around in the darkness.

"I think it would be better if you stayed outside and I stayed in the car for the night," she replied matter of factly.

"Are you kidding!" he said in a stern whisper. "It's terrifying out here. Let me in right now!"

"You're terrified?"

"Yes!"

"So now you know how I feel when I'm in the car with somebody who wants to see my vagina and I don't want to show it!"

"Okay, you made your point! Now open the door!"

"First I want you to promise that you're not going to try anything funny."

"I wasn't going to try anything funny before. Considering what we had just done, I didn't think asking to look at your privates was funny, I was actually quite sincere."

"And I told you no and you kept nagging!"

"How come you get to take out my penis and give me a blowjob, but when I want something I'm suddenly a threat?"

"Because you wanted me to do that. And you can't get raped and I can. You have an advantage over me."

"Okay," he said, not because he agreed with her, but because he knew the only chance of getting back in the car was by capitulating. She pulled up the button lock and Eric popped open the door. She slid to the far side of the seat as he got in. He locked the door and silently sat on his side facing one direction. She curled up on her side facing the other.

He tried sleeping, but the strange sounds of nature made him jumpy, which made her jumpy. After an hour or so, they both awoke from their shallow sleep to hear a steady tapping on the roof of the car. It had begun raining. Soon it was pouring. Lightning burst across the sky.

"Holy shit!" she said and after five minutes of continuous rain, she stopped herself from saying that she feared the weekend was going to be a washout.

Twenty minutes later the lightning stopped, but the rain kept falling and they finally both drifted off to sleep.

When someone whacked the roof of their car, both Eric and Anna bolted up like two pieces of toast. As the milky sky lightened, it was still lightly raining. Josh unlocked the driver side door and hopped in.

"Sorry, I was afraid you guys had left," he said, winded and wet. He was wearing a goofy Boy Scout outfit.

"What's up?" Eric nervously asked as his older brother fired up the engine. Anna looked out the window, fearful that he was being chased or that they had been discovered.

When Eric checked his watch, he saw it was already ten o'clock.

"What's up?" Anna asked.

"Because of the rain, no one can use the lake, so I'm free 'til it stops which, according to the weather report, will be in the next ten minutes," Josh said as he peeled out. "So I figured if I move like a motherfucker, I can get you guys to Bethel, and make it back before I get caught."

He zoomed out of the parking lot and down the highway to an empty gas station where he screeched to a halt before a lonesome phone booth.

"Need gas?" Eric asked.

"No. Just occurred to me that this is the last chance we're going to have to speak to Ma together, so we better get it over with now," Josh said and dashed to the doorless booth. He dialed their number spinning the spring in the rotary dial as rapidly as possible. The operator came on the line and gave him the cost of the first three minutes of the call. He slipped the coins into the slot. His mother picked up on the first ring.

"Hi Ma," Josh said casually. They spoke briefly about last night's scenic drive upstate.

"Hey!" she said. "I just heard on the news about some big rock-and-roll shindig that is happening up there. Near you I think."

"Near us?" He turned to his brother and asked, "Eric, you see any hippies?"

"Nope," he replied loud enough for her to hear.

Josh handed the phone to his younger brother, who chatted with her about how wonderful the clean mountain air was and that they had spotted cows, deer, and chipmunks, but surprisingly no horses. She continued to warn about the large army of hippies that were supposedly headed his way, Eric cut in, "Listen Ma, this call is costing us a bundle so..."

"... And it's raining!" Josh shouted out.

"I love you boys!" she shouted sadly. Eric held the phone outward so his brother could hear.

"We love you too," Josh shouted back.

"It's supposed to clear up this afternoon, so we're camping out in the woods tonight," Eric replied, "but we should call back tomorrow sometime."

"Well, if you're in the woods, don't kill yourself. But call me when you can." She said the magic words, giving them an excuse to miss tomorrow's call.

"See you Sunday," Eric replied.

"Yep, in time for Ed Sullivan, right?" she replied.

"'Course."

From a slightly redneckish gas station attendant working in the garage, Josh got basic directions—"Take 52 North to the blue farmhouse that turns into 178 East…"—Josh thanked him and sped up the highway, and only slowed down when he reached the turnoff. Once there though, Josh hit the brakes. Cars were lined up bumper to bumper all the way down to Bethel. What he thought would take ten minutes had already turned to a half an hour. Waiting, fighting the urge to honk, he kept looking up at the sky as the rain slowly tapered off. The clouds began breaking up and before they could reach their destination, the sun started peeking through.

"What am I going to do about Mom?" Eric asked to distract him.

"Call her tomorrow."

"But I told her we were going camping in the woods, so she said if I missed tomorrow that'd be okay."

"Oh right, good," he remembered. "But be ready to call her by Sunday. And since you're leaving then, when you get to Bethel you better find out the bus schedule so you can give her your arrival time back in the city. They like things like times."

"Hey!" Eric suddenly wondered. "What if I call them and they ask to speak to you?"

"Tell them I'm lifeguarding. They're worried about you, their baby, not me. By Sunday they'll have you back and I'll call, so they'll know we're fine."

"Right," Eric said.

They talked for another few minutes before Anna pointed out that the people in the vehicle in front of them were getting out. They weren't merely waiting, they were actually parking.

"Oh shit!" Eric said and looking into his rearview, he realized the folks in the car behind him were also unpacking their vehicles. "We're gonna be locked in here!"

"Guys, the good news is, I can see the town from here," Josh said, honking his horn to those behind him. "The bad news is, if I don't turn around right now and drive like a maniac I'm gonna be in deep shit." The car behind him backed up a couple feet.

"We'll walk it from here," Eric said to Anna who nodded in agreement, Josh did a 15-point U-turn and pulled onto the shoulder. It took Anna and Eric a moment to get their bags.

As Anna pulled on her pack, Josh whispered to Eric, "I got you all the way up here. Now just play it cool, don't push it and let her come to you."

"I owe you," he whispered back.

"Just get home in one piece on Sunday."

"That's the easy part," his younger brother replied. And Josh sped back to Narrowsburg as quickly as he could.

As they walked past the line of parked cars, pickup trucks and station wagons, Anna and Eric hiked about twenty minutes to the handful of little shops that legally made up the township of Bethel. At its center was an old, faded, blue building that had always been a general store.

"So where exactly are you meeting your friends?" Eric asked as they climbed up the wooden steps to the large open front porch of the crowded shop.

"Right here." She pointed to the old building. "A couple of friends said they'd be driving up separately."

"When?"

"Around two." She arbitrarily picked the time.

"You can't call anyone and confirm it, can you?" Eric asked nervously. A lot of people were on the street streaming up the hill.

"That's why I'm standing up here," she said, eyeing the crowd. Eric realized that she was actually on the back of a line that ended at an occupied payphone.

"Oh!" he suddenly realized. "I should use this opportunity to find the bus schedule and buy our tickets back home."

"First," she asked. "could you do me a favor and get me two dollars in quarters so I won't lose my place?" Sure enough, Eric saw that four more people had lined up behind her. Eric went inside, and, just as a new counter girl was tying on an apron, he held up a small bottle of icy Coke and a fiver. When she was making change, he asked for coins for the phone. Outside, he gave Anna the eight quarters and asked for her money to buy her bus ticket back to the city.

"Thanks but I don't need one," she said comfortably. "I can get a ride back with my friends. If you want to hold off, I'll get one for you too." Without asking, she took the cold bottle of Coke that he just opened and gulped it down.

"I can't take any chances," Eric replied, "I'm going to buy a seat now 'cause if I miss the bus on Sunday, my ass is grass."

"Do what you got to do," she said casually, returning his empty Coke bottle.

36

Kasabian, Moscow, 1922

It was during her third year in medical school that Masha Rodchenko took her only class in medical ethics. Since her focus was on obstetrics, for her term paper, she wrote an essay entitled, "A Modest Maternal Proposal," stating that since Russia was the first country to issue a driver's license, it was only appropriate that it should also be the first country to issue a mother's license. Her paper proposed that before conceiving, a prospective mother should demonstrate that she has the basic skills and knowledge needed for the formidable task ahead: "The state could offer a mental health test, as well as an assessment of root maternal instincts. Lastly, all would be given a class on basic pre- and post-birth care before being issued the license."

It went on to state: "The whole thing should take the same length of time as it would to get a driver's license. If a prospective mother appeared mentally imbalanced, the state should deny the license. If mothers truly love their unborn babies, they'd be happy to comply. By helping young mothers to raise and protect their infants are we not also securing the future of our great nation?"

The paper said nothing about enforcement or penalties of breeding without a license.

Her professor, a tacit, conservatively dressed academician who rarely gave elevated grades to women, awarded her an "A" and wryly wrote that she "demonstrated a great maternal conscience to our infant nation." She proudly showed the paper to Haig that night.

As one of the editors-at-large for *The Challenge Ahead*, one of the school's three revolutionary newspapers, Haig remembered during the last editorial meeting when deputy editor Apapov suggested that instead of just writing the usual stuff, the staff should try to "harvest the wild garden of students' radical ideas that were usually confined to the classroom."

"We need to bring revolutionary notions into the Revolution," Haig said to Masha.

"Absolutely," she replied absently.

"I think your essay would be a supreme addition to the next issue."

"Absolutely not!" she replied flatly.

"But it's a great essay. Do you know what the infant mortality rate is in Russia? You can almost see who's going to die before they're even conceived!"

"Look," Masha said, "I actually was being cheeky when I wrote it. I don't think mothers should need a license to have a baby."

"Really? That didn't come across at all," Morozov replied.

"That's why I called it 'A Modest Maternal Proposal,' I was paying homage to the satirist Jonathan Swift. I only wrote it for my teacher," she explained. "And these people nowadays, your so-called revolutionaries, they have no sense of humor. They seem to relish finding offense. It gives them unearned power."

"That's ridiculous. They're just vigilant. You came up with a great idea! It would vastly improve the quality of life for our country. It's your duty to share it, to be rewarded for it!"

"Let someone else have the credit for it. Tell you what, you like it so much, copy it and you can say you wrote it."

"This is what I mean when I say you lack a political conscience!" he chided. "They'll probably see it as a satire as well, but they'd also see the underlying value of it."

"Providing free medical skills for expectant mothers in the Ukraine, that's my political conscience," she fired back. Grabbing her book bag and coat, she angrily left and spent the night in her dormitory alone.

After hearing her admission that her paper was intended to be cheeky, Haig reread it and decided that the idea would be sensational if pitched seriously. He decided to accept her offer and rewrote it in a sterner, more severe tone. Then he proudly attached his own name to it. At the last minute, though, deciding it really was brilliant, he caught himself. He couldn't take credit for Masha's work. He loved her and the rewards she would reap from such a revolutionary manifesto would be immeasurable. He could see how over time, as compliments came in, he'd grow increasingly guilty and she would become more and more resentful. He crossed his name off and scribbled her name on the top of the page. She'd be ever so grateful afterwards, shy small-town girl that she was. All she needed was a little push.

When he submitted it to Yossif Apapov, his deputy editor, the older student read it and said, "Wow! Controversial!"

"But it shouldn't be," young Morozov declared. "It just makes complete sense."

"It's a little autocratic who gets to decide who can have a baby and who can't, no?"

"It simply advocates education and mental stability."

"Where exactly did you get it?" Yossif asked, seeing the name written above another which was crossed out.

"One of the female medical students here from the provinces," he said, not wanting to reveal it was his girlfriend.

"Oh, a nurse?"

"No, a female studying to be a doctor. She gave me permission to use the piece."

"A female doctor, it figures. You know what," the editor said. "Usually we put these in the back of the paper, but circulation has been dropping so I'm going to run this on the first page."

"Great!" he said thrilled. For the next three days he didn't say a word about it to Masha. He wanted it to be a big surprise.

When the new issue of *The Challenge Ahead* came out early the following week, Morozov grabbed the top issue from the first bundle and read it aloud in the editorial office. He was barely able to contain himself.

"Hey, Haig!" said one of the editors. "You filed this editorial, didn't you?"

"I sure did!" he said proudly.

"All the editors are talking about it."

"That's 'cause it's the best thing in the paper," He smirked. But the issue had not yet gone out.

That night he proudly handed her the school newspaper. When her eyes touched on her name on the front page byline she let out a bloodcurdling howl.

"I told you I didn't want this! You disobeyed me!" She ripped the paper down the middle.

"Disobeyed you!" he shot back. "What am I, some dog?"

"I told you I didn't want my name on the piece and that's my name!"

"And it's my Revolution!" he replied. "And I know you don't believe me, but I just did you a huge favor."

Ungratefully, she sprang to her feet, grabbed her coat, and dashed out the door. Morozov thought it best to let her cool her heels. Let her discover for herself that only good was going to come of it. Indeed, let her reap the benefits, when her fellow classmates heaped laurels and praise upon her for writing such an eloquent and socially conscious declaration. Over the following days, as others in his editorial office came to mention his discovery, more and more students stated that they felt no one was entitled to regulate a woman's god-given right to have a child.

149

"Do you believe that any insane woman should just be able to pop out a baby and torture it?" he argued to one fellow editor on the staff.

"No, but when that happens, the state takes the baby away. In fact, every country already does that!" he retorted.

"What about the benefits of making sure young women are educated in being mothers?"

"That's fine. There should be some educational classes, but she went too far with issuing a license."

He dismissed him and others who failed to see the imperative of state regulations. What worried him most was that Masha still hadn't called and asked his forgiveness.

After three more days of her silent treatment, he was summoned to the managing editor's office. Upon seeing him, Yossif winced and said they were in hot water.

"Why?"

"The editorial."

"What editorial?"

"You know, that piece by medical school student Rodchenko. Komosol has officially denounced it."

"What!"

Managing editor Apapov handed him an envelope with the notorious Communist Youth League seal on it. "You have to forward this to this Rodchenko character."

"What?!"

"Just give it to her."

"This can't be!" he said, looking at the envelope as though it were a death sentence.

"Relax. We only have to print a retraction, and an apology. But she's going to have problems."

"Problems?"

"It turns out the work is subversive."

"Subversive!" The managing editor was abruptly called away.

Once Haig stepped outside the office, he tore the envelope open and read it. The letter stated that counterrevolutionary charges were being weighed against Masha Rodchenko. "In the next 10 days you

150

will be notified of a disciplinary hearing for dispersing elitist anti-Bolshevik propaganda." He could barely decipher the signature—a Vladimir Mikhailovich Ostrowski, Chapter President.

Immediately, Morozov went down the hall and into the office of the Communist Youth League and asked to speak to Ostrowski. A student secretary asked what this was about. He introduced himself as an accredited party member and an assistant editor of the school newspaper who had selected the controversial piece.

"I'm just trying to understand the problem here," he said. "I mean her editorial really tried to help the Revolution, making Russia into a better, healthier..."

"Have a seat," she said tiredly, and picked up her phone.

After waiting twenty minutes, he was led into a corner office where a bespectacled youth who looked as frail as a twig introduced himself as the branch's political officer. Morozov took out the letter and asked how Masha Rodenchenko's opinion could even remotely be interpreted as counterrevolutionary.

"Surely you jest, comrade. Licensing the right to have babies? It's slavery! Utterly plutocratic."

"You're missing the point! It's about the safety of the infant."

"It's treason, pure and simple," the political officer said without raising his voice. "And don't think your name has passed unnoticed. We've already sent a report to the school's security committee."

"Treason how? She simply advocated for the mental and physical hygiene of..."

"Under the clever guise of maternal interest, she is trying to turn the inalienable rights of childbearing into a fascist commodity. Any fool can see that! No different than slavery."

"Where is fascist commodity even mentioned?"

"It's clearly implicit! It's in the very tone of her writing!"

"Tone!"

"Don't be obtuse! The very fact that she's from the Ukraine where the kulaks have steadily resisted the Revolution, and now here she is in Moscow, possibly an agent from the imperialist Kiev, dictating their own agenda!"

"This is bigotry!" Morozov fired back. "If she was from here, she never would've even gotten noticed!"

"Are you accusing us of bigotry, comrade?"

"Absolutely!" he fired back. "If she were one of us..."

"One of us? You're an Armenian passing as a Muscovite."

"I was born here!"

"It'd be well to remember that if it wasn't for us Russians, there would no longer be an Armenia. The Turks would've finished you all off. Does that make us bigots?"

"Where is Vladimir Mikhailovich Ostrowski?" Morozov asked, noticing for the first time by his name plate that the political officer was not the signatory of the letter. "I have the right to address my accuser!"

"You can write him an appeal. I'll see that he gets it."

"Look," Morozov said, hoping he could end it all here and now. "This was all *my* doing. She didn't even know I submitted it."

"Put that in your appeal," the little shit replied. "If you brought her piece to us directly instead of publishing it, we would've given you a commendation."

"She wrote this to help our nation! There's nothing political about it!"

"Everything is political!" he shot back, glaring at him. "When will people get that? Absolutely everything is political. Everything!"

It occurred to Morozov that he had better try to locate Masha before she learned of the charges against her by some stranger. He left the Komosol offices and dashed out the door, through the streets, straight to her dormitory. When he asked to see Masha, the front desk attendant pointed to the intercom phone. Four female students, also from the outer provinces, shared the single phone that was positioned in their corridor. When one of them finally answered, and he asked for Masha, she replied that student Rodchenko hadn't come home from classes yet. Morozov hung up and waited on the bench in the reception area.

As he reread the condemnation letter, he found himself fighting back tears. The severity of it was like a hard smack across the face. He hadn't seen her in a week since she learned he published it

152

without her consent. And now he was painfully aware of his own naiveté. Though she was fearful this could happen, he always had profound faith in the altruism of the Revolution. He only put her name on the piece believing that she would greatly benefit by it. Throughout the past week, he had been expecting people to present her with a bouquet of compliments, letters from fellow students commending the sagacity of her essay. But everything she had worried about had come true.

"How could I have been so arrogant!" he whispered aloud.

He knew that despite the constant vigilance against enemies foreign and domestic, this was still supposed to be a revolution of ideas and that the best ideas were supposed to prevail. For the first time he realized how wrong he was, how gullible he had been.

By the time Masha had finally returned from the school library around four p.m., he had nodded off. She spotted him dozing on the bench. He looked so delicate and boyish that she decided a week away from her was punishment enough. Softly, she awoke him with a kiss on his lips.

"Did someone notify you?" he asked, sitting up.

"Notify me about what?" She instantly sensed his fear.

"I'm so sorry," he said, rising to his feet. "I can't believe these idiots are doing this! It's all my fault, Masha."

"Doing what?" He handed her the letter.

She read it and immediately comprehended the gravity of her situation. She slumped down next to him in a daze and tried catching her breath. Tears came to her eyes.

"All it says is they're weighing charges. They're not pressing any. You've never done anything like this before, and there's no distinct sentence in your essay where you denounce the Revolution or any member of the Politburo. They really are just going after you because you're from the Ukraine."

"This was all done against my will," she seethed staring at him. "I'll tell them you did this! I can state that this was a stolen document. That I wrote it as a joke."

"I told them that. That I did it without your permission," he confessed. "I swear I tried to take the blame."

"What did they say?"

"They said that if I had submitted it directly to them instead of publishing it, I'd be commended. Instead, I am facing punishment as well."

"God damn you!" She crumpled the letter into a ball and threw it in his face.

"It even crossed my mind to say that I wrote the piece and put your name on it. But your professor already saw it and graded it. The truth would get out and he'd be put in a position where if he didn't turn you in, he could be arrested too."

"What have you done to me, Haig Morozov?!" Tears fell from her eyes. "I just wanted to be left alone! I just wanted to be a country doctor and help poor women in my district!"

"Let's not get ahead of ourselves. This isn't an arrest or a sentence. All that will probably happen will be a stern warning not to do this again and it'll all go away," he said earnestly. When she didn't respond, he finally whispered that he was profoundly sorry. She exited, refusing to even look at him.

Throughout the week, she got comments from fellow students, a few good but most were bad. She didn't respond to anyone. The following week, though, when the next issue of *The Challenge Ahead* came out, Masha's official student picture was printed alongside a retraction by the newspaper and a scathing editorial by Vladimir Mikhailovich Ostrowski, the head of the local Komosol, addressing "the crypto-fascist subtext" of her dangerous piece. Without so much as mentioning its editor, Morozov, it suggested that she might be a subversive agent of her renegade republic, which in turn was currently being manipulated by capitalist agents. The article concluded by giving out personal details about Masha Rodchenko, including the name of her dormitory and her room number.

The next day, the same article was picked up in the larger newspaper *Moskovsky Komsomolets,* the Communist Youth League's city-wide paper, which had a much larger circulation. There was also a sidebar article on the treacherous politics of the Ukraine, which had repeatedly subverted efforts of the Communist Party. Soon Morozov was receiving hate mail at the school newspaper office. By the second week, Masha started receiving death threats mailed directly to her dormitory.

Additionally, her classmates had stopped speaking to her, and she sensed that she was being followed.

"You might want to pack a bag," her best friend, Irena, also from the Ukraine, muttered without looking at her as they walked down the crowded hallway to an anatomy class.

"What kind of bag?"

"When they arrest you, they do it at night. They let you bring a change of clothes, stuff like that," Irena said as they entered the lecture hall. Masha sat in her usual seat in the front row. Instead of joining her as she normally did, Irena kept walking to the far side of the room. Masha was alone.

Over the next few days, when she wasn't cursing Haig's name, the growing notion that she might actually get arrested steadily paralyzed her with fear. What would her parents think? Would she actually be locked up in prison? She followed Irena's advice and packed some essentials in case the police came. She also wrote a letter to her mother explaining the hot water she had gotten herself into. She begged her parents for their forgiveness and their prayers. As that first week crept on, she refused to take any calls from Morozov and steadily came to believe that her fate was sealed.

37

Alexei, Woodstock Festival, 1969

As the rock music decimated all tranquility around them, the two older men sat facing away from it, along the grassy edge of the pond discreetly glancing at a flock of nude and semi-nude girls. The young ladies were giggling and bathing themselves. Haig said he wished Alexei had more film for his Minox. Sergei pulled out a second small bag of joints that he had bought and lit one up. Together they watched as young nudists splashed around obliviously in the pond.

"You know what I find most titillating?" Sergei asked softly, ogling at one young woman's bold immodesty.

"Their firm, just awakening breasts?" guessed Alexei also observing.

"That's good, but no, it's the pubic hair, so delicate it's almost like charcoal etchings, like god's own veil," he waxed. "So much more enticing than the genitals they cover. Rembrandt himself couldn't shade them so brilliantly."

"How about the thick, wiry tangle of pubic hair when they get older?"

"It's still better. Have you ever seen a hairless vagina? All you really have is a... I don't know... a kind of tiny, symmetrical ear," said Alexei who was clearly stoned. He turned his head and folded the top and bottom of his ear to demonstrate, "which I still find attractive."

"Wow! You have a very sexy vagina on the side of your head," Sergei said, and tenderly rubbed his finger along the outer edge of Alexei's hairy ear.

Alexei slapped Sergei's hand away.

Sergei chuckled and said, "Pass me your funny cigarette."

Alexei handed him the tightly rolled joint. Sergei inhaled deeply, coughed furiously then puffed again more delicately. Soon, when he learned how to properly negotiate the fumes, they passed it back and forth taking tokes. When they finished the sixth and final joint, Sergei pulled out a new bottle of vodka and they began taking slugs. As he started having hot flashes from the alcohol, Alexei pulled off his shirt, as did Sergei.

"That's some scar you got," Sergei said, staring at Alexei's war wound near his waist.

"Fortunately the bullet missed my intestines or I probably would've died. It was nearly a day later before I got stitched up. And the wound never properly healed," he said, rubbing his side. "It still feels numb."

Soon drunk and high, both men waded into the pond in their underwear where they laughed, splashed and chatted until they scared all the sexy young people away.

"This water is filthy!" Sergei suddenly noticed, prompting them to climb back up to the muddy banks where they laid down on the tall grass and passed out. As the sun began to set about an hour later, Sergei came to and, despite the booming music, he had no idea where he was. When he got his bearings, still a little drunk and high, he grew concerned about getting lost in the darkness. He grabbed both of their belongings, woke Alexei up and helped him back to his feet. As the constant music blared, they stomped back through the crowds and the two slowly marched up to the woods around the maze of parked cars, across the road and found their campsite.

"I don't want to spend another night sleeping in a puddle," Alexei said when they reached their leaky little tent. "Let's abandon everything and drive back to the city."

"No way, I'm as drunk as you," Sergei said. "Let's sleep for a while and sober up. Then we'll head out later tonight when the traffic thins out."

Before passing out, they needed to pee. As Alexei staggered behind a tree in the darkness, Sergei went to another. They looked down at the stage—two clueless brunettes with long flat hair and a pale male who seemed to be strumming the same four strings over and over.

"What's the custom here?" Sergei asked. "Do they give all Americans a guitar at birth?"

"You'd think one of them would try playing a zither or a damned harpsichord," Alexei replied.

One at a time the two men crawled back into their swollen tent and collapsed inside. While waiting for an occasional breeze against their hot flesh, they tried blotting out the persistent jumble of strings and ghostly singing to return to sleep. But periodically a new band would take the stage and started up with a whole new racket.

"That's it!" Alexei finally said angrily. "Time to go!"

When he got no response, he reached across the darkness to find his old friend was gone. He grabbed the flashlight that Sergei had placed between them, located his umbrella on the other side, and wormed his way back out of the tent. Although it had stopped

157

raining, the sky was black and the grass was soaked. Alexei strolled around for half an hour near the crowded stage before finally retreating back up to their little camp. After two days of living in this odd world of naive American children and annoying music, he remembered how young and virginal he himself had once been, which made him melancholy. In a few short days, he thought, he'd be returning to Moscow and all this would seem like a dream.

Although he was born the same year of the Revolution, he thought how it too was conceived in unforgivable innocence and because of this it had slowly become vicious. Now, just after the fiftieth anniversary of the CCCP, its once-sharp teeth had finally dulled. It had become bloated and corrupt as he himself felt, lying in that dark pup tent that was only a little bigger than his stomach. Feeling around for a liquor bottle, he found the slightly damp English-language edition of *Kasabian's Tales* that had somehow found its way into the tent.

Suddenly, the outline of a fat hippie paused before the tent. Alexei watched as the stealthy figure slowly, silently parted the flap, clearly looking for something to steal. Alexei lifted his umbrella preparing to jab the perpetrator in the face until he suddenly realized by the tangled mane of hair that it was his missing companion.

"What exactly are you up to, Sergei Hagopian?" He flipped on the flashlight, stopping him in his tracks.

"Me? What do you mean?"

"Admit it, you don't like this crap any more than I do."

"I admit it."

"So why exactly are you keeping us here?"

"I thought it might be fun."

"I've had my eye on you this entire weekend. I've seen you looking around all day. Who is it you're looking for? Fell for some underage Svetlana, did you?"

"No!"

"Fine, I don't care, but I'm done playing in this giant, noisy sandbox. We're leaving right now."

"Hold on now…" Sergei let out a deep sigh. "Frankly this is very embarrassing. In fact I can probably lose my job for this."

"At the embassy?"

"I have a daughter, Alexei. And she's here somewhere."

"You're kidding!"

Sergei pulled out his wallet and removed a color photo of an attractive young brunette that was less than a square inch in size. "When I first got stationed here in 1953, I met a beautiful young Irish girl, a secretary at the consulate, and I got her pregnant. She insisted on keeping the kid. We were briefly married, but it didn't work out. We kept in touch over the years. I've tried to give her money and support when I could. For the first few years she'd let me stop by for holidays, so I could give the little girl gifts."

"Wow, Sergei!" he chuckled. "You have an American daughter!"

"Now you know. And if the security officer at the embassy finds out..."

"What's her name?" Alexei took the photo and stared at it with the flashlight. She looked like a bosomy Natalie Wood.

"Anna. And I guess as I get older, the idea of having a kid strangely becomes more comforting."

"Particularly if you don't have to change any diapers."

"As death gets closer, you feel that at least you passed the torch, and your progeny might get farther ahead than you did."

"The only problem is they're usually even more lost than us."

"Maybe, but I also find myself worrying and wanting to care for her."

"Of course," Alexei replied.

"Over the past few years, the mother stopped returning my calls. I didn't think she wanted me around anymore. Depressing as hell."

"I can imagine."

"A few days ago she called me out of the blue and said she was desperate. Anna had run off with some guy on Thursday afternoon and they were coming up here."

"So that's what this is all about."

"That's it. It's my last chance to get back into her life."

"So you knew all along this wasn't a jazz festival," Alexei said with a smirk.

"I'm truly sorry, Alexei," Sergei said, "I was hoping to find her and then we could go."

"Shame on you, Sergei Hagopian, for not telling me the truth."

"Her mother was in such a state. She never called me before, ever! I didn't even know she still had my phone number. She gave me the updated picture. Last time I saw her she was a little girl!"

"It must be like looking for a needle in a haystack with all these kids," Alexei said.

"What else can I do?" Sergei asked. "I've been looking all over for her for the past two days with no luck, so if you want to leave…"

"We've been everywhere but down around that crowded stage," Alexei said.

"Actually I just spent an hour trying, it's useless. I can barely make out the endless faces – young people all look alike."

"Tomorrow in the daylight we'll descend into that snake pit. Give it our best shot. But if we don't find her – we leave. Agreed?"

"Agreed!" Sergei replied.

38

Kasabian, Moscow, 1943

Morozov left for the university early to avoid bumping into his good-for-nothing house servant. He was supposed to finally give his lecture on the development of Soviet literature of the Caucasus for the young professor's class in exchange for that lumpy bowl of oatmeal. He intended to review the index cards on the subject that were in his office, but on his way, he passed the faculty lounge usually filled with tobacco smoke and at least a few lazy pompous professors. For the first time he saw that the large oak-paneled room was completely empty. Not a single snoring bore. He went inside, took a comfortable seat and before him on an end table, he noticed a pile of school newspapers that had accumulated over the last six months.

Flipping through them, he was surprised to see a variety of articles about on-campus events, written by one Alexei Novikov, his annoying assistant. Unbeknownst to him, the youth was a precocious and productive cub reporter. Additionally, toward the end of each issue, he saw that the assistant had his own little book column. Morozov flipped through the pages, hoping to spot at least a single flattering reference to himself. After a few minutes he found nothing, but he was still impressed by the many books the youth had reviewed. Sometimes young Novikov critiqued as many as three new books a week. Crisply written, Alexei clearly had a knack for quickly identifying the key themes of each book, and specifically addressing how each work breathed a little life into the stale Revolution.

Morozov also noted that all his reviews were positive. Since each book was published by the state, they were little more than raves. Finally, to his surprise, he found a single negative critique. Of course it was a translated work by a young French communist, a nihilist who Novikov accused of being overly sensitive to bourgeois existence and thereby unwittingly corrupted by it.

Another stack of back issues also on the end table was of the *Literary Gazette*, something he would avidly read decades ago. While living down in Yerevan, Armenia, Morozov would only get them sporadically. He lifted the entire stack onto his lap and began scouring the pages, trying to catch up on the affairs of contemporary Russian literature over the past few months. Hastily he checked the reviews, readings, and directives from the Writers Union, as well as the seasonal lists of upcoming works. The paper would be far more informative if they also had another list of writers who had been arrested. But of course none of those things ever officially happened. Besides unsubstantiated rumors, he could only wonder about the fate of old friends and once serious peers who had vanished over the last few years.

Although he spotted a few names in the *Gazette* from his past, including one or two frail saplings that had somehow grown into literary oaks, he didn't recognize most of the new writers. On the last page of the winter 1941 issue, he noticed one small piece tucked in a corner:

"Marina Tsvetaeva, 48, onetime poet, was found dead in an apartment in Elabuga from a suicide on August 31. She was part of a group that was in the process of evacuating eastward ahead of the Nazi invasion. She had just returned to Russia after living in Paris for seventeen years…"

It went on to say that she had hung herself.

A full-bearded, large-bellied scholar puffing a smelly pipe, which resembled the smoke stack of a small locomotive, shuffled in. Haig grabbed the gazette and exited before the man could try to initiate a dull conversation. In a moment Morozov was back in his office staring blankly at the wall, too distraught to focus.

By just publishing her obituary, some sentimental old poetry lover had granted her a mercy. If this generation hadn't so effectively erased its immediate past, someone would've rebuked the obituary writer, if not demoted him, for slipping the Tsvetaeva notice in the paper.

As Morozov used the bathroom he ran cold water over his face. Looking at himself in the mirror, he remembered seeing Tsvetaeva at a few poetry readings over thirty years ago. The other poets were usually men. He distinctly remembered one time watching her march up the center aisle of a small room and boldly take the podium. Not more than six people were present. Tall, almost mannish, certainly no coquette, she read a cycle of recitations she had been working on. It was so memorable that when he later found the same poem printed in a tiny literary quarterly, he cut it out and glued it into his journal:

You whose greatcoats were lithely streaming,
Reminiscent of broad sails,
Whose voice and spurs were gaily ringing
Like silver bells
Whose eyes, like diamonds were leaving
On hearts their delightful traces –
The charming fops of vanished beings,
In time and space….
In a single gallop, fierce and risky,

You passed your shortest lives and glow —
And your ambitious curls and whispers
Now buried under layers of snow....

Upon remembering the poem, he remembered also thinking that there were so many promising young writers getting published in Russia back then, during the Tzar's final years, an entire literary generation who vanished under the Bolshevik snowstorm. There had to be at least a couple young Dostoyevskys and Tolstoys, not to mention a Flaubert, maybe even a Goethe. Such artists were rare hothouse plants who, left alone, might've eventually blossomed right here in Moscow. Unfortunately it was the wrong time and place to launch an artistic career.

Looking back, Haig saw Tsvetaeva's "greatcoats" poem as a valediction to them all: a brilliant age that couldn't survive the Soviet winter any better than the German army.

Although he didn't particularly care for Tsvetaeva as a person—she was far too self-involved—the fact that he took the time to glue her poem into his journal was the best tribute he could give to any living poet at the time.

She was part of that whole symbolist St. Petersburg fiasco that included Mandelstam and other writers whose names he had long forgotten. Haughty, effete, they were far more concerned with words and precious ideas than with publishing deadlines or the vagaries of the Writers Union. Like so many, Tsvetaeva was oblivious to the cataclysms of history that were occurring around her. The Revolution hit like a tidal wave. Instead of joining the right side and taking shelter, she and her aristocratic family fled to fashionable Paris, only to find that they were unable to adapt and sustain. They were eventually forced to return to Mother Russia. Although the worst of what he thought of as "the Refinement" was over, recriminations still awaited those who were foolish enough to come back from exile. He could only wonder what had become of her husband and poor daughter. Somehow, hopeless, she wound up all alone in an empty room in Elabuga, where one of Russia's finest poets quietly hanged herself.

When he arrived outside his office, Morozov saw the back of a young woman sitting alone in the anteroom at Alexei's desk. He watched her methodically flipping through pages of one of his books. He had seen it before—she was searching the marginalia for whatever might be incriminating.

The mysterious lady picked up a large red book by the Symbolist poet Alexander Blok. He and Lunz had once seen Blok reading aloud at the Pegasus Book Stall. He didn't know exactly how the poet had died but heard that he had contracted some mysterious illness that could only be treated in the more advanced hospitals overseas. Apparently he requested a medical visa, but permission only arrived after the poet had died.

"You okay, sir?" he suddenly heard behind him.

The young lady turned around and saw both Haig and Alexei standing outside in the hallway, staring at her. It was Alexei's girlfriend, Darya. She blushed and nervously slid the Blok book back on the shelf. Seeing her face again, he wondered why she looked so familiar, but thought all beautiful girls look alike.

"I didn't mean to be nosy, but I've always been amazed by what goes into the mind of a great writer such as yourself," she said. Haig nodded dismissively. She was secret police, pure and simple.

She grabbed her handbag and was off to class, leaving Haig alone with his assistant.

"You know she's read all your work," Alexei informed him awkwardly.

"She might like my writing, but she blushed when she saw you," he replied. Though he didn't trust her, he couldn't deny her radiance.

"I like her, but frankly, she's not really my type," Alexei said.

"Not your type! You're lucky she's even giving you the time of day!" Haig replied, grabbing his index cards from the top drawer of his desk and slipping them into his valise.

"I just mean..."

"Take me to Professor Slotkin's class before it's over!"

Alexei led the way. For the next three minutes, they walked through the crowded halls until they entered the packed lecture hall. The sharp, young professor rose to his feet, greeted him with a smile, and pointed to the front of the room where two chairs were positioned behind an old wooden podium. Under a large, airbrushed portrait of Stalin, Morozov took one of the chairs as the last students shuffled into the large room and filled the last of the seats. The young professor rose and began reading his introduction, "Not only is Haig Morozov the greatest living fiction writer from Armenia today but…"

As the starched idiot rambled on, Morozov reviewed the cards that he had prepared a while ago on "Literature from the Trans-Caucasus since the Great Revolution." If the students were expecting something original or exciting, he thought, that'll be their only surprise. Flat, predictable, conventional work was well rewarded by the new Soviet state, and he wasn't intending to disappoint any of the informers in the audience. If they were hoping to hear bold, courageous geniuses, the prisons were crowded with them, and he wasn't planning on joining them. As he was greeted with applause, he rose tiredly, skipped the perfunctory remarks, and began his lecture. It was little more than a reading of the uninspired Writers Union catalog. After droning on for twenty minutes the lecture was over. He put the cards away. A polite smattering of applause slowly followed.

"Would you mind if we asked you a few questions about your wonderful works?" Slotkin asked.

"Unfortunately I have a pressing engagement," he countered, having fulfilled his minimal obligation. In another moment, to the befuddlement of all expecting to hear him read his fiction, he marched out the door.

As he walked down the corridor to his office, Alexei caught up and said, "I just want you to know how honored I am to serve such a writer."

"As well you should be," Haig replied without a hint of sarcasm. Not surprisingly, the boring lecture inspired the boring youth.

"As you might recall, until recently I only did journalism," young Alexei said nervously. "And occasional reviews."

"More than occasional," he muttered having just seen a stack of them. "You've got a knack."

"Last year, while recuperating in the hospital, I wanted to do something more meaningful but frankly I didn't know how. That was why, when I heard you'd be here, I asked for this assignment."

"Wise."

"I wrote this," Alexei said, opening his book bag. He pulled out a stack of pages that was at least two inches thick—a goddamn manuscript!

Morozov groaned.

"It's my first novel," he said. "I just finished it."

"Unfortunately, I'm not a publisher."

"I know you're not, but I don't know who else... that is... would you consider reading it?"

"Let me ask you a question," Morozov said, coming to a dead halt. "Would you casually ask someone to take two weeks off from work and help you make repairs around your apartment?"

"No, but I..."

"I'm not a magician. I don't read quicker than anyone else. And the time that you want me to work on your writing is the same time that I won't be able to work on mine."

"Excuse me?"

"Put your manuscript in the bottom drawer of my desk and I'll try to get to it if I can," Morozov said tiredly and handing him the index cards from his Trans-Caucasus lecture, he added, "And please leave these there too."

Alexei considered trying to explain to Morozov that he could try his best to protect the older writer if he got a little help in return. But by just saying that he knew he'd be sticking his own neck way out.

He watched as Morozov walked down the hallway alone and finally exited the building into the snow-laden streets.

39

Squinting in the hot August sun, Anna watched Eric vanish in the growing crowd as he headed off to the Bethel bus stop. When the young girl in front of her hung up the pay phone, someone in the rear coughed. Five others were lined up behind her waiting. Anna snatched up the phone and dialed her home number. The operator came on the line and asked for a dollar eighty-five for the first three minutes. As she inserted all eight quarters, she reminded herself that she had to speak quickly before the coins dropped into the metal box and revealed to her mother that she had left the city limits.

"Hello?" Her mother answered.

"Hi Ma, Denise and I are out on Rockaway Beach." She assumed her little-girl voice. "We'll be back first thing tomorrow."

"The hell you are!" her mother replied. "I called Denise's house last night. Her ma said you left yesterday afternoon!"

"Yeah," she argued. "We went to her aunt's bungalow, but we aren't telling her, 'cause..."

"You must think I'm a bloody idiot that I don't know what you're up to! You're at that bloody concert upstate that you were blathering on about with that moronic drug addict Chicken."

"His name is Rooster and if you know that then why are you making me lie to you?"

"Get back down here at once or so help me God I will call the police on you, I will!"

"We're not doing anything!"

"You're a minor and he's an adult! I swear I'll have him locked away. I swear I truly will!"

"Well, for your information I'm not even with him! I'm with someone else so you don't know everything," Anna shot back.

"You're a dirty, little liar and I don't trust anything that comes out of your filthy mouth..." Suddenly all her coins dropped at once, causing the phone to go dead for a moment. When it stopped, Anna quickly said, "I'm not having sex or doing drugs, I'm safe and I'm staying here 'til after Jimi Hendrix plays on Sunday. Love you!" The line went dead and she hung up. As Anna walked away, the phone rang back.

The next person in line answered it and yelled out to her, "The operator says you owe another thirty-five cents!" Anna didn't look back.

Arriving at the Bethel bus station, which also doubled as a travel agency and notary public, Eric discovered that on the weekends, a bus from Bethel to New York City was scheduled to leave every other hour starting from six a.m. 'til midnight. The cost of a one-way ticket to New York was twelve dollars and seventy-five cents. All Eric had was the twenty-dollar bill that Josh had loaned him. For the first time after quickly tabulating the price of the bus ticket and then the cost of admission to the concert, he discovered to his horror that he'd only have twenty-five cents and he needed that for the subway token from Port Authority. He contemplated Anna's offer of a free ride home, but then decided against it and got on the short ticket line. The return ticket to the city was his sole life preserver if everything failed.

"Next!" said the clerk who looked like the actor Don Knotts.

"Can I get a ticket for the six p.m. bus to New York City on Sunday?"

"Well, you better be here not much later than six a.m.," said the clerk.

"Twelve hours earlier?"

"Yeah, in case you didn't notice, we got a lot of people here and they all made the same plans as you."

"Can't I just make a reservation? My name is Eric Stein."

"Reservation? This is Adirondacks Trailways, not TWA," the agent explained. "A seat on the bus is strictly first come, first served."

"Are you kidding?" Eric was astonished.

"No, and to be honest, I don't ever remember anyone being unable to get on a bus. But this weekend looks like it might be shaping into a very special occasion. We're seeing this huge crowd and frankly we just don't know what to expect."

"Don't you stop selling tickets once the bus is full?"

"We never stop selling tickets," the clerk said, "and we do our best to accommodate everyone, but like I said, the ticket isn't a reservation."

"Suppose I have my ticket, but there's no seat?"

"Sometimes they add an extra bus as I'm sure they will, but if someone misses a bus, they wait for the next available one. That's our policy."

"But as far as you remember, no one has ever missed a bus due to a lack of a seat?"

"True, but I never saw hundreds of thousands of people packed into our tiny hamlet either."

Since the bus ticket offered no guarantee, Eric thought that he might as well hold off on buying it and use the time to see if Anna really could get him a free ride back to the city. Then the windfall could be used for food and necessities. When he returned down the block to the General Store, Anna was standing out front sucking down another small bottle of Coke.

"Well, I got great news and not-so-great news," she said.

"What's the not-so-great news?" he asked.

"Rooster and my gang aren't arriving until tomorrow."

"Shit! Where are we going to sleep?"

"Don't sweat it, we'll find something, I always do. There are thousands of people here. And you brought your sleeping bag."

"That's true," Eric silently thanked Josh. "So I hope that's not the great news."

"No, the great news is that they just announced the festival is free! We just saved eighteen bucks!" That was good news, particularly since he underestimated the cost of the ticket. Despite it, though, Eric thought, *This girl is nuts, particularly after her little stunt last night. Say goodnight and take the next bus back home.* But then seeing how sexy she was, he thought, *I'm here anyway. And I already got to second base. Maybe I can round third and make it home.*

"So where is this concert anyway?" he asked, growing nervous.

"It's just up there," she said, pointing up the main road where the crowd of people were flowing.

"Shit!" He started freaking out at the thought of his situation.

"Come on. We're going to have a blast!"

"We're hundreds of miles from home, Anna, without food or shelter! This isn't what you told me it'd be like." Before she could respond, he joined the stream of hippies up the crowded highway.

"I didn't know it was going to be like this!" Anna said. "But it'll be great, you'll see."

"Please don't talk to me for a while, I just need to calm myself down!" Eric said, hastening ahead of her.

"Look, even if we had a car, we couldn't use it anyway."

"Just shut the hell up!" he yelled, causing all the hippies around him to stare. Someone muttered, *"That guy just told her to shut up!"* He stopped, so she stopped, and they let the crowd pass by until a fresh crowd was around them. Among the countless bare-chested hippies, he suddenly spotted a topless girl walking with a guy. Since Anna was staring off sulking, he kept stealing glances at the topless chick. Her breasts weren't particularly big, but they were firm and pouty, which somehow made the girl look smart.

After about twenty minutes of walking up the road, it cut right through what turned out to be a large dairy farm. Everyone was veering off between the barrier of parked cars. To their left was the campground, which was crisscrossed with parked cars. To their right was a grassy slope where most people were streaming. At the very bottom was a large wooden stage that young, long-haired workmen were still in the process of constructing. On both sides of it were two giant Jungle-Gym towers made of pipes rigged with lights and amps and slung with wires.

"What time is the concert beginning?" Anna asked aloud.

"Six p.m.," some old guy called back.

"What the hell are we supposed to do for eight hours?" Eric asked.

"I have friends here," she said, looking around. "We just have to find them."

"I thought you said Rooster wasn't coming 'til..."

170

"I have *a lot* of friends," she shot back.

"You sure?" he muttered. "I'm beginning to think you don't have any."

"Look, if you're gonna be..."

"Pardon me if I was led to believe that once I got here, all would be fine."

"Tell you what," she replied. "If this doesn't turn out to be one of the best weekends of your entire existence, you can do whatever you want to me! How's that!"

"Let's just find somewhere to unroll my sleeping bag before they run out of space."

Anna bee-lined to the high ground with Eric in tow to get a better view. She shielded her eyes and looked carefully around the sloping field slowly filling up, like a general scoping a battlefield.

"I'm starving," Eric muttered, not having eaten a thing that day so far.

"You wanna eat, follow me," she replied, wiping the sweat off her brow.

40

Kasabian, Moscow, 1943

Once he exited Moscow State University, seeing the latest white mounds of snow covering the city, Morozov realized that instead of sending his assistant back to his office, he should've had the little lackey drive him home—*Damn!* Struggling through the embankment of snow, Morozov slowly heaved one leg in front of the other until he made it to a long, narrow path.

Alexei's request for guidance compelled him to remember how when he was young he had longed for some magical mentor who could teach him all the tricks of the trade: how to draw out the complexities of a character like Dostoyevsky had, or how to chart an intricate plot through a thick forest of fictitious possibilities like Victor Hugo; or how to build a dramatic scene and bring it to a heartbreaking crescendo like Shakespeare. The closest he came to finding this magical guide was the drunken street thug Dimitri Lunz. The two were always together and both had great literary ambitions, so it made sense. But neither youth was qualified to do so. In retrospect, Morozov thought it was more like two cripples struggling to drag each other onward. Although they didn't say it, neither liked the other's work. Lunz's verse was little more than a sling of angry, awkward phrases, a narrow selection of antiquated themes hindered by a fuzzy concept clothed in a clumsy worn-out vocabulary.

"Quit writing and learn your craft!" Morozov once yelled at him. "Study the world around you!"

"That would only muddle what I want to say," Lunz replied.

"I know you're an iconoclast, but frequently your poems are little more than whiny insults," he criticized.

"At least they don't put people to sleep," Lunz countered. He detailed that although Morozov's work was majestic in intent, it was invariably wooden in execution.

One mildly intoxicated night, in an effort to remain civil, they agreed to read and write their critiques silently.

"The only proviso I ask," Morozov said, fearing the clash that would probably ensue, "is that after we read each other's work, we part in silence so we don't fight."

"Fair enough."

They both began reviewing each other's latest literary efforts. After about five minutes of reading, Lunz let out a loud editorial groan. Morozov resisted the urge to chuckle at the shlockiness of Lunz's poetry. Then he watched Lunz scribbling directly on his story—his only copy! He gasped in disbelief as the awful poet ran his pen first across words, then cut entire lines and soon whole paragraphs from his newest piece. To add insult to injury, Lunz began scribbling at length on his piece, apparently rewriting it in the margins.

Instead of grabbing his pages back and slapping the drunken halfwit across the face, Haig retaliated by crossing out entire poems, writing specific background information, replacing tired, redundant words and phrases with more idiosyncratic and euphonic ones.

As he was muting the cheap shock value that frequently overwhelmed Lunz's verses, the poet silently snatched his poems out of Haig's hand.

Lunz tossed the revised pages of Haig's story into the air and stormed out of his abode. Haig retrieved the rewritten pages and shoved them furiously into the trash.

The next day, after sobering up, Morozov began rewriting his story from memory, but he began to forget sections. This compelled him to reach into the trash basket and try to decipher his own story buried under the nearly illegible notes that Lunz had made on his original draft. Slowly he found himself reading the drunken poet's revisions. Despite his limited vocabulary, Lunz's rewrite really did bring the piece to life. He cut unnecessary expository paragraphs compelling the plot to speed forward. Soon the work jumped from the page. The drunk had loosened up the formality and let the language breathe. The result made his piece sound like a mix of early Chekhov and late Maupassant. Morozov wound up including most of Lunz's rewrites.

"Watch where you're going, fool!" some old teamster yelled at Morozov who was thoughtlessly crossing a slushy street. Haig paused as the man galloped his horse and wagon past him.

By contrast, sometime later, while rereading the finished poems that Lunz had rewritten, Haig saw that Dimitri didn't take a single one of his notes.

After a couple blocks of struggling through the muddy snow, Morozov passed a large familiar warehouse. His father had owned the old building over fifty years ago. He used it as a storage depot for his import-export stock. It was confiscated along with their home during the Revolution. The sound of hammers and construction coming from inside the old building made him aware that they were converting the space into something new, probably another small munitions factory. They couldn't turn out enough artillery nowadays.

He spotted a shortcut across a wide snowy field that led to Nevski Prospekt. Morozov cautiously moved down a steep embankment to reach it. As Haig was halfway across the field, he heard behind him, "Careful, comrade!"

He angled over to one side of the narrow snow-shoveled path and watched a construction worker pushing a wheelbarrow full of old bricks right past him.

"Coming through, comrade!" he heard again. Another giant troll in torn overalls was pushing a second wheelbarrow full of bricks from his father's former building. When Haig ignored the remark, the worker angled the bricks around him, nearly shoving him to the ground. Haig stopped as a third wheelbarrow also sped past. When it did, Haig actually felt the ground tremble below him. He turned and saw a couple more full wheelbarrows right on his heels. That's when he started hearing the faint sound of cracking. He instantly realized that this wasn't just a snowy path, but a frozen lake. At that instant, seeing the weight of the overladen wheelbarrows, he realized that the ice below could break at any moment.

The six men with their loads of bricks seemed to realize this as well because suddenly they all broke loose running, trying to get to the far side about eighty feet away. Panicking at the thought of plunging through to an icy death, Haig began dashing frantically too, overtaking the caravan of wheelbarrows. As he dashed, finally reaching the far bank, he heard cackling.

Looking behind him, he realized the entire crew of workers had stopped with their wheelbarrows and were laughing at him. The water hadn't risen any higher than the soles of their boots. It wasn't a lake at all, just a frozen field. And the laborers knew it.

"You should all be sent to the front!" Haig yelled furiously at them and stormed off. "I'll report you all!"

After a couple blocks along Nevski Prospekt, calming down, Haig found himself walking on long, narrow boards flanked on both sides by two trenches. One trench was deep. He figured a sewer pipe was in the process of being laid. The second shallow trench was where the new sidewalk was about to be poured. The entire city was being retrofitted and modernized. After a few more blocks, Haig turned off Nevski, which was packed with traffic. He opted for a quieter street that ran parallel— an as-of-yet un-upgraded street that seemed to have been overlooked.

It led him past a row of bricked-up doorways attached to one long low building. An ancient memory flickered. A small bistro had once been tucked into this block somewhere. The place was cheap, smoky, and crowded. Always noisy with excited conversation about the much-anticipated upheaval. It was as though the uprising were a hatching serpent, still coiled in its giant, leathery egg about to break out and rescue everyone.

"I must be seeing a ghost!" he suddenly heard in the distance.

He turned around. From a scattering of young people walking behind him, a single person grinned. A small, wrinkled man in an even more wrinkled suit caught up.

"I feared that you were dead, Haig."

"I guess we're it, the survivors from a forgotten age," Morozov replied, not sure who the man was.

"You don't remember me, do you?"

It was the man's deeply inset eyes that tipped him off.

"Critter!" At least that was his nickname thirty years ago when he was a young scribbler like himself.

"I haven't heard that nickname in ages," the withered man laughed. "I've gone back to my original—Yuri Petrovich Gallanski," his old friend reintroduced himself.

"That's right! Yuri!" Haig remembered and pointing to a vacant store front, he asked, "Do you remember a coffee shop that was here before the Revolution?"

"Frankly I don't."

"It had some illustrious historical title, like The Paris Commune of 1870."

"Don't remind me!" replied the smaller man. "I've put a lot of work in trying to purge my memories. I don't remember anything before 1940."

"I wish I could refine my own brain," Morozov replied.

"At my age, I find myself constantly reaching that point where I'm struggling to recall details. Now I just stop struggling. You should try it."

"So what are you doing now?" Haig asked.

"I'm a mid-level bureaucrat for the CWTPPPF3."

"You don't say!" Morozov smirked.

"I'm actually with the appellate division," he corrected himself, "of the Committee for War Time Production of Paper Products of Factory Three. In fact, I'm running late to an appointment a few blocks away."

"Toilet paper! I wipe my ass with sliced up newspaper like everyone else," Alexei replied.

"Well, someday we'll produce a special paper for the most important part of the body, 'til then we only have plans."

"How'd you wind up on the prestigious committee for sandy toilet paper?" Haig teased as they walked.

"After transferring out of more than a couple far colder postings, I finally worked my way back to Moscow and am grateful to quietly serve the Revolution without being a casualty of it."

"I'm surprised you weren't drafted."

"I have so many health issues, they knew I wouldn't make it through the induction."

He remembered an observation Lunz once made about Critter: "There were two ways a swimmer could get through a big wave, either by courageously rising up over it in glory, but risk having it crush you, or discreetly diving under it." Critter always went under, which was probably the reason that after thirty turbulent years, he was the sole person Morozov recognized since his arrival in his old hometown.

"I find myself wondering what I'd do if I knew the way things would turn out," Haig finally said.

"Learn to speak a *very* foreign language and move there?" Critter joked.

"With the entire world at war," Haig replied, "I no longer think there is such a place."

176

"I always wonder how Lunz would've coped," Yuri asked. "He was always so resourceful."

"You know he vanished one day about twenty years ago?"

"I'd hardly call it vanished," Yuri replied just above a whisper.

"You think he was arrested?"

"I heard that he was rounded up during a secret inquiry."

"Every inquiry is a secret inquiry," Morozov half-joked.

"That one was rather unusual, wasn't it?"

"How so?"

"'Cause it centered on something that actually happened before the Revolution."

"What are you talking about?" Morozov clarified. "It happened just before Lenin died."

"I don't think so."

Haig vividly recalled when the young poet had barely escaped being executed; he vowed he was going to devote his remaining years to poetry and little else. "Lunz told me he was arrested because he and his friends were drunkenly talking nonsense at some bar."

Critter chuckled. "Sounds like something he would say."

"After they freed him, he said he was going on a pilgrimage and would spend the rest of his life writing poetry in Siberia."

Critter sarcastically made the sign of the cross.

"Why do I sense you know something you're not sharing?"

"Of course it's not all hearsay, but I heard his arrest was due to his expropriations or more appropriately mis-expropriations."

"What the hell is mis-expropriation?" Lunz had rarely spoken about his pre-Revolutionary activities.

"He was a member of an outlaw gang who robbed successful businesses to finance the Revolution."

"I remember."

"Apparently one of his robberies went particularly sour."

"How sour?"

"A badly botched jewelry holdup. It was in all the papers. Something like fourteen people were killed."

177

Morozov vaguely remembered it—the Imperial Jewelry Heist Massacre. The bank robbers put the hostages in the windows and doorway so when the cops arrived and began shooting they were quickly killed in the crossfire. Since a number of gangsters were acting as lookouts nearby, a number of the tzar's police were killed as well but so were most of the gang.

Although Morozov knew Lunz was a part of some outlaw group that raised money for the Revolution, his friend never talked about it.

For all Lunz's bad behavior, Morozov simply couldn't fathom that his old friend was capable of killing anyone.

"He was just a lookout man," Critter said as if reading his thoughts. "I don't think Dimitri ever pulled a trigger."

"So why was he prosecuted for murder?"

"You have to remember that this was before the Revolution, so when the Tzar's government fell, their investigation stopped. Then years later, someone remembered all the missing loot. No one cared about the victims. All they cared about was the haul."

"What haul?"

"Supposedly he and the remaining members of his gang got away with a fortune."

"What fortune?"

"A big bag of diamonds."

"Diamonds!"

"Again it's all talk, and I heard that some of the loot was recovered."

"Lunz never had two kopeks to rub together," Morozov said.

"And he was a big drinker," Critter added. "When Lunz was drunk he was an even bigger talker. Never could keep a secret."

"But mainly he was an out-of-control hedonist," Morozov continued. "He'd spend everything on booze and girls. There's no way he could've sat on a fortune like that. The man utterly lacked self-control." But no sooner did he say this than he wondered if he ever knew Lunz at all. The former street urchin always had a natural gift at deception—all poets did.

Critter smirked and nodded.

"What do you think? He killed his fellow gang members and took all the remaining money for himself?"

"He didn't have to. Let's say for the sake of argument, from a gang of twenty, only six survive and years later they are rounded up. None talk, so three of them are executed. So there are three left."

"You think they split up the loot?"

"Lunz was the only person in the group that I knew, and I should add that even that was a rumor. Maybe he was only friends with one of the gang members."

"If he had loot he would've spent it," Morozov said.

"Unless he got his share after the arrest and execution. So there was no temptation to spend it," Critter replied.

"This is all utterly insane!" Haig said.

"I always liked Lunz," Critter said, "but frankly I never really knew or trusted him. And the fact that he vanished after being released is the only reason I thought the rumor might be true. But it's more likely he was scooped up during some mass arrests later."

Haig considered that Lunz took advantage of everyone, but only to the point that they'd forgive him—so he could use them again. That seemed to be his greatest gift, and though he had used Morozov many times over, Lunz never took anything Haig couldn't spare. And if pressed to admit it, Morozov knew he never would've become a writer if it wasn't for the drunk poet.

"What do you suppose this city will be like in another thirty years?" Critter asked, changing the subject.

"It'll either be a triumphant success," Haig said thoughtlessly, "or it'll be completely empty."

Critter chuckled and replied, "Maybe the two are the same thing."

As rush hour approached, the crowd around them thickened.

"The older I get," Haig said, "the older I wish I was."

"Remember the old poet, Leo Isaakovich Samioff?" Critter asked.

"The name brings a smile, but I don't know why."

179

"He only ate smoked fish. He was a few years older than us. A deep baritone voice, big hawk nose, deep-set eyes."

"The one who always used fruit in all his poetry!"

"That's him," Critter said. "He died the day after the Bolsheviks took over the Duma. No one knows how he died. They just found him dead in bed."

"Yes! He owed me two rubles," Haig suddenly recalled.

"I wish I were him," Critter said. "He must've died with a big grin on his face. Living just long enough to see the Revolution occur and going to sleep with the thought that an exciting new world awaited. There really is such a thing as a well-timed death. Not having to live through all this shit."

"Come to think of it," Haig revised, "*I* owed *him* two rubles."

"So you don't know what became of Anatoli..."

"I was never good with names," Haig replied, looking around nervously. It was nice to finally bump into another old-timer and quickly review the past, just to make sure it wasn't all a dream. Even the best NKVD team couldn't have planned a chance meeting like this. But they did have sophisticated listening devices nowadays. It was too easy to get overheard. Besides that, Haig had sacrificed too many old friends to save himself. He didn't want to ever have to bear witness against Critter.

As they strolled by another busy intersection, Morozov stared at an old church that had been transformed into another new bureaucratic office. Nowadays everything was some kind of government building. Critter suddenly pulled out a small flask.

"Normally I don't drink 'til after work, but meeting you calls for a toast."

Critter took a swallow then handed the container to Haig who gulped down the rest of it. He handed the empty vessel back to Critter who slipped it into his pocket.

"Hey, remember that place?" Haig asked, pointing to a small brick tenement.

"God!" Critter stared and grinned. "Are you trying to give me a heart attack?"

"If you survived that place," he nodded his head toward the old tenement, "I don't think I could give you a heart attack."

Suddenly, a curvy middle-aged Persian woman with a faint mustache turned a corner and started walking directly at them. Critter nudged Morozov who couldn't take his eyes off the voluptuous lady. As she moved her arm, her old fur coat fell open, revealing a pair of large, asymmetrical breasts. In another moment, she pulled it tightly around herself and passed between the two men.

"They still come here," Critter said, "the older ones at least. Even the Revolution can't erase the spirit of the place."

"But who has the rubles anymore?" Morozov half-kidded.

"They're very good about bartering," Yuri replied, knowingly.

The small brick tenement was once the location of what had been the cheapest bordello in all of Moscow. As poor, young men, maybe once a year, on their birthdays if they were lucky, they could leverage their boyishness and haggle down desperate ladies who were twice their age and weight.

"And this, my old friend, is where we must part," Critter announced.

"Your Paper Committee doesn't convene in the old whorehouse, does it?" asked Morozov.

"Since there are no whorehouses in Russia, it might as well. The question you should be asking though," said Yuri, "is who is following you."

"Following me?"

"And since my final goal is to try to outlive our fearless leader, I can't be a part of that."

Haig spun around and slowly scanned the foot traffic of people moving around. Everyone's head was fixed downward. No one stood out.

"Who exactly is it?" he asked. When his question got no response, he turned to find that Critter had kept walking. He could see he already reached the next block. Morozov turned a corner sharply, slipped into a narrow doorway and waited.

The notion that Dimitri Lunz, his oldest and dearest friend, could have been a part of such a violent robbery, and that he might've vanished with a bag of diamonds, was mindboggling. The very thought that he was sitting on a fortune while accepting Haig's charity made his head spin. Lunz was always broke and usually in some kind of trouble.

For the past twenty years, Haig imagined his friend living quietly in some remote fishing village in the Arctic Circle, like a monk whose prayers were his works of poetry, a calm center while Russia and the political world around him were crashing down. This thought gave Haig strength in man's ability to overcome his many vices and give his life purpose.

Critter's vodka began kicking in. Surveying the stream of people bubbling by in the afternoon twilight, he felt lightheaded, a warm glow. Suddenly one young face sparkled out from the rest: Although she was concealed behind a thick coat, scarf, and hat, her face stood out. It was his lost Ukrainian sweetheart, Masha.

As she approached, she looked up with a big smile of recognition and Morozov instantly embraced her. When she hugged him back, he planted a soft wet kiss on her neck.

"Professor Morozov!" She pulled away, smelling the booze on his breath. It wasn't Masha, at all, but Alexei's friend, the seductive she-agent.

"Oh god! I'm sorry. I thought you were..."

"Darya Kotova!"

"Of course. I'm so sorry. I thought you were an old friend," he said, trying to restrain himself. "What are you doing here?"

"Just walking by."

"Come now. This isn't a coincidence," he said softly staring into her eyes. "You followed me."

"Not followed, but..."

"I knew it!"

"I was on Nevski when I saw those workmen laughing at you. I was worried."

"You saw that?" If she had been watching him from that long ago, she must've been following him. On the other hand, why would she reveal this? "Is Alexei around?"

"I don't think so." She looked around innocently.

"Where exactly are you going?" He instantly sobered up.

"Right here." She pointed down the block to a large ugly building sliced through with many narrow windows. A filthy sign said, "Auxiliary Dormitory Number 3."

"This far from the campus?" he asked suspiciously.

"They shipped me to temporary housing until I get a permanent job assignment," she said, then quipped, "You don't need another assistant, do you?"

"If you like, I'll fire your boyfriend and give you his job."

"Please don't be paranoid, but I just saw you talking to someone." she said. She must've seen Critter.

"I was just asking directions," he replied, not wanting to involve him.

She grinned and asked, "May I ask you something?"

"Of course," he said.

"Who exactly did you think I was?" She looked deep into his eyes.

"A dear old friend from a lifetime ago," he replied and added, "The problem is I keep forgetting that time has aged us all. I'll see someone from long ago and forget that they're now thirty years older. I don't really know anyone who's young anymore. I guess that's why people have children—to remind them that they're old."

Inexplicably she hugged him. He went limp, utterly bewildered. Just as quickly, she released him and dashed into the old building without a word.

Over twenty years ago, Masha had awoken one morning to find an envelope had been slid under her door. He remembered his own terror when she showed up at his apartment and tossed it in his face.

"DISCIPLINARY COMMITTEE" was boldly written along the top. He remembered opening it and reading, "MASHA

183

RODCHENKNO IS SUMMARILY EXPELLED FOR ANTI-COMMUNIST SENTIMENT."

The letter went on to state that she had brazenly published "a crypto-fascist tract that undermined women's natural rights of childbearing." The letter stated that because she had no prior acts of unlawfulness, they had decided to be merciful. In their wisdom they chose to keep this transgression within the school's jurisdiction. Thankfully there would be no arrest. However, she had clearly violated the student conduct clause of her academic contract, therefore she would be barred from finishing her medical studies.

In a fine print, along the bottom of the letter, he read that she had two choices: She could make an appointment, appeal the decision, and risk an expansion of charges, which might lead to a civil arrest. Or she could confess her guilt, write a letter of contrition, accept the punishment, and re-apply next year to try to complete her final year of studies.

Before he could read the concluding paragraph, Masha slapped Haig hard across the face and shouted, "You did this to me!"

"I'll fix this! I'll make an appointment with Bukharin himself! I guarantee he'll quash this!"

"I only had one semester left! Just one!"

"Just hear me out!" Morozov pleaded. "I've been talking to important people, people of rank. And others who have experience with this sort of thing before!"

"I don't want your help!" she shouted furiously.

"We can try going over the disciplinary panel's head," he said somberly, "but most of those I've spoken to say the safest thing is to just take the punishment."

"What?!"

"They have a pattern of showing mercy in the face of guilt, if you explain you've learned from your mistakes, and they frequently arrest those who contest it."

"They're giving me three days to vacate my room!" she shouted, pointing to the final paragraph. "I can't even afford to remain here."

"Move in with me! Marry me! I'll spend my whole life making it up to you!"

"I only had one more semester!" she said, more to herself. "Just one! And I would've been a doctor!"

"They invested far too much in you. You're going to be a doctor for the state! They need you!"

She stormed off.

That night, Masha thought it over. She was faced with the choice of returning to the outer provinces of Ukraine and having to work on her parents' small farm for a year or staying with Haig in Moscow where he'd desperately try to repair the damage he had done. She chose to bottle up her anger. All she ever wanted was to be a doctor. And she was so close to finishing her degree.

Based on the information that Haig had learned, which she later confirmed, there was still a good chance she could re-enter the medical program next year and complete her studies with next year's class. Considering the fact that she was one of the youngest students in her class, she consoled herself with the thought that she still had time on her side. She told Haig that the only way she'd stay with him was if the old fold-out partition was stretched across the room again, like it was when his mother lived with him. She was not going to be his concubine. He humbly agreed.

Roughly a third of the parlor, where the sofa was located, became his sleeping quarters. Another third of the old sitting room, which held the bed and his mother's antique armoire, was her new living quarters. The dinner table before the fireplace was their common area. And they shared the bathroom and the kitchen in the hallway with another family.

Since Masha's food stipend was also canceled, Haig supported her with his modest salary. She took it as a loan and would periodically write him IOUs, which she vowed she'd eventually pay back. She refused to ever be in his debt. Secretly, once she was back in school and no longer needed him, she fully intended to refund him and then sever all ties with him.

After teaching classes every night, Morozov would come home and see Masha sitting at the dinner table, reading her textbooks and writing notes. He'd try to make small talk, but she'd barely respond. She clearly wanted to be left alone. He tried to give her her space. Days turned into weeks and months as he patiently waited for her to find the forgiveness in her heart so they could at least talk calmly. He hoped and prayed they'd eventually sleep together—this wasn't so much a matter of sexual desire as simple comfort—she had the only available bed. This became even more painful as winter grew colder since she also had the only thick blanket in the house.

At night, she could hear his teeth chattering on the couch far from the fireplace, which was in her part of the parlor. Initially she enjoyed hearing the sound—he deserved every damn shiver, every goose pimple he got for ruining her life. One exceptionally cold night, though, she put on extra clothes and was able to see her own breath. As she tried to sleep she was repeatedly awakened listening to him moaning in pain, rubbing his limbs together to retain sensation. She finally consented to letting him join her in the bed if only for her own warmth. But he had to keep his coat on and they slept back to back.

As the days grew steadily colder she finally allowed him to sleep with her. One night he thoughtlessly found himself spooning her and she didn't reject him.

She slowly loosened up as winter grew colder. True, she had lost a year of her life due to his arrogance and stupidity, but she saw that he had worked hard and was bending over backwards to reinstate her in medical school.

Also, the lesson wasn't wasted on Morozov. He had learned never to question her when she said something. So, even though she swore she would not, she gradually found herself reluctantly forgiving him.

One particularly cold night, he awoke to his surprise to discover that in his sleep he had hugged her. Though she seemed to be breathing in a halting fashion, suggesting she was awake, he gently released her. The next night, shortly after they went to sleep, he delicately reached under her nightgown. When she didn't protest, he ran his fingers across her bare thigh and down through her pubic hair. Her breathing grew unsteady. He sensed she was only pretending to sleep. When he slowly slipped his finger into her she

186

stopped breathing entirely. Abruptly she turned and kissed him on the lips.

"I love you," he whispered. She pulled up her gown and initiated sex. When he tried it again the following night, she stopped him, explaining that she was no longer on her period. They seemed to turn a corner. It simply required too much work to always be angry. Steadily, they began talking just as they used to.

They were intimate four times in December before she put a final stop to it. He knew she stopped it because he was about to leave the city. He had made plans to head north to a suburb outside of Saint Petersburg to visit his mother just before Christmas. Haig still hadn't broken the news to his mom that Masha was living with him, nor had he mentioned the whole ridiculous imbroglio of why.

After a slow train ride, he stayed with his aunt and mother in the country. He enjoyed the fact that they treated him like a young prince. Both his mom and aunt hated everything about the new government: the quotas, the coupons, the new restrictions on both actions and thoughts. His mom particularly despised the indignant stares she'd get in public if she said the wrong thing. Inexperienced, starry-eyed youngsters all conformed so easily, showing no spontaneity and spouting the same judgmental rhetoric about the Revolution, completely vilifying the tzar in order to give the current regime more license to shape some wildly ridiculous future.

"These kids should all be spanked!" she exclaimed. Fearful of judgmental stares, she entirely stopped making weekend trips to St. Petersburg. "I'd rather be a homebody and only speak honestly to my sister than have to silence myself for fools who don't even know the truth! This is far worse than it ever was under the tzar!"

One afternoon, while accompanying his mother to the local food commissary for their weekly quota of rock-hard potatoes and stunted beets—the only things that weren't out of stock —the woman manager released a bloodcurdling shriek. All grew silent as she announced, "Comrade Vladimir Ilyich Ulyanov, the savior of Mother Russia, is no more!"

"Oh my god!" Haig said. His mother rolled her eyes tiredly.

Russia's leader had been sick for a while. After a succession of strokes, he had clearly grown worse. Still, people were in utter shock wondering if the communist state would continue. Many wept openly. Even Morozov's mother who never supported the Revolution found herself growing quiet.

41

Kasabian, Moscow, 1924

Upon receiving news of Lenin's untimely death, Moscow was immediately overrun by hordes of mourners pouring into the city. The capital became one giant funeral procession. People wept openly while walking down the streets. Everyone except Haig, who was with his mother in St. Petersburg, lined up to bid farewell to the great liberator. Acutely aware of his mother's advancing age, he chose to remain with her and his aunt for a while longer than planned. He figured that Masha, who was always a homebody, might miss him and be kinder when he finally returned.

When Haig finally took the train south and returned home about a month later, it seemed like years had passed. Masha looked noticeably haggard. When he spotted some broken shards of glass on the floor of his living room, Masha informed him that his obnoxious friend had tried to jimmy open the window, which she had locked, so he broke in.

"Lunz?" he asked.

"Who else?"

"I thought he was gone for good, to devote himself to writing the new holy Bible."

"He came back for the funeral."

"I'm so sorry!" he said.

"He fixed the window the next day," she said. "And he apologized."

Haig also found two empty vodka bottles in the garbage can.

"How long did he stay?" he asked, astounded.

"Three nights."

"Was he a nuisance?"

"After the first night he behaved himself."

"He better have!"

"He didn't know about my..." Masha said, "my being expelled."

"What did he say?"

"Oh, he was quite sympathetic. He joked that it was the kind of blunder only you could make."

"Typical Lunz."

"We spent his last night just talking about it. He was actually very easy to talk to."

"You're lucky," he said. "My mother wasn't nearly as easy." He was going to mention all that had occurred but thought better of it. Masha knew his mother didn't care for her and he didn't want to get her started.

That first night when he was about to climb back into her bed, she firmly said no. The weather had grown warmer, so he returned back to the couch with the thin blanket on the far side of the room. Her former aloofness seemed to have mysteriously returned. He assumed that she had grown jealous of the time he had spent with his mother.

During that first week, when he would go to sleep, she'd make a point of regularly remaining, sitting up in front of the fireplace rereading her medical textbooks as though to remind him of the damage he had done. The following week, when the weather precipitously dropped, he made a renewed attempt to share the bed again. She relented but bundled onto her side. No physical contact, no more hanky-panky.

After the two went shopping one afternoon, as they approached their home, where fellow residents were chatting out front, Masha rushed ahead and entered alone. That was when he feared that she was ashamed to be seen by the other tenants. Even though he had initially introduced her as his fiancée, he deduced that she didn't want to be perceived as a kept woman.

"We'll remedy that when we get married," he replied, hoping to return to where they were before his trip north.

That night on the couch, he was awakened by the sounds of Masha intensely sobbing. When Haig asked what the problem was, she simply said she was feeling unwell.

As springtime rolled around, she seemed to be letting herself go, rarely grooming, steadily eating more and more steamed cabbage. Just reading and putting on pounds.

By late March, he received an invitation to come down to Yerevan and read some of his latest work at a big Armenian literary conference. When he informed Masha of the event, she simply shrugged. Remembering their last wonderful trip together, he contemplated inviting her along, but she had been so grumpy and ill-kempt lately that he decided against it.

A couple days before his departure, while searching for his latest manuscript, he found himself going through her papers and clothes that seemed to be taking over the tight apartment. Before leaving, instead of bidding her farewell, he muttered something under his breath.

"What's that?" she growled.

"Look at this place!" he finally broke. He pointed to her books and clothes scattered all around. Looking at her standing in her bathrobe, overweight, with her hair a mess, he added, "Look at yourself! It's all going to pot!"

"Going to pot?" She had a strange glimmer in her eyes.

"You haven't gone out in months. And this place is a pigsty."

No sooner did he say the words than he regretted it. Before he could apologize, she stormed out to the communal bathroom in the hallway, slamming the door behind her. He wanted to apologize, but he knew that would require a long and patient talk. If he wanted to make the train, he only had time to grab his bag and dash.

I've turned my beautiful, brilliant girlfriend into an old cow! he thought on the long rail ride south to Yerevan. During the entire trip, he simply remembered the wonderful time he had with Masha a few years ago and regretted not bringing her along.

When he returned a day early with a bouquet of flowers, he opened his door to find that the apartment was immaculate. All his linen and towels were washed and folded. Everything was put neatly

190

away. When he finally looked behind the partition, he discovered that Masha had packed all her bags. For the first time in a while she was dressed in a coat and scarf.

"I didn't think you were coming back until tomorrow," she said. "I had been working on a letter..."

"To whom?"

"My mother wrote me saying that she and my father desperately need my help. Since there are five more months before I can reapply to school I might as well spend the time down there helping them."

"You can't leave now!" he said.

"No, you were right," she said honestly. "I'm just driving us both crazy here."

"Why'd you pack everything?" he asked, noticing that she had completely erased all signs of her existence there. Even her stack of medical reference books was missing.

"I didn't have that much to start with. I tossed a lot of stuff out."

"Where are your medical books?"

"I just figured I might be down there a while, and this place is so packed. I sent them ahead."

"This is good. I'll go down there with you. It's time I meet your parents, isn't it?" he said, holding up his suitcase. "My bags are already packed, and I have two weeks without any work."

"Out of the question! They'd never allow it."

"I know that I made a mess of things," he said, handing her the flowers, "but there's only five months left before the university considers your readmission. There are no guarantees."

"You put a lot of work into the case, I'm sure we'll be fine."

"There's still a ways to go!" he said earnestly.

"I'm going to miss my train," she said simply and began walking out.

"I love you," he added tensely, blocking her and taking her hands. She looked away.

"We need a little time apart, Haig," she said softly. He reluctantly thought that maybe she was right, a little time apart usually helps.

"What's your parents' address?" he asked, grabbing a pencil.

"I'll write you once I get settled."

"Just tell me their address."

"If you send mail there, my father will just toss it out," she said. "And I'm probably not even staying there."

"Where will you be staying?"

"In Kiev."

"Where?"

"I don't know yet, with some friends. I'll have to see who has space. I'll write you when I know. Now I'm going to miss my train if I don't leave right now!"

He grabbed her bags and followed her outside. Then he flagged down a cab. When she sat inside, he got in next to her and closed the door. The taxi sped in silence to the terminal, where he carried her bags and followed her onto a crowded third-class car.

"What are you doing?" she asked, afraid he was going to come with her.

He silently hoisted her big sutcase up on the luggage rack over her seat.

"Look," she said, not making eye contact. "I'll be back here soon."

"How will I get hold of you?" he suddenly asked.

"I told you, I'll send you a telegram once I'm settled," she said, staring out the window. She didn't respond to his kiss, and another single woman took a seat across from her as the conductor yelled, "All aboard!"

As he stood on the platform and waved farewell, she stared, but didn't wave back.

42

"It sounds like we're approaching go-time for the IPO, no?" Eric half-rhymed to David Lande on the phone.

"We're getting close," Lande replied, "but before we have to do the whole dog and pony show, I'm taking some family time."

"Family time?" He tried to sound happy but was immediately concerned.

"My daughter just graduated from college, so my wife and I are taking her on a cruise in two weeks. We're sailing up to the Baltic, then we're docking in Saint Petersburg, Russia. I always wanted them to see the old country."

"When will you return here?"

"Once we hit Russia it's a train ride down to Moscow, then six weeks across the Trans-Siberian to Vladivostok where I've hired a five-hundred foot yacht and crew to pick us up, then we're off to Japan and across the Pacific on a plane trip from L.A. to New York."

"You're circling the entire globe?" he asked nervously.

"Eric, there's no need to worry. I'll call you as soon as I get back and we'll launch your IPO," he said. "Collect that free pile of cash, then start construction."

There it was, he thought. The countdown had begun.

That summer, too terrified that his once-in-a-lifetime deal was going to get away, Eric passed up an opportunity to join his wife, Edna, on a two-week trip to Peru. She was hiking up to Machu Picchu with a group of affluent friends from the neighborhood. As he drove her to the airport, she told him that he had to stay on top of Eriq Jr.

"Stay on him, why?" he asked while speeding on the Long Island Expressway.

"I spoke to him two nights ago and he sounded high as a kite. He needs a father."

"Where is he again?" Eric asked. "California?"

"Nevada, in the desert! We talked about this!"

"Right," he remembered, "at that rock concert."

"It's not a rock concert!" Edna yelled back. "He said he was going to some big art happening called Burnt Man."

"Right," Eric remembered. "His generation's Woodstock. That's what he called it. So I thought it was a concert. Big deal, he'll be back in a couple days."

"It's a week-long event!" she corrected him again. "Now who do you think influenced him to run off and do that?"

"Give me a break," he replied. "I was a kid, just trying to get laid."

"That's even more pathetic!" she replied.

"What is?"

"This was the woman you introduced me to on the street years ago."

"That's right, you met her. She looked a lot prettier back then," he replied.

"I hope so. I never had some teenager run off behind his parents' back and sacrifice four days of his life to lose his virginity to me. And I was older than Eriq when I lost my innocence."

"Give me a fucking break!" he said, honking at someone trying to cut him off.

After ten minutes of awkward silence, he pulled up in front of Terminal 2. She apologized for her outburst and he did likewise, telling her he loved her.

43

Kasabian, Moscow, 1943

Looking up at the old building where Alexei's girlfriend, Darya, had entered, Morozov began to suspect that this was the same dormitory where Masha had lived and got thrown out of all those years ago. It had the same style cornices and balustrade along the top.

Tiredly, he made his way home. After running into his old friend Critter on the street, he remembered the last time he saw him—an ambitious young man ready for whatever the world threw at him.

Meeting him this afternoon, he seemed fearful and shriveled. Life had crumpled him like a discarded sheet of paper.

"Is this really the same city where I was born and raised?" he muttered aloud, wondering what had become of his past.

As he looked around him, he tried to grasp details: the tracks of military vehicles in the snow, a wrinkled peasant woman completely shrouded in rags and headscarf scavenging through a garbage barrel, an ancient man poorly balanced on an old troika while his two heavy-set daughters put their shoulders to the side and pushed it like farm animals. Despite all the revolutionary zeal and painful refinement, nothing seemed to have significantly changed.

Hearing the sound of melting snow sliding off the shingles from a nearby roof, he looked up through various terracotta angles past half a dozen carefully positioned anti-aircraft balloons to the ancient cupolas and recent utilitarian buildings that now defined the Moscow skyline. In the middle of them, he recognized a lone spire that belonged to the old train station to Petrograd. For some reason, Haig thought of his father's childhood friend, Julius Martov.

Although he refused to believe it back then, he now regarded Martov as the last, best chance after Alexander Kerensky that Russia might've had at creating a government that didn't prey upon its citizenry. Morozov's father knew Julius when they were kids back in old Constantinople. As young non-Muslim teenagers growing up in an Islamic country, the two became natural allies, native guests in an unwelcoming land. Yet ten years later when they met again as young men in Moscow in the 1880s, their friendship instantly cooled. Where Morozov's father traveled in aristocratic circles, always striving to improve his business connections, marrying his mother, a beautiful young socialite, Martov became immersed in the growing revolutionary fervor of Russia. He was eventually arrested by the Okhrana along with his cohort and fellow revolutionary Lenin. Soon the two faction leaders were carted off to prison up in the Arctic Circle.

Both believed in a new Socialist-Marxist government, but Martov felt that it should be modeled after a European system, elected by the people and braced with checks and balances. Lenin, however, felt governance was too important to be left to the vagaries of the masses. It needed to remain above the fray and be managed by the educated elite, sacred trustworthy men who had suffered in prison and repeatedly proved their mettle during trying times. After the Revolution, as the Bolsheviks' power increased and opponents began to get rounded up, Martov finally fled to Germany. Within a year of his exile, both he and Lenin were dead. And now, twenty years later, a leader far worse than Nicholas occupied the Kremlin, an absolute monster.

When Morozov finally reached the Ulanov House, he was relieved to find that his servant, the voice of the commonest man, was nowhere to be heard. Haig peeled off his soggy shoes at the door and changed into slippers. In the bathroom, he stripped, hung up his wet clothes, and put on a robe. Although there was a giant chunk of strange meat floating in a small cast iron pot, Morozov heated some clear borscht and consumed it with the last slice of black bread. Then he went to sleep.

44

Alexei, Woodstock Festival, 1969

In the darkness with Sergei snoring next to him and rock music booming in the distance, Alexei flipped over so his face slapped against something square and hard. He realized it was a paperback book—the Morozov stories. The old writer was still haunting him. The commotion of the rock concert was throbbing outside like an injured monster that just wouldn't die. Though he tried to go back to sleep, he remembered when working for the curmudgeon, the Armenian would steadily taunt him with an endless stream of condescending remarks. Abruptly, the music came to a halt. A burst of applause signaled that another band had finished. A new one would start soon.

Hoping to get some cool air, Alexei squeezed out of the tent, careful not to awaken Sergei. Using the single flashlight, he walked down the muddy trail lined with tents and soggy sleeping bags toward the distant stage that was pulsing through psychedelic-colored gels. Although they planned to hunt for Sergei's daughter in the morning, he decided he might as well look for her alone while the crowd was calm. But all he remembered was the tiny wallet photo of a typical American girl.

The heat from the warm August night along with the day of rock and roll amid the constant flow of the pot and booze, had felled the children's crusade. Where the hell were their parents? he wondered.

As Alexei passed through an entangled mesh of sleeping hippies, he thought, except for the blood and body parts, this is what it looked like miles outside of Moscow after the Luftwaffe had strafed his position while surrounded in the Rzhev Pocket. He had crawled away, badly wounded, hoping to get through a forest filled with Nazi soldiers while trying to get back to his line.

As he walked through the valley of jumbled children, he tried paying special attention to young brunette girls, but it was hopeless. All young people with their tight little faces and flowy long hair looked too much alike. The process of aging to him really was a transformation into individuality. What he once thought of as ugly was actually a passage into uniqueness. All the kids here looked and were more or less alike.

At one time, Alexei flipped on his flashlight and shined his light into one young girl's small oval face. She blinked, shielded her eyes, and said, "What the hell, dude!"

"Is your name Anna Hagopian?"

"Hell no! What are you, some kind of creep?"

"Did you know the name of that last band that just played?" he asked, distracting her with a question.

"Creedence."

"Creedence?" He knew the word came from *creed*, meaning something to believe in. The band had completed their set, and a new band was loading in. He heard someone said, "Sly Stallone is coming on!"

Alexei continued walking around looking for Sergei's lost daughter. It grew increasingly difficult as the kids began getting up and heading toward the stage. The Sly Stone band seemed to form an immediate connection with the audience.

As more hippies rose to dance, Alexei watched and slowly found himself enjoying the music more and more. Before the set was over, finding himself too tired, Alexei trudged back uphill to his pup tent on the slope. As he squeezed in and lay back on his bag, he found the book again under his ass.

"Dance to the music..." he could hear blaring outside. But substituting his own lyrics, Alexei silently sang *Morozov's not my fault, Darya's not my fault, Morozov is not my fault...* until he drifted back to sleep.

45

Alexei, Moscow, 1943

As young Alexei rocked back and forth, his thoughts drifted hundreds of miles away to the remains of his division who survived only to be cut off in a surprise pincer move. Thousands of poor, young bastards like himself still fighting, whose limbs and heads were being blasted apart by German artillery, suffering brutal losses under the latest Nazi counteroffensive. Unable to stop thinking of what was happening, he rolled off Darya, who was grateful as she was getting sore.

"So tell me again," he said, ignoring their intimate activity, "what did he do after he left the university?"

"He met someone near the old Smolensky Market, some small guy around his age." She got up naked and went to the bathroom.

"Were you following him?"

"He asked the same question. I told him that I just happened to spot him and followed him a little."

"But you were following him?"

"Sort of, yes."

"When you do something and later confess to it, you're taking a big risk."

"Believe me, I know," she said. "He caught me."

"How'd he catch you?"

"He was hiding in a doorway," she said, turning on a faucet to hide the sound of her peeing. "But I covered my tracks."

"How?"

"I said I was heading into the auxiliary dormitory," she said from the toilet. "The old building at the far end of the campus."

"I wonder what he was doing all the way over there, in the middle of nowhere?"

"He seemed a little lost."

"It's a long way from home." Alexei opened the bathroom door, watching her as she was defecating. "Who exactly did he meet?"

"I didn't recognize him. Some skinny old guy. I would've followed him, but I was alone," she said, closing the door and cleaning herself.

"Shit, so he's connecting with old friends here," Alexei said, worrying that Ivan Lemokh might've been right. Was there more to the old writer than met the eye?

"He kissed me," she said playfully, jumping back into bed.

"Kissed you?"

"Right on the lips," she lied.

"What'd you do?" he asked tiredly.

"I'm just a young girl. What could I do?" she asked pulling the sheet over her mouth while grinning innocently.

"Sure you are."

"It was kind of an accident," she said. "He thought I was someone else."

"It sounds like you've taken a shine to our Armenian," he replied, taking his turn in the bathroom. She could tell he was no longer interested in sex, so she got out of bed and began to dress.

"I can say the same of you," she replied, hiding her anger. Alexei hadn't told her that he had just asked Morozov to read his manuscript, so her comment made him feel guilty.

"We have a job to do," he replied seriously. "And he's leaving soon so we have to hurry."

"Do you really think he's working for someone?" she asked, putting on an earring.

"Until today I had more doubts about you."

"Me?"

"Ivan Lemokh just told me that you wrote Morozov letters from the Ukraine years ago," he said and changing his tone, he looked at her and asked, "How come you never told me this?"

"I did tell you. I sent fan letters to a number of writers. They were actually part of a class assignment. He never wrote me back."

"A fan letter!"

"So what?"you don't get it

"It's just a little two-faced. You write him a fan letter and now you're working to arrest him."

"My country is currently under German occupation. I have no home to return to and my tuition has run out, so I'm doing this to survive. Not 'cause I want to."

"It's part of my job to keep an eye on you," he said in a slightly patronizing tone.

"You've been fucking me for the past two months. What do I have left to hide?"

Alexei let out a sigh.

"Can I ask you a question?" Darya asked, shifting her tone.

"What?"

"Isn't the great Commissar Zhdanov Morozov's patron saint?"

"You know he is."

"Aren't you a little concerned?"

"Of what?"

"That if you do arrest him, some of his more powerful friends might arrest you?" she asked. "Or us?"

"We've wheeled in much bigger fish than him to protect the Revolution."

"Is that what we're doing? Protecting the Revolution?"

"As far as I'm concerned that's what everyone is doing," he said earnestly. "That's what this is all about."

"After repelling Hitler's army with millions of men, do you really believe this cranky little Armenian is going to unravel Russia's great Revolution?"

"What exactly do you think the Revolution is?" Alexei asked earnestly.

"Overthrowing the stupid tzar."

"No, see, you don't get it," he said, clearing his throat. "The tzar really has nothing to do with this. The Revolution is a giant machine with countless moving parts."

"I know, and somehow Morozov is the single monkey wrench that'll bring it all down."

"You clearly haven't awoken to the reality of capitalism!" he said, glaring at her. "And I understand why. You can't see it here in Russia, particularly not today. But if you go to America, or any other Western country, you'll see that they never really ended slavery."

"Yes, they did, in 1863."

"No, they only let the slaves go home at night. The rich own all the governments. They send the poor to their factories and their children off to war. It's all about profit. That's all Hitler and this war is about. That's all any war is about. We alone have tried to stop this. We tried to give control back to the people, and I know it hasn't completely succeeded. The arrests, this very investigation seems crazy. So many innocent people have died. I'm not blind. I see that. I do! Many good people have been sacrificed. Morozov might be innocent as well. He probably is. He might also be guilty without even knowing it. This government, this dream of a better life for all, can only be attained through altruism and faith and—if all else fails—fear."

"How about if you get arrested?" Darya asked.

"If I too am arrested and die in the process, so be it."

"So be it?!"

"It's part of the price of constructing this dream of a just Russia, because if we fail, once they retake control—and they are always trying—then the dream is over, and we are lost forever. Not just us, not just Russia, and not just our children, but all mankind!"

"All mankind?" Darya echoed, trying not to sound sarcastic.

201

"Yes! Capitalism is killing this planet. It's big fish eating the little fish, eating the littler fish, killing the entire planet even more rapidly. That was Marx's whole point."

"Maybe so," Darya replied, "but some of the things we are doing seem so..."

"Extreme, I know, but Marx didn't give us the remedy, just the results. If you want to know the truth, I think Communism will fail. The entire world is against us. I think you'll see this for yourself."

"I've already seen it," Darya said angrily.

"Seen what?"

"I saw my mother nearly starve to death," Darya stated. "I almost did too. During the famine we used to see trucks filled with grain at night..."

Alexei looked at her with wide eyes, making her aware that the room might very well be bugged. She amended, "They were driven in from Russia to help us."

"If the Ukraine is cooperative then Russia is cooperative back," Alexei said sternly. "Communism is about cooperation. If we fail, the future of both our countries is over."

Before her eyes could start tearing up, she headed out the door. She never had any illusions about communism. It was just the latest form of tyranny. She hated it along with every other form of government.

46

Eric, Woodstock Festival, 1969

Throughout the afternoon, as mobs of kids kept packing onto the sprawling dairy farm and unraveling countless tents and sleeping bags, Anna led Eric on a wide sweep around the campgrounds, sniffing out food and supplies of the more prosperous concert-goers. She started walking down along the wide plywood stage, which was still being constructed. Then she headed up the slope, scoping out folks unloading ice chests, small grills, and shopping bags. Anna moved like a skinny pig sniffing for truffles.

"I'm starving," he murmured.

"I'll get you some food."

"Yeah, right." He no longer believed anything she said.

Tiredly, Eric spotted a staffer holding a bulky walkie-talkie. He headed toward him to see if he could suggest where they might find some free food, but the worker dashed off before he could reach him. All the employees were racing around, desperately sorting things out that should've been done a week earlier: the row of shitters, the medical tents, workers were even climbing up and down the amp towers, running wires, testing connections.

"Just wait here!" Anna finally said to him, seeing that he was sweaty and growing irritated. Her eyes were focused on something. "Don't join me no matter what."

"Why, what are you doing?" he asked nervously.

She hastened off. Eric watched as her beautiful little teenage body seemed to loosen up, walking absently like a child in the crowd who didn't even know yet that she was lost. She was slowly moseying over toward a campsite belonging to an older, responsible-looking couple.

Eric watched her pause until the husband walked off and the fuzzy hippie woman who had to be at least forty, was all alone. Eric fastened onto a small group of old hippies sitting like bullfrogs on a log screeching out a scratchy rendition of *"Blowin' In the Wind."*

From twenty feet away, he heard Anna say, "I swore my parents put up their tent right around here." Anna kept looking around, not facing the woman.

"Are you lost?" the older lady asked.

"Not really, I mean, the family car is parked along 17 so I can always just wait back there." Anna stared up at the packed road, "My brother and I went to Bethel to make some calls. We were supposed to rendezvous back here for lunch."

"What's your name, dear?" the older earth goddess asked.

"Annie, pleased to meet you." She shook her hand.

"Annie, I'm Martha. Are you hungry?"

"Not really, I'm more worried about my kid brother—he's starving."

"Tell you what, I think we can spare one sandwich." Martha reached into a large red cooler. "It's just liverwurst and onion, but we made too many of them."

"Liverwurst and... onion?" Anna said, trying not to sound horrified.

"With a little lemon juice squeezed on top. Ate them all through my last pregnancy. They're delicious."

The woman followed Anna's eye line to Eric who immediately joined in the hippie sing-along worried about being spotted. "...*before he sleeps in the sand. And how many times must a cannon ball fly...*"

"Liverwurst is great!" Anna said with a grin, taking the wrapped sandwich and squeezing it into her jacket pocket. "You are a life saver."

"Have you heard the word of God, Annie?" she asked.

"Every Sunday at mass," Anna shot back.

"Amen."

After a few more words of faith and gratitude, Anna marched off with the food in the opposite direction from where Eric was, compelling him to leave the older ensemble and catch up with her.

Once past some trees, out of Martha's view, Anna tossed the spongy sandwich to Eric who barely caught it.

"Now do you trust me?" she asked proudly.

"What is it?"

"Some kind of expensive Bavarian roast beef I think," she replied dryly.

"Want half?" he asked, eagerly ripping through the cellophane. Even with onions it looked great.

"All yours," she said, and continued looking for more opportunities. Slowly, Anna led Eric through the crowd looping along the outer edges. As people kept pouring in Eric took a big bite of the sandwich.

"Fucking liverwurst!" he yelled out to her amusement.

Still, it was better than nothing, so he silently chewed it down and wondered which he liked least, the liverwurst, the onion, or the lemon juice squeezed on it.

While eating, he kept following Anna, who marched ahead in her wide circle, periodically stopping, waiting, swatting away insects. He saw her occasionally interacting with wholesome-looking folks. Periodically, she was shamelessly collecting handouts of one kind or another, an apple here, a bag of chips there. She'd wave him over. He would dash over and collect the goods so that she would constantly appear emptyhanded.

"See if you can get some mosquito repellent," he called out swatting one from his arm.

"It's tough enough getting food." she yelled back.

Soon, Eric regarded the vast swirling crowd and the entire concert area the same way he remembered the river while rafting with his father and brother last year. Parts of the waterway were dead pools of standing people. Other parts of the grounds, people were able to rush easily through.

Although she didn't know anyone, several times Anna thought she spotted friends and would take off running. It was all Eric could do not to lose sight of her in the rushing mob. Unlike Anna, Eric was not a con artist, but he discovered he was actually a pretty good scavenger, picking up things on the ground that might prove useful later. Soon the giant amps started making noises. There was movement on the big plywood stage. People started applauding until some rugged bearded hippie who looked like a pirate said, "Sound check, sound check, one, two, three..."

His voice echoed through the vast field of kids. Everyone began applauding. The pirate welcomed everyone and pointed out where everything was located, the food, the outhouses, the medical tent. Then he began making other announcements: "Helen Savage, please call your father at the motel!" He was reading from a legal pad, a slow and steady stream of public announcements followed. Tiredly, Anna sat on a patch of grass and they rested.

Even though she wanted to ride in the cool old gas-guzzling tractor that shuttled lazy people around, Eric was secretly hoping to find a discarded tent, He insisted they walk, so he could scoop up more possibly salvageable items. She saw that he was constantly nervous about being separated, which she secretly found adorable so she demurred. At one point, they came upon a theater troupe of strident women wearing sexy yellow loincloths and bikini tops. They were evenly spaced out on the grass, each holding a daisy and simultaneously saying, "He loves me, he loves me not. He loves me, he loves me not..." Each time they spoke, they plucked a single slender, white leaf surrounding the bright, orange daisy.

"Is this some kinda statement on feminism?" Eric asked.

"Probably, they're usually pretty boring," Anna muttered.

"Hey! I think the first band is about to play," Eric said noticing movement on the bright stage. As they headed toward it, Eric scooped a couple more articles of clothing off the grass until they found a spot. Once sitting, Anna looked through the various things that Eric had recovered during his long walk: She selected a sky dyed tank top that she thought would fit her. Leftover were a kid's tee shirt, a single bright yellow sock, a bundle of knotted twine and, his biggest plunder, several large discarded sheets of thick plastic drop cloths, which workmen had been using to paint parts of the stage. Eric knew that if they could find a tree with low hanging branches, he might be able to fashion the plastic sheets into a lean-to in case it rained.

47

Kasabian, Moscow, 1943

"We're reaching the end of days!" Morozov heard from his bedroom. He was awakened by a bellowing voice from downstairs. The madman-housekeeper had entered and was ranting again. It was pitch black outside, around four a.m., and he had only just fallen asleep. Morozov rose, cinched on his robe, and went down to find his officially assigned drunk spread out on the dining room floor. He was uncorking a fresh bottle of vodka.

"What the hell are you doing here?!" Haig asked, groggily.

"Thank me, comrade," Mikhail got to his feet and proudly tossed a small carton on the table before him. "Chocolate! Got them for a steal! Worth their weight in gold!"

"The pub's closed." Morozov grabbed the vodka bottle out of the servant's clammy hands. "You're not allowed to be here now and I have to go to work in four hours." It reminded him of Lunz's middle-of-the-night drop-ins when he was too young and dumb to put his foot down.

"Don't worry. They're supposed to be here at any moment!" the drunk said playfully.

"They? Who is?" Morozov asked.

"Never mind. I work according to my abilities, comrade," he replied, snatching the bottle back. He took a long guzzle.

"You mean you drink according to your bottomless needs." Morozov grabbed the bottle back.

"Sieg Heil, Armenian Fuhrer!" With his finger touching his upper lip, the servant tossed up an angry German salute.

"What did you call me?" Haig couldn't believe the servant's insolence.

"I'm sick of all of you foreigners who were nowhere to be found when the invaders were outside our walls. But once we pushed them back, all you southerners came crowding in and giving us orders."

"Get the hell out of here before I throw you out!" Morozov had had enough.

"It just so happens, I'm with the secret police!" the drunken servant announced.

"Really?"

"In the name of Premier Stalin and the entire Politburo, you're officially under arrest!"

Morozov marched to the coat tree, snatched up Mikhail's old filthy overcoat, went to the front door, opened it, and tossed it out into the snow.

"How dare you!" the house servant snarled, rising to his wobbly feet. "We'll see who throws who out!"

The drunk snatched the small unopened box of chocolates from the table and marched out into the snow to fetch his coat.

"And take that with you!" Morozov said, seeing the full bottle of vodka that he left on the table. When the servant failed to do so,

Morozov grabbed it and dashed outside. As he did this the front door slammed shut behind him.

Wearing only his bathrobe and slippers, Morozov frantically tried the knob, then he checked the windows—all locked tight. He dashed out onto the thick mound of powdery snow yelling for Mikhail to return. But it was too late, the housekeeper had already pulled on his coat and vanished. In the past hour, the temperature had plunged. Another winter storm had abruptly swooped down from the north.

"Goddamn it!" Morozov stomped the frozen ground.

With vodka bottle still in hand, Morozov uncorked it and took a small swig. It burned his tongue. *You're going to freeze to death!* he thought. He considered using the bottle to shatter a window pane roughly five feet above the street, but he realized that he still wouldn't be able to climb up that height. He slipped and skidded through the snow halfway down the block, uncertain of where to go. When he took a second gulp, he spotted a white glow halfway up the long dark block. It was the ancient steam house that he had regularly passed on his way to the university.

With his bathrobe pulled tightly around him and teeth chattering, he shuffled over and dashed up the steps of the old establishment. Once inside, shaking off the snow, he heard the unsympathetic desk clerk mutter, "Five kopeks." The clerk didn't seem at all surprised that Haig was dangerously underdressed. When he explained that he forgot his wallet, he noticed the clerk eyeing his nearly full bottle of liquor.

"How about this?" Morozov plunked the vodka down on the worn wooden counter before him. The clerk took it and silently issued him a locker key and a gauzy, threadbare towel.

"I need to use your phone," he said.

"We don't have one," the clerk replied.

After rubbing the blood back into his frozen fingers, Morozov sighed and went down the narrow stairs to a big empty locker room that looked more like a crypt covered in mold.

His assigned locker was so rusty he was barely able to pry it open. He took a seat on an old wooden bench and slowly stripped.

After clearing out the cobwebs, Morozov put his cold, wet slippers on the bottom of the locker, then folded his wet pajamas and robe on top. He wrapped the towel around his naked waist and went down to the steam room. He opened the heavy, worn cedar door, entered, and closed it behind him.

Through wafts of steam, Morozov could make out several older men. They looked as if they were made of wax, just melting away drip by drip. He joined them on the worn slats that together served as a long bleacher. Resting his bony elbows on his thin knees, he closed his eyes, leaned forward, and inhaled slow deep breaths. When one of the old men dumped a pot of water on the manifolds of the scalding radiator, a wave of steam plumed up. The soaring heat made him lightheaded. All his concerns and trepidation dwindled in the vapors.

A lullaby seemed to rock him back and forth. He closed his eyes and returned to a worn-out memory of his beloved Masha and their little honeymoon in the empty train car as it snaked along the great Don to the southern city of Voronezh.

The conductor had said a detachment from the White Army was supposedly spotted in the upcoming distance. So they had to keep the train's lights off and were skipping stops until they were safely out of the region. Haig and Masha took off their coats and shoes and sat together. As the train chugged along the length of the glassy river, he worked his hands up around her narrow back. Soon he was able to reach around to one of her firm, ample breasts. Over the hours, since the car was empty, he undid the top of his pants and convinced her to sit on his lap. Over time he was able to work her dress up. After a couple hours, he had the head of his erection rubbing against her inner thighs. When he tried entering her, she stopped him.

"Don't be such a prude," he whispered. "A lot of girls do it."

"I want to too, but..."

"I can pull out before anything happens!"

"But if you don't," she asked, "are you prepared to marry me, because a woman can't raise a child alone?"

"If I got any woman pregnant, I'd certainly ask for her hand in marriage," he said chivalrously. "Any man worth his salt would do that."

"What a romantic proposal."

Despite the comment, she positioned her dress and undergarments just high enough to allow his penis to slide through her ample thighs, reaching under to the bottom bristles of her pubic hair. With more determined angling on his part, the bulb of his erection just penetrated her labia. Instead of a frantic coitus, through sheer force of will, he let the slow lurching of the locomotive bring them into a gradually sustained state of ecstasy.

Looking back on it two decades later, he realized that he should've bought a ticket and stayed with her when she boarded that train to the Ukraine. He should've stayed with her as though clinging to life itself. Because that's what she was, nothing less. She would've resisted, even fought him, but if he just stayed with her, let her slap and kick and scream at him—even call the police—she would've eventually calmed down. What else could she do? Back then, though, he thought a little time apart would heal everything.

Remembering back, just after she left, as the weeks apart turned to months, and she didn't send so much as a postcard, let alone leave a forwarding address, there was only one thing left for him to do. He had to fix the damage he had caused so that when she did return on September 1st, the problem would be solved. After all, she might've never wanted to see him again, but she wasn't going to quit her medical studies—that was her destiny.

Since she wasn't around to write her own appeal, he put all his pain and energy into launching a one-man campaign on her behalf. Over the ensuing months, he made appointments with influential men. He wrote reports and collected testimonials about Masha's dedication to her studies, detailing her exceptional gifts and grades, as well as statements of her relentless devotion and flawless character. She was no less a revolutionary than Comrade Lenin himself! All she ever wanted was to use her medical gifts to help peasants and recruit the local kulaks to the communist cause, bring light into the impoverished provincial darkness.

Morozov also undertook a private investigation of his own, eventually locating the vicious youth who masterminded Masha's expulsion. It wasn't Ostrowski after all, but an ambitious law student named Mikhail Michaelchevski, a rising figure in the Komosol who made a habit of lashing out wherever the opportunity arose in order to elevate himself. Morozov didn't have the clout to bring Michaelchevski down, so he did the next best thing. At various party meetings and rallies, he was able to gain an introduction, charm the man, curry favors, and eventually explain that he happened to know Masha Rodchenko and though she was a little naive, she was true of heart when it came to communism. He eventually got Michaelchevski to reconsider and soften his case against her.

Over months, as people forgot about the Rodchenko case, unable to gain anything by her loss, Morozov finally offered to write a flattering profile of Michaelchevski for the school's newspaper in exchange for a letter from him stating that upon review his zeal might've gotten the better of him. The opportuntist urged leniency for the young female student, stating that she had learned her lesson and that for the common good of Russia, she should be allowed to finish her degree and work as a female physician in the short-handed field of obstetrics.

It wasn't until nearly a decade later, during the beginning of the Great Refinement, that his eventual patron Andrei Zhdanov had a run-in with a group that Michaelchevski was affiliated with. Due to Morozov's false testimony against the old Komosol bully, he was finally able to get the little bastard arrested. He only wished he could've confronted him before the little prick was forced to sign his confession and say, "Remember that charge you leveled against that apple-cheeked beauty? This is what you get, you self-righteous piece of shit!"

At the time, though, nearly powerless, through persistent petitions and requests, Haig actually got two of the old Bolsheviks to write letters of recommendation to reinstate Masha in the medical program "for the good of the Revolution." Ten months after her expulsion, having waited the prescribed length of time, and submitting his impressive packet of letters, the Moscow State University Disciplinary Committee, the Komosol, and the Admission Committee all granted permission for Masha Rodchenko to return to classes and complete her final year of studies.

A violent clamor yanked Morozov upright in the steam room.

"What the hell's going on?" he yelled aloud.

"Sorry, comrade!" a lone voice called back through the clouds. "One of the boilers is out, and this is our least busy hour." He realized that while napping, all the other ancient insomniacs had melted away. He was alone in the old steam room. A multitude of hammers proceeded with an unsynchronized pounding.

He cursed as he marched back into the dressing room. There he opened his squeaky locker only to remember that he was still locked out of his house and since he had just fired his servant, there was no one waiting for him, no one to let him back in. Worse still, he was too under-dressed to combat the biting cold. Scavenging around, opening some of the other rusty lockers, Morozov found a baggy pair of trousers then narrow shoes with thin socks tucked into them. The shoes pinched his toes but were better than the still-moist slippers. A filthy, buttonless overcoat crusted with what might've been dried vomit was hanging from a corner hook.

He brought the clothes into the bathroom where he examined them under a light for fleas, bedbugs, and lice. He saw none. Without a choice, he pulled the garb on, and grabbed an old towel that he used as a scarf over his mouth and neck.

Daylight slowly brimmed and spilled over the city's edge. Resembling a common beggar, Morozov traced his steps between the last of the retreating night workers and the growing stream of day workers.

By the time he finally reached the university he could barely feel his ears and toes. The campus was empty. Although he was able to enter his building, a security guard was puzzled by Morozov's gypsy-like apparel. The guard explained that it was an official holiday—Red Army Day. No classes.

"I need to get to my office!" Morozov insisted. "It's an emergency!"

The guard allowed him to proceed to his office. Once there the Armenian writer began making calls to Housekeeping hoping to locate someone who might have a key to the "historic" Ulanov House. Different numbers kept ringing and ringing. He finally got one maternal operator who listened patiently to his confusing complaint about getting locked out, half-dressed in the middle of the night due to his crazy servant.

"Let me try to find someone to help you and have them call you back," she replied softly.

Haig thanked her. Exhausted, he dropped into his chair, laid his head on his desk, and immediately dozed off.

48

Eric, NYC, August, 2001

On the morning of August 15, 2001, Eric checked his email for new messages from the Lande Properties LLC and was surprised to find one from his son Eriq: "Just heard on the radio that today is the anniversary of Woodstock! I wish you had conceived me there, I'd be thirty-two years old, minus nine months – Luv Eriq."

Eric Sr. found the message amusing because the Woodstock Festival was also the thirty-second anniversary of losing his virginity.

The last time he saw Anna O'Brien was fourteen years earlier, in October of 1987. He remembered because Halloween was coming. She stopped him on the northeast corner of Eighty-sixth Street as he was walking down Broadway to take his wife out for dinner.

"Oh my god! Is that my old Woodstock boyfriend?" he heard from behind. Turning, he saw a middle-aged woman dressed in a whirlwind of uncoordinated colors, waving at him with one hand. Her other hand was pushing a carriage with a baby and two toddlers in tow. Anna was wearing undersized jeans that truly were in distress and a low-cut top that did little to corset her rolling belly and breasts.

As she got closer, her perfume overwhelmed him. Under a runny watercolor of mascara, her face showed clear signs of both sun and alcohol damage. Although she couldn't yet be forty, she looked noticeably older. The infant in the carriage looked worried. The two kids behind her were fighting, screaming. She couldn't care less.

"I haven't seen you since high school!" she said in an unmodulated voice.

"You avoided me like the plague," he reminded her.

"I was convinced that you told everyone I was a slut!"

"I don't kiss and tell," he smiled.

"So what are you up to?" she asked, blocking the sidewalk so a bottleneck of people was forced to slowly edge around them.

"Married with a kid too," he replied, holding up his ring finger.

"Too bad," she smiled. "'Cause I'm back on the market."

"Really?"

"My second divorce just came through," she said. "At least this one had a job, so if I get a decent settlement with child support, we should be okay."

"So what do you do now?" he asked.

"Only the most important job in the world," she replied, waving a hand at the kids.

"Hey, how's your crazy dad?" he asked, remembering the time the wild-haired Armenian strangled him.

"He had a heart attack about ten years ago," she said. "A five-pack-a-day smoker."

"Oh, I'm sorry."

"Wasn't that a wild freaking weekend?" she whispered, smiling.

"The Mount Everest of weekends."

"We were a part of rock-and-roll history!" she yelled.

"The amazing part to me was just staying alive without food or even shelter really, in that ocean of hippies, surviving for four days by our wits, actually *your* wits."

"Oh God!" she winced, "my life is still like that."

"And who is this?" he heard his wife coming up behind him. Eric introduced Anna to his wife, Edna.

"So you're the lucky lady who took Eric off the market."

214

"Yeah, I have all the luck," Edna replied. Anna gave Eric a farewell peck on the cheek and continued down Broadway pushing the carriage, with the kids in tow.

49

Eric, Woodstock Festival, 1969

As Anna was leading Eric near the crowded stage, he spotted something unbelievable. A small and isolated tree with one thin, low-hanging branch and no one camped under it.

"That's our spot!" he said. "I can rig a lean-to to it!"

"Do it," she replied impatiently, not caring what the hell "a lean tube" was. She followed him as he carefully laid out his finds: rope, plastic, and other stuff.

As he started cutting the twine, though, the sound engineer began to check the amps again, and Eric quickly realized the location was no good.

"Why not?" Anna asked, exhausted after all the walking.

"We're right under the speakers, it's deafening," he explained. "We won't get any sleep!"

"Screw sleep! This is where all the action is!" she argued, pointing to the stage dead ahead.

"First of all, it'll be mobbed."

"It is mobbed!"

"And we'll be stuck here for the next two days. We'll need sleep."

Anna cursed but relented. They packed up their acquired survival gear and resumed the walk back up the grassy slope as clouds began to roll in. It took them another forty-five minutes of pushing through the crowd, looking for an available space that had the right balance between trees and a good view of the stage.

"Anna!" Someone shouted.

She turned and saw a towering teenage girl with blonde bangs, waving to her through the crowd from a hundred feet away.

"Isla!" Anna hollered, dashing over. Eric watched as they flew into each other like a pair of pigeons crashing midflight. They hugged

215

and kissed and laughed. Isla appeared to be a part of a larger group of at least six adults, all in their early twenties. Her bunch turned out to be a pack of foreign exchange students from northern Europe who were attending a summer liberal arts program at NYU. Anna had met them one Sunday afternoon in Washington Square Park and they hung out while listening to street performers and getting high.

Isla introduced Anna and Eric to her compatriots: Rolland, Amandine, Pierre, and Sandrine. They had a couple uncorked bottles of wine, three loaves of French bread and two big wheels of creamy brie.

"Looks delish," Anna said, eyeing the appetizers.

"Help yourself," said Isla. As a sprinkle of rain began to fall, Anna tore off the heel of a baguette for herself and then a second piece for Eric. He grabbed the knife and sliced off two wedges of the brie. There was also a big bag of Granny Smith apples just for the taking.

"Where are you guys sleeping?" asked Rolland, who looked like the subject of a van Gogh painting.

"We haven't really found a spot," said Anna.

"If I eat the wax will I get sick?" Eric asked, having cut a second wedge of cheese.

"It's fine," Rolland said. As he started eating, the Europeans chatted among each other in French, so Anna whispered to Eric, "Look, there's a tree, right behind them. Let's set up camp here."

Before he could swallow his Brie, the amplifier towers suddenly screeched, causing acute mass deafness. The bearded pirate who was master of ceremonies finally announced that the Woodstock Festival had officially begun. Cheers, then silence.

"We're still too close to the stage to sleep," he replied. Anna would've argued, but she knew that he was already touchy as hell and didn't want him high-tailing back to the city before the first night. They thanked the Europeans for their generosity and continued heading up the slope through the steadily growing crowd.

50

Morozov was awakened by the faint sound of ringing. He jumped up realizing it was the phone in his outer office — Alexei's desk. He snatched up the silent extension on his desk, but he could barely make out a distant voice on the far end.

"Please help me! I'm locked out!" he shouted. Suddenly loud static bursts like artillery fire nearly deafened him then the line went dead. He hung up and a moment later, the phone rang again.

"I called you at your house a week ago and you hung up on me then too." It was the man who asked for help with his poetry but it wasn't Lunz.

"So sorry. How are you doing sir?" It was High Commissar from Leningrad Andrei Zhdanov, his old friend and patron.

"My fault. The reason you didn't understand my question was because my idiot secretary sent the poems to your office in Yerevan. She just resent them to you there. So how are they treating you in Moscow, Haig?"

"Things are a bit sticky."

"I warned you it'd be dangerous," he said. "But I tried to get you extra rations. I personally asked your chairman for the nicest house he could find. He said he got you in for some newly created residency grant."

"I'm grateful," Morozov replied. For the first time he was aware as to the mystery of some of his added amenities.

"In your file it says you wrote a review for one of Akhmatova's old books."

"Anna Akhmatova?" You mean, *Bulrushes?*" Morozov recalled. "That was nearly thirty years ago."

"So now you'll review her again."

"Over the last twenty years, I've pretty much confined my reviews to writers from the Caucasus," he said. "I haven't reviewed poetry since the Revolution."

"No   matter."

"In fact, she wrote a positive review of one of my story collections twenty years ago," Morozov recalled.

"So much the better. That shows that you're not returning any favors."

"Returning favors?"

"I need some scribblers from her generation."

"I can't believe she has a new book out," he said.

"Actually she doesn't. In fact, it was murder scraping together her poems. I got them from her file."

"I don't understand. You want me to review her uncollected poems?"

"She's regarded as something between a doyenne and a sacred relic from the Imperial Age," he explained.

"Last I heard, she gained a ton of weight and talks to herself."

"There's a growing underground swell that has lifted her onto a pedestal. I need you to knock her down."

"Andrei, why would some Armenian short-story writer up from Yerevan have anything significant..."

"It's not just you. I'm assembling a whole team. Kushner wrote a solid review of her decadent influences. I have a second writer, a leading young poet working on a longer piece detailing her cryptic capitalist symbols," Zhdanov explained. "But yours will be in the *Gazette*. You're head of the smaller Soviets brigade. We need a coordinated assault. She's been repeatedly warned. Her stuff is circulating! This is absolutely necessary!"

"I must confess, Andrei, I'm a little overwhelmed right now. I have only a couple months to finish editing my memoirs, which has a May deadline. I'm also working on a lengthy appreciation of Fedin, which is due in two weeks."

"Forget Fedin! He's more popular than Koba himself!"

"Andrei..."

"Have you ever been to his dacha?"

"Where?"

"In Peredlinko—the kennel for all the top dogs."

218

"Andrei, can't you give this honor to someone else—maybe some influential critic? I can put you in touch with one."

"Nonsense! I need you!"

"Why are you even wasting any time on her?"

"You don't know what's been happening. Since the invasion, we put all our efforts into just trying to stay alive, so we haven't had the resources to focus on domestic security. All the bedbugs are crawling out, Haig! Even in the arts, we're seeing a resurgence of selfishness that can only be termed cosmopolitanism at its worst."

"Cosmopolitanism?" he echoed.

Before the Revolution, he thought of Russian culture as a subdivision of European culture. It was only when the Revolution shifted its focus, and the refinement went from the military to the Arts that Soviet culture began to truly emerge. Countless articles that he and others had written about how European art from the decadent cities of the West had clouded the minds of so many Russian writers.

When he heard the term "cosmopolitanism" he pictured the lurid images of Egon Schiele, the confused and frenetic forms of Pablo Picasso, the voodoo theories of Sigmund Freud, and the harebrained mysticism of Carl Jung.

These ideas were as far removed from the Slavic peasant life as one could get. Ultimately though, Morozov knew that underneath it all, this anti-cosmopolitan obsession was all just another power play to please the big boss.

Anticipating him, Commissar Zhdanov replied, "You're from little Armenia, way out in the sticks. You probably don't see the importance to this," Zhdanov said. "But cosmopolitan influences have steamrolled through little cultures like yours. It drains away all the local color and sets up these look-alike colonies of modernism right in your backyard. Do you want that?"

"No, Andrei, but we're still at war with the Nazis!" Morozov reminded him.

"The generals will handle the war. Our job is the home front." Zhdanov went on to explain that since the invasion, all the insects have crawled out of their cracks—spies and instigators have grown emboldened by the thought of an imminent fascist liberation.

"You must've heard about Andrey Vlasov?" he asked.

"I heard the name."

"He was one of our best generals until he was captured by the Nazis. Then he defected to their side. They say there are no counterrevolutions. That it's all paranoia, but Hitler has recruited a whole army of them! We've had villages who've turned in their party leaders, flying swastikas from town halls. They 'Seig Heiled' the Germans as they came marching in! Hell, I've had reports as far away as Siberia of people openly ridiculing their NKVD officers, vowing to turn them in when the Nazis arrive!"

As the Commissar yammered on, Morozov remembered how this short, fat, red-faced man had initially gained importance years ago by purging the "Deviationist" from the Leningrad Komsomol League. A few years later he launched an attack on the arts, particularly non-conformist painters, musicians, and filmmakers. That was when the term "cosmopolitanism" was first bantered about.

"I know you think I'm being a bully, Haig, but we repeatedly tried to work with Akhmatova. She simply won't play ball."

"You tried working with her?"

"Stalin himself approved of her last book of poetry to be published. And that was just a few years ago."

"What book?" he asked.

"It was called *From Six Books*," Zhdanov said.

"I don't remember hearing about it," Morozov replied.

"I think it was from six of her books," he reasoned. "Anyway, instead of showing gratitude and working with us, the old crow kept openly disparaging the Revolution, so we pulled the book before it could leave the printers. Pulped the entire run."

"Good! The ingrate deserves it," Morozov said, and added, "but by publishing a volley of essays condemning her you'll actually be introducing her to a whole new generation of readers who don't know of her."

"Haig, she continues to write! We still have informers telling us about her private readings. Literary salons she still holds. We've

220

gotten reports of her fans who openly recite her work in public. Her poems are getting out, spreading like lice! We've actually found new verses of hers getting published abroad. Hell, we even found a poem of hers recently published here, in a small unsanctioned journal. She's too trivial to arrest but too influential to ignore!"

If this was truly the case, he couldn't blame Zhdanov.

"If she's still living in Leningrad, that sounds like punishment enough," he replied.

"Actually she's not, she was evacuated to Tashkent. Truth be told that's one of the reasons I think making an example of her is merciful."

"Merciful?"

"She probably won't survive to see your review or the others."

"What do you mean?"

"I heard she has typhoid and isn't doing well."

After recently reading about Tsvetaeva's death, the thought that Akhmatova was going to die as well silenced him, which Zhdanov interpreted as arrogance.

"If you're not going to help me, Haig," Zhdanov charged, "it would compel me to completely review our relationship. Do you understand?"

"It's not that. It's just…"

"I'm going to assume the war and maybe your resettling has thrown you off a bit," Zhdanov said more sternly, "but I need to see some party-mindedness, Haig. I really do."

"Of course."

"Five hundred words should be fine. Nothing you can't do in your sleep."

"Andre," he abruptly got up some nerve. "Do you happen to know of a writer named Daniel Kharms?"

"Why would I know him?"

"He's from your city and I heard that maybe he was arrested…"

"Wait a second," Morozov could hear the sound of papers shuffling. "I've got his file around here somewhere. He's that nonsense children's book writer, isn't he?"

"What would be the prison sentence of a nonsense writer?"

"We don't sentence people for that anymore," the Commissar replied.

"So five years, tops?"

"I don't have time for this silliness, Haig. If he's been arrested, it's for something a lot worse."

"I'm pretty sure he was arrested."

"You don't have any idea what's going on up here, do you, Haig? We're completely cut off. Unable to feed our people. And the Nazis are constantly shelling us. Bombs falling every hour."

"I thought I heard that things were getting better. That you were finally getting food supplies through," Morozov replied. He had read about the heroic convoy of trucks that was steadily driving over frozen Lake Ladoga.

"You haven't read that on warm days, trucks break through the ice!"

"My god."

"You don't know the half of it," the Commissar went on. "Leningrad requires at least a thousand tons of food per day. Less than two hundred tons are getting through! We're starving up here."

"I'm so sorry, Andrei."

"The other day my secretary stumbled over a corpse in the snow. It was sliced up. Butchered like a pig, right on the sidewalk near my office."

"I'm truly sympathetic but Andrei, what does that have to do with one silly nonsense writer?"

"Here it is..." He paused for a moment.

"Here what is?" Morozov asked.

"His arrest report! As I thought," Zhdanov said reading the file. "Here's a testimonial given by a reliable witness who heard Kharms say—and I quote—'The USSR lost the war on its first day. Leningrad will either be starved to death or it will be bombed to the ground, leaving no stone standing! If they give me a mobilization order, I will punch the commander in the face...'"

"Oh, god!" Haig murmured. Goddamned Voronsky had lead him into a trap.

"'LET THEM SHOOT ME,'" Zhdanov angrily continued reading Kharms' quote, "'but I will not put on the uniform nor serve in the Soviet forces...'"

"I thought it was just his writing," Haig uttered, embarrassed.

"Don't interrupt!" the commissar angrily replied and added a final quote: "'I would not shoot at the Germans, but at us!' meaning Russians."

"Was he executed?" Haig asked, cutting the man loose.

"We don't execute people, Haig. You know that."

"A lot of people are terrified of the Nazis," Haig replied, trying to make a defense for him. "Making all sorts of crazy outbursts. I've heard them saying one thing one day and then recanting it the next."

"You think I don't know that? Leningrad is turning into a tribe of cannibals."

"It sounds like your job is cut out for you, Commissar."

"They're never going to publish the official casualty count," Zhdanov lowered his voice, "but it's heading toward a million."

"A mill..." No official statistics had ever come anywhere near that. Suddenly a muted alarm bell went off in the hallway.

"According to my file, your cowardly friend..."

"I never even met the man..."

"His cell block was evacuated to Novosibirsk."

"He's still alive?" Morozov asked in disbelief.

"Do you think I'm lying?"

"No, I didn't mean..."

"Tell you what I'm going to do," he said almost angrily. "I need some forms anyway, I'm going to have someone in the records department call you directly, to tell you about your traitor, Haig. In exchange I want that damn Akhmatova essay immediately!"

"I wasn't challenging you, Commissar!" The line went dead. All he could hear was the unfamiliar bell that had been softly ringing in the hallway.

When he stepped into the hallway, his phone began ringing again. Haig raced back inside, and immediately said, "Commissar

Zhdanov, please accept my apologies. You don't need to have anyone call me."

"I'm sorry, I might've called the wrong extension." It was a man who introduced himself as Montov, Deputy Director of Housekeeping. He said he had learned that someone at this phone number was locked out of his home.

"Yes," Haig replied. "That was me."

"Don't you have a servant?"

"I fired him last night," Morozov said.

"You don't have the authority to fire him."

"Last night he woke me up ranting. He has repeatedly come in drunk, and when I asked him to go home, he started insulting me."

"Oh," he sneered, embarrassed. "You must mean Mikhail Kamenev. I'm sorry."

"So he's acted this way before?"

Instead of responding, Montov said, "I think I can take the department car for this. Why don't I swing by your office and let you in myself."

"I'm obliged."

Ten minutes later, a clean, well-dressed man in an old-style bowler hat showed up at his office. He introduced himself as Deputy Director Samuel Montov and didn't say a word about the strange apparel Morozov had pulled together from the bathhouse. Since it was still quite cold outside, the deputy director brought his car around front and Haig jumped in.

"I have to confess," Morozov said as they drove, "I've never had a servant before, so I think I might've behaved inappropriately with the first housekeeper you sent."

"Kata."

"So I take it Mikhail was your way of punishing me."

"I certainly can understand why you'd think that, but the truth is we're suffering from a severe labor shortage. All available workers have either been enlisted and shipped west to fight the war or were sent east to work for the war effort."

"Aren't there any students who need jobs?" Haig asked.

"They tend to go after the more prestigious ones."

"If I can locate a student who'll take the housekeeping job, can she apply it to her school labor contract?" he asked, suddenly thinking about Alexei's attractive friend.

"If she can cook and clean, have her speak to me. I'll show her the list of weekly chores she has to complete, then if she's interested, I'll push it through."

Montov double parked in front of the Ulanov House. The supervisor got out, took out a large ring of keys, unlocked the front door, and Morozov dashed inside without thanking him.

51

Alexei, Woodstock Festival, 1969

Still asleep, Sergei grumbled and rolled repeatedly, shaking the little tent back and forth until he woke up Alexei.

"Hey!" Alexei said, shaking him.

"Huh!"

"You were yelling in your sleep."

"Oh, sorry." Sergei said. "I dreamed I was in a building that was on fire."

"Why didn't you jump out a window?" he kidded.

"It was too tall..."

"Wait! Hear that?" Alexei interrupted, hearing only the pitter-patter of raindrops. "No rock and rolling! Maybe they gave up."

"Oh no!" Serge said in panic. "We have to find Anna before she leaves!" He wiggled out of the tent like a snake sloughing off its old skin.

Alexei joined him outside. They discovered that though many surrounding tents had indeed vanished, the concert was still in effect. Because it was raining, they were just taking another break. The good news was the vast ocean of youths was finally draining out of the giant grassy lawn. Hiking up through the soggy mud, Alexei used his umbrella as more of a walking stick. Since both men had to relieve both bowel and bladder, they got on the shortest line and chatted for forty minutes before they were finally able to use one of the filthy stalls. While Alexei was sitting on the can, desperately trying to crap, the concert began blaring again.

"Shit!" he yelled, and did.

Living outdoors like an animal was not healthy, he thought. Running a slight temperature, he knew that something was wrong. Once they were able to wash off, Sergei said, "I'm famished."

"I didn't sleep at all last night," Alexei countered, rubbing his side. "My old war wound has been acting up."

"Sorry to hear," said Sergei. "Let's find Anna and get you back to your nice hotel in the city."

Before they began their descent into the crowded area around the stage, Alexei reached into his pocket where he had just shoved some toilet paper. Sergei watched as he tightly balled up two pieces, wet them in his mouth, and wadded them into his hairy ears.

"Me too." His Armenian friend reached out. Alexei tore off some squares for him as well. Their plugged-up ears did nothing to reduce the noise as they headed down into the loud fray.

Some curly-haired fool named Joe Cocker was singing and lurching around on the stage. Sergei, who kept staring at him, finally said, "He's going to bite off his own tongue!"

The two stout, gray-haired men shoved through people less than half their age and weight, feeling as welcome as two beetles in an ant colony.

"Conventioneers!" one young rebel said to Alexei.

"Conventional!" he misunderstood. "You all look the same! We're the only ones who are different!"

As Cocker finished his set and another band took the stage, the two men slowly inched along, trawling back and forth, in a giant zigzag pattern, angling, squeezing, and nudging their way through the loud crowd; staring into hundreds and soon thousands of tight, bright little faces who were all focused on the stage. Since Alexei was exhausted, it was all he could do to keep up with Sergei who moved frantically, like a black bear searching for its cub. Several times when the Armenian father was combing through the more distant corners of the viewing area, Alexei would pause and wait for him to loop back. He spotted a nice bonfire that some kids had set to dry their wet clothes after the last downpour. Alexei opened his hands toward the flames.

"How are you doing, old dude?" yelled one tall hippie kid with a wispy starter beard.

"Tired, wet, and hungry," Alexei replied over the music. "Like everyone else I imagine."

"You're not a Republican, are you?"

"Just the opposite," Alexei responded. "I'm a communist."

"Yeah!" the youth responded making a fist. "Want some bread?"

"Bread?" he asked, suspecting it was slang for something else.

"Yeah, we got a bunch of day-old loaves from the Hog Farm." He held up a loaf.

"Sure, I love bread."

The hippie reached into his rucksack and pulled out a broken loaf of slightly moist, mainly stale bread.

"Thanks, here," Alexei said, offering the kid a quarter.

"It's free! *Viva la Revolucion!*"

52

Kasabian, Moscow, 1943

Arriving at the university the next morning, a slim yet large envelope was sitting on Morozov's desk. Zhdanov's photostats of the Akhmatova poems had arrived. Despite the distastefulness of the assignment, Morozov decided that maybe a break was for the better. Working on his memoir—constantly measuring the grim present against the hopeful past—as extracted from highlights of his journals—was becoming an ongoing source of melancholia. To spend the next few days on his latest assignments, namely the condemnation of Anna Akhmatova and a glorification of Konstanin Fedin, might be strangely therapeutic. Though he felt conflicted about attacking the poet, he liked the novelist.

He actually met Fedin when the novelist was a part of a group called the Serapion Brothers. Even then he was a formidable writer and an exemplary revolutionary. He was a part of the Education Comissariate and later, due to his experience in the war, Fedin joined the Red Army and fought against the counterrevolutionary army known as the White Guard. Afterwards when he served as editor of the journal *Books and Revolution*, Fedin published one of Morozov's early stories. Fedin lived with a group of nonconformist writers in a former aristocrat's palace on Nevski Prospekt in Saint Petersburg. The writer Evgeny Yevgeny Zamyatin ran the collective. Despite the single misstep of criticizing Stalin's increasing power—which one could still delicately do in the very early 1930s— Fedin played his cards right. His military service, which underscored his courage, his slightly subversive roots, which allowed him to come in from the outside, his steady output of work, all smart moves. This was while other more talented, less compromising writers started "disappearing."

Fedin seemed to sense what was coming and he steadily adopted techniques that the Writers Union strongly recommended. The more Fedin fell in line, the more successful he grew, as he steadily moved his way up to the forefront.

Anna Akhmatova was a dismal study in contrast. Once formal, popular, and romantic, she steadily opposed the new regime. Over time, she and her writing became more isolated. Many writers moved up in the cliques they had joined early on. Yet Akhmatova's wily group steadily slipped down and away.

Although the poetess wrote a favorable review of one of his early collections of stories, Morozov never had the dubious pleasure of meeting her, primarily because she was from St. Petersburg and he was from Moscow. He flipped through the folder Zhdanov had sent of her poems. Most were copies of copies of copies of poems. Some pages were barely legible; typed poetry with rewrites crammed in the margins. Occasionally, entire lines were X-ed out.

Examining the photostats of the poems, with their many folds and strange smudges, he suspected they had been fished out of garbage cans and smoothed out. Others were written in frenzied handwriting as though quickly heard then hastily scribbled down before they could be forgotten. He found it absurdly amusing that he was reviewing work that had never been and never would be published. It was like digging up a dead body to put on trial. The works covered a broad range, both her early and later poetry. Although there were a few older poems that he recognized, he hadn't read most of them.

As he took notes, he kept thinking of her as dead. It was easier that way. What other writer had a growing reputation and continued writing, despite the fact that she no longer had a chance of being published? The vast majority of working poets nowadays wrote bland imitative odes to state-sponsored projects---productive factories or newly dug canals—subjects passed down by the Ministry of Cultural Affairs that the Writers Union routinely recommended.

Morozov remembered Zhdanov mentioning that Stalin himself had gotten Akhmatova's last book published, so presumably, at one time he even might've liked her. Morozov remembered reading that the Roman bard Virgil had a tricky friendship with the emperor Augustus, as did Louis XIV and the wily playwright Moliere.

Sifting through her many gathered poems, he soon found himself strangely identifying with Akhmatova's predicament. Instead of focusing on her works, he thought of the countless acts of betrayal by cloying students, like Alexei and Darya, who pretended to be enthusiasts of her poems. A generation of secret police-larvae feasted on the bodies of these few genuine writers. As all thoughts of intrigue and plotting slipped away, he just started simply enjoying her poetry, even her weakest pieces felt liberating by today's standards.

Clearly she was just writing for herself, not giving a damn how she might be perceived. For a moment he found himself growing envious of her. He'd never enjoyed such freedom. The joy of writing had died so long ago for him and only been replaced by doubts and concerns regarding how his work might be deliberately misinterpreted for someone else's political gain. Yet for all its compromises his writing was still in print. And there was always a modicum of originality that might be called Morozov-esque. As long as he remained loyal to Stalin and stayed safely in little Armenia, his big-fish-in-a-small-pond life was infinitely more comfortable and completely protected.

Suddenly the annoying intern popped his head in, compelling Morozov to slip the forbidden pages back into the envelope.

"What!"

"I just wanted to see if you needed anything?" asked the little bloodsucker.

"Yes," the older writer said. "Drive me home."

He didn't feel safe reading her poetry at the university while his backstabbing bootlick was around. He slipped Akhmatova's pages into his valise, grabbed his coat, and followed the younger man out to the car.

That night he looked around the house for another bottle of vodka, but only found a disgusting apricot aperitif. He regretted trading the first bottle to the bathhouse attendant as he drank down the syrupy liqueur. When he grew sufficiently lightheaded, he absently reached into his bag and pulled out the Fedin manuscript.

After twenty minutes of reading the novel, he decided that Fedin could use a critical essay to remind him of his former fearlessness, while Akhmatova was long overdue for praise. But the world didn't work that way.

A headache compelled him to lie down on the sofa in the study and shut his eyes for a moment. When he awoke it was the next morning. He tossed the empty liqueur bottle in the trash and carefully stacked his unwashed dishes in the sink. Although he didn't know if firing the annoying oaf was a wise move, he was grateful to be rid of him. He dressed and slowly walked to the university. While still in the hallway he saw his office door was ajar. Looking inside, he saw the shapely derriere of young Darya. She was replacing a stack of books onto his bottom shelf.

"Nope, I didn't hide the evidence there," he said, startling her.

"If evidence is dust," she grinned, "then you're very guilty. I don't think they ever dusted here." She was holding up a dirty rag.

"Books look more distinguished with dust on them," he replied.

"I have to confess I'm bewildered about your selection," she said, scanning his shelf. "Mainly new writers, conventional, frankly pretty boring. Not what'd I'd expect from you."

"What would you expect from me?"

"Your work is more genuine. It's not contrived. You don't shy away from pain or darkness." She paused, looking at one book. Although he didn't utter a sound or a make an expression, he was moved by her summation.

"I'll eventually figure out what exactly you see in these new books," she finally said.

"And I have no doubt that when you do, I'll be getting a visit from the Cheka," he quipped.

"I know you don't believe me, but I don't report people, particularly while my country is being occupied by the filthy Huns."

"You mean the Germans?" he whispered and immediately regretted it. She gave a wide smile but didn't say a word.

"Let me ask you this, can you cook?"

"Not very well, why?"

"I might have a job for you." She snickered, compelling him to ask, "Didn't you say you're still looking for work?"

"I just got offered a position as a research assistant for an archaeology professor on Byzantine studies, but I frankly have no interest in any more vanished empires."

"I need a housekeeper," he said, without mincing words.

"I don't think the school will authorize cooking and cleaning as fulfillment of my student employment service. They want something scholarly."

"I spoke with someone named Montov at Housekeeping. He said that if I could find some student who was willing to do the job, he'd authorize it as fulfillment of their academic requirement."

"Between dusting broken tiles, and dusting your dusty shelves, I'd rather do the latter," she joked, as the school bell rang. "And that's my next class."

"Drop by the Housekeeping office, ask for Montov. Look over the list of tasks he'll expect of you and if you want to do them, fill out the proper paperwork. They'll give you the keys to my place. You can try to poison me by making me dinner tomorrow night."

"Mr. Montov in Housekeeping," she repeated.

He nodded and watched the odd, yet beautiful young woman grab her things and dash out.

53

Eric, Woodstock Festival, 1969

"Richard Moss and Barbara, please meet at the information booth," Eric heard over the PA as he led Anna up the hill, still searching for a place to camp. "Greg Holland, go to the Ferris wheel at noon. Your sister has your medicine."

"I hope Greg is okay," Anna muttered, as a chopper flew in and touched down to the rear of the big stage.

"If you got food, feed other people!" the pirate organizer said over the PA. "Keep feeding each other!"

He went on to say that there were seventeen food lines. When Eric brought this to Anna's attention, she replied that she preferred hitting on the "softies" rather than standing in one of the long lines.

"...the rain and mud glues us all together. We're all in the same puddle," the Pirate continued what was turning into a riff. "We need volunteers for lots of stuff and everyone can help out if you want."

"Want to volunteer for something?" Eric asked Anna, who didn't bother to respond.

"Let me give you some idea of what I'm talking about," the Pirate continued on the PA, "A half an hour after we release anybody having a bad trip from our first aid station we turn them into doctors and they care for people who are tripping like they were when they came in. Though people have been saying some of the acid is poison, it's not poison. It's just bad! It's manufactured poorly so anybody that thinks they've taken some poison, forget it. And if you feel like experimenting, only take half a tab..."

Anna pointed to Eric as new waves of kids came dashing down over the road. "Every fucking minute it's going to get harder and harder to find a spot!"

"Okay! I give up," Eric conceded. "Let's crash with your foreign exchangers."

Eric and Anna turned and raced back up to the Europeans. As Anna got permission and then schmoozed with them, Eric ran his hands along the grass under the lone tree searching for any sticks and stones in their prospective sleeping area. Then he unfolded one of the drop clothes and put it down as their ground cover. Next he unfurled Josh's sleeping bag on it to make sure the enclosure would be wide enough. Borrowing a knife from the exchangers, it took another hour to carefully fashion the other pieces of plastic into a kind of overlapping three-sided tepee. Lastly, Eric cut stretches of twine and found several sticks to use as stakes. He carefully poked holes in the thick plastic and braided the twine through the overlapping sheaths of plastic to keep the rain from getting on Josh's sleeping bag. Afterwards they angled inside the little enclosure to make sure it held together. Some of the foreigner exchangers came over and complimented his lean-to. He said he was always handy with crafting things.

"You know, you could patent this thing," said Rolland, admiring Eric's ingenuity as he ate a muffin.

"Why didn't you bring a second sleeping bag?" asked Amandine, seeing the single one inside.

"I'm meeting some friends here who have an extra one," Anna replied. "They just haven't arrived yet."

"Did you guys buy that?" Eric asked, looking hungrily at the muffin.

"No, the Hog Farmers were giving it away."

"There's a hog farm here?" Anna asked, looking around, hoping to see pigs.

"No, that's just what they call themselves," Rolland said.

"They said they were part of the security here," said Amandine, who turned and pointed up the slope. "I think if you go up there they just set up another food booth. You should go get some while they still have them. They're free!"

"At a hog farm?" Eric repeated, grateful for the information.

Suddenly they saw a commotion on stage. Apparently the first band was about to perform. Anna was excited that it was finally going to commence.

"You guys wanna come with us?" she said to the Europeans, even though Eric wanted to first get some food at the hog farm.

"I never head of this Sweetwater band," said Rolland, the oldest member of the contingent.

"They're good!" Anna replied, even though she had never heard of them either.

"We'll watch from here," Isla said.

"Keep an eye on our stuff," said Anna. The two were about to march down to the stage, but before they could take three steps, Eric pointed out that no musicians had yet appeared.

"When's this fucking thing going to begin!"

"Come on, we can still get some hog food and be back before it begins," Eric urged.

No sooner did he say this than a tall, righteous Black dude wearing a dark dashiki and carrying an old guitar strode across the wide wooden stage. A backup guitarist, also Negro, followed him. They sat on side-by-side stools, but the backup musician's mic didn't seem to work.

"Please welcome Richie Havens!" said the pirate on the PA.

"He looks so cool," Anna cooed, immediately entranced.

Although Eric felt self-conscious, he followed Anna who shamelessly barreled past others angling as close as she could to the stage. They watched Havens who began a heavy strumming, while turning his guitar into a kind of drum. He began a soulful rendition of "Motherless Child," interspersing it with the refrain, "Freedom, freedom..."

Soon, he began instructing the audience to clap along, which Anna did. Eric closed his eyes, rocked to the beat and savored the power of Havens' mellifluous voice. At one point they heard a twang, and Anna pointed out that he had broken one of his guitar strings, but kept playing, which for some reason seemed to attest to his artistic devotion. Too soon his set was over. After a wave of applause slowly subsided, some Indian guru, Swami Satchidananda, came up next. It began to mist as they listened to the divine, exotic mystic give some rambling hocus pocus, in which he namedropped Gandhi's second cousin or someone and concluded by awkwardly saying, "America is helping everybody in the material field, but the time has come for America to help the whole world with spirituality also!"

"We make the rest of the world more spiritual," someone joked, "by bombing the shit out of them!" A big laugh followed.

Next, the band they thought was supposed to play first, Sweetwater, appeared.

"They look like virgins," Anna joked.

When they started playing, Anna put her thumbs down and said, "Next to Havens they got nothing."

"That's probably why they were scheduled to play first," Eric reasoned.

"Shit, I need to tinkle," she said, which pissed him off since he wanted to eat earlier, but he knew if they did, they would've missed Havens. He said he'd go with her, but she said no, worried that they'd lose their prize spot.

"I'll bring back something good to eat."

Alone, he watched the rest of Sweetwater until some springy-haired kid with a delicate voice replaced them. Springy Hair strummed a guitar along with a second guitarist. Eric thought he wasn't particularly special until he started singing a moving rendition of Simon and Garfunkel's "America." Tears came to his eyes as he sang the line, "We've all gone to look for America..."

The second guy didn't look like Paul Simon.

Nearly an hour after leaving, Anna finally returned.

"Sorry, I bumped into someone I knew at the bathroom, so we stood on the hog line and I got you these." She handed him four little green apples.

"What!" He was expecting a hearty sandwich.

"Shit, I missed Bert Sommer," she said as she watched Springy Hair bow deep to the applause.

"And I thought it was Garfunkel," Eric said before biting into a hard, sour apple.

54

Kasabian, Moscow, 1943

When Morozov arrived home, the day after informing Darya about his housekeeping job, he saw the lights on and heard the sound of pots and pans banging. When he entered the kitchen, he was delighted to see Alexei's beautiful girlfriend wearing Kata's old apron preparing food. Sliced cabbage was boiling. A small side of pork loin was roasting in the oven, and she was mincing something.

"I hope you like bigos?" Darya asked.

"Sure," he replied, just glad to be free of the old drunk.

As he removed his coat and shoes, unlike with the prior two housekeepers, he instantly felt at ease with Darya. She radiated a light whimsical quality as if her life was only a first draft and could easily be revised later.

"Did Alexei tell you anything about me?" she asked out of the blue as he took his first forkful of her food.

"He told me that you read all my books," he said.

"He didn't tell you that I once sent you a fan letter, did he?" she asked, casually sitting across from him and taking a sip of his water.

"You're kidding!" he said, amused. "When did you send it?"

"A couple years ago, while still in high school. I actually sent two letters to your office in Yerevan."

"Two!" he said. She blushed and rose to stir a pot.

"Over several months. The second one was basically a copy of the first letter."

"I'm so sorry," he said, amused and beguiled.

"It's probably for the best, I was going through an annoying period back then. I was reading a lot. I would obsess on a living writer and look for little holes in their works and pester them with annoying

236

questions. It made me think I was very clever. I think you were the only one who was smart enough not to respond."

"I used to get a lot of fan letters," he explained. "And initially I'd reply to each of them. That's the truth, but then they'd write back. Some days I'd find ten new letters responding to my response! Plus new ones. Soon I no longer had any time to write, so I finally stopped reading them completely."

"Makes sense," she said. "It's just odd that I'm here now cooking and cleaning for you."

"Now you have me all to yourself."

She listed different dishes that she knew how to cook: stuffed cabbage, pierogies, potato pancakes, and so on. She was trying to put together a shopping list as the Housekeeping office had issued her that month's ration cards and requested that she submit a weekly menu.

"All your dishes sound delicious," he playfully rhymed.

"I have a lot of schoolwork," she said, "so I'm a little concerned about how late I am expected to stay."

"Just start dinner and if I'm not here by six p.m., leave it on the stove." By six p.m., it was dark outside and she was a young girl in an empty city.

He included that she should make enough food for herself as well. "We'll just say I have a healthy appetite."

"You're a good boss."

After he finished eating, she cleaned up and left. Morozov returned to his study and pulled out the big envelope of Akhmatova's poems. On the last page of her packet was a photograph of the poet when she was still in her twenties—statuesque, sexy, with a superior grin, and those dark, alluring eyes. He wondered at the time if her career would've taken off as it did if she were short, fat, and ugly. It's easy to be successful at anything, he thought, if you're beautiful.

He remembered the scandal she had caused when she initiated a divorce against her husband—the Acmeist poet and war hero, Nikolay Gumilyov. Then, if this wasn't bold enough, she swooped down and clenched some other handsome devil, marrying him before the ink on her divorce papers had dried. Rumors poured forth that she was having multiple affairs, behaving like a common trollop.

A few years later, her jilted husband Gumilyov, who supposedly coauthored some counterrevolutionary manifesto, was rounded up with a group of others. He was among the first wave of writers to have been executed by the new government, supposedly before Lenin could pardon him. Dimitri Lunz was grabbed with his group. Soon afterwards, Morozov remembered connecting the two events.

Akhmatova's second divorce soon followed. By 1925 she had made enough contrary remarks to seriously hamper her career. But still she was able to find employment. As a fluent polyglot she translated major works by a variety of important writers including Victor Hugo, Rabindrathath Tagore, and Giacomo Leopardi. It didn't pay a lot, but because of her superb language skills and deft poetic abilities, the works kept coming. But translators could be a slippery lot, frequently using the subversive ideas of foreign writers to vocalize their own seditious beliefs. She also wrote occasional essays and criticisms, but could only get them published in small, hard-to-find journals.

As the government grew increasingly suspicious, she eventually found herself officially banned. Ironically, because of her censure she survived the worst of the Refinement. Included in her file, Zhdanov noted that they had literally received countless denunciations detailing how she had regularly railed against the Revolution in public places. She had even mocked the Great Leader once, while in a trolley. She laughed aloud about the state of contemporary poetry, openly denigrating it as "propaganda trash." All these reports must've made it all the way to the top. And though they arrested her son and then another companion and steadily denied her basic privileges, Morozov found it odd that they refused to touch her. To them it was as if she were already dead.

55

Eric, Woodstock Festival, 1969

"I**f you were a carpenter, I wouldn't even date you," Anna whispered as people were still applauding to Tim Hardin's song, "If I Were a Carpenter."

"Well, you're no lady," Eric replied.

Ravi Shankar came on next. Neither Eric nor Anna was acquainted with his work, and were first amused to see his crazy, antiquated instrument, which some guy said was a sitar. Eventually though, when someone nearby passed a joint around, both took big hits and really started losing themselves in Shankar's ancient tunes, closing their eyes and just letting it pass through them like an exotic breeze.

As the mist turned to rain, the crowd, particularly some of the more liberated girls, started pulling off their shirts, belly dancing in their sweaty bras: Anna did likewise. Even though she didn't take off her shirt, Eric felt uncomfortable, wishing she wouldn't put her ample self out there for older creeps to ogle. Sure enough a middle-aged pervert with an incredible beer belly danced over and offered her his joint. When she tried to take it, he wouldn't let it go, wanting her to suck it while he held it to her beautiful pouty lips. She snatched it away from him and took the hit anyway. As she closed her eyes and held in the fumes, he danced closer and closer looking as if he was coming in for a kiss. Eric thought, if he fucking touches her, I'm gonna punch the fat fuck in his face. Anna glimpsed at Eric and seeing his rage, she walked over to him and said, "I can handle myself, man!"

"I didn't say anything," he said over Shankar's sitar.

"I could see it in your face!"

"The guy was about to grab you."

"And I would've kicked him in the balls."

"You shouldn't've smoked his joint."

"You're probably right, but after this long day, I really needed to let loose."

"Well don't let me stand in your way," he replied dryly.

Still stoned, she took his comment at face value and kissed him on his lips. Always horny, he instantly forgave her and wrapped his arms around her slender waist and plunged his tongue in her mouth, which tasted like ashtray. In another moment, they were making out. He dropped his hands down her back and cupped her tight, round butt cheeks. Both were horny, but tired after the trying day that started in Josh's backseat.

They headed back to their lean-to behind the foreign exchangers who were wrapped up in their own European reality. Squeezing together in the oblique plastic tarp, Eric felt like they were encased in a giant condom. Exhausted, they hugged and kissed and grinded groins together before they both finally passed out.

When they awoke, not long afterwards, the sky was black. A cutie with long brown hair wearing a sexy red jumpsuit was up on the stage belting out a powerful song called *"Lay Down."* As Melanie sang the line, "We bleed inside each other's wounds," Eric tongue kissed Anna who reciprocated. It wasn't easy wiggling his arm and hand around until he was able to run fingers along her big, firm breasts and pointy nipples then down the front of her shorts, where he was able to unclasp the tight brass button, and pull down the heavy metal zipper and rub along the outside of her damp panties brushing his fingers along her glistening curly hairs. He couldn't believe that she was even allowing it, let alone getting into it. His cock felt like it was going to burst.

"God! You are the most beautiful girl in this whole world," he whispered into her ear.

"I know," she whispered back unsarcastically.

If you only acted just a little bit saner, you'd be perfect, he thought.

When he slipped the top of his index fingers into her, she finally stopped him. Instead of pushing him away though, she pulled up the sleeping bag. Next, she lifted her hips up and to his amazement, slid off her cut-offs and panties. He wiggled and pushed down his own pants and underpants, then angled further until his tender erection was rubbing through her sharp intricate coils of pubic hair.

240

"Wait a sec!" she grabbed his dick, "you're wearing a rubber, right?"

"Oh, right!" he said nervously. Rummaging through the bottom of his knapsack he found the rubbers Josh had given him. He took the little sealed packet, tore it open, and rolled it down his cock. She opened her legs, touched his erection and for the first time ever, he slipped the tip of his boner into a female. She made him go slow at first, but she was wet and he steadily moved quicker. Soon he was fucking her frantically. The music blotted out her moaning. He thrust as hard and deep as he could and orgasmed. She pulled him onto her, exhausted. Eric slept deeply for about five minutes before the sticky heat compelled Anna to shove him off and open the tarp, parting her legs in the darkness to let a stray breeze cool her down. After a few minutes, he re-awoke and he started fingering her. And they began fucking again, this time slower. They fucked as Melanie finished her set and fucked harder through Arlo Guthrie's entire set as well. Finally, when Joan Baez began to play, Anna said she was getting sore and needed a breather. Eric kissed her all over her beautiful radiant face and down her big insanely perfect breasts, and ran his outstretched fingertips down her strong, perfect body.

"I love you," he said.

"Don't ever say a word about this to anyone at school!" she retorted.

"I won't!"

As raindrops began to tap on the outer plastic drop cloth, he wanted to ask her to marry him right then and there and be with her forever, but he knew she'd be angry and end it right there. He lay quietly next to her for the next few hours as she snored. When the stage finally went dark, she got up and walked about ten feet in the darkness, squatted behind the slim tree and peed as people were still zipping around.

After falling asleep awhile, he awoke when she held open the flap of plastic to let another breeze inside. He gently touched her breasts and soon they were having sex again. Then they briefly napped again and awoke again. Anna said she could hear either Isla,

241

Sandrine, or Amandine screwing either Rolland or Pierre. Soon one of them was screaming ecstatically which made Anna horny again. People in the vicinity began applauding and blurting funny comments.

In a moment, Anna and Eric were screwing again, then Eric came, then napped. Then they began screwing again. This continued until the sky began to lighten up. The entire time Eric used the same sperm-bulged, over-stretched condom, which soon resembled a deflated white snake skin.

When Anna saw it, she was amazed it hadn't snapped, saying, "Those mothers are strong!"

56

Kasabian, Moscow, 1943

In 1938 it was easy to turn in people who he barely knew. All Morozov had to do was fill out an arrest warrant, which he called the De-People Form. Most of his victims he never even knew. They were just names on lists compiled by others.

It started in 1937, when a short, quiet man, Sarkis Tomian, the chief political officer of the Armenian Communist Party, unexpectedly died and Moscow failed to appoint a replacement. As the Refinement was just beginning, it quickly led to a lengthy bureaucratic backlog. Two weeks later, one of two other Moscow appointees, technically his superior, contacted him to say that Morozov by default was the interim political officer. This meant he was authorized to co-sign the stack of disciplinary forms until a new officer was appointed.

He knew what was happening and wanted no part of it, but when it began, all looked to see who wasn't participating. He knew — between killer and killed, he had to pick a side. This meant he was expected to add to the list of the guilty. So he initiated his first warrant — a grumpy old poet with bad breath whose work was highly derivative and no one liked. When it was done, one of his co-signers asked, "Just one? We're each supposed to do eight names."

So the next day Morozov filled out another arrest warrant. The guilty party for this one was a cloying memoirist, who was constantly pushing him for publishing opportunities. He never learned of the consequences. The man simply disappeared. But in the mornings just after waking up, he'd envision the man's bewildered face as he was pushed down onto the oil-blotched asphalt surface of some truck garage with other doomed men. When the truck ignitions were turned on to cover the sounds, the shooting began. The thought paralyzed Morozov with guilt. After that, his conscience got the better of him, and he only served as a co-signer for others, consequences be damned.

Soon quotas came down from Moscow, numbers had to be met. This spawned a theory that the real reason for the arrests was simply a matter of numbers. Russia could not support its current population. The fewer the amount of people, the more resources per capita. Stalin was simply thinning the herd, slimming down those who weren't behind the new government in order to make labor equal production. Haig sensed that once they reached a magic number, the arrests would stop. Fortunately, the other two members of the local Party were more than happy to generate names. On a weekly basis he had to clench his teeth and sign a small stack of warrants as quickly as possible.

He tried not to even look at the accused, covering them up when he signed the forms. But soon he realized friends were vanishing and he feared he might be responsible, so after a few months, before signing the warrants he started checking the names of the guilty party. On four occasions, instead of trying to halt the sentence, he simply asked if others could sign the forms. But then he'd have to sign other warrants in return. It became harder when he learned that not only the accused, but sometimes their entire families, were also wiped out, whether they were killed, arrested or simply exiled, he didn't know or want to know.

It was around this time, in late 1938, that his writing began to change. He'd begin writing a story the same old way: He'd draw up a mysterious character. Then slowly a story would take shape, but before it'd go very far he would find himself killing off the side characters. Soon his central characters started dying as well. He didn't feel as if he was writing it, just observing it. They'd be struck by cars, or suffer a fatal heart attack, or just die inexplicably in their sleep.

Murdering characters in fiction was actually much harder than signing De-People Forms. He would have to humanize them first. No matter how he would try to protect his protagonists, his instincts would draw them to an irresistible death. Soon he didn't know why, but he was only really writing characters to kill them. Love, missteps, intrigues, amusing misunderstandings—all seemed irrelevant next to their sudden demise, which would bring him great relief and calm. With each character, the two points drew steadily shorter, just characterizations and executions. In several stories he simply erased the deaths, but he couldn't conceive of any more fate for the characters, they no longer had a purpose. It wasn't that he wanted it to happen, it was more like being a witness.

He accepted their deaths and tried continuing the stories by focusing on grieving family members or friends, promoting them to central characters, but soon he'd find that they died as well. There was no mystery to him as to why he was seeing this. He knew it was because of the arrests. Yet, since he loved writing, he hoped his writing disorder would pass. So he kept turning out the stories with the unexpected deaths, which he would dispose of after finishing. Finally when his two good friends Yeghishe and Aghasi were eliminated, he stopped writing altogether.

Life was strange back then. Fearful that they too were at risk, friends of the arrested usually stopped mentioning their vanished friend. There would be these sudden pauses in conversation, where someone brought up the missing person and no one would respond. After a conversational bump of silence, the talking would resume. It was like a silent epidemic sweeping Russia. By 1939 the great invisible peril of counterrevolutionaries was essentially over.

Now, four years later, instead of signing a De-People Form, he had to write a convincing condemnation of Akhmatova's work, poems that he actually liked and respected. The worst of it though was the fact that his byline would openly be printed on the review. No one ever knew he was responsible for the arrests of so many. Now all of Russia was going to see what a coward he was.

The next day at the university Haig spent the entire morning rereading all of Akhmatova's poems. As he did so, he found himself repeatedly glimpsing her photograph until Anna's large eyes seemed to be growing sterner. They appeared to be judging him.

With a violent sweep of his arm, he pushed everything off his desk onto the floor.

"You okay, sir?" Alexei asked, hearing everything fall.

"No! Hold on!" As Alexei began to pick up his telephone and other items and put them back on the writer's desk, Morozov asked, "You said you were in combat, didn't you?"

"Yes. Two years ago."

"Did you ever kill anyone?"

"Yes—the enemy."

"Did you actually shoot someone and see him go down?"

"Yes."

"Tell me about it."

"May I ask why?"

"Private business."

"On October 15, 1941, my combat group was holding our position outside of Zubtsov. We were stuck way out ahead of the rest of our company. We didn't know the Germans had just gotten resupplied. They were moving down a thousand-mile line, closing up the salients."

"What are salients?" Morozov asked.

"Bulges where our troops pushed out. We were exposed on three sides."

"What happened?"

"We learned that the 4th Panzer Group along with some infantry were advancing and would be moving against us within the next few hours."

"Why didn't you retreat?"

"We should've, but there was a standing no-retreat policy. We were told we had support coming. Air cover and reserves moving up," he said nervously. "We were also expecting tank support."

"This was your first conflict?"

"My only real conflict, yes. We were fresh meat, replacing more experienced troops. We didn't know it was all lies. We dug in and waited. Very nerve racking."

"What happened?"

"We finally saw a formation of advance fighters passing overheard, but we did a pretty good job of camouflage. I can't tell you how relieved we were when they flew right over us. A battalion of T-34s was supposed to protect us. But it turned out they were knocked out by those fighters. About an hour later, those same planes circled back. They swooped down and strafed us over and over with machine-gun-fire. We were pinned down."

"So you were wounded by the planes?" Morozov asked.

"They wiped out most of my brigade, but after doing their worst, they flew off. And those of us still alive figured we were lucky 'til we saw the black clouds coming over the hills—a column of Panzers had finally arrived and systematically worked their way up our lines, blowing out our trenches, hitting us with close range machine-gun fire. We were just sitting ducks."

"And after that you ran for it?" Morozov asked, trying to get him to finish.

"After that they sent in their infantry for cleanup. You work your way down the various war machines, until you finally go man to man. The five guys to my left were all wounded or dead. So it was just Piotr and me and we huddled among the dead and dying until two Nazis jumped in our trench. I bayoneted the first."

"Where?"

"Here," Alexei grabbed his stomach. "He's screaming. His buddy jumps on me and Piotr grabs him. They're wrestling."

"Why didn't you help him?"

"I yanked my bayonet out of the first guy and jabbed it into the back of the big one who was fighting Piotr, but..." Alexei couldn't speak any longer.

"What?"

"It snagged on his bone, up here," Alexei pointed to his left scapula.

"You probably weren't doing it right," Morozov said, and standing up, grabbing an umbrella and holding it like a rifle, he demonstrated. "You're supposed to use your whole body when you thrust!"

"It was my first time in combat," Alexei said.

"Then what?"

"Just as I'm about to stab him a second time, two more Nazis rush us. So I shoot them."

"Where?"

"First guy up under the chin, the second square in the chest. Next I feel this sharp snap in my right side and then it's all numb and wet. The son of a bitch who was fighting with Piotr had killed him and shot me in the side."

"Let's see where you were hit." Alexei lifted his shirt and showed the wound near his appendix.

"So what'd you do next?"

"When you're hit by a bullet it's like being kicked by a horse! I fell to the bottom of our trench."

"Then?"

"I laid there and wondered if I was dead."

"The German soldier didn't try to finish you off?" Morozov asked.

"He thought I was dead and he ran off to help one of his comrades. That's when I scrambled up out of the hole. But all around me it was a slaughter. The Germans were executing the wounded."

"What'd you do?"

"Dragged myself into the woods. Over the next day, in agony, I crawled through the mud and leaves until I found some others who dragged me back to our line."

"Is this what your novel is about?"

"Oh no, I couldn't write about that."

"Too painful?"

"No, we lost. They'd never publish a defeat."

Haig paused respectfully before saying, "It must've been gratifying, killing Germans."

"My single day of combat experience was mostly boring, until the Germans appeared, then it was pure fear. By the time the Panzers rolled in, most of my buddies were dead or dying."

"It sounds awful."

"You spend months training and becoming a tight group of guys, then in one afternoon you watch them get slowly torn apart bleeding, weeping, and then dying."

"What happened to your guns!" Morozov argued. "Why didn't you shoot back!"

"You can't shoot a tank or a plane," he said tiredly. "We were out of mortar shells by then. No medical supplies left."

"Why didn't you retreat?" Morozov grumbled.

"Those who retreated got shot in the back, those who tried to surrender got shot in the front."

"Do you feel any guilt?"

"Guilt? About not helping Piotr?"

"No, shooting the Germans."

"They killed all my friends and almost killed me! Hell, I was only defending myself!"

"Yes! You were only defending yourself," Morozov repeated with the thought that this was essentially his situation with Akhmatova. *If I don't write this essay, I'll be the victim here. At least she has a choice in the matter. I don't!*

"The only guilt I have is not killing more of them," Alexei added, slowly growing angry as he reflected on the worst day of his entire life.

Morozov thought that the key reason this Akhmatova essay was so difficult was the fact that he actually liked her poetry. But, after a moment, even the thought that he was only defending himself didn't relieve his guilt.

Morozov abruptly remembered the stack of school newspapers in the teachers' lounge, each containing one of Alexei's sycophantic little book reviews, the perfect size. And Alexei didn't know Anna

Akhmatova! To him she was just another name. If Alexei, the spying bootlick, could spin out all those little novenas pertaining to the Revolution, what was one more?

"I'll make you a deal, I'll read your novel and give you my wealth of experience, if in return you write a review for me."

"Of your book?"

"No, you moron! Someone else's book."

"Who?"

"Here's the new German in your foxhole." He slid Zhdanov's envelope of pages across the desk to the youth.

"What, who is this?" he said, wondering if it somehow factored into his investigation.

"Anna Akhmatova," he said, "the witch poet of Leningrad."

"What's a witch poet?"

"She's a grotesque creature with a hook for a nose, and big dark rings around her eyes. And her poems are spells of selfishness," he said, vilifying her as best as he could. "We must defend the motherland from her spreading her lies."

"I never even heard of her. Where is she published?" He flipped through the strange photostatted pages.

"We must stop her from being published! But her disciples are still copying her work by hand. They are scribbling her spells onto public places! We need to put a stop to it!"

"And you want me to kill her like I did the Germans?" Alexei asked calmly, trying not to sound sarcastic.

"Just write a negative review, but not too negative." He suddenly decided to expand on his idea. "'Cause afterwards I'll have another job for you that you'd probably like."

"What's that?"

"How'd you like to write a laudatory review of..." Haig reached into his drawer and took out the thick sheath of new pages making up Fedin's latest manuscript. "Konstanin Fedin's great new masterpiece!"

"Hold on..." Alexei said, pointing to the pages of poetry. "Suppose I like the poet witch, and I don't care for Fedin?"

"Welcome to your first lesson as a writer. You like what you're told to like," he paused, "besides, you're not writing either review under your name, you're writing them for me. And don't tell me you haven't done assignments before, I've seen your column. In the past six months you reviewed enough books to fill the Library of Alexandria."

"This is a lot of work," Alexei said, looking at the two manuscripts. He was too embarrassed to mention that Darya had written most of the reviews for him.

"Okay, just focus on the poems. I'll handle Fedin." Morozov put the manuscript back in his desk drawer.

Alexei took the Akhmatova poems and flipped through them: "When do you need this by?"

"Immediately! Fast as you can. Only three hundred words. It'll be done before you begin it."

"This looks beyond me," he said, flipping through the verses. "I don't really get poetry."

"Nobody does. It's a mystery."

"I just don't know how to..."

"I know what you're saying. Poets are sneaky. They'll write something annoying and then in the next sentence recant it all or contextualize it in a way to neutralize the original offense. Don't let them off!"

"I won't," he replied, without a clue to what this meant.

"Even moody poems can be regarded as emotionally subversive."

"Moody poetry?" To Alexei all good poetry was moody.

"Think about it. If a poem creates depression or doubts, those are all treason of the soul. Life is hard enough. Poets should be encouraging, stabilizing for our country."

"I never thought of it that way."

"And you bring in your war manuscript right away! I'll fix it for you. I know a couple editors who owe me."

"It's not really a war novel," he replied. But Morozov had turned his attention elsewhere to that day's newspaper, straightening it out nervously.

Without a word, Alexei walked behind Morozov's desk and opened his large bottom drawer, where he took out the hefty manuscript—just where Morozov had asked him to put it after the Slotkin lecture weeks ago. He placed it in front of the writer.

Glancing at the new burden of pages before him, Morozov winced.

Alexei scooped up the Akhmatova envelope and proceeded back to his little desk out front.

Feeling relieved that he no longer needed to worry about the Akhmatova piece, Morozov shoved the newspaper in the trash. He slid Alexei's manuscript into his valise and headed home.

It was relatively warm outside so he walked, but Akhmatova's poems of heartbreak made him think of Masha.

By the time he arrived home, he immediately went to his journals. Flipping through one of his diaries, he soon found what he was looking for. It was the May 3, 1924, entry, the shredded pieces of Masha's letter from Kiev. At the time, he tore it up after reading it and wept painfully. Later, he fished the pieces out of the trash and glued them into his journal. He would periodically re-read it when he felt the need for punishment.

It had been a month since he had gotten her readmitted into medical school. He still hadn't learned her address so he couldn't notify her of the wonderful news. But he kept expecting her to return from the Ukraine any day, excited to resume her medical studies. Instead, he received a brusque note:

Haig Morozov Kasabian:

My plans have changed and they no longer include you or your communist medicine. I fell in love with a good man who would never betray me and we are starting a family. If you attempt to pursue me I will file a complaint at the local CPA Headquarters requesting that they strip you of your sacred party membership. I've moved on and strongly suggest you do likewise.   —Masha Rodchenko

Masha kept her word about one thing, she provided her return address in Kiev. His first impulse was to travel down to Kiev immediately and plead with her in person. But he also sensed that this would only fill her with rage. And the thought of arguing with her in front of her new husband was too much. After crying himself into a fever and then falling asleep, he woke up, dressed, and went for a walk. As a cool breeze blew, he tried to accept the situation. When he returned home, he sat down and wrote a response:

Masha, I understand if you don't want to ever see me again. Painful though it is, I accept your decision. But being a doctor is your life's dream. You had this calling long before you met me. Don't deny it! And you're so close to getting there! Forget about love and me – I'll never bother you again, but if you don't follow your destiny, your life will steadily become unbearable. Mark my words, you'll never forgive yourself!"

He mailed the letter that afternoon.

A month later, his letter was returned to him unopened. He sent her a second letter with a message written on the letter saying, "POSTMAN! If you know Masha Rodchenko and she lives on your route, could you please deliver this letter to her?"

It too was returned with the same stamp that said, "RETURN TO SENDER—No one of that name lives here."

She didn't provide the address to her parents' little farm in the Ukraine, only the return address of the one letter she had sent. He began to wonder if she was lying. Maybe she hadn't met another man. To walk away from all those difficult years of medical school, then abruptly find a husband, sounded absolutely nothing like her. She must've suffered some kind of severe mental collapse. Nothing she had done or said made any sense. He paid for a long-distance call and contacted the Kiev Police Department, asking for the Missing Person's Desk. When the constable on duty answered, he explained how he feared for a young woman's life. She had recently moved to Kiev. She sounded delusional and might need immediate assistance.

The constable asked how he was related to the subject in question. He honestly replied that he wasn't.

"Notify her immediate family and have them contact us. You can't file a missing person's form yourself," he said. When Haig explained that he had no way to contact her parents or any of her family members, the constable replied that there was nothing he could do and hung up.

All that was left for him was the remote hope that she might calm down and eventually come to her senses. Her destiny was waiting, but it wouldn't wait long. It was weeks away and then days. Finally, the deadline for her re-admission arrived and passed. All his tedious work and relentless campaigning to get her back into school had been for nothing. Soon, months passed and the semester ended. Still not a word. When the day arrived for that year's medical school to graduate, tears came to his eyes as he thought if she'd only returned, she would've been a doctor by now.

It was as if she had slipped off the caboose of a train that he was still on. He could only watch her broken body, laying on the tracks behind him, growing smaller with time, as his own life went on without her.

One day, a year and a half later, while in the student cafeteria, he bumped into one of Masha's old classmates, Irena, the only other female student from the Ukraine, who happened to be back in Moscow visiting friends.

"So you're not in touch with Masha Rodchenko?" He tried not to sound desperate.

"No, but I ran into her and her beautiful baby, which made me think of you."

"Me?"

"Well, you dated her so it crossed my mind."

"We broke up after that whole editorial debacle..."

"Right, I remember when she got expelled."

"Anyway," he said without updating her, "was she alone when you met?"

"Just her and the baby."

"Did you meet her at work?"

"No, on Sikorsky Street. Only for a moment. In passing."

"And you thought I was the dad."

"It crossed my mind. Sorry." She smiled.

"Did the baby look like me?" he asked softly.

"It looked like a baby."

"How old did the baby look?" Haig pressed.

"Well, I only saw it for a moment but it could've been two years old," she said. Then seeing her friend approaching, Irena said goodbye.

"Did you get the baby's name?" He blocked her exit.

"No."

"Do you know where Masha lives? An address?" He placed his hand on her elbow.

"Like I said, I saw her on Sikorsky Street in Kiev for a moment." She looked nervous. "We barely said hi."

"She didn't say anything about me?" She saw the panic in his eyes.

"Haig, I was never very close to her. We really said little more than hi and bye, I swear." She stepped around him and left.

57

Woodstock Festival, Eric, 1969

As she heard the foreign exchangers moving around in the early morning, Anna was grateful to have an excuse to stop Eric from slipping it in again. Apparently, due to the intermittent drizzle, they had postponed the morning's schedule of performances yet again.

"What I would give to take a goddamn shower!" she said, feeling icky and sticky down there from all the sex.

"It's still early. Let's head down to that Filipino Lake and take a dip." He had heard people calling it that.

"I didn't bring a towel," she said.

"I might have something," Eric said, and went through a little pile of items he found that were still dry. He pulled out two clean children's tee shirts and biting their edges, he tore along the seams turning them into two thin hand towels. They carefully wiggled out of their little lean-to and walked over to the big pond. Several people were already floating around, some nude, some not. Eric stripped off his shirt and shorts and tossed them onto the grass. Naked, he stepped into the still cold waters. His toes slid through the squirmy, muddy bottom. Slowly, he sat down in the water. Anna looked around the filthy pond, let out a sigh and since there were other naked females older than her, she pulled off her top and bottom and quickly went in, submerging herself as best as she could.

"Fuck it's cold," she murmured.

"I don't know about you, but I really needed this," he said as the water chilled his clammy body. In lieu of soap, she ran her fingers along her curves and cracks then got out. She dried herself quickly and pulled on her shorts and shirt. Eric continued floating on his back, feeling his pecker bobbing on the surface.

The gentle sounds of water dripping, insects, and birds chirping only made Anna nervous. Looking around, Eric suddenly realized that a lot more people also decided to take a morning dip. The pond was filling up by the minute, so he got up, toweled off and caught up with Anna. They waited on the bathroom line, but the food line was way too long and slow. Since the ground was still spongy wet, they returned to their narrow plastic tepee and squeezed back into the sleeping bag. When Anna started snoring Eric slowly moved his finger along her body.

"Hey! I was sleeping!" Anna barked. "You had enough!"

He sulked. Seeing that the rain had subsided, she started dressing saying she was starving and needed some chow. He dressed as well. Looking up the slope, they could see the line hadn't moved at all; the same wet people were still waiting.

"I read that a group of people who were starving to death on a life raft focused on..."

Not wanting to hear it, Anna needed some alone time and began walking around the noisy sea of concert-goers. Within minutes she spotted an older couple and began making small talk. She quickly got an apple. She thanked them and kept moving, collecting some crackers here and seeded grapes there. After an hour, she returned to find Eric eating a sandwich and scratching his latest mosquito bite.

"Where'd you get that?" she asked almost surprised.

Eric explained that he hiked up to the road just as the New York State Troopers were handing out thin wrapped sandwiches, but he could only get one.

"And you didn't have the decency of even saving me half?" she said, appalled. "I thought we were a team."

"I just figured you were getting fed." She handed him some mushy grapes that she had gathered, only to make him feel bad. The foreign exchangers were eating a fresh wheel of cheese and another loaf of bread.

"They never run out of that stuff," Anna said, eyeing their food.

Around noon, it started to clear up again and the festival resumed, so they waded down into the crowds before the stage and watched as five colorful white boys with shaggy hair dumped a bag of junk onto the vast plywood floor. They began picking up sticks and pieces of wood and banging them together. The band soon strummed guitars, clapped hands, and shook mariachis.

"Hippie shit," said Anna, not caring for improvised instruments.

As Quill played, new clouds appeared and a new mist began to fall.

As the clouds thickened and the sky soon grew darker, the spray continued until the band finally finished. Eric could see the pirate from yesterday come on stage and as he talked, all could hear a distant boom.

"Oh shit!" Eric said, unable to spot where in the sky the sun could be hiding.

"Come on! Let's go back to the lean tube!" she said nervously. They went up the hill where they still had a clear view of the stage, but the mist was now a light rain. And the foreign exchangers were missing.

As the showers increased, the pirate suddenly grabbed the mike and in a frantic voice said: "Everybody sit down and wrap yourself up. We're going to get hit and we'll have to ride this out! Hold on to your neighbors, man!"

Eric, who was always looking for an excuse to touch Anna, gently wrapped his arm around her slim feminine back. She hugged only herself.

"Please get off those towers," the pirate yelled into the mic, referring to the kids who had scaled up the six thirty-foot amp-and-light scaffolds that surrounded the stage. "We don't need any extra weight on them." About a half-dozen skinny kids who had scurried up there to get the best view of the stage were slowly working their way down.

Suddenly lightning flashed before them, compelling the reluctant ones into a hasty descent. "Please move back! Please move away from the amps." He was clearly worried that the wind would knock over the towers. Although it had been stifling in the August heat, a cold wind started blowing in out of nowhere. Instead of a soothing presence, the pirate was clearly tense, like he was preparing for Armageddon. "Put the mic stand down and cover all the stuff." Now he was talking to the techies scrambling around the stage.

Quill's equipment was still in place. "We'll be back in just a sec! Soon as we get set up again." He paused a moment as the cold rain steadily increased and the wind began to whip the vast sea of hippies around. Bracing for the inevitable, people had pulled out ponchos, raincoats, and umbrellas. A sudden gust violently tore the top of the lean-to, compelling Anna to grab the plastic sheathe that had come loose. Eric tensely looked up at his make-shift home bending in the wind and wondered if it could withstand.

"Hey, if we think really hard maybe we can stop this rain," the pirate said, getting back on the mic. "Let's all focus on that. No rain! No rain!"

Some people in the crowd started chanting, "No rain! No rain! No rain!"

"The wind is blowing this way," the pirate pointed to one side of the field, "Please get away from there and be on that side of the towers." People began migrating to where he was pointing. About a dozen techies began roping down tarps as though the stage was the deck of an old clipper ship.

"No rain! No rain!" Eric and Anna joined in, but it only seemed to make the wind stronger until drops began trickling in.

"Hey! Flip off the power!" the pirate said to his staff as the storm seemed to turn into a Nor'easter. "We're going to have to turn off the microphone for a minute!" he said to the concert-goers battened down before him.

"Oh jeez!" Eric said nervously as their little tree began to sway, stretching the lean-to until the twine was tearing through the plastic holes, increasing the water coming in, and soaking their clothes and sleeping bag. Anna reached up and tried to clamp up the holes with her hands.

As though the pirate was the captain of the sinking ship, he earnestly said: "God bless you!"

"If anything happens to me I want you to know that I love you," Eric whispered.

"Oh shit!" Anna said, nodding her head in disgust, while trying to keep from getting wet.

Eric felt foolish.

"Watch those towers!" were the Pirate's parting words before flipping the mic off yet again.

"At least we're away from those fucking towers," Anna said looking at the nearest one to see if it was shaking.

As the wind picked up, people held each other. It blew for about five minutes then, for no apparent reason, the whole thing was over.

The rain tapered, the wind ceased and the sky began to lighten up. The sense of relief made everyone instantly euphoric. In a matter of minutes the temperature warmed up again to its former August heat. Eric and Anna watched hippies tripping on the warm water flooding the grass, dancing and stripping off shirts and pants. As streams of water began flowing down the grassy dale, Anna pointed out that young guys were dashing and jumping down the muddy slopes as though they were water slides. Soon, the less inhibited ones stripped off their undies and were walking around buck-ass naked. All were wet and the ground was pure mud. All seemed to be having a blast.

After another twenty minutes, the rain stopped entirely, blue skies peaked through, and the pirate got back on the PA system and announced: "The forecast for this afternoon is intermittent entertainment between intermittent showers!"

Some began to dry off the stage as others started toting equipment and instruments back onto it. A young, cocky guy in a worn GI shirt with a bushy mustache strutted up to the mic with a guitar in hand.

"Hey! That's not Santana," Anna said. She began wringing water out of the sleeping bag as Eric started making repairs to his lean-to.

Without any backup, the GI-shirted performer with the bandana strummed through one song followed by the next until he reached his final song, *"And it's one, two, three, four. What are we fighting for? Don't ask me, I don't give a damn, next stop it's Vietnam!"* He stopped singing and shouted, *"I don't know how you expect to stop the war if you don't sing any better than that! There's about three hundred thousand of you fuckers out there! I want you to start singing!"*

People down front sang along. Suddenly, the foreign exchange crowd reappeared. Apparently before the storm of the century could blow them back to Europe, they grabbed their possessions and took shelter up near the first aid tent.

As the lone hippie continued singing, Anna commented that behind him, it looked like the roadies were assembling some kind of electro-tentacled machine. People applauded as Country Joe left and a squad of new musicians took his place and checked their instruments.

After a quick intro, the band Santana began playing. They were the first minority act after Richie Havens. The large-afroed-drummer, a Black guitarist, a Mariachi guy, even some dude on a cowbell, instantly harmonized together as though the instruments were all being played by a single crisp musician. After the hippie improv and country rags, Eric was impressed by how tightly this Latino band played together. One of the neighboring concert-goers said it was a rock-and-roll update of the uptown Latin dance hall music.

"Well I never heard any Latin music," Anna said. "So it's all new to me."

Hearing the male chorus sing "You Got to Change Your Evil Ways" was powerful and when Eric sang along, he looked at Anna hoping to send a message that she didn't get.

The next number, "*Soul Sacrifice*" all instrumental, was nothing short of stupendous, compelling Eric to close his eyes and keep pace by thumping his fists on the grass. After Santana was finally done, both Anna and Eric agreed that though it was great, they needed a break. Both said their ears were ringing and they weren't even near the stage. Still, it was hard to squeeze out of the crowd.

"This festival is like going to a wedding and eating and drinking nonstop until you can't eat another bite, then you get served dinner," Anna said.

"There's an old English painter named Turner," Eric replied, trying to impress her with his erudition. "Apparently in order to get a fresh perspective on his work he would spend hours in a dark room just trying to blot out his brain."

"Yes! We need to do that with music! Silence for the next hour!" Anna shouted. But for the next hour and a half, as they strolled around the vast dairy farm, there was no escaping the rock and roll: the Incredible String Band, then Keef Hartley, and finally John B. Sebastian kept playing on and on. And the crowd just seemed to grow bigger and thicker.

During a silent interlude, as a new band started loading in, Anna and Eric watched a seated group of serious mystical types spaced out on a patch of grass, practicing what Eric swore was called "cunnilingus yoga."

Anna said that was bullshit. "Who would name a type of yoga after eating pussy?"

"That's what the guy told me," he insisted.

"They look like they've gone deep into themselves," Anna said softly. Eric knew they were all faking—it was just an act.

"They know we're watching them," he replied.

This new brand of yoga seemed to mainly consist of sitting up straight, closing one's eyes, and doing "controlled breathing." And it appeared really boring. Suddenly someone bumped into Anna. She turned to see some goofball who turned out to be at the rear of a long line.

"What are you waiting for?" she asked.

"Hog Farm line," the long-haired goofball replied. They turned around and stood behind him.

"What are they serving?" Eric asked.

"Whatever people from the area donate," he replied. "The Hog Farm heats it up, throws it on a paper plate, and hands it out."

After not moving at all for about ten minutes, the line suddenly took off. As Anna looked over, she spotted one girl leaving from the front, holding what appeared to be a big bowl of lasagna smothered in melted mozzarella and thick tomato sauce.

"Holy shit!" said Eric, famished.

The line was long, but it didn't seem to slow down.

"Please don't run out of lasagna! Please don't run out of the lasagna!" the goofball began praying aloud.

"You're gonna jinx us by saying that," Anna countered.

The line kept moving, but after five minutes Anna saw that they were giving away something else. When they finally reached the home stretch, their hearts sunk. Instead of a plate of fresh lasagna, each of them were handed a small can of tuna with a plastic fork and a hard roll.

"Where's the fucking lasagna?!" the goofball cried out.

"All out. Step aside," replied a Hog Farmer.

Eric and Anna sat on a log and watched the inescapable concert in the distance. Canned Heat played as they ate their hot cans of tuna.

"I feel like a fucking cat," Anna muttered, as crowds walked past.

"Not me," Eric said in an upbeat tone. "This is the best meal I ever had." He forked it into his mouth.

"Are you a moron?"

"No, I'm employing the technique of FDT."

"STP?"

"No, fantasy displacement therapy."

261

"What's that?"

Eric explained that instead of tuna, he was fantasizing that he was eating a grilled medium-rare steak. Forking down a chunk he said, "Oh my god, this is the best piece of filet mignon I've ever eaten."

"Here," she said, handing him her can. "You can have it with my cat food."

"You should try it—fantasy displacement works!"

"I'll try it the next time we have sex," she muttered.

Before returning to the concert, the two went to a second even longer line for the row of port-o-sans. After five minutes of waiting, Anna struck up a conversation with some girls in front of her while Eric chatted with some Black youth named Benny behind him. He was telling Eric that he was moving up to Canada after the concert ended.

"My number just came up. There's no way I'm gonna risk my life so some fat cat in Washington can get richer."

"Just get a deferment," Eric said. His brother had one as did everyone in his college class.

"I'm a high-school dropout," Benny confessed. Eric didn't reply. All his friends had graduated high school and went on to college, so he just assumed everyone did.

After forty-five minutes, it was finally Anna's turn to go. The lady who was exiting the shitter advised her: "Take a deep breath and try to hold it for as long as humanly possible." When the next toilet became available, Eric also followed her advice.

As soon as he stepped outside, Anna said, "Let's get our sleeping bags and camp over by the big pond."

"Why?" he asked.

"Those girls I met on line are doing it," she explained.

"Why?"

"All these top acts who were supposed to play during prime time were pushed back cause of the storm, so they aren't going on stage 'til late tonight."

"So what difference will it make if we camp by the pond?"

Anna explained that it was quieter there and if they slept through the next two boring bands, Mountain and Grateful Dead, they could watch Creedence and Janis Joplin. And though she said she was ambivalent about Sly and the Family Stone, she really loved The Who and Jefferson Airplane.

"The Guess Who?" he asked.

"No, just The Who," she said.

"I prefer the Guess Who."

"'Cause you're a moron!"

"Do you think we'll be awake for Jefferson Airplane?" he asked. Grace Slick was so hot, she could sing the phone book and he'd listen.

"I don't know, but I don't want to watch these clowns," she said, pointing to the stage. "I mean, they have great voices, I'll admit it, but let's face it, they're ugly. Who wants to look at them?"

Eric silently agreed. The sun had come out, so they grabbed the sleeping bag and left the rest of their things in the lean-to under the semi-watchful eyes of the foreign exchangers.

As they walked to the pond, Eric spotted an epic line in front of the small bank of phones. He remembered that he was supposed to call his mom and give her a specific time that his bus would be returning tomorrow. But then he remembered that his mother said he didn't have to call if he was camping out with Josh, so he walked past.

Anna was chattering on about how cool Santana had been, but even more excitedly, she couldn't wait to see Janis later that night.

"Janis and Jimi are the absolute best," Anna said as they found a dry place on the banks of the pond to unravel their bag.

"We'll get close to the stage tonight," he replied.

"I saw her once down in the Village."

"At the Fillmore?" he asked, trying to get comfortable.

"No, another theater a few blocks from there. She was rocking out the roof!"

"I wonder if I can find a cardboard box," Eric said.

"The grass is dry here," she pointed out.

"No, not that." He explained that when he called his mother tomorrow he needed to find some way to block out the rock and roll in the background.

As they squeezed into their single bag, Anna was still blathering on about how cool Joplin was. All he could think about was how he was going to explain all the booming music in the background when he spoke to his mom tomorrow. Maybe he could call her during a rainstorm, he thought.

"If we're going to get some rest for tonight, we should stop talking," he finally said to shut Anna up.

But she kept mumbling poetically about how the distant stage was throbbing with music and the sky was vanilla with shooting stars.

"Shooting stars?" he replied, looking upward. "There's only sunlight."

"Janis' perspective is my perspective." Anna ignored him, "And mine is hers. And that's really the most important thing with these concerts, with the whole phenomenon of rock and roll shows when you really think about it."

"Interesting point! Sleep tight."

"It's like there's a giant mirror, and they shatter it and scatter the pieces to each of us. We see them but all we can really see is ourselves in them."

"Okay, then..."

"When The Beatles sing the song "*I Am the Walrus*, you are the walrus" —you know that line?"

"Yep," he said, praying she'd tire out.

"I am *he*, as you are *he*, as you are *me*, and *we* are all together. Do you know that line?" she asked emphatically.

He tiredly nodded yes.

"No, I mean do you know that specific line?" she asked pointedly.

"Shouldn't we try to rest for Janis?" he asked, almost maternally.

But Anna continued yammering quickly and quietly, nonstop. Soon she started laughing at her own thoughts quicker than she could put them into words.

"Are you okay?" He put his hand on her forehead to see if she was hot.

She mumbled on, lying on her back, occasionally laughing, sometimes cursing until finally he realized she was on something.

"What'd you take?"

"A tab with the girls," she said.

"Huh?"

"Licked a tab."

"Oh, shit, it wasn't the brown acid, was it?" They had been making announcements, all day, warning about the brown acid.

She ignored the question and resumed muttering then singing more of the lyrics from "*I Am The Walrus*."

"Why did you take acid if you wanted to nap?" he tried reasoning. "It's a stimulant!"

She just kept laughing and whispering until she stopped. Then the two just listened to the distorted echo of Canned Heat, which consisted of two male vocalists. The bearded, chubby guy had performed first, but now the soprano half was singing, *I'm going up to the country...Where the water tastes like wine...*"

Anna seemed to finally calm down so, despite the fact that the sun was still in the sky, Eric began to get groggy.

Just as he began to drift off, Anna let out a bloodcurdling scream. She pounced to her feet and flew off like a kite that broke its string. Shit! he thought, she must've taken the brown acid.

58

Alexei, Moscow, 1943

Thrilled by the notion that one of Armenia's most influential writers was going to read his novel-in-progress, Alexei Novikov read Anna Akhmatova's poems but quickly found himself startled by her narcissism and brazen sentimentality. They weren't verses. It was emotional exhibitionism! Every word hung out exposed. Had the woman no shame! Did she walk out into the streets naked every morning? How could any self-respecting woman proudly chronicle every little humiliation of her life? When did this become poetry? Her disappointment seemed to take precedence above the great, yet beleaguered nation of Russia. "Decadent selfishness!" he wrote on a notepad as Darya entered.

"What are you doing?" she asked, seeing him underline his own comment.

"As I see it," he grumbled, "I'm doing your job."

"My job?"

"Weren't you brought in to help me with the Armenian's literary affairs?"

"What are you saying?"

"He asked me to write a review of some old lady's verses and I have no idea what I'm doing. I don't read poetry, and I've never written a poetry review."

"Let me see it."

He tossed his fountain pen on the desk and headed into the bathroom.

"Like the book reviews, keep this confidential," he called out. "Also, technically I'm the only one who is supposed to read that."

But Darya wasn't listening. Almost immediately, she found herself rapt in Akhmatova's words. Each poem seemed to cry out what Darya had learned to keep to herself, poison that she had learned to digest, always in pain yet never dying. Akhmatova's poems seemed so powerful and empathetic that tears came to Darya's eyes as she flipped through each of them. As Alexei showered, Darya pulled out a sheet of paper and a pen and began copying lines that grabbed her.

Roughly twenty minutes later when she had sped through most of the poems, the ring of the phone compelled Alexei to open the bathroom door, soaking wet and answer it in the nude.

"Report to Ivan Lemokh's office at seven a.m. tomorrow," he heard.

"Who is this, please?" It wasn't his superior.

"You'll find out when I see you."

He hung up without mentioning the call to Darya who discreetly wiped her tears and continued reading. When he flipped

266

off the desk lamp, she got up, silently took off her dress, and joined him in bed.

"So what do you think of her poetry?" he asked as she pulled up the blanket.

"Remarkable."

"Remarkably bad?"

"No, they're amazing," she said. "They really capture the feeling of..."

"We'll talk about it in the morning," he cut her off. He was beginning to obsess about this mysterious appointment tomorrow morning. Who was this new guy? Where was Ivan Lemokh?

Early the next morning as instructed, when Alexei entered the university, he went down to his superior's office in the basement. Instead of seeing his young friend Ivan, who had selected him for this sensitive assignment, there was a short, chubby, middle-aged man, shiny under a gloss of sweat, who he had briefly seen with Ivan Lemokh a couple times from afar. They were never formally introduced, but now he was sitting at Ivan Lemokh's desk.

"Sit down, Alexei Romanovich Novikov," the man commanded, without looking up from whatever he was reading.

Alexei nervously did as told.

"My name is Arkady Leonovich Petrov," he introduced tiredly. "From now on, you'll be reporting to me."

"What happened to Ivan Ivanovich Lemokh?" Alexei asked nervously.

"You tell me." He finally looked up with a sneer.

"Tell you what? I don't know." For the first time, he realized it had been a while since he reported.

After a long unblinking glare, he asked, "Are you sure?"

"Of course I'm sure."

Petrov stared at him, squeezing the moment to its fullest before saying, "A couple nights ago, Lemokh had the audacity to send the police in to arrest Morozov."

"Send who where?"

267

"He sent the police to the Ulanov House without even telling me! Fortunately, the Armenian was gone. But he jeopardized everything on the ravings of some drunk!"

"Where was Morozov?"

"Apparently he got locked out and spent the night in some bathhouse nearby."

"I hadn't heard."

"I warned Lemokh about taking shortcuts. I didn't authorize him to do that!"

"Was he trying to get him to confess?"

"Not with Morozov! I went through this with him! I sent a boy in to do a man's job."

"What shortcuts did he take?"

"He installed some halfwit servant named Kamenev." Alexei remembered Morozov complaining about Kamenev—the drunken housekeeper.

"He's some incompetent brute who swore in some insane affidavit that the writer was a spy. Thank God I caught it before it got out of hand."

"He didn't tell me anything about it! I swear!"

"You're probably lying, but since Morozov has already gotten used to you, I don't have time to replace you without jeopardizing whatever progress we might've made." Petrov rose, walked around his desk, and sat on its edge so that he was staring down at Alexei. "This is because this is an extremely delicate case. I repeatedly emphasized this to Lemokh when I first assigned it to him, but clearly he didn't get it."

"I know Ivan was feeling great pressure," Alexei tried defending his friend.

"This isn't like the old days!" Petrov started yelling again. "The three signatures don't cut it anymore! Understand?"

"Yes sir."

"Yezhov was shot. All high-level arrests get passed around and thoroughly scrutinized nowadays. Zhdanov is going to meticulously check and double-check whatever he got and if he finds anything

268

fishy, who do you think gets released and who is arrested in his place?!"

"So," Alexei said hesitantly, "I report to you now?"

"That wasn't a rhetorical question!" he yelled furiously. "Who the hell do you think got arrested instead of the Armenian?!"

"Ivan?"

"Exactly. That leaves me and you! And I have no plans to get shot due to some over-zealous youth. Understand! Your job is to collect evidence and then you give it to me. That's it!"

"Yes sir."

"You tell me everything! That's your *only* job. Period."

"Will do."

Opening a file with the title: ARMENIAN on it, his new supervisor said, "It says here you are still active in the military."

"Yes sir, I was wounded in Rzhev last year. I'm still officially recuperating."

"Any unseen problems or lack of progress and I will have you back in uniform so quick it'll make your head spin."

"Yes sir!"

"So what's the latest with the Armenian?" the chubby man asked. "He was going to mention Darya's assignment but since Lemokh brought her into the case, Alexei wasn't sure if she was apart of the official investigation.

"Speak up!" Petrov barked.

"Morozov just asked me to write a book review," he finally said, unable to think of anything else to say.

"On who?"

"A poet from Leningrad — Anna Akhmatova."

"A poetry review?"

"Yes sir. He said it was to be a condemnation of her work."

"Has the girl helped?" Petrov asked out of the blue. "She's supposed to be a literary asset."

"What girl?" Alexei replied cautiously.

Petrov glanced at the file. "According to Lemokh's notes, a Ukrainian student, Darya Lebedova Kotova, was assigned to help you trap the Armenian, but I don't see any notes of her participation or reports from her. And since he's been granting her a free dorm and tuition it sounds like a good time to cut her loose."

"Oh, no! I'm sorry. Yes, Darya Kotova is on the team."

"You didn't recognize her name a moment ago," Petrov snarled.

"I just don't think of her as a girl. Darya's an integral part of this investigation."

"Integral, how?"

"Morozov fired the drunken housekeeper and hired her," Alexei said, grateful to hear that Darya was officially sanctioned.

"What else do you suddenly remember?"

"Just that he likes and trusts her."

"Why are there no reports of any of this?" He flipped through some pages.

"I told Lemokh everything."

"You told him! No! You must submit clearly handwritten reports every single day. I have to type my reports in triplicate, so the least you can do is a single handwritten report, and if you don't write it clearly you'll have to type it too!"

"Yes sir, sorry," he said nervously.

"Now write an update of everything you just told me about Kotova and her participation in all this."

"By participation, you mean..."

"Every conversation that she had with the Armenian, every sneeze, every twitch! In fact, have her write daily reports as well. We're paying her more than enough for them."

"Yes sir."

"So the next time I summon you, I'm expecting two clear handwritten reports, from you and from her – understand?"

"Yes sir."

"Dismissed," Petrov said in a military fashion, something Ivan never did. Alexei said that he was looking forward to working with him and exited.

59

Eric plodded down the hill like a tired grandparent trying to keep Anna in his sights as she raced through the mob wildly. About a hundred yards away in the crowd, he saw some tall, bare-chested, wavy-haired Adonis surrounded by a group of friends. He spotted Anna and opened his muscular arms as though summoning her.

Anna leaped into the air and he caught her with a big deep laugh. She kissed him full on the lips. She wrapped her bare thighs around his tight muscular waist. Then, after swinging her in a big wide circle, he lowered her onto his sleeping bag as though she were a Barbie Doll.

"So where the fuck were you!" she shouted. "We spent the past two days looking for you guys!"

"She's on brown... on the brown acid!" Eric yelled, racing over, trying to catch his breath.

"The festival only started last night," an attractive older blonde named Matilda joined in. It turned out this was Anna's legendary group of friends.

"This is Eric Stein, my high school classmate," Anna introduced them. "Eric, this is Rooster and gang."

While Anna with her shapely figure looked like a young woman in full bloom, standing next to her, Eric knew he still resembled a skinny kid. He modestly waved at Rooster's group, which consisted of three young women and two men, all long haired and older, in their twenties. They nodded back showing even less enthusiasm.

"I can't tell you how hard it's been, Roost!" She used her little girl tone as he caressed her arm. "We slept in a car and then a bag."

"You slept in a bag?" kidded one of the older hippies named Micah.

"A sleeping bag," Eric added.

"We lived like bums since we got here."

"Bums in bags?" repeated Micah, amused.

"We've been eating whatever crap we could find! Tell them, Eric!"

"We weren't really prepared for this," Eric replied, not adding that this was all her fault.

"Well you don't look like you're starving," muttered the attractive blonde Matilda, who Eric sensed was not as excited as the others to see her younger, more buxom rival.

"Rooster, are you going to offer us some chow or what?" Anna asked, looking at the smoky grill with various pots simmering on it.

"Sure, we got a little chicken gumbo and some wild rice that Jasmine made."

"What did I tell you?" she said to Eric proudly. "We'd be fine once they got here."

"So I guess you don't want to nap for later tonight?" he asked her softly, preferring their being alone.

"Nah, we'll be fine," she replied, still racing.

The hippies resumed their former conversation, which was about the moon launch just weeks earlier. Micah explained how the much smaller landing vessel discarded the towering fuel tanks once they broke free from the earth's gravitational pull.

This compelled Eric to realize *he* was little more than a propulsion system designed to shoot the tiny capsule called Anna to Rooster, her lunar target. Now that he had served his purpose he knew she'd rather he'd discreetly fall away as well.

He watched Anna as she grabbed a plastic bowl and started doling herself a large serving of the gumbo out of a big pot. All he could do was watch as Anna sat next to Rooster and asked him a million moronic questions: Were they here during the big rainstorm? Did they catch Richie Havens' amazing performance? When exactly did they arrive? Who had they seen perform? What time did they plan to leave? Was there any room for her to return in the car? She didn't include him in that question.

As Anna chirped away, still on the tail end of her little acid trip, Eric finally grabbed a bowl and spoon and scraped up the last crusty bits and drips of gumbo juice over the overcooked rice. He then retreated behind a tree and tried to savor the flavors of the tasty dish.

After about ten minutes he realized he could no longer hear Anna's needy, cloying voice. The two had vanished. After walking around, he saw that Anna had followed the hippie Adonis behind the tent out of view and they were making out. Rooster's strong arms were slithering around her sides like a pair of tropical snakes. Likewise, their tongues were entwined.

Fuck this! he thought, tossing his empty bowl to the ground. *She's officially on her own.* He walked all the way down to the pond, yanked up his sleeping bag and headed back to their former encampment, behind the foreign exchange students where he angrily shoved his bag back into the wind-torn lean-to. Though the festival was still in full swing and kids were still pouring in, he thought, *I came here to get laid and did it. I was never some rock-and-roll halfwit and I probably incurred some auditory damage being here this long. This is actually a perfect time to dash.* She had left him, so it was a guilt-free out. He had a comfortable margin of time to get back to the Bethel bus station and catch the last bus to the city. And since they weren't even halfway down the list of shitty bands, he should have no trouble getting a seat. And he wouldn't even have to lie to his mother on the phone tomorrow, it was a win-win.

Before he could collect his stuff, though, Amandine stopped by holding a plastic bowl filled with more lasagna!

"Those hog farmers are giving out freshly baked mountains of pasta, and no one's even on line!"

"Thanks," he said, reaching for it.

"No! This is mine," she said. "Get your own."

Hungry even after the tuna and hungrier still after the dregs of gumbo, Eric raced up the hill and onto the one short line. Before he could get near the front, the line came to a dead halt.

"Shit!" someone yelled out. Just five people away from the server, they ran out.

"Just hang on!" one of the Hog Farmers announced from behind the wooden counter. "Another pot is on its way."

"Another pot of what?" someone yelled back, but no one answered.

273

Eric waited ten minutes as the line lengthened behind him. He feared the worst. Maybe a can of beans this time. Then the line started moving again. When Eric finally got served, it was a big paper cup filled with some kind of soup. He automatically asked for a second cup. For his sick girlfriend.

"Everyone's got to get their own!" another Hog Farmer cited the rules. He eagerly slurped down several more spoonfuls. It wasn't bad, but he wasn't sure what it was. He slurped more, trying to categorize it. It seemed to taste differently with every bite. First he thought it was a chowder, then he came across small strands of chicken, so he thought it was chicken noodle. But at the bottom of the paper bowl he found lentils and beef. It turned out the Hog Farmers had poured every can that was donated into a giant pot.

60

Kasabian, Moscow, 1943

Haig Morozov was sitting at his desk at the university just before noon and tried reading his intern's clunky novel. Almost immediately, he was disturbed by the ringing of Alexei's phone from the outer office. As usual, the assistant was nowhere to be seen.

"Who is it!" he finally picked up his extension.

"Is this Mr. Morozov?" He could barely make out the faint voice breaking through the wall of static.

Before he could respond, the line went dead.

"I was out in the hall and thought I heard the phone ring," Alexei said, just returning from his first meeting with his new and terrifying boss.

"What's the status of the Akhmatova essay?" he asked.

"I've been following your advice and just zeroing in on suspicious lines," he began hesitantly.

The phone began ringing again. Morozov snatched it up before the assistant could, and he yelled, "What?"

"Mr. Haig Morozov?" Except for a repetitive pounding in the background, the gruff voice came in loud and clear.

"Speaking," he said.

"I'm calling from the Bureau of Prisons in Leningrad, specifically the Office of Records, in compliance with a request from Commissar Zhdanov's office."

"Oh," he said. He waved away his assistant.

"I got a request to give you an update of one of our prisoners."

"Yes?"

"A prisoner number K-2378-6140, named Yuvachyov." It was Voronsky's traitor who went under the alias Daniil Kharms.

"Go on."

"May I ask you a question?" the paper shuffler asked. "Are you the Armenian writer— Morozov-Kasabian?"

"Yes, I am."

"I'm Armenian too," said the clerk in Armenian. "I've enjoyed your work for years, sir."

"Thank you," Haig replied. "What can you tell me about Comrade Yuvachyov?"

"It says here he was arrested for spreading libelous and defeatist sentiments."

"Yeah, I know that part. I just want to know his current status."

"He pretended to be nuts," the fellow countryman said. "Do you know that part too?"

"No, how did he pretend to be nuts?" he asked.

"Personally that's what I would've done in his shoes," the clerk replied. "And he must've done a pretty good job because a military tribunal dumped him in the Kresty Prison psych ward."

"And from there he was shipped out to Novosibirsk?" Morozov anticipated, remembering what he learned from Voronsky and Zhdanov.

"Novosibirsk?" he said. "No, I don't see that."

"It doesn't say he was transferred?"

"No, there'd be a blue transfer sheet here. Oh, wait!" the clerk suddenly grew silent.

"What is it?" Morozov asked. He could hear the clerk shuffling more papers and then saying, "Hmmm."

"What?"

"My mistake, you're probably right. He probably was transferred."

"Transferred where?"

"Probably to Novosibirsk, like you said."

"When exactly was he transferred?" Morozov asked suspiciously.

"Not sure."

"What does that blue transfer sheet say?" Morozov tried not to lose his temper.

"Look, I just don't want to get in trouble."

"How would you get in trouble?"

"Why don't I send the file to the commissar's office and you can talk to him yourself?"

"Not necessary. Comrade, this isn't something regarding me personally. I've never even met this Yuvachyov fool. Is the blue form not..."

"There is no blue form." Lowering his voice to a whisper, the clerk said, "See the problem is, what I'm telling you isn't in the file. It's my own speculation. And I'm not supposed to speculate."

"From one Armenian to another," Morozov said softly, "just tell me off the record: What do you think?"

"Well, as I mentioned, there's a customary blue transfer sheet when people are moved from one facility to another and I don't see it here."

"Are you saying..."

"I'm not saying anything."

"But you speculated that he was transferred," Morozov replied.

"I just repeated what you said," the clerk replied and asked, "Where did you hear it?"

"I heard that his wife was informed of this."

"Okay, so maybe that's what happened. Maybe someone forgot to fill out the blue form."

"Well, let me ask you this," Morozov changed his tone. "Would there be a death certificate if he died?"

"Technically yes, they are supposed to include one, but I've never seen one."

"Never?"

"Almost never."

"So you're saying what exactly?"

"Unless there's a clerical error, it looks like Kharms never made it out of the psych ward of Kresty Prison."

"There must be some information in that goddamn file!"

"The last status report is dated February 2 of the past year."

"If he died why wouldn't they include a death certificate?"

"Look, I don't want to get pulled into this. All they include is a yellow entrance form and a blue transfer form signed by several people."

"Who?"

"The duty officer, his commanding officer, and the warden. Unless there's another transfer form I've come to assume that the exit date on the yellow form usually signifies that they died there."

Morozov couldn't follow him so he simply stated, "Do you think he was executed?"

"Absolutely not. They don't execute anyone anymore, but if they did there would've at least been a gray disciplinary report. You have to read between the lines a little. He wasn't executed."

"So where is he?"

"Think about it, comrade. They can't feed the law-abiding citizens. How are they supposed to feed prisoners accused of treason in the psych ward?" With that the Armenian clerical worker hung up.

The probable date of Kharms' death was over a year ago. He never should've pushed. Now he had some new information, so there was a new bit of ugly business. He had to track down old Voronsky and inform him that this children's book writer had died. Starving to death, giving someone nothing to eat for months on end actually sounded much worse than being quickly executed. Morozov went through his desk, located the old critic's work number and called him. He decided to simply tell him that the man passed away.

The female operator from Gosizdat greeted him.

"Aleksandr Voronsky please."

"Who?" He repeated the name and explained that Voronsky was a custodian. After a pause, the receptionist said that no one by that name worked there.

"Please inform Mr. Aleksandr Voronksy that it is with great regret that on February 23 of last year, his friend Daniil Kharms passed away."

"I told you!" the operator replied impatiently. "We don't have anyone name Voronsky working here."

"He called me from here just a few days ago."

"Sir, I don't know what to tell you."

Morozov suddenly hypothesized that perhaps due to his criminal record, he might be working under a false name. "Could you just give the message to the head of your custodial staff, maybe they could post the message in their locker room. Maybe one of them might know him."

The operator sighed, took the message, and Morozov thanked her. The job was done. After hanging up the phone, feeling some sense of relief, he got up and quietly walked into the outer office. Alexei was not at his desk, but the envelope containing the Akhmatova poems was on his blotter. Looking inside he saw several hastily handwritten pages. They were numbered lines that Alexei must've pulled from the stack of Akhmatova's poems.

He read them:

1) *As if with a straw you drink my soul...*

2) *One heart isn't chained to another...*

3) *Hail to thee, everlasting pain!*
The gray-eyed king died yesterday.

4) *Both sides of the pillow are already hot... I haven't slept all night.*

5) *We are all carousers and loose women here: How unhappy we are together!*

6) *Here everything is the same as before, just the same... Here it seems useless to dream.*

7) *I came to take your place, sister...*

8) *Weak is my voice, but my will isn't weakening...*

9) It's become easier for me without love...
10) I seldom think about you now.
And I'm not fascinated by your fate...
11) We don't know how to say goodbye-
We keep wandering arm in arm...
Give me bitter years of sickness,
Suffocation, insomnia, fever,
Take my child and my lover and my mysterious gift of song...
12) I don't know if you're living or dead –
whether to look for you here on earth
Or only in evening meditation,
when we grieve serenely for the dead.
13) A voice came to me. It called out comfortingly,
It said, "Come here.
Leave your deaf and sinful land.
Leave Russia forever.
I will wash the blood from your hands..."

The isolated lines by the old female poet touched Morozov. Even more though, he was impressed by his slow-witted assistant's sensitivity. He hardly thought Alexei was capable. Looking up, he saw him standing in the doorway with his typical mule-like expression.

"So how far along are you on the essay?" Morozov asked.

"I'm still exploring possible approaches of attack."

"For god's sake! You've isolated all the key lines here! You're not writing an arrest warrant, just a little poetry criticism."

Coming over, for the first time, Alexei saw the numbered verses, but had no idea what they were or how they got there.

"I just don't understand, sir, if no one is ever going to read her poetry," Alexei asked, "why am I even writing this?"

"Because we have a deal, you moron! My name is going to be on the byline, not yours! Now finish the goddamn essay!" Still angry about the whole Kharms debacle, Morozov grabbed his coat and valise with Alexei's novel in it and headed out the door.

61

Eric, NYC, 2001

During the last week of August, Eric Stein got an email from David Lande. The old man wrote that his trip across Russia had stiffened his resolve to build his dream project.

DavidLandesJr.@LandesPropertiesLLC.com:

"Slowly crossing the infinite space of Siberia felt like passing through time itself and made me aware of how brief life was, so, in short, I want to launch the IPO as soon as I get back which is Saturday, September 5. (I'm currently in Tokyo.) I've come to realize that we are only given enough time to erect our headstone and then it's over."

Inasmuch as Eric never saw Lande so firmly resolved, he used the opportunity to shift gears on the IPO. Over the course of the next week, his team at K&O cc'd countless messages filled with facts and figures to Merrill Lynch, the Lande Properties, and the various newly appointed financial officers at Jamaica Bay Estates LLC. Once the prospectus was finally cleared by the Davis Polk lawyers, Eric would have the completed draft of the IPO on his desk on Friday, September 7.

On that date, Eric emailed Lande that the complete prospectus was ready once and for all, and asked if he wanted to iron out all the details with the FAA before making the big launch.

DavidLandesJr.@LandesPropertiesLLC.com

I'm back in the States, but need a week to get my bearings. Due to my physical limitations I'd like to hold the signing at my office. Can you and your team join me on Monday, September 10 at 7:30 a.m.?

EricStein@Kaye&Oden.com

Absolutely! See you then!!!

On the night of September 9, Eric got a follow-up email:

DavidLandesJr.@LandeInc.com

Turns out I have my annual dental appointment tomorrow. Can we make it the same time on Tuesday?

EricStein@Kaye&Oden.com
See you Tuesday morning.

62

Alexei, Moscow, 1943

When Darya returned to Morozov's office, she snuck up behind Alexei sitting there, slowly studying the list of Akhmatova verses. He had no clue how he got the verses, or how to write a condemnation of them.

"I was looking for that," Darya replied, snatching the list out of his hands.

"You wrote this!" Alexei asked, surprised.

"Yes, I copied them out the other day while you were in the shower. I must've accidentally left it in the file."

"Why did you copy them?"

"I liked them. I would've copied them all but didn't have time."

"Damn it, these poems are highly classified."

"Too late," she kidded. "I sent them to the Germans."

"Morozov read your damned list. He thinks I wrote it and now he wants me to write a review condemnation based on your goddamned lines," he shouted at her. "And I have no clue what to do."

"Those are the most beautiful lines I could copy in the time you took to wash yourself," Darya elaborated.

"I don't care!" The pressure was getting to him. "I'm screwed! You're supposed to help me!"

"Alexei, she's a wonderful poet," Darya appealed. "Don't do this!"

"Are you willing to protect her in exchange for your tuition and your dormitory?" he asked. "Because if you don't help, you're going to be tossed out of here and I'm going to go be sent back to the front. And I'm not kidding!"

"Okay," Darya said, and with a short sigh, she let the hope go. Then she flipped through the loose pages of Akhmatova's photostats while muttering, "There was something."

281

"What?"

"There was one poem and I remember thinking that she was really pushing it." She finally held up one page. "Here. This is the closest thing I read that might be... a way to get her."

Alexei slowly read the poem aloud:

"Not for weeks or for months have we parted
But for years, Here at last is the day
That chill of true freedom has started
And the wreath at the temples arise gray.
There's an end to betrayal, to treason
And no more do you hear, rain or shine,
Irrefutable torments of reasons
For that unrivaled rightness of mine."

"If there's any chance of arresting her, it's with this poem."

"Okay, good. Write a critique and..."

"I can't do it! I won't!"

"Darya!"

"I've written reviews for you and helped with your novel, but I can't do this! I just can't! You do it. It should be easy. Just read the words! They're the very description of treason!"

Alexei snatched up the pages and mouthed the words, reading it slowly. Then he nodded his head.

"It sounds like she's attacking the tzar."

"She wrote this poem recently. There is no tzar."

"What exactly am I supposed to attack?"

"She writes about the end to betrayal, to treason," Darya said. "How much clearer can she be?"

"Who exactly is committing this betrayal and treason?"

"Who do you think?" Darya asked.

"Counterrevolutionaries!" Alexei replied.

Darya smirked and nodded her head. "How about the chill of true freedom... what does that sound like to you?"

"I don't know!"

"Don't you see! It's not freedom. She can't call it captivity or tyranny, can she?"

"Why not?"

"'Cause she'll get arrested!"

"By who?" he asked, bewildered.

"By us! Isn't that what we're supposed to do?"

"What does," he read the line slowly, "'the chill of true freedom has started' mean?"

"It's irony!" she replied. "She's being ironic! There is no true freedom here!"

"Of course there is! What are you talking about?"

"You know what has a chill," Darya hollered, "Something that's dead! Freedom is a hot and living thing!"

"Not necessarily in Russia. Everything here is cold!"

"My god, you're tone deaf," Darya said, as she pulled on her coat.

"Where the hell are you going?"

"I have to fix a *courageous* and *decent* man his dinner. See irony in that!" She stormed out of his house.

The more Alexei read and reread Anna Akhmatova's betrayal poem the more perplexed he became. He initially thought that Darya must be wrong—the poet was referring *to* the counter revolutionaries, but the "unrivaled rightness of mine" seemed far too egotistic, and he realized it had to be just the opposite. Was she making a confession?

He sensed she was mocking something, but her language, her very voice was clearly out of touch with contemporary locutions and ideas. Although she had some interesting poetic phrasing, it was hardly anything he'd call incriminating. He had no clue what Darya found so incendiary. The poem was baffling at best. Darya had to be wrong.

What he found most unforgivable about Akhmatova's work was what it lacked. For the past few years, her city was suffering from one of the most barbaric sieges in modern history, one that was slowly killing her fellow Leningraders, yet she didn't write a single poem about it! He took out a pen and scribbled a draft of his condemnation:

"Anna Akhmatova's poetry is largely sentimental and irrelevant, but the most egregious aspect is its selfishness. While her city is slowly being starved to death by fascist monsters, all she can focus on is the many loves who have abandoned her and the countless shades of melancholia. In her many poems, instead of mentioning the vast struggle of her great, beleaguered race, she dwells on her own personal frustrations. Is it any wonder why all her mawkish poems are filled with teenage heartbreak? What man would waste any time on such a whiny and needy woman?"

He went on to insert some lines from a few of her moodier poems and, counting out three hundred words, he was soon done. It was what Morozov had asked for, a straightforward condemnation that served the minimal requirements.

After the piece was finished, Alexei began to write a detailed status report of that day's progress for Petrov. Although she didn't actually help, Alexei fabricated some details on how Darya had assisted him with the case. He hoped it would be enough for his new boss. Soon as he finished it, he found himself remembering that Ivan pressured him to persuade Darya to entice the writer in some sexual escapade. He warned Ivan against it. Now he wondered if his old friend and former supervisor was dead or in prison and what would happen to him and Darya if they didn't find some way to trap Morozov soon.

63

Eric, Woodstock Festival, 1969

Checking the time, Eric realized he could still catch the eight-thirty-five bus, but feeling calmer after eating, he decided it was only fair to inform the cheating bitch of his imminent departure—even though she probably wouldn't even notice him missing. He decided to leave the information with the foreign exchangers and let them tell her. But when he returned to their torn lean-to, he saw Sandrine all alone reading a book. All the others must've gone down to watch whoever was currently performing.

"Could you do me a favor and tell Anna that I've gone back to the city?"

She replied in French. Her book was in French and hard as he tried, he was unable to impart the message.

"Isla, Rolland, down to music," she struggled and pointed to the stage.

He again headed down toward the stage where Mountain was performing. *What a stupid name for a band!* he thought. *If The Beatles were called Mountain they never would've made it.* As he reached the concert area, he found that it was as packed as a rush hour subway train. No foreign exchangers in sight but suddenly, a couple hundred feet from the stage, he spotted Rooster who was a head taller and a brain dumber than everyone around him. He watched him, rocking in the distance. Angling slowly up around the human penis, he could see most of his entourage including Anna also dancing. Eric slowly pushed through until he was only about twenty feet behind her. He tried calling to her over the deafening music, hoping simply to wave goodbye. But it was just too loud.

As he shoved closer still, he heard, "You're a cheap ass slut, aren't you!" He realized Matilda, who was just in front of him, was hollering angrily at her.

"We were already together, you dumb cunt!" Anna shouted back just in front of Eric without turning around to see him. "I was balling him for two weeks before your skanky old ass ever met him!"

"And you left him, whore!" the blonde fired back. "We've been fucking for the past week. He's done with you, bitch!"

"This is great!" Rooster mouthed cluelessly, rocking his head to the music.

"Why don't you go fuck yourself, you fat slut!" Matilda shouted into her rival's ear.

The song that Mountain was performing abruptly ended just as Anna smacked Matilda across the face and yelled, "FUCK YOU, CUNT!"

After a beat, everyone applauded.

But all heads in the immediate vicinity spun around. Before Matilda could recover, Rooster jumped between them.

"She just hit Matty!" said one of the other members of Rooster's little cult.

The human penis stared at Anna in disbelief as Matilda started wailing painfully as though she had been stabbed.

"Not cool!" said Micah, the oldest male in Rooster's hippy tribe. Rooster hugged Matilda, holding her in his arms.

Instantly aware that all eyes were on her, Anna turned and pushed her way through the crowd. All she could do was retreat. It was over. She was unofficially expelled from the community of love.

"Oh shit," Eric muttered and gave chase.

When she squeezed out of the human gridlock, she just walked numbly up the slope, her eyes fixed painfully to the ground. Eric circled around and lingered before her, looking away. In a minute she nearly bumped into him.

"Where the fuck did you go!" she shouted, instead of hello.

"I was watching Mountain. They were great..."

"They sucked!" she shot back. He could see her eyes were red. "I was looking all over for you."

"I kind of felt like you wanted to be with your friends."

"They are so fucking phony. That peace and love shit! What bullshit! Hippies are living proof that rednecks fuck goats!"

"Hey, I like goats!" he replied.

"Then go fuck one!" she yelled, suddenly transferring her anger onto him.

"Hey, they were *your* friends," he said, tired of all her crap.

"I fucking HATE them!" she hissed, and almost as an afterthought, she added, "and to be honest, I'm pretty tired of you!"

"And Matilda was tired of you screwing around with Rooster and called you on it." Eric shot back, sick of her shit. "That's why you slapped her, isn't it?"

"Who told you that? It's a dirty lie!"

"I saw it!" he yelled back. "Just now! So don't bullshit me, Anna!"

"Well, I was with him first!" She instantly broke down and started weeping. "I mean, I know I should've told you but..."

"Told me what?"

"I met Rooster about a month ago in Washington Square Park and we dated. But he needed a place to crash so I sort of introduced him to Matty. I mean, she had her own place in the Alphabets, so he crashed there but we kept seeing each other on the side."

"While he was dating Matty?"

"He was just fucking her raggedy ass to pay the rent, but we had something real!"

"I really don't care," Eric said tiredly. "Why the hell did you even invite me up here?"

"'Cause Matty's brother, Micah, owns the van, so I couldn't come up with them. But this was all my idea. I told them about it, so we agreed to meet up here." She spoke through tears and sobs.

"So you used me?"

"Used you! I asked everybody I know for a ride and you called me back! I told you my plan was to meet my friends up here and ride back with them."

"But we were intimate for the past two days," he pointed out. "And you never said you had a boyfriend."

"Look, I didn't know we were going to get it on. I mean, I just figured we'd come up here, meet up with them, and listen to music."

"How would you feel if after making it with you, I met some girl up here and started getting it on with her?" he asked.

287

"Okay! I'm sorry if I'm just a dumbass fat slut! Okay! Is that what you want to hear?" she started crying. "I'm a stupid fucking cunt. Does that make you feel better!" She began bawling until people started looking at them.

He felt embarrassed so after a minute he stepped close and hugged her and whispered, "I just felt kinda hurt, you know."

"I didn't fuck you for the ride, okay? I'm not a skank!" she said softly. "I liked you and that's why we did it! But god help you if you tell anyone at school!"

"I won't, so please stop saying that!"

Although he was still furious, she had a point. She never made any offer of sex. And she did mention connecting with friends up here. And looking back at it, she all but described her heartbreak in that sappy poem she read. She even mentioned Rooster by name. He just didn't want to believe what he was hearing. But still they did ball, they spent an entire night balling, which according to Arnold Toynbee's study of societies, is tantamount in some Western societies to an engagement and in some tribal societies, balling is marriage itself! And though she turned out to be a user, he was actually grateful that he was able to say to Josh and his friends that he finally lost his virginity.

"I got to tell you," he said. "I was just about to leave."

"Leave!"

"Yeah, the last bus is going back to the city at eight thirty-five. I can just make it."

"No way, man!" she said. "I mean, I'm not leaving 'til I fucking see Janis Joplin and Jimi Hendrix!"

"Well you can stay. I mean, you have the French Foreign Legion," he said, referring to the foreign exchangers. "And you can hold onto my sleeping bag." Now that there was little chance of Rooster balling her in Josh's bag, he didn't mind lending it out.

"Come on, I'm just a girl! I can't stay here alone without you." She employed her little girl voice. "We're a team! You have to stay!"

"Sorry, but all obligations officially ended when Rooster fingered you!" he shot back.

"He did no such thing! We just kissed! Forget about all that bullshit! Have you ever heard Hendrix, I mean, he's fucking mind-blowing! I mean, it's truly transcendental!"

"Yeah, but he's the very last act and at this rate he probably won't be performing 'til next week. And I frankly don't like rock music enough to endure another night of this." Eric started walking back up their little lean-to.

The thought of remaining bothered him even more than being cuckolded by Rooster.

"Are you kidding?" she asked in disbelief. "This is the best thing ever!"

"No it's not. It's awful! There's no food, no privacy. I'm filthy. And I have a nonstop headache!"

"You're with the coolest people ever!"

"We're all stuck in this big outdoor prison."

"This is a huge outdoor party."

"Bullshit! This is like Auschwitz with loud music!"

"Listen to me, I know I haven't been easy, but I promise you, one more day and it'll be the best twenty-four hours of your life."

"Look," he said, hoping to convince her to join him. "I haven't had a solid meal or a night's sleep in three days. I've been having diarrhea. I'm achy and wet, and my clothes are filthy and..." As he felt his pockets he suddenly realized that his lumpy wallet was missing. "Oh fuck!"

"What?" she asked as he frantically looked through his pockets.

"My wallet!"

"What about your wallet?!"

"You took my wallet!" he instantly deduced insanely.

"I what?!!!"

"Give it back!" he yelled, no longer trusting this cheating scammer. She must've grabbed it in order to hold him there.

"What the hell are you talking about?!"

"You have it in your pocket! Don't deny it!"

"Check me," she said, clenching her wallet in her right hand and holding them both in the air. After he thoroughly patted her down, she said, "Satisfied?"

He snatched her wallet out of her hand.

"What the hell are you doing?!"

"How much money do you have?"

"Around ten bucks," she replied. He opened her wallet and counted eight dollars and forty-six cents. Not even enough for a single ticket.

"Fuck!" he handed it back at her.

"Don't worry," she said facetiously. "I won't fucking abandon you."

"You won't abandon me? We're both abandoned!"

He couldn't believe he was going to have to spend more time with these spongy-headed hippies in this noisy swamp, at the mercy of this manipulative tramp! All the frustrations of the past two days culminated in him yelling: "I fucking HATE rock and roll!"

64

Kasabian, Moscow, 1943

As Haig Morozov walked home, all he could think was that although the arrests had slowed down, the Refinement was never going to completely end. Although Darya had dinner waiting for him, he was too disturbed by the thought of the child book writer starving to death and having to tell Voronsky. In fact, he was in no mood to even deal with the always cheerful Darya. So instead of going to the Ulanov home, he just kept walking into the empty night.

For years, Morozov wanted to write a great novel, his own updated *Brothers Karamazov*, in which Russia would be the main character. But he knew such a book would never get published and would probably get him arrested. Still he kept returning to the idea, writing it in his head: His great nation would be represented first as an abused child, beaten by his tzar father who allowed its aristocracy to molest the boy. He'd be bullied by his school teachers who'd be the secret police. They'd punish him capriciously for no real reason, constantly tossing him in detention. The child would grow into a scarred and deeply scared youth, who, on one desperate night, would finally lash out and kill his father.

And just like that, the boy would become head of the household. He would want to learn from his father's mistakes. He'd want to correct all his father's injustices and be a good father himself some day. He'd want to create a new order for his children and his children's children, a new freedom from all brutal fathers. Unfortunately, the father still had brothers, his White Army uncles were still alive and vengeful. He'd be repeatedly forced to beat them back. If this wasn't enough, counterrevolutionary cousins would try to undermine his autonomy from within. So the young man would have to be on his toes, hitting others before they got him.

Raised in this increasingly treacherous world, his physical wounds would heal, but irreparable psychological damage would've been done to him. Even though the young, slightly demented man still harbored hopes for a happy future, by the time he reached his late twenties, he understandably would grow steadily paranoid. In place of his once innocent demeanor would be a sinister temper. As he keeps avenging his enemies he soon comes to relish it, growing into a bonafide sadist. By middle age, the man that is Russia has developed an unquenchable thirst for the blood of his newly born children. Where the initial victims were once strong and real enemies who deserved their fate, the new focus of his rage would be the easy targets, the slow and awkward ones who lacked guile and were unable to defend themselves.

Suddenly. peals of laughter awoke Morozov to the fact that he was on a dark street. Lost in his thought, he had ventured much further than intended. A couple of older women were on the corner, chatting, huddled in a deep doorway. Their loose faces were streaked with garish cosmetics. Among them was the pear-shaped Persian — the painted women who he first saw with Critter a while ago. Although she wasn't young or pretty, she had dark, alluring eyes heightened by sharp, black brows. In the night, her shapely red lips, so thick and full, popped out. It was easy to understand why Islamic men wanted them under veils.

As he kept staring, she tilted her head back just a bit and parted her lips, revealing brown teeth that were snaggled and missing. The tip of her tongue flicked a bit.

"Five rubles?" he asked just above a whisper.

"Seven," she countered. "Up front." He nodded and she led him in silence a block away into a small, dark rooming house, then up a long narrow flight of rickety steps. The entire building seemed to creak and shift underfoot as though they were in an old wooden ship. Finally they reached the unlit top floor that ended at the roof door, which had a small panel of unwashed glass in its center.

He counted out the rubles. She rolled them up and slipped them into some invisible pocket then turned around. Shoving her ass upward she put her hands up against the roof door frame and stared out the little window over the low unlit rooftops. He stopped her before she could lift up the rear of her long, frayed dress. Gently he rubbed his hands down along her ample thighs. He caught her face in the dirty square of glass on the door: Her eyes were clenched. She was biting her lips, braced for come what may. Although her skin was splotched and wrinkled, it struck him more as an expression of sadness rather than age. For a shining instant something about her, her anguished expectation of pain and pleasure, reminded him of poor Masha. Something far sadder than he could ever imagine must've brought her to stand prone for defiling. He pondered how many hard hands and penises had pawed and penetrated her in the course of her life.

She didn't budge as he gently massaged her hips and caressed his fingers up along the edges of her loose body. He ran his lips along her neck and the tips of his fingers down along the top of her brassiere, freeing her loose breasts. His left hand played with her dark brown nipples as his right hand came down, pulling up the front of her dress. His fingernails slowly combed through her ample pubic hair.

"Putting it in or what?" she asked tiredly.

"This'll do for now," he finally whispered.

In another moment, both were outside walking in different directions. He hadn't even unzipped his trousers.

65

Eric, Woodstock Festival, 1969

"DID ANYONE FIND A LOST WALLET?!" Eric hollered to all packed around him when Mountain finally ended their set. "Anyone see a lost wallet!" None responded. It was too dark to even see the muddy ground.

Eric manically shoved through the crowd trying to retrace his steps. Without his money there was no chance of buying a ticket out of this loud and slippery hell. After walking around slowly in the darkness for about fifteen minutes, staring at the muddy earth, the next band, the Grateful Dead, took the stage. Looking around in the crowd, Eric suddenly realized that he had lost all trace of Anna. Feeling a hopeless panic, he screamed out her name.

"I'm right here!" he heard in the distance.

Eric looked up the slope and saw her walking toward him, extending a paper plate with rice and beans to him. Only when he saw it did he realize he was starving.

"No fork or spoon?"

"They ran out," she said.

"Where'd you get it?"

"The pig people," she pointed up the hill.

"Did you get some for yourself?"

"I'm good."

Using the tips of his fingers he brought the plate to his mouth and scooped the bland food in. Then, seeing her eyeing the food, he said he was done and gave the plate back. In a moment she spooned the rest down her gullet.

"You know, they added some new shower stalls," she said, pointing up the slope.

"Really?" She was being uncharacteristically kind.

"Yeah, no line if we dash now."

Eric tiredly accepted the loss of his wallet. Both commented that they felt dirty and clammy, so they returned to the semi-transparent lean-to, grabbed one of the damp children's t-shirts he had found and hiked up to the newly installed showers stalls only to discover a long line had formed. They got on anyway and waited for almost an hour in the dark as they got closer, to the end where they discovered that everyone had a two-minute water limit. Once inside the stall, on the floor, he discovered a tiny button of soap to use on his armpits. After little more than a chilly baptism of water, they toweled off. Then they dressed and hiked back down to the stage in the dark where Anna pointed out a dry spot on the grass that had just opened up.

"I really miss clean, laundered clothes," Anna whispered.

"Me too."

They took a seat and listening to the Grateful Dead, Anna tried not to think of Rooster, and Eric tried to forget he was completely broke and miles from home.

"So," he blurted out in the middle of one ridiculously long and clumsy guitar riff. "Do you think you can ask your friend if she can give us a ride home?"

"No fucking way!" she said tensely. "Fuck Rooster and the van he rode in on!"

"No, not him, Isla."

"Oh, the exchangers," she said.

"If you'd rather not, I'll ask them," he said.

"No, it'll probably be best if I do it alone," she sighed.

"You want me nearby?" he asked.

"No, just stay here and enjoy the music. I'll come back when it's done."

After twenty minutes of hating himself for losing his wallet and finally just listening to the Dead, Eric found himself unimpressed. They were still playing when Anna finally came dashing back down the slope in the darkness.

"Bad news. They're not going to New York," she said, winded. "They're heading up to Boston."

"You're kidding!"

"Sorry, nothing's working today." She appeared clearly agitated. Eric could see her looking up the hill repeatedly.

"Did you run into Rooster again?" he asked.

"No, I saw someone else even worse."

"You have a lot of angry exes."

"No, this creep dated my mother. Then the guy tried coming on to me."

"You're kidding!"

"Nope."

"Where is he?" he asked, looking around, concerned.

"Up near the tents." She pointed. "A gray-haired prick."

"Oh shit!" Eric said, wondering if he'd have to fight some older man now.

"It's okay. He's with some other fat fuck. The two stand out like a pair of sore thumbs. He didn't see me, but I can spot him a mile away."

"Maybe we should report him to one of the troopers," Eric suggested. "I saw some along the road."

"No, I just need to keep away from him," she said. "But listen, I saw something else and figured out a way we can easily get home."

"How?"

"There were a whole bunch of people lining the road, holding signs or just waiting for people to get into their cars then asking for rides back to the city."

"That's not a bad idea," he said.

"There must be a million people here. And ninety-nine percent of them are going back to New York. There must be one car or truck with some space for two, and we look like a sweet pair of innocent kids."

"Maybe," he said, not revealing that he knew that if they did this, they'd be murdered within hours. The only other safe idea Eric had was to appeal directly to the troopers for help. If worse came to worst, he could call his mom—which would put him and Josh in serious hot water—but she could wire money to the local Western Union.

They listened to the Dead or, more particularly, watched the outline of a bunch of stoned kids dancing mindlessly in the dark to them. Before they were done, Eric nodded off. When he awoke, Creedence was leaving the stage and Janis Joplin was just coming on. Anna was fast asleep, snoring next to him.

"Hey Anna!" he yelled. "Get up, it's what's-her-name!"

"Oh shit!" she said, barely able to open her eyes.

"It's Janis!" he said.

"Okay," she said, sitting upright with eyes wide open, but after a few minutes she was nodding off again.

"I thought you didn't want to miss this!" Eric said, waking her up again.

"I don't!" she bolted up. Janis was singing her second song but, hard as she tried, Anna couldn't keep her eyes open. She loved listening to Janis' rough, raw voice. It slowly melded into a blurry audible texture and soon became a wonderful pillow to sleep upon. She and Eric were periodically awakened by the booming moments of Sly and the Family Stone. Back to sleep and then the sun rose. Eric awoke for a moment during the end of "White Rabbit," but went right back to sleep again. For him, only weird dreams bubbled out of the percolating cauldron of incredible sounds.

66

Kasabian, Moscow, 1943

Back in 1924, shortly after his beloved Masha had vanished in the Ukraine, Morozov began getting his short stories published in steadily more prestigious magazines throughout Russia. Soon he finished his first novel, *The Worker from the Caucasus*. It earned him favorable reviews and growing influence. "A genuine hero from the revolution," one critic said. Another wrote, "Young Armenia has found its voice." He won the prestigious Vittig Award, then several smaller accolades. Just as steadily, he found himself moving up the party ranks, getting a minor teaching post at the Moscow State University, but the job would only last for a year.

After Lenin's death, the party itself was rapidly changing, growing increasingly more capricious, at times suspicious, at times forgiving, but steadily audacious, echoing the sentiments of those in the Politburo as they slowly jockeyed for power.

Although his father had wanted him to shun his Armenian past and embrace Russian pride, the older Morozov grew, the more nervous he became amid the perilous whirlwind of Moscow politics and the more he found himself taking shelter in his paternal heritage. As a Russian in Moscow he was lost in the crowd, but as an Armenian he stood out. He read everything he could on the history of ancient Armenia, and its importance in the region. When the great Roman Empire in the East had flourished, he was happy to discover that an Armenian Emperor, Leo, had actually ascended to the Byzantine throne.

The tiny, landlocked wedge of a country that happened to be strategically located in the southernmost tip of Russia was all that was left of the kingdom, which was founded four millennia ago. At its peak, its territory had extended from the Mediterranean to the Caspian, almost to the Black Sea.

One day, his old friend and colleague from Sverdlov University, Aleksandr Sergeyevich Shcherbakov, inquired as to whether he had ever traveled to Yerevan. When he said that he had, adding that he had turned down a teaching post there, Shcherbakov asked if he spoke the mother tongue.

"Of course, my father taught me when I was growing up."

Aleksandr said the party desperately needed someone down there who they could trust.

"For what?" he asked. Despite the fact that Shcherbakov hadn't even published a book, everyone liked him, so he had steadily risen to a prestigious post of the growing Writer's Union. Recently he had been put in charge of the Caucasus region. He explained that the Union needed someone to represent Moscow in their southernmost outpost.

"You'd be perfect for it. Everyone in the party trusts you and you're famous enough to influence your countrymen down there."

"Is this a permanent position?"

"Only the great Koba can grant that," he replied.

"But you're in charge of the region?"

"These are all Comrade Stalin's jobs, no one else's. I'll put you in touch with Andrei Zhdanov. He'll get you a meeting."

"Zhdanov?" he asked nervously.

"Just look Andrei in the eye and ask him if you could help organize the Writers Union down in Armenia. Confidentially, he's not that bright, but he's easy to work with," he explained. "He just wants someone to blame if all goes wrong."

That was how he first met Zhdanov. The two had a long talk about the function of literature in the new communist state. Or rather the commissar talked and he listened. Morozov knew exactly what the man wanted to hear so he said it. The commissar quickly endorsed Haig's appointment, personally introducing him to the Great Leader.

Although he knew of the great man going back to the Revolution, Stalin really had made little impression upon him. Of the many heavenly bodies orbiting around the great sun of Lenin, he was at best one of the outer planets. Lunz, who had briefly worked with Stalin on the expropriation committee years earlier, had referred to him as the Revolution's Strong Man, and said that the only reason he was appointed to the General Secretariat of the Party was because no one perceived him as a serious contender for any significant job.

After Lenin's sudden passing, the founders of the party—Zinoviev, Kamenev, Trotsky and Bukharin—spent years jockeying for his power while Stalin remained in the shadows. Although the politburo was divided by those to the left and those to the right, throughout the 1920s, they compromised and humanely navigated Russia from capitalism to communism through the New Economic Policy (NEP). It was Stalin who finally declared that it was time to cut capitalist ties and make Russia the communist state all had envisioned—enacting his ruthless policies of collectivism and steadily crushing all those who resisted. After he got his appointment, Morozov remained silent as the government grew increasingly autocratic; different colleagues shook their heads in horror at some of Stalin's actions, but none protested. "This would never have happened if Lenin was still alive," many said as the government edicts steadily grew more ruthless.

The final genuine attempt to neutralize the Georgian ruler was made by one truculent old-timer, Martemyan Ryutin, a candidate member of the Central Committee. Stalin's final endgame occurred when the economic visionary of the NEP, Nikolay Bukharin, was put on trial. That's when Ryutin rallied some of the old Bolsheviks for a final stand. They initiated a coordinated campaign against Stalin, trying to oust him, but by then it was too late. After Ryutin was arrested, the great Zinoviev followed, then all the others fell like dominoes. With Stalin as victor, all believed that at least the arrests would wind down. Like other kings, they assumed that now that he confidently won the crown, he'd grant amnesty to all transgressors in order to unify his kingdom.

But it was not to be. Stalin's protégé Sergey Kirov, the man who many felt might have become his successor, was suddenly and mysteriously assassinated. The Great Leader explained that the counter-insurgency was far from over. Indeed it had only just begun. He warned his countrymen that a vast nation-wide conspiracy was underway to extinguish the communist hope and take over the largest and greatest nation in the world. He unleashed his bloody dwarf, Nikolai Yezhov, the newly appointed head of his NKVD who was in charge of "rooting out all the counterrevolutionaries."

The Great Refinement—as Haig called it—had begun.

Luckily for Morozov by this point, he had kissed Stalin's ring and was firmly in his camp—his man in charge of the Armenian Writers Union. By the late 1930s, amid widening waves of mass arrests, Morozov no longer saw himself as a writer, but rather as a professional survivor. His only priority was to get through this at any cost.

During this time, despite what was going on around him, Morozov read about the horrible drought occurring in the Ukraine. Though it was not far away, there were no shortages of food there. He heard the rumors that this was Stalin's private retaliation for their disloyalty, but he preferred the official reports. On a positive note, he hoped that the famine might compel his beloved Masha to finally make contact, and request help for her and her child. By this point, his books were on shelves all over Russia—they all listed his home in Yerevan, so it would be easy for her to track him down. He'd be glad to use his acquired influence to make sure she and her family were safe. Of course he never got a call or a letter. All he could do was pray that she and her kid were okay. At one cultural event he was introduced to an artist, Alexei Rodchenko. He immediately asked if he was from the Ukraine and was related to a Masha Rodchenko.

"Alas, no, Saint Petersburg is my hometown. No living Mashas in my family."

When it was announced that the Ukrainian Writers Union was holding its third annual conference and it was extending invitations to the neighboring republics—provided they pay their own way—Morozov, as head of the Armenian Writers Union, pulled strings to go.

It was a four-day trip, a train to Batumi, then a ferry up along the Black Sea to Odessa. When he stepped off the boat, he was surprised to see government agents checking large parcels and crates. Innocently, he inquired what exactly they were looking for.

"Your papers," said an aggressive agent in Russian. He barely got them out before the man snatched them out of his hands.

Upon seeing that he was a founding member of the Armenian Communist Party, his papers were returned and he was ushered out. Immediately he suspected something was up. As he strolled down the streets of Odessa, he saw folks malingering along the sidewalks, sitting on curbs, leaning in doorways. He thought they were vagrants, mainly men, in loose, worn clothes, hollow-cheeked, emaciated. He heard the famine was bad, but this wasn't the first time crops had turned. People had survived them before. He stopped at a nearby diner, took a seat at a table and ordered a bowl of chicken soup.

He barely noticed the bedraggled children quietly queuing up in the rear of the place. When someone finished eating, the child at the head of the little line raced up to the vacated plate and licked it clean, then went back to the rear. When Morozov realized this, he set his spoon down leaving his bowl half full for the next kid on the line, and departed before he'd see which child would get it.

Finally boarding his train to Kiev, he thought things didn't seem too bad. But, as the train would pull into the small towns and villages along the way, through his window he'd spot groups of men and women in baggy outfits with sunken eyes and hollow-cheeks. They could be lingering on the platforms in a daze, lying on benches, occasionally spread out inexplicably on the ground. It was the strangest thing he ever saw, an island of starvation in a sea of well-fed people. The train pulled into one station and a portly, well-dressed man took a seat across from him. The gentleman checked his pocket watch, took off his hat, and unfolded a newspaper which he began to read. Morozov reviewed the short scholarly essay he was going to present on the achievements of the Armenian Writers Union and its relationship to neighboring unions in the Caucasus. Halfway through it, he casually looked out the window as the train was still sitting in the station. A tall, pale, sunken-cheeked woman in a shawl was standing before him like a ghost.

When their eyes met, she opened her mouth and pointed inside. He held his hand open, gesturing that he had no food. In another moment, a railroad official came and shooed her away.

"I'm told it's worse in Kazakhstan," said the older gentleman sitting across from him, still reading.

"It's odd," Morozov replied. Food was in short supply in Armenia as well, but he hadn't seen anyone starving.

"That's why I don't leave the house without my newspaper," replied the older man, holding it up like a shield.

Morozov was hoping the older man might comment on the situation but Morozov didn't dare share his thoughts.

As soon as he arrived in Kiev, he pulled out the only letter he ever got from Masha and had a taxi take him to an address on Melnikov Street, where she had lived ten years earlier. It was a small apartment building. Once there, he knocked on the door and found a family who had just moved in. They never met or heard of Masha

Rodchenko. He brought along four pictures he had of her and showed them. They had no idea who this young woman or her child were. He located an older super, who remembered the pretty young girl and her baby from a decade earlier, but he had no idea what had become of them.

"She wasn't very friendly, but she was very pretty," he said.

"Did you see her with her husband?" Haig asked.

"I never saw the husband but I think I remember her saying he was working in Odessa. Maybe she moved there."

"Do you have any records of how long she stayed? Maybe a forwarding address?"

"Sorry, no." The superintendent then turned and left.

As Morozov walked through the city, he thought, I know she still has to be here somewhere. I feel it. She probably walked down these very streets in the past few days. He carefully checked everyone and kept turning around hyper-vigilant, not wanting to miss a single face. I bet one of these people know her. He began to utter her name aloud as he passed others, "Masha Rodchenko, Masha Rodchenko..."

Suddenly, he had a brainstorm and dashed into a nearby pharmacy where he was able to browse through the pages of the local phone directory and see if he could look her up. There was an entire page of Rodchenkos, a popular name. His heart began pounding as he counted out no fewer than six Masha Rodchenkos. One of them had to be her! Hope renewed, he made change, went to the pay phone in the rear and started dialing them up, one by one.

Each voice that answered the phone was male. Two said women named Masha were their wives. But neither of these women matched the description of his Masha. A third man said his mother's name was Masha. Three others denied knowing any Masha at all. They weren't sure why that name was posted in the directory. In all three cases, in the event that the men might be lying, Morozov explained that if his friend Masha did live there, he could help her. He could get food for her. One of the men then added that he actually had a cousin named Masha.

"How old is she?"

"In her sixties," he replied.

"No, she's too old," Morozov said.

"Oh, I mean she's forty!" he revised.

"Does she have any children?" Morozov asked desperately.

"Please," he finally broke down. "Our rations aren't enough. If you can spare some food!"

Morozov delicately hung up.

Since he still had a couple hours before reporting for the conference, he hiked around the capital city. A lot of lean, lanky people walked, slept, and lounged along the public squares, just trying to look inconspicuous. After a while he realized the starving population here was probably no fewer than anywhere else in the country. Turning a corner, reaching one small park, he saw something that surprised him. Some smartly dressed man, possibly a tourist, was holding a big circular loaf of black bread. Morozov paused as the man began breaking the loaf apart. When a youth caught his eye, he tossed a chunk of bread on the ground. The kid picked it up, when he started eating it, others came over. The man kept tearing and tossing pieces of bread. Soon others were racing over and snatching it up as though it were gold.

Before the feeder finished his offerings, a well-dressed man started running toward him, chasing him off. He had to be an official trying to suppress the appearance of the famine.

That was seven years before the Nazis invaded Ukraine; he could only wonder what it must be like now. They had sent in countless Panzer divisions, which had decimated the capital, far from the safety of Moscow. Civilian death rates were staggering out there.

Walking down one empty, poorly lit street not far from the Moskva River, Morozov saw an endless procession of military trucks rumble by one after the next: A steady interval of headlights stretched as far as the eye could see. Before him in the distance, Morozov spotted a bright square of light revealing a small diner, the only shop still open. Through the greasy glass he saw someone eating. After remembering his trip to Kiev during the famine and all those sad children, Morozov found himself feeling hungry.

As the lone patron was leaving, he held the door open for Haig who went inside. He hung up his coat, scarf, and hat and took a seat away from the window. The place was little more than one long Formica counter that ran parallel to a narrow stainless steel kitchen. The cook who doubled as a waiter said, "We're serving dinner."

"Great," he said. "Got any vodka?"

"Dinner's one ruble, wine is two rubles." He nodded yes.

A moment later, a bowl of stew was placed before him. It was a watery mix filled with hairy strands that had to be chipped beef. Bits of potatoes, shreds of carrot, and strips of cabbage were just visible. A hard crust of rye bread and a sour cup of burgundy in a water glass followed. Usually he began with a sip of wine, but this time, cold and hungry, he couldn't spoon the stew down quickly enough. Afterwards he used the crusty bread to sponge up the last of the broth. The old vegetables and chewy bits of meat tasted delicious but it was more of a broth. In a moment the entire bowl was clean.

Not wanting to go back into the cold and then sit alone in that museum of a house, haunted by the ghosts of a purged family, he took Alexei's manuscript out of his valise and placed the stack of pages on the counter before him.

This Must Be Done!

A novel

by Alexei Romanovich Novikov

Ugh! he thought, awful title. Trying to skim through Alexei's clumsy style, he read the first few pages slowly, trying to get a fix on the time, place, and central characters. The sentences were as monotonous as the succession of military vehicles still rumbling by outside, but he couldn't entirely blame Novikov. The writing precisely conformed to the social realist style as dictated by the Writers Union. It took him about forty pages before Morozov got the basic setup: A young hero is a quiet veteran of the war, trying to recover psychologically and physically from his injuries. This was the most authentic part of the book.

Morozov skimmed through the opening chapters, identifying the key players; a rosy-cheeked virgin who believed that the revolution would save them all and a cynical old intellectual who is exiled there, constantly disparaging "the new system."

As soon as Morozov was able to recognize the plot he could skim through whole pages and just focus on the predictable plot twists. By the time Morozov was two-thirds of the way through with the manuscript, he saw how it was going to end, but continued skimming. Then, out of nowhere, to his utter surprise, even shock, the cook who ran the diner suddenly slung a second ladle of hot stew into his empty bowl, without his even asking.

"Wow, thanks!"

"You've been sitting there for nearly two hours," the counterman replied. "I figured you wouldn't leave unless I did something."

"I'm sorry, I have to read this monster." He slapped the pages.

"It's all right. I can use the company," the cook replied. "And it might not be the best stew, but we have a lot of it."

"How come I got no beef the first time?" Morozov asked, spooning up large chunks of meat. He also saw a broader variety of thick vegetables.

"I usually save the bottom of the pot for my regulars," the cook replied unapologetically, "and I've never seen you before. But 'cause of the cold, no one is coming out tonight and I'm closing soon."

"Lucky me."

"Want more?" he asked, holding up the large jug of Georgian burgundy. "The stew is free, but you'll have to pay for the wine."

"No thanks." It tasted like vinegar.

"You can keep reading but be prepared to leave when I'm done."

"Fine."

Alexei's novel basically followed all the other books of the early 1940s literary catalog. They were frequently mailed down to him in Yerevan where Morozov would periodically skim them. The central characters this year were all war heroes who were always wounded. After taking some time to recover, they eventually returned to their native villages. In Alexei's book the town is in Siberia not far from

Tomsk. Once he arrives he finds that the community is demoralized. Due to the war, the region is drained of both human and agricultural resources. The local economy is in shambles. In these books, Morozov reflected that although there is an array of identifiable characters, there's always an attractive young woman who happens to be a zealous young party member—and they were always virgins. In two novels that he could think of, these virtuous women were engaged to be married, saving themselves for their nuptials, but both lost their fiancés in the war.

To his credit, Alexei gave his virgin a twist, she had brought some shame upon herself with an earlier debacle—initiating a reduced rations drive, which everyone already living in austere conditions ignored. Now she was no longer taken seriously at the local party meetings. Still all these wonderful Joan of Arcs harbored a dream of bringing their shattered communities together and pulling them out of their rut. But alone they can't perform miracles.

Also there is always some central failure, like a broken-down mill or a large, untended field, but with no working plow or draft animals, or for complicated reasons, they can't get it working. And though the local commissar is sympathetic, he points out that there is no simple fix. Complex plans have to be drawn up in Moscow: Those above must make hard choices. Sign countless forms. Go through various committees. Find and bring in heavy equipment, which is usually rusting in some other field. Throughout the opening pages of these books, symbols of inertia abound against the background of war.

Usually about halfway through the novel there is some early, impulsive, and ill-conceived event that the virgin, or others like her, concoct. But invariably that half-cocked attempt also ends in failure. And frequently when it does, a beloved horse or elderly figure dies in the effort. The plots roll sadly like a child's marble toward the edge of a table.

But little things are at work: The girl, who has an unrequited crush on the hero, provokes him to join her, but due to his disability he's reluctant. Others applaud his wisdom in refusing to try to do the

306

impossible and more importantly into reigning in her rambunctious nature. A girl like her needs to be tamed like a wild horse.

Clearly the war took a big toll, leaving a great weight on these neglected heroes; guilt, shame, anger left him confused and aggravated. They all believed they should've died on the field of honor, with countless other comrades.

Steadily though, as Alexei's hero learns how to handle his pain, he begins to tap into a hidden strength. Although he disparages the girl for her petulance, he has a begrudging respect for her. As the plot thickens, and the shrill virgin continues advocating for change, some stodgy member of the local committee brings charges of "upstartism" against her. It's then that the hero reluctantly stands up for her and pleads for calm. That's the twinkle of light that always appears at the end of these long, dismal tunnels.

67

Eric, Woodstock Festival, 1969

Eric awoke hours later to a single cold drop of water on his face and then a third. Raindrops were falling again. Clouds had covered the bright morning sky and the rain rapidly increased. The music had ceased and people were moving to take cover as Anna also stirred.

"Come on," he said to her taking her hand. As they tiredly trudged back up to their lean-to, it was just beginning to pour. They each carefully slid inside, lying heads and tails on the sleeping bag. Though it kept raining, it didn't storm, and his minor repairs seemed to keep the lean-to dry, so they were able to sleep a while longer. Eric finally awoke feeling his legs shaking gently. It took him a moment to realize that Anna was silently weeping.

"What's the matter?" he asked, gently rubbing her leg.

"I can't believe I fucking slept through Janis!" she finally said. He didn't buy it, but didn't say anything. He knew she was crying because she had lost her big shaggy lover—Rooster.

"Due to the showers..." The pirate was back on the PA. A loud boo went up. "Due to the showers, we're forced to delay today's show. But even if Mother Nature doesn't hold up her end, we're holding up ours. We got the performers. And if worse comes to worst, we'll extend the concert for one more day!" The pirate wanted to leave the stage before getting electrocuted. "That's the best we can do, folks. Thanks!" Sporadic boos slowly mixed in with the wave of applause.

"Fuck!" Eric muttered.

"Shit! You have to get back today too, don't you?" Anna asked.

"They're expecting me for dinner tonight," he muttered. Both their mothers were expecting them back home tonight. In another minute, the rain and wind started whipping the crowds, compelling both of them yet again to hold their little plastic shell tightly around them as water trickled down from above. Hungry and tired and dreading to fight to survive for another day, they waited for the storm to subside.

Anna kept thinking, *If the rain stops right now! And they cut the crappier singers from the lineup, maybe we can still catch Hendrix before evening and make it home tonight.*

When the storm finally died down, Anna was able to doze off, which allowed Eric to gaze at her perfect face. Beauty always seemed to epitomize truth and meaning and worth, but as he stared and thought of her actions, he knew this was simply not the case. How could anyone so mercenary and immature and just plain selfish be so unfairly attractive! he wondered. She was a living, breathing lie! Still, his erection told him otherwise. It was pulsating like a small oblong heart that had ballooned out of his pelvis.

With one hand, he parted the plastic lining of their little teepee, allowing a gentle breeze in to cool his sleeping Aphrodite. With his other hand, he slowly ran the edge of his fingers down along her nude back, to her bra strap. One of her large, tight orbs was pressed up against his shoulder. Running his free hand up her front, he gently stroked along the outer edge of her right breast, which was hiding just below the sleeping bag. Her perfect red nipple hardened. To be able to just run his lips over it, to taste its cherry tip with the tip of his tongue. Suddenly she turned away nearly tearing the plastic sheathe down. He pulled his numb hand up and contemplated extricating himself. But in another moment she leaned back making herself even more exposed than before. Her perfect protruding butt was now pressed against his rock-hard boner.

He delicately angled his erection so that it was rubbing parallel with her firm round cheeks. She didn't seem to notice, much less mind, so he slowly lowered his underpants down freeing himself from the elastic band and rubbed himself against her bare flesh. Pretending to thoughtlessly hug her, he was able to place his right hand on her left breast, which he just left there as he rocked his pelvis back and forth against her ass. He did this off and on for about five minutes at which point, without intending to, he clenched his teeth and began to ejaculate right on her lower back.

"What the hell!" she muttered as he suddenly grabbed himself and reluctantly squirted into his own palm.

"Shit!" he said, grabbing the child's tee shirt.

"What the fuck!" Anna sat up.

"Sorry, I... I had one of those... nocturnal things!" he whispered.

She rolled out of the lean-to only wearing bra and panties into the rain.

"Sorry," he said, self-conscious of those passing by. The place offered absolutely no privacy.

"Fuck!" Anna shouted, wiping herself off.

Embarrassed, he cleaned himself and pulled his pants on. It was still raining outside, but they both had to use the toilet. And neither wanted to be alone with the other. She marched ahead of him up the hill, where they waited on separate lines silently until they were drenched. Then they relieved themselves. Afterwards they agreed that they were hungry so they spent another hour in the rain waiting for the Hog Farmers to hand out more food.

"They should consolidate the lines so you can wait for the crapper, take a dump, and still be waiting for the food line," Eric kidded. Anna didn't respond. At one point, she felt uncomfortable and Eric noticed that several of Rooster's asshole hippie friends were traipsing about. By two p.m. the rain finally began to taper back to a mist. The organizers moved quickly and mopped down the stage and flipped back on the electricity.

"They should just let Hendrix go now, then all the unknown acts can take their time," Anna reasoned. "Don't you agree?"

"Absolutely," Eric replied without thinking, he just didn't want any problems.

But instead of Hendrix some long-haired dude wearing a funky tie-dye shirt with fuzzy sideburns leaped onto the stage. And, in a matter of moments, he began belting out a soulful ditty. Eric heard his English accent. Neither knew who he was.

"Shit! This is what I'm talking about! No one wants to hear this freak!" Anna yelled, and noticed his jerking movements as he sang. "I didn't know Frankenstein was performing."

But gradually they came to enjoy his quirky interpretation of *"With a Little Help From My Friends"* which made Anna sad because none of the people she thought were her friends had helped her.

"I'm really sorry for... coming on your leg," Eric said earnestly, seeing the tears in her eyes.

"If it makes you feel any better, you're not the first guy to do that."

Almost as if the sky waited for Joe Cocker to end his set, the rain started to pour again. Instruments and equipment were hastily covered or whisked away. The electricity was again shut off. This time Anna and Eric took shelter with a group near the medical tent. Since there was no background music, Eric pondered borrowing a couple bucks from Anna and waiting on one of the endless phone lines to call his mom. But what would he say? *I can't come home today because I lost my wallet and am stuck with some nutty tramp at the big, wet hippie rock concert that you warned us about?* He knew that when dinnertime rolled around, without hearing a word from him she'd start growing concerned. So he actually thought he would make the call and come clean to save them the worry. But once he got on the hour-long phone line he decided no: his confession would also put Josh in jeopardy and he just couldn't do that to his brother.

"Want some chips?" He heard Anna munching from a half empty bag of Lays barbecue potato chips.

"Where'd you get those?" he asked, grabbing a handful.

"Someone left them. They're a little damp."

"Sure," he said, few were any bigger than fingernail clippings.

They finished them before they got back to the lean-to where they squeezed back into their soft plastic cone. With nothing else to do, they were barely able to play the hand slap game 'til Eric almost elbowed a hole in the plastic. Then they thumb wrestled and finally played the animal alphabet game while waiting for the rain to subside. Finally when Eric said "penguin," Anna couldn't think of another P animal. Still she couldn't concede, so she started kissing him. Heavy petting ensued, then finally they got under the damp sleeping bag where Eric opened the other condom and they began fucking again as the rain began to pour. After he quickly orgasmed, they took turns standing naked outside for a brief and cold shower. The rain soon slowed down so they pulled on their clothes. Everything was wet. That's when the rain finally stopped and the next band was finally announced—Country Joe and the Fish.

"Isn't that the guy who sang, "One two three four. We don't want no stinking war?" Eric asked, seeing the hippie in the army shirt from yesterday.

"Yeah! He already played!" she declared as if calling foul.

"Yeah, but he was alone. Apparently he needs a whole 24-piece orchestra to bring his subtle beauty to full bloom," Eric kidded.

Anna spotted a couple near the front get up and leave, so they dashed in and grabbed their spot because it was still kind of dry. They were able to lie down. Just as Eric started nodding off, Anna started screaming at the top of her lungs. Eric awoke to find some older, hairy man pinning her down in the mud.

68

Eric, NYC, September 10, 2001

In the two years since Eric Stein's son, Eriq Jr., was admitted into Cornell University in 1999, he changed his major three times. First he studied drama, which compelled him to be more expressive and less inhibited. Then he majored in African-American Studies, which left his hair dreadlocked, and finally he wound up in Business Administration before he took a leave of absence. To celebrate his temporary liberation from school, he got a series of primitive pattern tattoos up and down his arms and lower back. Then he decided to travel around the world on the cheap.

"All I'm asking is for you to go back and finish your degree before doing your big On-the-Road thing," Eric Sr. said over the speaker phone at his office in Midtown.

"By then there won't be any road to be on," young Eriq retorted.

"That's ridiculous!" his father replied.

"We've increased the population by tenfold in the last hundred years. If the Earth was a human being, then in just the past century, by its increase of carbon emissions, pollution, and deforestation, it has aged forty thousand years."

"Why is it always 40,000 years?" his father laughed.

"Every major scientific study indicates that this country is going to be a desert with nearly ten-billions mouths to feed by the time I'm your age," Jr. said. "I'm really just trying to say goodbye to this great planet before it's gone."

"People have been peddling that shit forever," Eric Sr. retorted. "Your future will wait till you finish your degree, trust me."

"You ran off with some girl and went to Woodstock when you were younger than me!" his son yelled back, playing the one trump card he always played.

"And believe me I paid for it!" Eric said. "When I got home my mother had been medicated. My father was so angry, he wouldn't even talk to me for two days!" He remembered his father had donated his new high-fidelity stereo to the Salvation Army as a penalty. They really punished his brother, Josh, who admitted to being the mastermind.

Josh forgave him soon after, but that was the most difficult aspect of it. His father never fully trusted his older brother again. Years later, when he sat next to Josh on his deathbed, he apologized a final time for missing that final bus back to New York City that Sunday night just as they had agreed he would.

"Don't ever apologize for that," Josh replied with a chuckle. "Helping you lose your cherry to the girl of your dreams—that was one of the best things I ever did. Tell people about that at my eulogy, you'll get a big laugh."

Suddenly a "You Got Mail" mailbox icon appeared on his computer screen. As Junior wailed on about his elaborate travel plans, Eric read the email from one of Lande's accounting people. He said that a bill was going before the New York State Assembly that was giving a big tax break on new buildings that offered an increase of square feet to non-for-profit and mixed-economic class tenants. Another minor detail that might be helpful for his upcoming Jamaica Bay prospectus. He interrupted Eriq to say they'd have to continue this discussion later.

"How'd I know you'd say that?" his son said, and hung up without a goodbye.

By eleven p.m., Eric Stein was still at the office exhausted. He had told his wife that he was going to be spending the night here as there was still too much to do. She wished him a good night and went to sleep.

He still had a team of young associates and proofreaders working around the clock to finish the final documents before sending them to the printers and having them ready for tomorrow's big signing at Lande's office. Eric knew he wasn't going to get any sleep that night. His right-hand man, a brilliant twenty-eight-year-old Wharton grad named Ronald Mann, was verifying the financial projections, as was someone from Merrill Lynch, while a lawyer from Davis Polk reviewed the latest pie chart figures. His other trusted associate Bob Ames was checking the explanatory footnotes, and

Jessie Kingston was combing all the data tables for any glaring inaccuracy. Despite this crack team, he knew that he had to personally go over everything himself or he'd be in for a painful surprise at the last moment—which was always the case.

After all the revisions and re-revisions, he knew there still had to be half a dozen inconsistencies just waiting to spring up at the last moment when it was too late to fix them. Sitting at his desk, he hoped to read the prospectus as though it were a thriller, but the pea-soup legalese was too thick to move through, and the charts and graphs and endless tables were too plentiful to check. Sipping coffee to combat his exhaustion, he'd read through it for a few pages, until he'd nod off for a few minutes. Then he'd awaken with a start and begin reading it again and nodding off again.

By one forty-five a.m., Mann tapped on his door awakening him.

"Yep?" Eric asked, pretending to be wide awake.

"We're done and we have to take the contracts to the printers right now if they are going to be ready at eight a.m. for the signing."

"Oh shit," Stein said, realizing he'd barely scratched the surface of the document. But on a positive note, he hadn't found any glaring fuckups. "Okay send it!"

When Mann left, Stein curled up on his couch and drifted along the surface of a shallow sleep.

An hour later, Mann woke him to say the document had been sent to the printers and should be ready at go-time.

"Good."

"We should start heading down to Lande's Properties and set up for everyone," Mann said, looking at his wristwatch.

Eric checked his wristwatch and said, "Call for three cars. Let's get everyone down to the lobby." His team consisted of Mann, Ames, his two associates, three paralegal temps, and an in-house proofreader. As a fiery orange sun rose over steamy Manhattan, they boarded the Lincoln Town Cars and headed south. This was it. After years of hard work, luck and patience, it was finally going to happen.

On the ride south he thought, after the documents were all signed, while the drafting team is going to bed, he'd have to spend

314

the rest of the day making sure the shares were selling without a hitch.

69

Alexei Novikov's first novel sluggishly wrapped up just as Morozov knew it would: The wounded soldier and the idealistic virgin managed to hatch some harebrained scheme to fix the village's broken-down windmill, but the two of them alone simply couldn't do it. Gradually though, each of the other oddballs in their Siberian village started joining in on the endeavor, each contributing some trivial yet vital part to make the whole stupid plan work. Even the old skeptic contributed something, an antiquated mechanical tool he found buried near the mill called a "bachelor's crank." He had no idea what it was, he simply liked the way it looked. But at a crucial moment, the virgin is able to insert the rusty ratchet into some cobwebbed hole and, with the hero, they slowly spin it and are able to get the old mill grinding again. By the end of the story, the young couple fall in love and they rename the tool—the lover's crank.

"All done," the old counterman said to Morozov, upon wiping down the counter. He was ready to close the diner.

Morozov thanked the cook for the extra bowl of stew, shoved Alexei's manuscript back into his valise and put down his rubles and a couple kopeks as tip. In another moment he had his coat, hat, and scarf on and stepped outside into the chill. The procession of military trucks heading to the front line was still rolling down the street, a series of paced headlights, though it was moving now at a slower frequency. The convoy had to be at least a couple miles long, packed with artillery and men—fuel for the never-ending war.

It was just about nine p.m. and as he walked onward, only drunks and prostitutes were still floating down the empty prospekt. In fairness to Alexei's literary skills, Morozov imagined that it would take a virtuoso to find something new within the narrow confines of the current literary conventions. The book could've been much worse. Energized by the oily meal, as Morozov walked past the corner of the old whorehouse, he checked to see if his Persian harlot was around. But the streets were empty as it was bone chillingly cold. Soon Morozov reached the banks of the glassy Moskva River. Darya must've finished her housekeeping chores for the night and had left by now. Morozov was about to head home when he spotted a large bonfire in the distance. Black silhouettes were held in its warm, tight orbit. For a moment, he imagined that they might be the lost poets and intoxicated artists of his youth. As he grew closer, he saw that most of them were veterans missing a limb or elderly drunks. Groups were sharing common bottles. As the flame died down, one of the men fed a broken placard into the dying bonfire.

"Behind Us Is Moscow! There is no room left for retreat!" the sign warned, as flames engulfed it. A second sign stating, "Remember Borodino!" followed. They had been mottoes of the Communist Youth League to inspire people as the Germans raced toward the capital several short years ago. Morozov found a place to sit and take in the heat. The stars were beautiful tonight. Someone generously offered him a bottle, he graciously passed. The soothing heat and odd companionship brought him as close as he could get to calm. The thought of Kharms' death had finally stopped haunting him, another dead writer that no one had ever read.

After ten minutes of quiet company, a high-pitched whistle penetrated the darkness. A narrow stick figure of a man in a uniform raced toward them plucking a whistle out of his teeth.

"ARE YOU ALL INSANE?!" he screamed. Evidently, he was the local air raid warden for the area. As though he were a robot, he walked right into the bonfire and started kicking the burning pieces of wood apart.

"Do you idiots think German recons aren't flying over every hour? I should have you all arrested! You're probably deserters!" He continued ranting against the dozen or so men, as they broke off into their little groups and splintered into the darkness.

Alone, Morozov rose and resumed crossing the Moskvoretsky Bridge nearby. From the top, he could see both the domes around the

Kremlin and the Bell Tower of Ivan as if warning him to go no further. Tired and cold, he turned around and headed home.

It was late when he finally approached the small, stately home. He was surprised to see an upstairs light still burning. Darya must've forgotten to turn it off when she left. He unlocked his front door, took off shoes and socks, then headed upstairs to his bedroom. He froze at the door when he saw her lying on his bed, curled up like a black cat. Darya was fully dressed and snoring away. He only felt tenderness for the poor girl. He was going to cover her with the blanket and sleep downstairs, but then he saw the empty wine bottle on the end table. On the other side of the bed, initially out of view, he saw three small leather-bound books on the floor.

"What the hell is this?! Those are my…." He picked one up and confirmed it. "How dare you read my private journals!"

She awoke. "I'm so sorry!"

"How dare you!"

"I didn't mean to… Let me explain…" She struggled to her feet.

"Get the hell out of my house!"

Clearly she was still intoxicated as she passed him. He grabbed her shoes and overcoat and tossed them down the stairs.

"It's not what you think!" she said, groggily.

"Just get out and never return!"

"I'm…"

"I know who and what you are!"

"If you read the letter I sent you, you'd understand."

"I don't need to read a letter! Get out!"

He let her put on her coat and shoes as she said, "Just let me explain!"

"That you're a drunken snake and will do anything to further your own career!"

"No, that's not it. It's…"

"If you don't think my journals have already been checked for anything that can be used against me, you're very much mistaken."

"It wasn't that!"

317

"You're a generation of backstabbers and opportunists," he said and slammed the door in her face.

When he returned to his bedroom, he noticed that the three journals that she had been reading from had been carefully placed face down. When he studied the pages, to his surprise he found that they all pertained to Masha Rodchenko.

70

Alexei, Woodstock Festival, 1969

Despite his few remaining teeth and shaky bridgework, Alexei slowly began chewing down on the last of the hard French bread that some hippie kid gave him. He moved away toward another group of silly kids, drumming on their bongos to the beat of the yellow-shirted man on the big stage. Though he didn't hate this country, Alexei thought that if the Cold War ever warmed up, Russia would roll over it in a matter of days.

Suddenly, over the drone of the music, he heard a shrill shriek and then Sergei's frantic voice cursing in Russian. He looked through the crowd from twenty feet away and made out Sergei wrestling in the mud with some skinny savage. When another wet kid jumped on his broad back grabbing his thick mane, Alexei charged through like an old bull. He froze when he realized that it wasn't a second guy, but a beautiful raven-haired girl clinging to the Armenian's back. She was desperately trying to get him off a boy, who Sergei had pinned down into the mud.

"Sergei! Stop it!" Alexei lifted the girl off his back.

"This piece of shit is sleeping with my daughter!" Sergei yelled in Russian still holding down the boy.

"They're kids!" Alexei replied, pushing him off the young man, and helping him to his feet. "We were kids once, remember?"

The music drowned out the comments of the surrounding hippies who watched the incident in dismay.

"I hate you!" the girl hissed, slapping her father's shoulder.

"Good. Then I'm doing my job!" Sergei replied. "We're going back to the city right now!"

"The hell we are! You're not my father! You're just some old dude who balled my dumb mom sixteen years ago!"

"How dare you!" Sergei said grabbing her skinny arm. Eric grabbed him and Alexei separated them all. Some of the concertgoers in the vicinity yelled for the old guys to leave the kids alone, but none got involved.

"Someone get the troopers!" her teenage boyfriend yelled out, stepping between Sergei and his daughter. Even though Eric didn't want to be there any longer, he wasn't going to be pushed around by this hairy creep.

"Hey!" Alexei grabbed Sergei's arm as he was about to punch the kid. "Let's all just calm down, okay?"

"You're a minor!" Sergei said to his daughter, then turning to the boy, he said, "And you're a rapist!"

"Fuck you!" Anna shot back.

"And you're a child molester!" Eric yelled back.

"This is Anna's father," Alexei said softly to him.

"You mean, her step-father?" Eric yelled back.

"Her real father," Alexei replied.

Turning to Anna, Eric asked, "This is your father?"

"Technically, but that's all!"

Alexei calmly asked her boyfriend his name and how old he was.

"Eric Stein, eighteen," he lied.

"I'm Alexei Romanovich Novikov, fifty-eight," Alexei shook his hand. The youth looked like his younger son. "So how'd you get here?"

"A friend drove us up," he replied, not implicating his brother.

"That boy can go straight to hell for all I care," Sergei said in Russian, then switched to English. "Anna you're coming back with us right now!"

"No fucking way!" she shot back. When he grabbed her the process replayed. She started screaming and Eric grabbed him until Alexei got between them all again, pulling them apart.

319

"I don't know who you are, but you ain't telling us what to do!" Eric yelled, and turning to people around them, he repeated, "Help! Someone please get the cops!"

"Yes! Notify the police!" Sergei replied. "They're both minors! I'm her father! Anna is a runaway!"

"She's not a runaway!" Eric said.

"I have an idea, let's all go to the police," Sergei yelled at him. "Anna's mother asked me to come get her! Once the police arrive, I'll call her and we'll have *you* arrested as her abductor!"

"Calm down, everyone!" Alexei said. "Sergei, just take a breath!" As the Armenian turned and slowly exhaled, one of the hippies asked Eric and Anna, "Do you guys need the cops or what?"

"We're fine, thank you," Alexei said, and turning to Eric, he said, "Let's try to work this out, okay?"

"Okay," Eric said, realizing his own vulnerable.

"Where'd you two kids meet anyway?" Alexei asked as Sergei tried to reason with his daughter.

"At school. We attend high school together. We were in a poetry workshop."

"You wrote poetry?"

"We both did."

"Do you read poetry?"

"Sure. Lots."

"You're going home right now!" Sergei yelled to Anna as their discussion flared up again.

"I'll get a cop and have your Armenian ass deported!" his daughter shouted back and yelled to all around. "This man's a no-good commie spy!"

"Let's all calm down," Alexei said again.

Embarrassed by the prying eyes of surrounding hippies, Eric tried to quiet her down.

"She refuses to leave!" Sergei said in Russian.

"We're here anyway," Alexei replied softly. "Let's let them watch their show, then we'll all drive back to the city together."

Sergei let out a curse. Still speaking in Russian, Alexei suggested he compromise with the kids so as to appear the hero. The Armenian sighed, nodded, and stepped over to his daughter and Eric.

"How about we watch the music 'til dinnertime," he said to his daughter, "then we all drive back to the city? My treat! Does that sound fair? A nice meal and a warm drive back?"

"Hell no!" said Anna.

"Actually," the boy whispered, taking the girl aside, "that would make things a whole lot easier for us." He was still clinging to the hope of making it home before midnight to avoid the full wrath of his parents.

"We missed Janis, I'm not missing Hendrix!" she fired back.

"When exactly is Bendick performing?" Alexei asked, looking at his watch.

"Hendrix, Jimi Hendrix! He's the last performer," Eric said, almost shamefully. He wanted to leave as much as either of them but couldn't admit it.

"This is ending today, no?" Alexei asked.

"Unfortunately not," Eric explained. "They announced that due to all the rain they were going to play all night and into tomorrow."

"So when is he playing?" Sergei asked.

Eric produced a list of players he had found and began making calculations.

"Assuming the monsoon season is over," he announced, "sometime tomorrow morning." Worried that the youth wasn't being fully forthcoming, Sergei asked if he could see the lineup.

The two men examined the band names:

"Ten Years After
The Band
Johnny Winter
Blood, Sweat & Tears
Crosby, Stills, Nash & Young
Paul Butterfield Band
Sha Na Na
Jimi Hendrix

"There are seven performers before him," Eric said.

Switching back to Russian, Sergei muttered, "Just our luck! Hendrix is the last. That's at least nine hours away. And if it rains it could be longer."

"I don't like it any more than you," Alexei also spoke in Russian. "But if you want to be a hero to your daughter and win over her mother, I don't see any other way out."

"But you could miss your flight!"

"It's departing at nine p.m. tomorrow night. The skies seemed to have cleared up, so if we leave here by noon tomorrow that's seven hours to take what is supposed to be a three-hour trip back to New York."

"There's going to be a lot of traffic, Alexei."

"Well, I'm willing to risk it."

"If I pulled something like this when I was a kid, my father would've strapped the hell out of me right where I stood!" Sergei said softly.

"If you were married and raised the kid yourself, you'd have more leverage. But now, if you want to develop a relationship with this angry girl, you have no choice."

"I don't know. Her mother asked me to do this. Maybe I should just call the police."

"Do that and you'll never see your daughter again."

"I'm sorry for pulling you into this, Alexei. I wish we could've spent a relaxed day together in the city."

"Nonsense, I'm happy to help you, Sergei. And after a lifetime of reading about America and studying their society in textbooks, this is probably the best place to understand this strange country."

"There's two more bottles of vodka in my trunk," Sergei said.

While the two men talked, Anna gestured to Eric that they should dash, but he didn't want to lose his meal ticket or his ride home, so he finally asked, "So what do you guys want to do?"

"We'll stay with you 'til Hendrix finishes," Sergei said to his daughter, "then we'll drive you back to the city."

"That's acceptable," the boy said before Anna could louse it up.

"I was talking to my daughter," Sergei said, annoyed that he had to indulge this little toad.

"That's acceptable," she repeated unappreciatively.

"So we have a plan," Alexei said calmly to Sergei who was still staring severely at the young man who he knew had been defiling his daughter.

"Great," said Eric, actually relieved that they had a safe way to get back home. Even though he secretly hoped that they would've coerced her to leave right now.

"Let's all shake on it," Alexei said, extending his palm, trying to usher in a new spirit of good will. Everyone took turns shaking everyone else's hand. Sergei and Anna, who were the last to shake, did so quickly.

"Would you do me one small favor?" Sergei asked his daughter directly.

"What!"

"Can we go up the hill to the line of phones and call your mother?" he asked softly. "She's worried sick about you."

"Long as you don't touch me!" she said, still pissed.

He held his hands in the air to show compliance. Eric wanted to join them to call his mother as well, but respected that Sergei wanted to be alone with his daughter.

"So Eric Stein, you're a Jew?" Alexei began chatting as the two departed.

"I'm Jewish," he clarified. "My faith is one of the many qualities that make up my identity, but it hardly defines me."

Alexei nodded. Being a Communist Russian in the United States, he fully understood the youth's sentiment.

71

A late-night knock on the door made young Alexei jump to his feet.

"Who is it?"

"Who do you think?" Darya said through the door. He opened and saw that she was disheveled. Her coat was wet with melted snow. He immediately knew that something was off. She had been sleeping with him regularly for the past two weeks, but before entering, she had always taken the time to make herself attractive.

"It's almost midnight. You never come by this late."

"What's the matter?" she asked, wondering if he smelled the wine on her breath.

"Ivan Lemokh was removed, very probably arrested," he replied.

"Arrested!" she said.

"Morozov did it."

"For what!"

"Treason? Who knows?"

"Oh my god!" she said, terrified. "When did this happen?"

"Yesterday I think," he replied. Briefly believing the arrest had something to do with her reading the Armenian's journals, she gave a sigh of relief realizing this wasn't her fault. Then, he added, "We're next."

"What are we going to do?" She was petrified.

"We just need to go slow and follow orders," he said, rubbing her arm.

"From who?" she asked. Ivan had been their supervisor.

"A real bastard named Arkady Petrov. Very by the book. He wants us to turn in daily reports."

"Oh my god!" Darya suddenly panicked and asked, "He didn't call you, did he?"

"Who?"

"Morozov!"

"About what?"

"Me?"

"Why would I hear from him about you?" Alexei asked.

"I don't know," she said, unable to reveal what he had just caught her doing. "Maybe he didn't like my cooking."

"No one gets arrested for burning pierogis."

"Hell!" she blurted, sitting on the edge of his bed. She removed her shoes. "I didn't think I'd be working as a cook and maid. I was just supposed to get close and provide information about him. This isn't what I bargained on."

"Relax, let's just go to bed," he said, seeing that she was clearly frazzled.

She hung her dress on the back of a chair. In a moment they were both under the sheets, with the lights off, staring at the ceiling in silence.

"I wish there was some way I could quit this job," she muttered.

"Me too but we're in this together. And together we'll get through this," he said, flipping off the light.

72

Eric, NYC, September 11, 2001

As Eric Stein and his IPO crew wheeled three carts with the ten hot boxes containing the freshly printed contracts into the spacious elevator of Two World Trade Center and soared up to the Sky-Lobby, Eric could feel his heart beating. He had always been one of the experts, one of the consultants, never a quarterback in the game until now. From the Sky Lobby on the seventy-second floor, his entourage wheeled their carts to the second elevator then up to the ninety-third floor, just seventeen floors shy of the top.

During the entire ride, as others chatted, Stein kept thinking. *This is it! This is actually, finally, really going to happen!*

In a matter of minutes the group brought the IPOs into the chilled offices of Lande Properties LLC where the sexy short-haired secretary led them all to a conference room offering a stunning view of New York Harbor. Upon a long collapsible table, two caterers had placed trays of fresh bagels, platters piled with cream cheese, slices of tomato, onion, and lettuce. Select cuts of lox, ham, and turkey were displayed as well. On another table was an assortment of just-baked danishes and two large steaming urns of coffee.

Stein had his team take the various contracts and documents out of their boxes and organize them on a long oaken conference table. His team moved furniture and chairs around so that when everyone finally arrived, the process would occur quickly and efficiently.

Promptly at eight o'clock, using two canes, one in each hand, Lande slowly hobbled in and was warmly greeted by Eric and his entire team. It wasn't until eight-thirty that the principals finally began to arrive. Eric's assistant Paul Mann contacted the offices of three underwriters on a conference call so they could listen in.

When the last one arrived, they sat around the large conference table, where everyone was provided with a thick copy of the IP offer. When all were settled, Eric sat at the head of the table, introduced himself, and explained, "To start, I'm going to read this aloud and summarize the details. These include the risk factors, use of proceeds, and the capitalization structure. Then I'll review the financial data and the management structure, and wrap things up with legalities."

"Sounds good. Let me just say," Lande interrupted, "Mr. Stein has put a lot of time and effort into this deal and I was looking over his shoulder every step of the way, so he has my utmost confidence."

"Thank you sir," said Eric, who began: "For tax purposes this entity is being structured as a real estate investment trust. Parties of the first part, known as Landes Properties LLC..." He spent the next fifteen minutes going through the documents. Some followed along, but most of the older men at the table did not.

By eight forty-five, the IPO reading was complete. After a few questions, Eric said it was time for the signing. All the principal signatories were instructed to flip through their copies to pages with red "Sign Here" arrow stickers and they began affixing their John Hancocks to the bottoms of sixteen separate pages. A mere twenty minutes later they were all done–every contract was officially signed, dated, and occasionally initialed. The public offering was ready to go.

"That was a lot easier than I thought it'd be," Lande said, tiredly looping his signature like vines wrapping around the signing field of the last financial instrument. He had scribbled out his signature twenty-two times in eighteen minutes.

"I told you it'd be…" Suddenly, a massive explosion made the great building shudder. Deafening silence. All looked out the window, south over Lower Manhattan and New York Harbor–their only view–it was still a beautiful summer day.

"What the fuck was that?" Lande asked his assistant who dashed out of the office. Within minutes all were informed that a plane had accidentally struck the uptown face of the northern tower only a few hundred feet away.

"Unbelievable!" said Stein, staring out the window at the clear blue skies facing the opposite direction of the North Tower. "How the hell do you crash into a huge building on such a clear day?!"

"The pilot must be goddamned blind!" said Mann, Eric's number two.

Although anxiety filled the air, Mr. Lande assured everyone that they should remain calm. Their building was completely separate from Tower One. All were absolutely safe.

"For the record," Lande announced, "these buildings are more solid than the bedrock they're standing on."

"Those poor bastards," said someone, referring to those across the way.

Although the tragedy was evident, the sense of fear and urgency was nervously allayed. Within twenty minutes, before most of the signatories or others affiliated with the signing could leave the office, the floor's designated fire marshal announced that he had just been notified by Port Authority police that everyone needed to remain where they were: The building was sound. The plaza however was covered with the carnage from the plane's wreckage as well as people evacuating from the North Tower, which was still on fire.

Once the plaza was evacuated and opened up, they would notify the residents of the South Tower and give them the opportunity to vacate as well. Eric took out his cellular phone, looked up his speed dial, and hit the name Q, his nickname for his son. The call wouldn't go through.

73

Kasabian, Moscow, 1943

That night, after Morozov ejected an intoxicated Darya out of his residence, he was unable to sleep. After all these years, he well knew how the secret police worked. He had seen them move as delicately as butterflies, extracting tiny bits of truth to lace around their own web of lies. He had also seen them rolling in like tanks to simply pulverize their targets with relentless accusations.

Tonight was very different. The sloppy display of finding the strange girl passed out in his bedroom would never have been sanctioned by the secret police. The fact that she had opened his journals on the pages exclusively detailing his relationship with Masha, the one romance in his life, left him utterly bewildered. This girl was just a mindless teenager, probably with an infatuation, who should've just been sent to bed without supper.

By contrast, Alexei, her boyfriend, probably was secret police. Everything about him underscored it—the way he dressed and carried himself, even his cloying attempt to win Morozov's trust by showing him his own rancid manuscript. Someone else probably wrote it.

The single most enigmatic details, what he found mind-boggling, was what Darya had mentioned, that she had written Morozov a fan letter years earlier. She referred to it when he tossed her out. The secret police, or more particularly Malenkov's thugs, could never have pre-established a back story from that long ago.

Over the past couple of years, he still had gotten a few fan letters, not as many as in his heyday. Even now, years after he stopped writing, he'd receive one every couple of months, probably because his stories had been adopted into so many primary and secondary school anthologies.

When he first started receiving them, these juvenile missives were a real boost, but they quickly became a burden. Yet he couldn't bring himself to toss them in the garbage, so he'd simply slip the unread, unopened letters in the bottom file drawer of his desk in his Writers Union office in Yerevan, Armenia.

After a shapeless night of wondering what Darya could've written him in her letter, he recalled that she said she had sent the same letter a couple times. The next morning, he made an excursion. On his way to school, he stopped by the local post office and paid for a long-distance call. Then he headed to his office. He knew Lucille, the secretary of the Writers Union, had arrived. She always came early. Morozov placed a long distance call from his office at the school to the Yerevan branch of the Writers Union.

"Lucy, how are you?" he asked in Armenian.

"Kasabian?" She recognized his voice and always called him by his Armenian name. There was an echo as though she were speaking through a wide tunnel.

"I'm wondering if you could possibly do me a small favor?" he asked.

"Here in the outer republics," she replied, "we have all the time in the world, particularly when the boss is away. You know High Commissar Zhdanov sent you a package."

"Yes, I got it." It was the Akhmatova poems. "Go into my office and pick up the extension."

A moment later, she was sitting at his desk. He instructed her to take the huge stack of letters that had been accumulating in his file drawer and pile them on his blotter. She counted out nearly fifty sealed envelopes.

"Shame on you, Haig, for letting all these go by. They're schoolchildren! Many go back years!"

"Look for the older ones with a return address from the Ukraine," he instructed. Within five minutes she located seven of them, which was not surprising as he had made friends there when he visited for their literary conference.

"I'm looking for one letter in particular from a Darya Lebedova Kotova," he said. He spelled the name out for her. "She said she sent me two, but just find..."

"Found it!" she said after a minute.

"Cut it open and..."

Lucille, a middle-aged woman, suddenly said, "Oh, it has a picture!"

"A picture?" he asked.

"Yes, a photograph of a young girl and she's holding up something small and shiny. It looks like some kind of gem."

"A gem?"

"It looks like a diamond, probably cut glass."

"That's odd..."

"Dear Mr. Morozov," she began reading, "I am a young girl living in the Ukraine, where your works are eagerly read. I personally have enjoyed your stories immensely..."

The letter went on for a while, flattering his literary gifts and detailing several of her favorite stories. After a few minutes of the usual pleasantries, she finally touched on one of his shortest and most widely anthologized pieces, The Greatest Mystery. It opened in a small cafe in Moscow. A handsome lad named Yuri meets a beautiful girl named Galina who just arrived in town. She is from Kazakhstan and knows no one there. They strike up a friendship. And though Galina is reluctant to pursue romance, they enjoy each other's company. Gradually though, they venture through the city having different adventures. Slowly they grow more comfortable with each other. Over time, without being aware of it, Galina comes to rely on Yuri. And one day, without intending it, Galina finds herself growing attracted and an affair ensues.

Before their romance can deepen, Galina announces that she would be shortly returning to her hometown.

"Why are you leaving?" he asks bewildered. She never mentioned leaving before.

"It's time to go."

"Why is it time? Are you sick or something?"

"No."

"Are you homesick?"

"No, nothing like that," she seemed amused.

"Is it because of me?"

330

"Why would it be because of you?" she asked.

"Just that if you think I'm playing with your feelings or something?"

"I don't think that, I know you're honorable."

"So then why are you leaving?" he asked.

"Do I need a reason?" she asked blithely. With that remark he found he wanted to shake her and say yes, but didn't want to scare her off. Galina was a strong-willed girl, so he decided that the best way was to pull back and give her the time to explain why she was leaving. Over the next week or so, they continued seeing each other, but he didn't even ask her departure date. Then one day, he went to her boardinghouse and knocked on her door but there was no answer. When he returned later, he met the landlady who explained that Galina had left earlier that day.

"Left?"

"Took her bags, returned her keys, said goodbye, and left," she said. And that's it, but the story doesn't end there. As he grows older, and has other relationships, Yuri keeps measuring other girls against Galina; one way or the other, they always come up short. He has imaginary conversations with her. He also imagines having children with her, raising a family. The story ends at the end of Yuri's life with him wondering what he did that led to his being abandoned by the girl of his dreams. Morozov wrote the piece shortly after being abandoned by Masha.

Lucy read Darya's letter in which she asks what could have inspired him to write such a painful piece:

"The Greatest Mystery focuses on Yuri's pain of losing Galina. In doing this though —you remove him from the realm of blame or fault. You make him a victim. Not once in the piece do you have him wonder if maybe he did something to drive Galina away since she seemed to dump him. I can't help wondering if something happened to Galina that you're leaving out. I know it's impertinent for a reader to question an author regarding the fate of his characters. All we can do is accept and ponder his results. But I keep thinking that maybe there is more. Galina's demeanor does seem to shift suddenly near the end of the story. You mention that she starts showing up late for their appointments, but you don't say why. At another point you state "that day, she let her appearance go." Is there a cause for this? I've read enough of your work to know that this isn't carelessness on your part. Of all your stories that I've read I've always felt that this one was the most troubling inasmuch as it was the least resolved. Maybe this is why it was always one of my favorites. It offers no resolution hence the title. Still you must understand that the reader needs these questions answered or like Yuri the reader is haunted forever."

Most letters he received were simple messages with flattery and thanks. This one was far from that. Aside from an analysis of the story, her comments seemed to go deeper than the realm of fiction. Morozov found his heart racing and suddenly he broke into a sweat. The girl had sent him the message in 1938, five years ago, and she had been waiting ever since.

"So why did you need to hear this letter?" Lucille asked after his protracted silence.

"I met the girl who wrote it," he said. "And I pretended that I read it and just forgot its contents." Before the secretary could inquire any further, he asked her for the latest news of life back home. Everything was the same. In another moment, he thanked her and hung up.

When he stepped into his outer office, he saw Alexei sitting at his desk reading that day's newspaper.

"Is Darya here?" he asked, not revealing last night's incident.

"Not yet. I was waiting for her because I have to run to class myself," the young man said, collecting his books.

"I just wanted to talk about her dinner menu this week."

"So everything is working out with her?" his assistant asked.

"Yep," Morozov said and, feigning a yawn, said, "I could really use a pot of tea."

"I'll get you one before I go," Alexei said and exited.

Morozov flipped through Alexei's newspaper, examining the headlines. For the third year, poor Leningrad was under siege. Although the Red Army was steadily gaining traction on all fronts, the Germans had finally mobilized around Kharkov-Smolensk after the winter counteroffensives. The Japanese had landed in Singapore. Thankfully, they still hadn't invaded Russia. Leon Blum, the socialist prime minister, was being put on trial by the Vichy government. The Allies were finally getting their feet wet in North Africa as all hoped. But they weren't coming to the rescue any time soon. Both the Americans and the English were being routed by Rommel's tanks in the desert, truly pathetic.

Alexei returned, quickly setting the tray before him. Morozov saw a pot of tea and a roll with a knife and a pat of butter.

"So," the youth said, "I just wanted to…"

"Ask if I finished reading your novel?" Morozov anticipated.

"Actually I was going to say that I completed your Akhmatova review."

"Hand it over," Morozov replied. Alexei eagerly opened his schoolbag and took out the typed review. Morozov immediately began reading it. After seeing all her most touching lines, he was surprised to see that Alexei had sidestepped her poetry entirely and simply addressed Akhmatova's poetic negligence of her beloved city. Morozov knew that Zhdanov would hate it, but it fulfilled the requirements and he knew that no one else would take this approach.

"I should have some critique of your novel soon," he replied.

"Fine," Alexei said, and instead of asking for his newspaper back he quickly left.

Morozov poured himself a full cup of tea, but before he could sip it, the phone rang and he answered it.

"Haig!" It was the commissar's almost impatient voice.

"I'm happy to inform you that I finished the Akhmatova essay," he greeted him.

"Did someone from the Prison Records Department call you?" Zhdanov brushed him aside.

"What?"

"You heard me!"

"Yes, someone did," he said, "Just as you instructed."

"A new letter attached to Yuvachyov's file was just brought to my attention."

"I think you told me you were going to send me the file. I didn't ask for it."

"It's not the file that concerns me," he said. "It's a letter by some clerk named Aram Tomissian who wrote, 'Please remember what we talked about. Any speculation on my part is strictly confidential.'"

"Oh, we briefly chatted about..."

"I don't know what you're trying to pull, Haig, but if this Tomissian told you anything about this file, about the Kharms case— if any information gets out, I am going to hold him and you directly responsible. I don't like my kindness being taken advantage of. Do you understand?"

"I would never do such a thing," Morozov said.

"I'm gonna deal with this clerk personally, but God help you and anyone else if this information gets out and circulates in Moscow." Morozov sensed that the commissar was speaking through him to others listening in.

"Of course not," Morozov said, and trying not to leave things on a tense note, he said, "Regarding the Akhmatova essay..."

"Too many balls in the air. I'll get back to you when things settle down," Zhdanov hung up.

Morozov remembered the disparity between what the commissar had told him and what he had learned from his fellow countryman–that Yuvachyov had not been deported north but had starved to death all alone in a prison psych ward. Why the hell did he allow the Armenian clerk to send him the file! Now it was too late to help the man but, picking up the phone, he realized he still might be able to get ahold of the former critic and keep him from spreading the message of poor Kharms' demise.

When the switchboard operator at Gosizdat answered, Morozov said, "I know you said he doesn't work there, but I left a message for Voronsky and..."

"One second please," the clerk replied.

"I was trying to show my gratitude by not calling to thank you," the former critic said as soon as he picked up the phone.

"Did you call Kharms' widow?"

"No, she's out of town with her family. But I'm going to be seeing her this weekend."

"We have a problem."

"I know. Her husband was murdered."

"The problem is you can't tell her about it."

"Can't tell who about what?"

"You can't tell Kharms' wife that he died... You need to keep this confidential."

"What are you saying?"

"The source was unreliable," Haig lied. "I was mistaken."

"He's alive?"

"Not necessarily."

"He's either dead or alive," Voronsky shot back.

"The clerk wasn't forthcoming, so let's say I extrapolated that he was dead."

"How did you extrapolate such a thing?" Voronsky was indignant.

"The clerk thought Kharms' penal record looked fishy."

"How so?"

"I can't disclose any more than that," Morozov said, fearful his line was tapped. Voronsky didn't say a word, so Morozov added, "If false information goes out that Kharms was killed, you'll be putting all our lives in jeopardy, including Kharms' widow."

"So Kharms was executed and you're complying with the official lie," Voronsky said, incriminating both of them.

"At worst it was an accident, but it was unconfirmed."

"Fine, I'll tell her that."

"No! Alex, you were in the camps," Morozov reminded him. "The constant hunger, the freezing cold, the years of hard labor. He wouldn't want to live like that."

"He was murdered and you want me to keep it from the poor woman. Say it!"

"I'm worried for Kharms' widow!"

"No, you're not, you're only concerned with your own precious life!" Voronsky replied angrily. "Admit it!" Morozov realized that the old critic was suffering for the loss of his young friend, so he tried to cushion the impact.

"I'm not just sorry because of his passing, I'm sorry that our state is so... cautious," Morozov said, trying his best.

"Our state? Oh, you mean the mustached thug who stole our government and publishes every shred of paper that you wipe your ass with!" Voronsky didn't care who was listening.

"That's enough!"

"You're a regime hack! And whoever is listening knows this!" Voronsky flew into a rage. "'The State' has bestowed this artificial, overinflated reputation on you!"

"I've tried to help you as best as I could."

"They murdered a very original young writer and... and I can't even ease his wife's suffering by telling her of his demise."

"You seem to think I'm somehow benefiting from all this!" Morozov finally broke. "Well I'm not! I'm just trying to stay alive."

"The only reason you can pretend to be a writer is 'cause all the real writers were killed or silenced..."

"If you don't think that this is a burden I carry..."

"A burden you carry! Your ink... is *their* blood!" Voronsky's words were like daggers. "But don't worry, they're all gone now, so it's just a matter of time before your blood will be someone else's ink. Someone less talented and more obsequious than you–if that's even possible." Voronsky hung up.

Rising from his desk, Morozov slowly stepped to the outer office and walked over to Alexei's desk where he took his seat and just breathed slowly. His eyes glanced at the small shelf of books he had placed there showcasing his fellow frauds.

He saw a mediocre melodrama written by some grinning fool named Charov, a bland party functionary. Yet the book immediately brought tears to his eyes. It was a memorial to his dear old friend the courtly Yeghishe Charents. He had picked up the fake book and flipped through its pages and remembered Yeghishe, who had somehow evaded the Turks during their monstrous genocide. After fleeing into Russia, Charents joined the Red Army and fought valiantly in the Civil War. He then studied briefly in Moscow with Morozov in the Institute of Literature and Arts under the tutelage of the esteemed poet Valery Bryusov.

Although Charents joined him down in Yerevan and helped establish the Armenian Writers Union, Morozov noticed as the poet's work slowly veered from the party line. At the time, he tried to warn him. Careerists were constantly on the lookout to turn in others in order to elevate themselves. And sure enough, soon one did. Charents' work came under attack. The great Gorki tried to help him, bolstering his sagging reputation, saying what a fine writer he was, but it didn't help. Steadily Charents' output declined.

Whenever Morozov thought of Charents, he also remembered his other close friend and co-worker Aghasi Khanjian–who became the First Secretary of the Armenian Communist Party. Morozov was too frightened to even find a memorial book for Aghasi as the man was grabbed by the devil himself, the head of the NKVD, Lavrenti Beria. In arresting the first secretary, he demonstrated for all to see that no one was safe, no matter how high they climbed.

Usually all the big fish were given show trials, but Khanjian never made it to court. Supposedly he died while waiting to be interrogated, yet everyone knew the truth. Soon after Aghasi's death, against Morozov's stern advice, Charents courageously wrote a requiem poem to his old friend, pinning a bullseye on his own back.

As Charents saw his end looming before him, he anesthetized himself with morphine. One day in 1938, when the Refinement was in high gear, Morozov came to work to find a stack of death warrants on his desk, just waiting for his signature; among them was one for Charents, who was incarcerated in a prison hospital due to his addiction. To his own peril, Morozov signed all the warrants but that one. Each day he grew even more fearful wondering how much time would go by before being arrested himself. To his great relief, he was informed that Charents had politely died before he found someone signing his own arrest warrant.

Overnight, the Armenian poet's books seemed to magically vanish from the shelves as though they had died with him.

It was this particular detail, the erasure of his life work, that Morozov found truly exquisite. At first he thought of it almost as a form of torture after death. But one day, he read the Irish philosopher George Berkeley's famous quote, "If a tree falls in a forest and no one is around to hear it, does it make a sound?" With that single phrase, Morozov had a revelation: If the greatest artistic works of an entire generation are erased, did that society–the people in that time and place–ever really exist? Rather than erasing Charents and countless others, Morozov took a strange comfort in the thought that those thugs in power were effectively eliminating all records of themselves and the despicable age they had lived.

74

Alexei, Woodstock Festival, 1969

On the evening of Sunday, August 17, 1968, Alexei Novikov, Sergei Hagopian, his daughter, Anna O'Brien, and her friend Eric Stein stood along the outer edge of the crowd and listened to a bunch of mop-headed boys on stage, playing tunes loosely reminiscent of Elvis Presley.

"What's the name of this band?" Sergei shouted into his daughter's ear.

"Ten Years After," she yelled.

"Ten years after what?" Alexei asked. None answered.

In the warm, packed darkness as Alexei was halfway through a bottle of vodka, the band's name compelled him to remember ten years after Morozov's death. That was when Stalin himself finally croaked. The entire nation went into a contest of mourning. And Georgy Malenkov, his own boss, finally took over the reins of power. Quickly though, Malenkov's spinelessness and obsequious personality emerged. This in turn seemed to awaken everyone to the prolonged horror of what they had suffered while at the hands of the Georgian monster. Overnight the flat and charmless Malenkov was pushed aside by the ebullient and gregarious Khrushchev. Aside from a lucky group of Jewish doctors who had just been rounded up in Moscow due to Stalin's final paranoid conspiracy, who were suddenly set free, no great repudiations occurred. There was no mass amnesty of all those unlawfully incarcerated over decades. The millions who had been sent away on trumped-up charges still had to finish their sentences or die trying.

Beria, the sadistic head of the secret police, was discreetly put down like the lecherous little rat that he was.

Even though the prisons throughout Russia still remained packed with victims of the former leader's paranoia, the full extent of Stalin's damage to the country was cautiously being addressed in the secrecy of the Politburo, resulting in a tentative "thaw." Communism was given a new hiccup of freedom.

The works of writers and artists and thinkers from the past twenty-odd years, who were abruptly dispatched and had their works redacted from history as well, were reconsidered. By the mid-1950s as the leadership tried to modestly repair the damage, certain books began to magically reappear on bookshelves throughout Russia. It was during this period that an announcement appeared in the *Literary Gazette*, an anthology of stories by Armenian writer Haig Morozov would be republished. Several months later, someone who decided that Moscow needed to show a spirit of inclusion to its tiny border republics decided to ignore the writer's chosen moniker and resurrect his family name. Overnight *Kasabian's Tales*, a selection of his best stories, appeared and became a bestseller.

"He did it to himself," Alexei whispered over the blaring rock music. "It wasn't my fault."

If his time with the Armenian writer had taught him anything it was simply that, though he actually enjoyed doing it, writing fiction just wasn't worth it. The labor was too great, the rewards were too small, and there was far too much political risk.

Shortly after the Morozov fiasco in 1943, Alexei Romanovich Novikov was returned to the military, but in a noncombatant position as reporter for the military newspaper in Moscow. There, after the war ended, he met a girl, fell in love, and with the patronage of his young bride's father, a powerful figure in the Moscow Communist Party, he landed a coveted job as a cub reporter at *Pravda*. With his own work for the party and favors done for various big politicos, he slowly moved his way up the ranks, covering the city beat in Moscow. Gradually, he got onto the prized editorial board and by the early 1960s, with the birth of his second son, he was offered the assistant editor position on the prestigious international news desk.

No sooner had Ten Years After finished its noisy set than another band, unironically entitled The Band, began loading onto the stage. Perhaps it was the booze or the lively crowd, but Alexei found himself emulating the kids around him, slowly stepping to their beat. Soon he was clumsily dancing familiar steps with the surrounding tribe of young hippies who were amused by the old dude's low-key folk dancing steps.

"Are you Russian?" some kid divined from his hop-kick choreography. He nodded yes.

"Hey man, we're going to have a revolution here too someday!" the kid said.

"You better hope not," Alexei replied, laughing.

The kid lit up a joint and offered it to him. He took a puff and kept dancing until a sharp pain in his side compelled him to stop–his old war wound was flaring up again. Alexei sat down next to Sergei's daughter's boyfriend who was lying on the mud fast asleep. He felt sleepy too, but didn't want to get his clothes muddy.

Near the pond, Alexei spotted Sergei chatting quietly with his shiny new daughter. Neither was listening to the music. She was finally relaxing. Alexei walked over intending to ask the Armenian to keep an eye on the boy so he could head up to the tent, but he overheard Sergei say, "Your mother is trying her best, you know. It's not easy for her alone."

"You don't know! She's a monster!"

"Come on, be fair. She's a good woman who deeply cares about you … And I know I haven't been there for you, but so do I, if you'll just give me a chance…"

340

"Everybody deserves a second chance," she replied, thinking more about herself specifically when she'd return home tomorrow to her angry mother.

Alexei could hear tender tones rising in Sergei's voice, a pitch that he hadn't heard in twenty years. Sergei was clearly in love with his lapsed daughter and he wanted to get to know her. At the same time, she also seemed to be slowly, cautiously reciprocating. Concerned for the spongy-haired Jew who had come close to getting stepped on by surrounding hippies, Alexei returned to the sleeping lad.

"Wake up, kid," said Alexei to young Stein, helping him up from the mud.

"What's up?" the kid asked groggily.

"We have an empty tent where no one will trip over you."

"A tent!" Stein sighed. After two days of sleeping in the sticky raincoat of a lean-to, the idea of an actual tent sounded luxurious.

75

Kasabian, Moscow, 1943

From outside Morozov's office, Darya noticed the Armenian writer staring at his library of fake books wracked with palpable sadness. Silently, she stuck a small, weathered photograph in his face.

He looked at her severely, then down at the photograph. It was his beloved Masha, still young, holding an infant in her arms.

"What the hell!" he said, snatching the photo from her hand.

Darya put a finger over her mouth then pointed at the baby and then at herself.

He took the photo and held it up to the light. It looked like it must've been taken about twenty years ago, not long after she had left him. He didn't recognize any of the surrounding buildings. It didn't look like Moscow. He assumed it was taken in the Ukraine.

Before he could utter a word, Darya took out a scrap of paper, scribbled on it and held it before him: "TALK OUTSIDE."

She stepped back and pointed out of his office window to a distant street corner. Her beautiful young face was filled with apprehension. He couldn't say no. Alexei hadn't yet returned. He tensely nodded yes. Still in her coat, she left the office, exited the building, and ducked into a nearby doorway across the street. Five minutes later, she watched Morozov in his coat and hat exiting as well. She hastily walked up from behind. In a moment, they were walking side by side.

"That's a picture of my mother holding me," she said simply. "She died about ten years ago."

"You're..."

"Yes."

"Masha Rodchenko died?" he whispered, unable to look up. It felt as though a giant plug had been pulled from his heart, draining a lifetime of hope from his world. At the bleakest, loneliest times over the past twenty years, his survival rested on the blind belief that she was still alive somewhere. He lost any faith in god long ago, when his people were slaughtered, but the notion that somehow he'd eventually find his way back to Masha, if only for a final farewell, that still endured.

"She had psychological problems," Darya explained. "She died there."

"When did this happen?"

"November 20, 1933," she said.

"Not because of the..."

"No, her mental state deteriorated before that," she said, knowing that even talking about the famine was unofficially taboo.

"I'm so..." he couldn't speak. "I tried finding her." He realized he had waited too long.

"I'm sorry about last night, but I had my doubts too, which was why I had to check your journals," she replied as they walked. Both of their eyes discreetly searched along the streets and windows for anyone who might be watching.

"Why didn't you just tell me who you were?" he asked.

"I thought it'd be better to approach you gradually over time, to win your trust. I mean I didn't even know if my mother was telling

342

the truth, or if it was just delusional, that my father was an Armenian writer. But once I saw my mother's name in your journal, I couldn't stop reading."

"This morning," he replied. "I called my office down in Yerevan and had my secretary locate your letter and read it to me…"

"My mother told me how she left you suddenly, but I didn't believe her," Darya said. "And years ago when I read your short story for the first time, I thought maybe it was true."

"You know, she was just six months away from finishing medical college, from getting her MD," he muttered.

"She told me that every day," Darya said. "How she came so close to being a doctor."

"It was my fault that she got expelled. All my fault!"

"She said that too." She paused. Darya stopped at the corner and looked at him, but he refused to make eye contact or say anything. "You don't believe me?"

"Why didn't you put that in your letter?" he asked, coldly.

"And say what, 'Dear Writer Morozov, My psychologically disturbed mother says you're my dad. Please rescue me from the state orphanage. Sincerely, Darya'?"

"Exactly and I would've!" he replied emphatically.

"You didn't even open my letter," she replied.

"You're right."

"It's okay. People think orphans are children whose parents died, but my orphanage was filled with girls whose fathers and mothers had given them up. So aside from being unsure if you were my father and trying to convince you who I was, I also feared that you knew about me and simply wanted no part of it."

"I tried looking for her. And you as well!" He didn't mention that he thought Masha had a son, not a daughter.

"Well, I figured that I only had one chance so I was hoping that if you replied we could correspond and slowly become friends. And I could make my case."

"You need to understand, if you had told me about this earlier, I would've been much more inclined to believe you."

"So you still don't believe me?"

"Since I've arrived here I've been under constant surveillance," he said, searching around. "Indeed you work with the very team investigating me. *You are* investigating me. That's correct, isn't it?"

"Yes, but…"

"What are the odds of this happening? My long-lost daughter being one of the investigators on my case?"

"I'm not an investigator. I'm a student. I'm only doing this to cover my tuition."

"Your tuition?"

"I came here on a partial scholarship 'cause my mother went here."

"Okay."

"It was only for one year and at the time, I happened to be dating Alexei so I told him that I loved your work."

"I see," he resumed walking and she followed.

"He informed me that you had been picked as the first writer in the Ulanov Residency Program and I thought that this was finally my big chance to meet you."

"So what happened?"

"You apparently belong to another faction so they were looking for someone who they thought might be able to earn your confidence. Alexei asked if I wanted the job. He said it was all information-gathering. And I couldn't go back to the Ukraine anyway. So it made complete sense. I figured I could help protect you and at the same time I could finally meet you."

"Perhaps you're telling the truth. Perhaps not. But you and your boyfriend will be rewarded if you manage to find some way to put me away, won't you?"

"True, but…"

"And now of all times, you've conveniently come forward with a photograph of some young woman who everyone knew I had dated twenty years ago, holding a baby. And you're telling me you're that baby?" He looked up at her and asked. "Would this be enough proof to risk your life?"

344

"Wait! I have better proof!" She reached into her purse. As they kept walking, she discreetly pressed something sharp and small into his palm. He examined it. To his shock, it appeared to be a diamond– a sizable one at that. It was the same one that Lucille had described as being in the photograph sent five years earlier.

"What is this?" He handed it back to her.

"My mother said you gave it to her," Darya said.

"I gave her a...?"

Morozov froze, and just studied her beautiful face: The eyes were hers, but her mouth and nose, they were his. He dropped the diamond, which she immediately retrieved. He instantly confirmed three details: First, that Lunz had in fact stolen diamonds just as Critter had reported. The second and third details made him clutch her to keep from collapsing: Twenty years earlier, when he was away at his mother's house outside St. Petersburg, the drunken son of a bitch, his best friend, had probably forced himself on his beloved Masha: Darya wasn't his daughter–she was Lunz's daughter! For a moment, looking around him, a flash of fury, blinding hatred filled him. As he caught his breath, he was about to lash out and tell her: *Your father was a filthy, drunken, backstabbing thief and your mother was worse!*

The betrayal must've occurred during Lenin's burial week! Further comtemplation revealed the age-old mystery of why Masha abruptly left him. She knew she was pregnant and in the ensuing weeks and months, she was beginning to show. Then, when he went down for the job interview in Yerevan, she wasted little time packing her bags and leaving.

Staring into Darya's face, he realized that despite the soul-twisting agony he felt–she had been betrayed even worse–by the same exact couple. Yet she didn't even know it. He took a deep breath to get his bearings and said, "I have something difficult to tell you, Darya."

"Just hear me out," she pleaded. He could hear a tremble in her voice. "I understand your doubt. I really do. I had a plan to win your trust."

345

"And how would you do that?" he uttered just above a whisper.

"By helping you get through all this," she said, pausing at a crosswalk. "I mean, you're not going to be here much longer. I can let you know what they're going to do. I can try to help you navigate this until you return south."

"This all happened because of me," he muttered, still in shock at Masha and Dimitri's betrayal.

"Because of you?" Darya asked, still thinking he was talking about the investigation.

"I got your mother expelled from medical college. That was all my arrogance. I put the Revolution above her! What loyalty did she owe me after that?"

"But you tried to fix things."

"I'm glad you read my journal, so that you know that," he said, grateful to finally be able to share his burden with another. "But let's face it–I killed her."

"I always thought that I had killed her," she replied softly.

"You?"

"Everyone said that when I was born she changed. Her personality changed. Everyone says that having kids transforms you." Thinking about it a moment, Darya added, "You must've had some idea that she was pregnant."

"I really didn't," he replied. "I mean, she was gaining weight. I should've guessed but we were always so careful."

"But you knew she had a baby," Darya asked.

"I learned about it a year after she left Moscow. Someone told me she saw her in Kiev with a child." Suddenly, he froze. Without even knowing it, he knew that by talking about this, he was letting Darya accept that she was his daughter, which was neither true nor helpful.

"Look," he said. "I don't want to hurt you, but I don't think you want to hurt me either."

"I never would."

"You need to understand that over the past twenty years, I've seen so many of my friends get arrested…" He didn't add that he had signed off on countless arrests himself.

346

"So you still think I'm making all this up just to arrest you?" she asked, clearly distressed.

"That's not even the issue," he said.

"It is to me!" She grabbed him. Tears were in his eyes. "I waited all my life for this moment! To be able to meet my father. To not feel all alone here." He looked down both sides of the street to see if anyone was watching and gently removed her hands.

"What kind of father would I be if... This is really what's best for the both of us," he said, believing he was giving her a bigger gift by allowing her to continue to believe the lie–that she was his daughter.

"This is awful," she murmured, looking to the ground.

"It's not that bad," he said. "I mean, we both know the truth– that's all that's important. And by not announcing it, we'll be out of their reach."

"But you're my father," she half-announced, half-appealed.

"Yes, I am," he replied softly. "But for now that's our secret."

"So you do believe me?" she said desperately.

"Of course, but..." Before he could finish, the illegitimate daughter of Dimitri Lunz and Masha Rodchenko threw her arms around his neck as though hanging onto a slim branch over a great height. Everyone on the street around them stared. Only when he hugged her back did she release him.

"Thank you, Dad!" she said.

"Please don't call me that."

"But you are!"

"But it could get us both in trouble."

"You don't understand. For me this is a dream come true. Maybe my greatest dream!"

"Listen!" He was trying to keep this from getting out of hand. "My sabbatical here in Moscow ends shortly. This is for your sake more than mine. I mean, you don't have the same level of protection that I do. So I want you to promise that for the rest of my stay here you're not to going to come near me. I'm under steady surveillance. If we're together, they'll catch us. This must be our secret."

"It would be smarter if we just kept doing things as we usually did," she replied.

"Absolutely not! Being together is just not safe," he said. "When I get back to Armenia, after some time has passed and all this has blown over, I can send you some money. You can come down and perhaps we can get to know each other." Then he paused and asked, "Did it ever occur to you that they already know that you're my daughter and they're just waiting to catch us?"

"If they did know I think they would've already made some move. And I also think staying apart is a big mistake. They're going to wonder why we're apart. I'm supposed to cook and clean for you."

"It'll create all sorts of problems," he said nervously.

"You're my father so I'll do whatever you want," she said, preparing to stay away from him. "Maybe when you're alone only with your thoughts, you can think about the fact that you have a daughter who is very proud of you."

He nodded, unable to look at Dimitri Lunz's child, instead of the daughter he should've had, and briskly walked away.

76

Alexei, Woodstock Festival, 1969

As some new band blared in the middle of the night, the groggy teenage boy and corpulent Russian journalist tiredly climbed up the crowded, dark slope to the campgrounds on the far side of the concert area. As they walked, they discovered gaps had opened up in the quiltwork of wet campsites. People had left to beat tomorrow's closing rush. Quickly, Alexei found their pup tent situated along the edge.

"My bed is on the right, you're on the left," he said as the kid scurried in and stretched out on Sergei's slightly damp sleeping bag. Alexei kicked off his shoes and slowly followed, laying down on the comforter next to the youth. With the music still blaring in the background, both quickly drifted off to a deep sleep.

Apparently a large bird, perhaps a falcon, had flown into the tent. It was whipping its wings and claws against the fabric trying to get out. Alexei flipped on a flashlight and saw it was the kid struggling with the canvas top of the tent.

"Relax, son! You're in a tent. Remember? We're at the Woodstock Hippie Dippie Festival."

"Oh right," Eric remembered, and began to calm down. "Sorry. I just woke up and thought I was trapped in some kind of large underwater net."

"It takes three days of sleeping here before you get used to it," he kidded.

"Gosh, my heart is racing," the kid said.

"Want a little vodka?"

"Sure," the kid replied.

Alexei handed him the remains of one of the nearly empty bottles that lined the side of his sleeping area. The kid unscrewed it, took a swallow, and said, "So what's your deal anyway?"

"My deal?" Alexei said, trying to grasp the idiom.

"Are you a commie?"

"Very proudly."

"Why?"

"Cause it's the only chance mankind has of enduring in a world being steadily strangled to death by capitalism," he replied calmly.

"That's funny 'cause communists seem to be strangling freedom from those they rule."

"I won't deny that there are sacrifices, but much of what you read is propaganda."

"See this is the big problem, I really can't wrap my head around capitalism versus communism."

"Let me ask you something," Alexei said after a pause. "Have you ever seen this motion picture called *It Is a Wonderful Life*?" It was the movie he had seen at the hotel just before driving up here with Sergei.

"*It's a Wonderful Life*," he corrected. "Sure."

"You know the character George Bailey?"

"Yeah, Jimmy Stewart."

349

"Right. When he's just about to kill himself, the old angel comes down..."

"Clarence," Eric said.

"Right, Clarence. And he gives George a kind of gift. He shows him what the world would've been like if he had never been born."

"Sure," Eric said, not sure where all this was heading.

"The two worlds we see, with and without George, perfectly highlight my perception of communism versus capitalism. In communism we see George Bailey who makes personal sacrifices to support his community. Ultimately, he ends up being rescued by those he helped."

"Right, he becomes the richest man in Bedford Falls," Eric added.

"But had he not been born, we see the true nature of unchecked capitalism–a terrifying place where the crippled banker..."

"Mr. Potter... Pottersville!"

"Right, Potter buys everything and he simply lives to exploit everyone for the most he can get, without breaking the law, yet without any regard to community or any sense of duty to others."

"That's your idea of capitalism?"

"To me that film holds our two economic systems side by side."

"Where are the prisons?"

"Prisons?"

"You people have all these prisons."

"That's not true. The UN released a study a few years ago that showed that far more prisoners are incarcerated here than in Russia."

"So you're saying that if you're a good communist you get to nail Donna Reed?" Eric joked instead of argued.

"I'm not sure what nailed or who Donna Reed is. My point is that in one world individuals live for the good of the group. Whereas in the other world the greediest individuals essentially live at the expense of the group. They turn the group into their slaves."

"But George Bailey owned things too. He drew a salary. And Potter worked for a living," Eric replied.

"We have ownership and salaries in Russia too," Alexei explained. "I'm just saying it's unfair for Potter to be able to own

350

everything and make more than he can ever spend while so many others work constantly and can barely survive."

"You're showing Russia as this ideal place..."

"I know my model is a little simplistic and biased but we don't have millionaires and we don't have vast ghettos. We certainly have our injustices and problems."

"We have open elections!"

"So you support your President Nixon?" Alexei asked.

"Hell no."

"How about the fact that the government of New York State is headed by a multi-millionaire? Do you think that's just a coincidence?"

"Rockefeller's not as bad as he could be. Sometimes millionaires can be quite decent 'cause they can't be corrupted. Bobby Kennedy was a millionaire, he was my first choice for the presidency."

"I read all about his war on poverty."

"Then he got assassinated, and with it we lost our best chance for peace in Vietnam and fixing this broken country. We still thought Humphrey would win, but that asshole Daley ruined his chance with his police riot."

"I studied many articles about last year's election," Alexei said, "and I have to say that liberal infighting seems to be your country's undoing. You radicals all seem to undermine your own success."

"Just the opposite, man," Stein said confidently. "We're the ones strengthening our nation. Think about it, this country can only work if we as a people truly believe that it belongs to us."

"Oh, I like that!" Alexei said, envisioning the lad's remark as a pull quote for his big article. Stein struck him as the embodiment of every youthful idealist, far more articulate than most of the long-haired potheads he had interviewed so far.

"You know, I've never been able to do this with my boys," Alexei said.

"Do what?"

"Just talk. Exchange ideas."

"Well I've never been able to talk much to my father so I guess it's typical," Eric replied.

"Would you mind if I interviewed you?"

"Ask away!"

The two talked about everything from the latest trends in fashion to the future of America. As Stein kept talking, his responses grew more involved until poor Alexei finally passed out in the humidity.

77

Alexei, Moscow, 1943

When Darya failed to show up in Alexei's flat that night as had been her usual routine, he remembered how frazzled she had been the day before when he mentioned that their supervisor, Ivan, had been arrested. He assumed that she just needed a little time alone. The next day though, when she didn't stop by Morozov's office, Alexei became concerned. Petrov wanted progress in the case, not to mention reports, and she was the inside operative. Alexei called her dormitory, but the supervisor on duty said calls were not forwarded into the student's room after ten p.m.

Early the next morning, when Alexei called her dorm room, she answered groggily.

"You didn't show up," he said. "Are you okay?"

"Oh yeah," she said, sounding a little odd. "I just got a bad head cold. I'll be fine in a couple days."

"Do you want me to bring you some soup?" he asked tiredly.

"No, just give me a little time to recover," she replied. "I'll be fine."

"Well, if you need anything, just give me a call," he said. "I can pick up some food and drop it off by your house."

"Not necessary," she answered, and thanked him for the offer. "I'll be fine in a few days."

By the end of the fourth day, he was summoned by Petrov who asked where his reports were. He replied that Darya was out sick and there had been no progress in the case.

"No progress!" roared the new supervisor. "Your job is making progress, which means you're not doing your job!"

"I'll just go arrest him for being a German spy!" Alexei fired back. "Is that what you want?"

"Don't you dare talk to me like that! I'm not your old school chum!" Apparently Petrov had learned about his friendship with Ivan Lemokh.

"You told me you didn't want me to make the same mistake as Lemokh."

"I asked you to be cautious, not lazy," Petrov roared.

"We're trying our best."

"If this is *your* best," Petrov replied, "I'll get some other nitwit from your army group to shadow the Armenian. And I'll make damn sure you're in his foxhole fighting the Germans."

"I can have them ready tonight, so I'll deliver them in the morning."

"My office door is unlocked. Put them on the desk as soon as you're done."

"Yes sir!"

As he left Petrov's office, he found himself feeling furious toward Darya. The fact that she hadn't provided any new information on her cranky boss was now putting his life in jeopardy. After the meeting, he called her dorm room. When she didn't pick up, he left a message with her switchboard operator. An hour later, when she didn't return his call, he called again and again, each time leaving a new message. When he closed his eyes briefly he dozed off. He slept later than he had intended and she still hadn't returned his call. Angrily he dressed and walked into the freezing night.

Upon entering her dormitory, the night matron, a large woman in a nurse's outfit with an unapologetic mustache, sat before him stating he wasn't allowed up; visiting hours had ended twenty minutes earlier. She would however permit him to speak to her on the phone.

"This is urgent!" he replied.

"You can *ask* her to come down and talk with her in the lobby for five minutes," she said. "Under supervision."

"Okay," he sighed. When the matron rang her room, Darya didn't pick up. The matron said, "You'll have to see her in the morning."

"No! This is an emergency!"

"Of what nature?" she asked, not easily moved.

"She's sick with a fever. She hasn't been returning my calls all day! She could be unconscious."

"I'm sorry, but if she's asleep..."

"If she's asleep I'll just wake her up. But if she's on the floor unconscious, burning up with a fever, I'm going to report you. I can't tell you who I work for but I guarantee heads will roll!"

"I have rules..."

"And we both know that during exigent circumstances, like a possible medical emergency, you're allowed to make exceptions."

She had recognized him from prior visits so she agreed. He was allowed to go up, but she insisted that he had no more than fifteen minutes. "No funny business!"

Within five minutes, Alexei was up two flights of steps knocking on her door. But after another five minutes when his knocks turned to bangs, she still didn't answer. Pressing his ear to the door, he didn't hear a sound, so he kicked the door and yelled, "I know you're in there, Darya! If you don't open up this instant I'll get the pass key. I swear it!"

Within a few seconds, she opened the door and walked past him without acknowledging him, out to the communal bathroom. Alexei entered her room. He examined it and seeing her pillow with its indentation, he touched it and realized it was moist. It might've been fever sweat, but it also could've been tears.

"What's the matter?" he asked when she returned.

"Nothing," she said without making eye contact.

"Come on! Out with it," he said, placing his hand on her cheek. "You've been out sick for days and you don't even have a fever."

"I just learned that my dearest girlfriend down in the Ukraine was killed, okay! Satisfied?" She started crying uncontrollably.

She got back into bed. He took off his coat and scarf and sat on its edge and started unlacing his shoes.

"What do you think you're doing?"

"I don't want you to spend another night alone."

"It's against the rules. And I'll get in trouble!"

"No you won't. I'll take care of it!"

"I want to be alone!" she shouted. For a few minutes, he lay quietly next to her.

"All right," Alexei finally whispered, aware he had overstepped his fifteen-minute limit and that the matron would come up and drag him out soon. "But promise me you'll spend tomorrow night with me even if you're sick!" He had a small apartment of his own, without a monitor restricting his comings and goings. She relented and he left, gruffly thanking the mustached matron on the way out.

The next day at the university, he overheard Morozov mutter something about how much he hated eating food from his local diner.

Alexei kept waiting for Darya to show up at his office, but the morning hours passed and she didn't appear. By late afternoon, with still no sign of her, he knew something was wrong. She was clearly working out some problem, so he tried to be patient and wondered if her situation was somehow connected to the case. Darya had always seemed immune to melancholia. Indeed she was always cheering him up.

Although he initially thought that he'd give her another night alone to try to sort things out, after dinner, he got a call from Petrov who again asked about the reports. Not taking any chances, he bought some flowers and headed over to her dormitory again. Again it was just after visiting hours.

Just like the prior night, she refused to answer his call from the main desk. Because he had complied the day before, the night matron again let him pass, giving him fifteen minutes to return or else. When he knocked, Darya opened. Immediately he could see by her messy hair and all the soiled tissues that she had spent yet another day in bed. The single detail that grabbed him was that even though Darya never mentioned her before, there was now a picture of this dead friend, a sweet young girl with a candle burning before it. Although she spoke little about the past, Darya always was very open. If the friend had suddenly been killed, it was more in her nature to call him immediately, seeking comfort in his arms.

"What was her name?" he asked, picking up the photo, inspecting it closely.

She looked at him nervously. "Elena."

"I don't remember you ever mentioning an Elena," he said.

"My childhood was not a pleasant one. Pardon me if I chose not to be forthcoming."

"Come to think of it, I don't remember you ever talking about it at all."

"I grew up in the state orphanage," she said.

"Wow, you never mentioned that," he said sympathetically.

"Frankly, I'm ashamed of it," she said.

"Why?"

"It was like a training school for harlots," she said flatly. "The old bastard who ran it fed us and looked after us according to the favors we did for him."

"Just awful."

"I was just a girl. Elena was older. If it wasn't for her, I would've starved to death."

"How did she go?" he asked.

"Like I said, she was killed in an air raid," she repeated, not unlikely as the Ukraine was still experiencing some of the worst of the combat.

"How old was Elena?"

"I told you," she replied, "a little older than me."

"She was very pretty," he said, staring at the photograph.

Darya took the picture out of his hands and put it back behind the candle.

"So sorry," he said. "What was Elena's last name?"

Darya froze. In that moment, she knew he had her. She could've easily produced a name, but knew he'd call to check to see if she had actually been killed. She silently returned to bed. In another moment she began bawling her eyes out.

He waited for her to tire herself out, then he softly said, "If Ivan Lemokh was still in charge I could deal with him, but Petrov is on me like a hawk. I can't cover for you much longer. Just tell me the truth. I can help you."

She didn't respond.

"Did you get into a fight with him, is that it?"

She considered telling him he caught her going through his private papers. She could say she was looking for evidence.

"He raped you, didn't he?" Alexei asked.

"No! Nothing like that!"

"What did he do?"

"He didn't rape me," she said slowly.

"What then?"

"He..."

Tell me!" He pushed, not letting up. "Tell me, or I'll confront him myself!"

"He rejected me."

"He can't do that! He's not authorized to fire you! You were appointed by..."

"Look, I got into a fight with him, okay? We worked it out. I'm going back in a few days so there's nothing to worry about."

When he asked her more about their fight, she started weeping again. When he tenderly touched her back, she pulled away. He realized she was done for the night. She had put the whole thing behind her and was as tight as a drum.

The next day at school, Alexei listened as the Armenian writer said that he heard there was a big Spring Faculty Luncheon at the VIP dining room next week and wondered why he hadn't gotten an invitation.

"It's usually just for the senior faculty members," Alexei said.

"Can you get me an invitation?" he asked.

357

"I'll look into it, but from what I hear the food isn't special, just sandwiches."

"Don't patronize me, I just want to get to know the faculty."

"I was just worried that something was wrong with Darya's cooking," Alexei casually said.

"It's fine," he mumbled.

"What did she make for you last night?" he asked.

"An Armenian dish called 'mind your own damn business,'" he said with a scowl.

78

Eric, NYC, September 11, 2001

Five minutes after the horrific airplane accident, all could smell the thick smoke as the North Tower burned. Despite the fact that the South Tower was sealed, the thick black smoke permeated the building, coming in through the vents and into the air ducts. Though much of it was filtered, the noxious fumes of the burning airplane fuel was soon overwhelming the entire ninety-third floor. Soon it began stinging Eric's eyes and irritating his throat. Using his cellular phone, he left a message on his wife's voicemail, but she was still in Peru. He repeatedly tried to call his son, but the calls weren't going out.

"If you got a minute," Lande's sporty secretary approached Eric who was sitting in the outer reception area. "Mr. Lande would appreciate it if you could join him."

"Sure," Eric said, snapping his phone shut. Twenty minutes had passed since the deafening explosion across the plaza. The distant wailing of countless sirens echoed up from the street. All knew about the freak plane accident across the way but were finding a silent comfort in the fact that the fire was isolated to the North Tower.

Eric entered Lande's spacious sun-flooded corner office. Lande was sitting at his desk studying the hefty IPO all had just signed. It was like a half-billion-dollar phone book. For a moment, Eric froze as he saw the paperback on Lande's desk. It was the copy of *Kasabian's Tales* that he kept in his Midtown office.

358

"Oh, no," Lande said, seeing his expression and sensing what he was thinking. "This isn't your book. I just bought it on the computer. You can buy books through computers nowadays."

"So I've heard."

"It's just like yours. That's why I got it."

"It is," he said, inspecting the edition. It was a recent reprint from just a few years ago, in much better shape.

"So the IPO is finally signed and done–and as far as I can tell, you did a splendid job."

"Thank you, David."

"You were beginning to doubt I'd ever do it. Don't deny it," he said with a grin.

"Maybe a little," Eric tried to show a bit of levity.

"Since we're stuck here, I thought I'd use the opportunity to understand a couple things."

"Of course. What did you have in mind?" Eric assumed he was referring to the public offering.

"Frankly, though he was old, my father's mind was sharp as a tack to the very end, so I can't fully understand what compelled him to believe that you were his son. And I do remember you saying that you were friends with Kasabian." He held the paperback out. "But you couldn't've been friends with Kasabian, could you? I mean, he died seven years before you were even born."

"It was late in the day when I said that. I had three cocktails at lunch and I slipped up. I'm sorry."

"The fact that you turned down a considerable sum of money demonstrated that you are an honest man, which is why I trusted you with my IPO, but how the hell can you say you knew someone who died years before you were even born halfway around the world and then call it a slip-up?"

"Remember the big Woodstock Music Festival back in 1969?" Eric explained.

"Of course."

"I went up there when I was just a kid. I ended up spending two days with a small group that included an older Russian journalist named Alexei Novikov who, happened to be Kasabian's assistant over twenty years earlier in Moscow during the war. We briefly became friends that weekend. Alexei was the one who signed that book in Kasabian's name. He wrote that inscription in Russian. He was kidding around. Someone told me later that what he wrote loosely translated to something like 'I was his son,' which your father must've read when he opened my book."

"Ahh!" David replied. "Dad told me that when he was very young he had a sexual liaison with the writer's girlfriend. Then afterwards, he said he deeply regretted it. He must've learned that he impregnated her and thought you were the son."

"Your father had an affair with Kasabian's girlfriend?" Eric asked.

"That's what he told me just before he died. He mellowed out in his later years, but when he was younger, everyone said he was a tiger. He would cheat on my mother until she finally left him, which was why he stopped drinking. But back in Russia when he was still young, I can only imagine the crazy things he must've done."

"If he felt guilty enough to leave me half his estate," Eric said, "he must've felt pretty crappy about the liaison."

"When we visited Russia last month, I tried to look up Haig Morozov–Kasabian's son–I figured that maybe I could give him a small endowment assuming he was a half-brother–but by all accounts the writer never married or had a family."

"If I'm not mistaken," Eric said, trying to remember. "Alexei, the assistant, said he dated a girl who claimed to be Kasabian's daughter. And I think he spared her from getting arrested."

"Glad to hear that," Lande replied.

79

Alexei, Moscow, 1943

Over the next week, Alexei found himself making calls to get Morozov an invitation to the Faculty Lunch. At the same time, his overbearing boss Petrov had him retroactively write a full dossier of his investigation of the Armenian, starting from when he first picked him up from the train station weeks earlier. Alexei parsed out some of the minor information that he picked up along the way, such as the fact that Morozov stated that he liked the subversive poet Mandelstam. With a slightly different writing style, he also wrote a second set of reports loosely echoing his first reports in Darya's name to account for all the time and diligence she had spent on the case.

Throughout the week, in the evenings, he also kept visiting poor Darya at her dormitory, bringing her soup and trying to help her recuperate. Every time he gingerly mentioned seeing Morozov at work, he could see the stress in her face as she pretended nothing was wrong. He had no doubts that whatever was bothering her was directly related to this case. By the week's end, he got an angry call to report to Petrov's office first thing Monday morning. His tactics weren't working and his boss was clearly out of patience.

That evening, he went down to Petrov's office, ostensibly to drop off another useless report. As expected. his supervisor wasn't there.

Without wasting a moment, Alexei opened the drawers of his small wooden file cabinet and began thumbing through the files. He quickly found the file marked ARMENIAN. Opening it, he sorted through the reports he had submitted and finally found a sheet with a brief description of himself and behind it a brief description that Ivan Lemokh had written of Darya Lebedova Kotova. It was taken from her school records. The file detailed that she was orphaned at nine years old, had lived in the state orphanage, then had been adopted at age fourteen by the Lebedova family. She attended the

Taras Shevchenko School in the Ukraine, where she had graduated with honors.

The next day, paying out of his own pocket, he called the school outside of Kiev, and assuming his old boss's identity, he introduced himself as Secret Police Lieutenant Ivan Ivanovich Lemokh.

After half a dozen more phone calls and three calls back, he discovered that ten years earlier, Darya's biological mother had died in the state insane asylum outside of Kiev. Because of the war, one clerk stated, a lot of records were lost. Nothing else was known about her.

He soon concocted a plan. That afternoon Alexei got a piece of stationery from Housekeeping that said, "From the Desk of the Deputy Director of Housekeeping." He also secured a Staff Appointment Requisition Form, which consisted mainly of little boxes that had to be checked. He carefully filled it out and, two days later, he called Darya.

By way of apology for his recent insensitivity, he asked Darya if he could take her out for a nice dinner that Saturday night. She suspiciously consented. He was rarely contrite. The dinner ended with a cheap bottle of wine and a lot of sweet talk. She loosened up. Soon they were laughing and affectionate as they used to be. Once they reached his apartment, he gently began to kiss her, caressing her arms and rubbing her back. When they had sex, Alexei put all his efforts into trying to please her–the girl he was attracted to, before her recruitment. After she drifted off to sleep he delicately crept out of bed.

Still asleep, she dreamed she smelled cigarette smoke, an aroma she usually liked. Opening her eyes, just a bit, she saw a tiny orange glow burning in the darkness. She made out a ghostly form. When she flipped on her bedside lamp, Alexei was sitting at the foot of her bed staring at her.

"What are you doing?" she asked.

"I'm in one hell of a bind," Alexei said tensely.

"What bind?"

"I just got a letter today from Petrov, the new boss."

"What letter?"

"I have no idea what he'll do to me," he said, rubbing out his cigarette.

"What are you saying?" she asked, surprised after such a light, romantic evening.

"He got notified from Housekeeping that Morozov has requested a new housekeeper."

"He what?"

"Quit lying to me, Darya!" he shouted, and punched the foot of the mattress she was sleeping upon.

"I told you I had problems with him, but we worked it out," she said earnestly.

"My boss yelled at me this afternoon asking why I hadn't told him that Morozov had fired you! He threw the letter in my face."

"I don't believe it!"

"Don't worry, you can ask him yourself. He wants to see you."

"Me!"

"He said time is a factor! And that because you and I were romantically linked I've compromised the entire investigation."

"You what!"

"He's going to have me arrested! You too, probably."

"Why didn't you tell me this earlier?"

"Under the circumstances I didn't want to upset you. I wanted to enjoy a final evening together."

"Show me this Housekeeping letter!" She got out of bed and put on her robe.

He pulled the envelope out of his jacket and tossed it on the bed. She opened it up and read the fake requisition form saying Morozov requested a new housekeeper. Under reason he wrote, "Housekeeper stopped coming to work."

"This makes no sense," she replied. "I'll have Morozov..."

"I can make up my own lies, Darya! From you I expected the truth!" he said, clearly disappointed.

"Look," she said timidly. "I never would've put you at risk or done any of this, but I was in a difficult spot."

"Done any of what?"

"Taken this job."

"You told me your tuition was almost gone. The Germans were occupying your country! I thought I was doing you a favor!"

"You were!"

"You told me that you had some added knowledge of the Armenian."

"I read his books. But he hadn't written that much."

"You gave me the impression that you knew something more."

"Oh, you mean the letter," she said.

"What letter?"

"I told you I wrote him a letter years ago."

"You never told me that–what letter?"

"I told you about this. I even told Ivan! He never even replied."

"Why'd you write him?"

"It was a fan letter," she said. "I was just a girl. I'm sure many wrote him. All of Russia reads his stories."

"You had some sort of connection with him, didn't you?" he asked.

"Connection?"

"Did you meet him somewhere earlier? Is that it?"

"No, I met him here, with you."

"But before this?"

"No! Never!" she swore.

"Then what!" Alexei rose to his feet. "Don't lie! You're connected to him!"

"I'm... I'm…" She was tongue tied.

"You're what?!" Alexei got up and grabbed her shoulders so he was staring directly into her eyes. "Darya, you're my girlfriend. If you're in trouble let me help you."

"I'm not in trouble."

"I'm in trouble, so you are too. What the hell is going on?!"

"I'll get Morozov to vouch for us," she said.

"You think getting the subject of a police investigation to vouch will help us?" he asked sarcastically.

"I'm sure I can!"

"Just tell me the goddamn truth!"

"This is very difficult to explain," she said and taking a deep sigh she sat back down on the edge of his bed.

"Just say it."

"Twenty years ago, before I was born, Morozov... dated my mother."

"What! Where?"

"Here! At the university," she said. Alexei's mouth fell open.

"Wait a second," Alexei said.

"She was a student, he was her tutor. She left him before he even knew!"

"Knew what? Say it."

"That she was pregnant."

"Your mother left the writer Morozov?"

"Yes. They were together, but I never met him."

"And you knew this!"

"I did, but..."

"Oh my god," he suddenly realized why he couldn't find anything out about her past. "He's your father!"

She sat perfectly still staring sternly at the floor.

"Darya! How could you do this to us!" he yelled.

"I didn't plan it. I never met the man before. And the opportunity just fell into my lap."

"The opportunity to meet your father? Say it!" Alexei said.

"Yes! My father! I didn't even know he was my father for certain until a few days ago."

"Only a few days?"

"My mother told me some stuff, but I wasn't sure what to believe. Most of it I got from his journals!"

"*His* journals?"

"I read them."

"When was this?"

"Remember the other night when I came over. You first learned that Ivan Lemokh was arrested?"

"You came over later than usual. You looked disheveled."

365

"Yes, earlier that night I made him dinner but he didn't come home."

"So?"

"I waited for him. As the hours passed I grew more bold 'til I went into his bedroom and flipped through his journals. He wrote all about my mother and what he did and her leaving him."

"He could've walked in and caught you! You jeopardized everything we're doing," he said sternly.

"I didn't do it for the investigation! He knows we're investigating him! I needed to get to the truth for myself."

"You should've met him on your own time. And you should've told me this at once!"

"I've been poor and powerless all my life," she yelled. "I never had money to travel to Yerevan. I tried writing to him twice, but he didn't reply."

"Darya, you've insinuated yourself into a highly sensitive investigation that was initiated at the top level!"

"I really just accepted this job to be able to finish my studies because the Germans are making my home into a wasteland. What else could I do? I can't go home."

Alexei empathized as he was in a similar situation, terrified of being shipped back to the slaughter. But it was all he could do not to focus on the awful situation that Darya had put them in. "When Petrov learns that you knowingly became a part of this, he's going to demand our heads!"

"And how would he find that out?" she said, glaring at him.

"He's on me every single day!" he shouted. "Every morning he makes me submit a report about this goddamn case! Hell, I've been writing yours, covering for you. You put my neck in a noose!"

"I never lied to you."

"Does Morozov even know you're his daughter?"

"No," she lied, intent on keeping him out of it.

"It doesn't matter. You lied by not immediately disqualifying yourself and telling me that you were his daughter."

"Look, the truth is, I really didn't know for sure! He might not even be my father!"

"You're not an idiot and neither am I! Even suspecting it was enough!"

"Fine, I was wrong, but none of this has to do with you or Morozov's guilt or innocence," she said earnestly. "He didn't betray the state!"

"Maybe not, but impregnating some young foreign student twenty years ago and abandoning her with a child..."

"He didn't abandon her! She left him! She went nuts!"

"Right now you should be worried about your own future," he shot back.

"You don't understand. You were raised with two healthy parents. My mother went insane and died when I was a little girl. And he didn't even know he was my father!"

"You used an internal police investigation to meet him!"

"That doesn't mean I didn't do what was required of me."

Alexei let out a long sigh and just stared off, hoping she'd calm down. After a moment, he said, "The only good thing about this situation is the fact that Petrov doesn't know any of this."

"Nor will he," she said sternly.

"Hold on," Alexei said. "This is perfect!"

"You only discovered this three days ago reading his journals. That's why you're revealing this now."

"What does that have to do with anything?!"

"When did he discover you reading his journals?"

"About a week ago?" she said, not volunteering that it was so painful, she drank a bottle of wine she had purchased for him and passed out on his bed.

"Good! So that will provide a reason as to why you weren't forthcoming."

"What reason?"

"You're going to say you suspected this and you told me but we chose not to disclose it 'til we were certain. Now that we know for certain that this is the man who impregnated your mother, we're ready to come forward with this accusation of paternity! That's not much, but it'll be enough for us to embarrass the Armenian, which should get our necks out of the noose."

"Well, I lied," Darya suddenly renounced. "The Armenian knows who I am and he's no longer speaking to me anyway."

"That's even better. He's turned his back on his only daughter!" Alexei said angrily.

"It's more complicated than that!"

"Did he leave your mom when she was pregnant with you?"

"My mother left him! He didn't even know she was pregnant! She broke his heart!"

"How do you know she left him?"

"It's in his journals."

"That can be a manipulation."

"Come on, all his stories are filled with heartbreak!"

"His stories! You weren't even born when he left your mother so you don't really know who left who."

"She left Moscow and moved back to the Ukraine. That's a documented fact!"

"Doesn't it make more sense that he left your mom after impregnating her and then she returned home and became unstable due to the situation he put her in?"

"That just didn't happen. She told me."

"Mightn't she have lied to you, to save face?"

"No!"

"Just consider it. I mean how old was she when you were born?"

"Twenty-two."

"Can you imagine the shame? Going off to college in Moscow and coming back
pregnant and unwed?!"

"You have sex with me and we're not married," she shot back.

He ignored her remark. "And you just said that when you told him all this, he denied being your father."

"If he had impregnated and abandoned my mother, I'd go after him with all I've got. I'm not a forgiving person, believe me!"

"You said she was a student here."

"She was studying medicine, a year away from becoming a doctor."

"And she dropped out?"

"Yes," Darya said, not wanting to reveal the entire editorial debacle that Morozov had caused, which got her expelled.

"He got her pregnant! That's why she dropped out!"

"No, it was something else. A year before that."

"What?"

She sighed and gave him the whole truth. "He made a mistake and got her tossed out of school, but he let her stay with him and he worked to get her pardoned. They permitted her to return to school the following year, but instead she went down to the Ukraine, gave birth to me, and broke his heart!"

"If you learned all this 'cause your mother told you, I might believe it, but the fact that you got this information from his journals means it's unreliable," Alexei replied. "Can't you see that?"

"My mom was crazy. He, on the other hand, had no reason to lie," she replied angrily. "What do you think? He wrote his journal entries thinking some illegitimate kid was going to sneak into his house and read them one night?"

"No, but who doesn't cast themselves in a sympathetic light?"

"Look," she finally said exhausted. "If you want to fabricate some arrest warrant you don't need me. Just do it on your own. This whole place is held together with lies, so just write your own version of events but leave me out of it!"

"When we go to Petrov's office we need to have a single story that'll free us from this mess, or we're going down together! Do you understand?!"

"I'm not betraying my father!"

"But nothing will happen to him! Trust me!"

"Tell that to Ivan. I'm not going to sacrifice my father to this stupidity!"

"Okay, maybe he didn't do anything wrong to your mother, but he's still technically your father and you said he knows it, right?"

She didn't respond.

"If you were my daughter, I'd die to protect you!"

"But instead you're also pulling me down with you!"

"You don't have to tell Petrov any of this!"

"That's not going to get us out of this," he exclaimed. "Only one thing will work."

"I'm not doing it!"

"If that's your choice, so be it," Alexei yelled, "but I refuse to be punished for your actions either."

"No one is punishing you," she replied. "We don't have to say a word about it, no one will know."

"Look, we're in trouble and as I see it, there's only one way for us to get out of this alive."

"He's going to be returning to Yerevan soon. Just let him go!"

"Listen to me, Darya. Petrov is far more attentive than Ivan ever was. If I can catch this in time, so will he."

"You're scared of this bastard!"

"Terrified. He can read me like a book. And he won't let this go. When he realizes what you've done, Darya, punishment will be swift and we'll all go down. So I'm warning you. There's not much time and only one slim possible way out!"

"Are you threatening to turn me in?" she asked. "Your own girlfriend?"

"I'm not going to die for your arrogance."

"My arrogance! You're the one who needs to wake up!" she shouted. "I watched your country starve my people to death and you monsters still don't even acknowledge it! Like it never happened!"

He grabbed her by her slender shoulders and staring deeply into her eyes, he pleaded, "Damn it, Darya, I'm begging you!"

"Don't touch me!" She shoved him back. "I'm not going to sacrifice my father to this monstrous state!"

Alexei silently grabbed his coat and left.

80

The pounding of the rock music seemed to be in sync with the throbbing pain in his side. When Alexei Novikov flipped over, an intense, cutting pain ran through him like a bayonet. He rolled to the former side where it abated. Sunlight was streaming through the narrow slit at the front of the pup tent. The teenage boy Eric was lying next to him on Sergei's sleeping bag, casually reading a book.

"What are you reading?" Alexei asked stiffly, desperately trying to hold it together.

"Just found it here." He held up the copy of *Kasabian's Tales* that Sergei had given him.

"Never heard of the guy before."

"How is it?"

"Interesting when he's not shoveling all the commie guff."

"Agreed. Ideology has no place in fiction."

"I've got to try to find a copy of this," the kid said, handing the book back to Alexei.

"You know what," Alexei said. He picked up a pen and scribbled something inside the title page. "Sergei gave the book to me and I'm giving it to you." He handed it back. Eric tried reading what the old Russian wrote, but it was written in Cyrillic. He did notice that Alexei had jokingly signed it "Haig Kasabian."

"Thanks," said the young man.

"Where the hell is Sergei? He's supposed to be back by now," Alexei wondered.

"Oh! He and Anna popped their heads in about a half an hour ago while you were still asleep. They slept in the car."

"My side is killing me," Alexei said, clutching the scar tissue of his old war wound.

"Anna said they heard of a small diner in some nearby town called Eldred. They were going to try to get some food for all of us."

"I couldn't eat anything anyway," Alexei said.

"I hope they get back soon." Eric paused. They could hear the band playing outside. "It's still Sha Na Na! And they've been playing for over an hour!

"Will it ever end?"

"Hendrix is up next. And I want to get a good spot."

"I'd go down there with you, but I'm in too much pain."

"Pain from what?" Eric asked.

"Old war wound." He pointed to his right side. "Acts up from time to time."

"You sure that's all?" Eric asked. "You look really sweaty."

"The heat in this tent is like a steam bath," said Alexei, wincing at the pain. "It's really just the nerves. When a large-caliber bullet tears a hole through you, the skin heals but the nerves stay shattered forever."

"You know I might have something for that." Stein rustled through the zipped-up pockets of his knapsack. "Here we go!"

Stein pulled a small corncob pipe out from the bottom of his bag. There was something packed in the pipe's tiny belly. "This'll calm your nerves."

"More pot?"

"No, this is opium, straight from Afghanistan–the real deal."

"Real what?"

"Just try it."

Eric lit up the pipe and passed it to Alexei, who inhaled and held the smoke in his lungs 'til his face turned red. Then he released it slowly and took another hit, then a third, then a fourth and in a moment, all the contents in the bowl was reduced to ash.

Eric opened up the small aluminum foil ball his brother had given him and put the rest of the dark brown substance in the tiny bowl of the pipe and handed it to Alexei who lit it up. After a while, as the journalist smoked, his pain gradually vanished.

Eric picked up the copy of *Kasabian's Tales* and began reading the back cover copy.

"That book has haunted me," Alexei said. "I don't even know how it got here."

"It must be pretty good."

372

"It's not that, it's just that I got stuck investigating him."

"You! So you arrested him?"

"No. Oh god," Alexei said, feeling the euphoria of the drug in his system. "He never was arrested. It's difficult to explain."

"If it's too personal..."

"Well, I know this sounds odd, but he's the reason I'm here this weekend, putting up with this whole fiasco with Sergei and his daughter."

"Why?"

"Let's just say, I once knew another Armenian father and daughter. Only I did them a grave injustice, so now I'm trying to make up for it in some little way."

"Another Armenian father and daughter? Did Morozov have a daughter?"

"He swore he didn't. I mean, when he looked into my eyes, I really believed it when he said Darya wasn't his daughter."

"Derriere?" Eric kidded.

"Her name was Darya," Alexei pronounced solemnly.

"So if he denied it, why do you think she was his daughter?"

"'Cause he sacrificed everything for her."

"What exactly did he sacrifice?"

With nothing else to do, Alexei told him the entire story of Morozov, Darya, and himself over a quarter of a century earlier.

81

Kasabian, Moscow, 1943

The Armenian writer was awakened by pounding at his front door downstairs in the middle of the night. He initially thought it must be the air raid warden notifying him of another impending Luftwaffe raid and chose to ignore it. But it grew so loud and persistent he finally pulled on his robe and slippers. He shuffled down the stairs, flipped on the outside light, and opened the door. Two men in black leather jackets shoved past him and into the foyer as though they owned the building. The bigger one closed and locked the door.

"What the hell?" Morozov asked, unable to accept what he feared the most.

"Haig Kasabian Morozov?" spoke the larger man with a wandering eye.

"Yes?"

"Get dressed, or we'll bring you in the way you are."

Morozov walked up the stairs to his bedroom with the two NKVD agents close on his heels. They stood a few feet behind him as he pulled on his shirt and pants. His fingers trembled as he knotted his shoes.

"Am I under... arrest?" he finally asked, nearly done.

"Sure," said one of them, casually.

"Can I grab some things?"

"Chop! Chop!" For years he had been warned to have an overnight bag at the ready by his front door, yet he never thought to heed the advice. Now, five years after the worst of the Refinement, he was finally being hauled in. His brain went into survival mode: *If I got a lengthy sentence, I'll need warm clothes.* He grabbed his second overcoat and wool pants and socks and underwear.

"Are you nuts!" the smaller, neurotic agent said, seeing him place the items on his bed. "Take whatever you can fit in your pockets and let's go!"

As he stuffed his gloves and socks into his pockets, he tried to think what they had gotten him for. Was it for associating with Voronsky and the whole Kharms fiasco? Despite the recent Darya debacle, he hadn't said anything incriminating, or done anything illegal.

He wondered if there was any chance of quickly calling the commissar. But then he thought Zhdanov might actually be behind this. When he shoved everything he could into his coat pockets, the larger cop finally swung him toward the door and he headed down the stairs. Although they weren't touching him, the agents were at his back. When he turned sharply into the kitchen, toward the telephone, the bigger cop again grabbed him by his neck and swung him like a rag doll back toward the front door.

"Out!"

It didn't matter. He just remembered that he had disconnected the phone and didn't know Zhdanov's number anyway. A moment later, he was sitting in the back seat of a black sedan pressed next to the larger agent with the wandering eye. The shorter one drove insanely.

These two thugs were old enough to have seen the worst of it, he thought. He could only wonder how many people they themselves must've tortured and executed between them.

Morozov remained silent and just tried to compose himself as the car finally screeched to a halt in front of Lubyanka, the notorious police headquarters. In silence they pulled him out of the car. They led him into the building through the security post and down a flight of stairs to a dank, chilly corridor. He remembered the last time he was here decades earlier when he was coerced into giving a false testimony. Since then he had never stepped foot inside the notorious jail. This is what they all must've went through, he thought, remembering all the warrants he had signed.

He smelled the faint odor of turpentine just as he remembered it years earlier and he wondered if they somehow used it on the prisoners. They shoved him into a small windowless room and locked the door. After a brief claustrophobic pang, he closed his eyes and thought how life over the years had steadily grown more challenging and far less rewarding. If existence was only ever-increasing pain and fear and ever-decreasing joy and happiness, was it really worth it?

Two hours passed before he heard the heavy bolt outside slide open. A pudgy, chinless, middle-aged man with thick glasses was in the doorway clutching a folder.

"Comrade Morozov?"

"I'll sign," he said as though dropping a giant anchor.

"Sign what?"

"Whatever is written on the warrant."

"I'm sorry, comrade," he grinned, "did you think you were under arrest?"

"That's what the officer said."

"Lebitov!" the interrogator yelled out. Suddenly the large agent with the wandering eye filled the doorway. "Did you tell Comrade Morozov that he was under arrest?"

"Did I?" he asked.

"You dolt!" the interrogator yelled out. "Apologize to esteemed writer Morozov. He is our guest here."

"I apologize, esteemed writer Morozov," said the officer flatly, who then exited.

"I just wanted to ask you a few questions if I may."

"May I ask who it is I'm speaking to?" Morozov asked.

"I'm Comrade Arkady Leonovich Petrov. I'm the Deputy Supervisor of Political Security here at the university."

"Alexei works for you?"

"Precisely. He was in charge of your security."

"So he's the one who found evidence of my…"

"He found that someone denounced you, which we now know to be a lie. That person was arrested and is being held as we speak."

"What did he say I did?"

"That you were recruited by the ROA -- Vlasov's scum."

"General Vlasov?" He was the general that Zhdanov had mentioned who had defected along with many of his troops outside of Leningrad, joining with the Nazis. They had started the Liberation Army of the People of Russia.

"We knew these accusations were absurd. That's why I sent for you. Let me apologize for your being put in this cage. I told these morons to bring you to my office down the corridor, but they don't seem to be able to follow simple instructions."

"What are you saying?" Morozov still couldn't grasp the situation.

"We simply wanted you to clear your name so we can properly arrest the real culprit."

The belief that he was about to be summarily executed had been like a hand clamped over his throat. Suddenly, finding that it was the complete opposite, he had to restrain himself from letting out an audible sigh of relief.

"You must be aware of the frenzy of arrests that occurred just a few years back. So many innocent people were locked up for nothing," Petrov said. "We've put an end to all that nonsense."

"Over-prosecution, they called it," Morozov replied sternly. "It was supposed to have ended when Yezhov was executed."

"Precisely! Denunciations are no longer enough."

"So all this happened 'cause one half-wit denounced me!"

"In fairness a little more than a denunciation occurred." Petrov tossed the thick folder he was holding on the small table before him. "Actually it was a very elaborate timeline with detailed statements and a lengthy list of supporting witnesses. We couldn't just ignore it. That's why I sent for you. We needed you to refute it and help us prepare a counterstatement against your detractors. And we're going to try to round them all up."

"How can I help?" Morozov flipped through the typed pages of the file.

"What can you tell me about..." Petrov carefully read the name from his notepad, "a Darya Lebedova Kotova?"

It was like a punch in the gut. This flabby little jellyfish staring at him was barely able to hide his smirk as he relished every detail in this surprise checkmate.

"My cook?"

"Did you give this to your cook?" Petrov asked, placing something small on the folder. Even in the darkness, he knew it was the diamond.

"What exactly is it?" Morozov lied, holding it up. It was Darya's inheritance from her real father.

"It belongs to your cook."

"I haven't even seen her in a while."

"I just learned that," the loathsome creature replied, and snatched the diamond back.

"Where exactly is she?" Morozov asked. "I'd like to hear her denunciation for myself."

The chubby NKVD supervisor picked up the file and flipped on a discreet light switch that made the room slightly brighter. Then he read the opening statement: "I, Darya Lebedova Kotova, attest that while working as the housekeeper for writer Haig Kasabian Morozov, I repeatedly saw him abuse the State University of Moscow and the Cultural Ministry's gift of the Ulanov House. He used it as a base to survey our capital and provide vital information to enemy provocateurs. He did this by leaving messages in the pages of his private library of books, which were on display in his anteroom at the university."

Petrov read on that this Kotova girl alleged that his library of fake books was regularly picked up by a carousel of couriers who posed as students. "The purpose of his accumulated information was instrumental in the recent bombing runs on our factories to the east."

"Insane," Morozov muttered.

"It gets better," Petrov replied, and flipped to another page. "It's fair to assume that Morozov might actually have been using his surveillance information to stage an assassination plot of both our great leader and esteemed members of the Supreme Soviet..."

"I don't believe any of this!" he said in disgust.

"Neither do we."

"No! I don't believe she said this."

"Look for yourself," he said, showing him her signature at the bottom of the neatly typed up confession. There was no point in replying.

"She claims that you secretly allied with the former convict Aleksandr Konstantinovich Voronsky," the pompous dwarf added.

"Voronsky?"

"Fear not," Petrov replied. "Voronsky died five years ago. That's how we know she's lying."

"He died?" Haig could barely talk.

"Back in '38."

No one died in '38. One way or another Voronsky was executed. He must've been communicating with some NKVD impostor. He should've suspected it from the start. So there never was any concern about Kharms' incarceration at all. It must've all just been an elaborate ruse to embarrass him in front of Zhdanov—which was exactly what had happened.

"May I see that?" the writer asked.

Petrov handed him the file. He flipped through the confession that he knew was fake and read an appendix filled with affidavits of various witnesses who systematically denounced him. They included his old friend Critter A/K/A Yuri Petrovich Gallanski, and Kossima Yekta, who he deduced was the name of the older Persian prostitute. Another affidavit was from Laslo Panteleimonovich Kas, one of the construction workers with the wheelbarrow on the sheet of ice. They even had a statement from the counterman during his late night walk, who recounted, "Regrettably I gave the traitor an extra bowl of venison stew." Clearly one silly teenage girl from the Ukraine couldn't have surveilled him all the time and located all these patriotic citizens on her own. Morozov realized they must have had a full roster of agents following his every move around the clock.

"What I need from you, and you can do this at your leisure," Petrov said, "is a full denial of her accusation and hopefully some remarks about her on your own behalf."

"What kind of remarks?"

"Perhaps you might dwell on why she might be so obsessed with you and would make such malicious accusations. Also maybe you can shed some light on your relationship with her."

"Shed light on what? She cooked, I ate."

"She's an attractive young thing from the provinces. Be frank, did she try to seduce you as well?"

"As well?"

"Alexei said she beguiled him."

"Is Novikov here?" Morozov-Kasabian asked.

"Outside, yes," the deputy supervisor replied.

"If he said she seduced him that's a lie," the Armenian writer replied. "They were romantically involved."

"And thank god he was," Petrov replied. "He's the real hero here."

"Can I thank him personally?" Morozov asked tersely.

"Absolutely, I can't spend another moment in this closet anyway." Petrov led Morozov out of the airless room. He walked the writer through the dark, silent corridor that was lined with reinforced metal doors all spaced about ten feet apart, each cell presumably holding a prisoner. Finally at the end of the hallway they came to a clean, well-lit administrative room. When Petrov opened his office door, Morozov saw Alexei seated calmly reading a book.

"Your own girlfriend! Shame on you!" Morozov murmured to the youth.

"Shame on him for what?" Petrov said, turning to the writer. "He saved you! If he hadn't brought this to my attention and instead the girl had brought all this to some other investigator, you could very well be sitting in the jail cell that your accuser is now occupying."

"His kindness is an inspiration to us all," Morozov said, glaring at him.

"All we need right now is for you to deny her charges. Then you can leave," Alexei said softly, trying to expedite the process.

"May I speak to her briefly?" he asked the deputy supervisor, restraining his increasing anger.

"Out of the question. We just need for your denial," Petrov said. "We can interview you more later."

"I'm not denying anything," he replied flat out.

"Haig Kasabian Morozov, either she is lying, in which case you're innocent," Petrov reasoned. "Or she's telling the truth and you're guilty. Now which is it?"

"Neither," he replied. "And if she were here we'd get the truth. That this is all a set-up."

"Well I'm sorry you feel that way…"

"Why the hell am I wasting my time here?!" Morozov finally burst out. "Where's a phone? I intend to call Commissar Zhdanov and have you all locked up!"

"This isn't Leningrad, comrade," Petrov replied, sounding authoritative. "He has no authority here."

"You think I don't know what's going on?! You're all Malenkov's stooges! His little lackeys! Nothing more."

Petrov's face grew beet red as he slid his phone over to him and said, "Call your commissar. It just so happens that I spoke to him last night. We told him that we stumbled upon this elaborate plot to frame you."

"Did you?"

"He fully supported our efforts to prosecute the instigator."

"Did he?" Morozov was unimpressed.

"He was greatly relieved to hear that we were doing everything in our power to protect his old friend." Suddenly one of the leather-jacketed thugs who had brought Morozov in signaled to Petrov who said, "If you'll excuse me for a moment."

The jellyfish stepped outside. As soon as he did, Morozov said to his aide, "She loved you, Alexei Novikov. Do you really think you can live with what you've done?"

"*Live* with it is exactly what I'm doing!" he replied fiercely.

"You probably feel relieved today, but believe me when I tell you that you just took on a burden that'll increase each day until you die."

Alexei silently counted backwards from one hundred.

"I'm not a fool!" Morozov said. "I knew I was targeted as soon as I stepped off the train. But you couldn't get anything on me, so you did the next best thing, didn't you?"

"And what's that?" Petrov asked Morozov, returning in time to hear him.

"You discovered this poor delusional girl."

"Delusional, how?

"She thinks she's my daughter."

"And why would she think that?" Petrov asked.

"Because twenty years ago, I had an affair with her mother. I wanted to marry her, but she left me for someone else. Darya Lebedova Kotova is not my daughter, I wish she were– but she's not."

"There's no law against impregnating some cute kulak," Petrov replied with a smirk. "That's why god created kulaks."

"If Darya's not your daughter, why does she even matter to you?" Alexei interrupted.

"Because she has no part in any of this," Morozov said, "but I was friends with her father. "A backstabbing drunk named Dimitri Lunz who vanished twenty years ago."

"Comrade, nothing you said exculpates her," Petrov replied, and sternly added, "and even if she is an innocent, we still need to send a message, don't we?"

"What possible message are you sending?" the writer asked. "And to whom are you sending it?!"

"To pesky upstarts from the outer republics, like the Ukraine, who think they can just waltz into our capital, our turf," Petrov said, pointing into Kasabian's chest, "and step on our toes like they own the place."

When one of the leather-jacketed thugs entered and briefly chatted with Petrov, Alexei whispered to Haig, "I didn't sacrifice her for you, if that's what you're thinking."

"You could've fooled me."

"I begged her to help turn you in, but she refused. Wouldn't budge."

Morozov didn't say a word until Petrov returned, at which point Alexei exited.

"Darya Kotova was right," Morozov spoke up. "I admit it now. I was sent here by Vlasov to kill Stalin. Now arrest me and give her a medal."

"You know the answer to that. I can't arrest you, can I?" he replied. "What I want to know is why do you even care?"

"Because you and I, comrades, are done. We're nasty, old men who killed others to survive–and for what?" Morozov asked. "She still cares about others. That's why she's in this mess. And she is someone's daughter."

"Hopefully not anyone whose literary works can be pulled from the shelves throughout our great country, not someone whose name can be stricken from the record of history for all time," Petrov replied. Alexei reentered and took his seat.

"Do you think Darya should be executed?" Morozov asked him.

"She's not going to be executed," he replied softly. "She'll be sentenced and hopefully grow up along the way."

382

Realizing that his fighting to free Darya only gave Petrov pleasure, Morozov finally said, "So be it. Do what you will. Am I free to go?"

"Actually, I changed my mind. I'm going to break our rules and grant you the one request you made earlier. Come with me, please," Petrov said, and nodding at his two thugs, they followed. As Alexei rose, the deputy supervisor said, "No, you stay."

Petrov then led Morozov and the thugs out into the dark corridor and down the hall. After walking down a flight of stairs to the basement and through a maze of hallways, he stopped at one cell door. There he took out a key and opened it.

A small figure was lying on a cot. In the dim light it was hard to determine her age or sex. But her crudely cut hair still had long strands attached. As his eyes adjusted to the light, Morozov saw that her face was bruised. Her eyes were swollen shut. Her nose and lips were split.

"You wanted to confront your accuser," Petrov said to Morozov. "Here you are."

The Armenian just stood frozen in the doorway. He wasn't sure if she was awake or not. She laid perfectly still.

"Darya Kotova!" he feebly called out. She didn't so much as twitch. He sensed that she was on some sedative. Morozov stumbled back into the hallway clearly shaken.

The pudgy man closed the steel cell door and said, "Fear not, the human spirit is more resilient than steel." It was the title of one of Morozov's more popular stories. The Armenian was silently driven back home by the two who had arrested him.

82

Alexei, Woodstock Festival, 1969

"So you turned in your own girlfriend?" Eric asked the Russian journalist after he relayed the full story of the Armenian writer and his possibly secret Ukrainian daughter.

"I begged her to work with me. It was either her or me," he replied tiredly. After three days of surviving with Anna O'Brien, Eric had some idea of what it was like trying to navigate a self-absorbed personality.

"And the Armenian writer couldn't help her?"

"Nothing he could do would change the outcome at that point," Alexei said, feeling relaxed due to the opium he had just smoked. His pain was all but gone.

"Oh shit!" Stein suddenly blurted, bolting upright in the tent. Eric was suddenly aware that Sha Na Na had stopped playing. "I can't fucking believe Anna's not back! And Hendrix is coming on now! Shit! Well, I waited through this whole concert for this guy! I'm gonna go." He grabbed a couple things.

"Wait," Alexei said, letting out a great sigh. "I'm coming with you!"

"Are you sure?"

"I waited eighteen hours to see to see this magical Hendrix. And I'm suffocating in here."

Eric crawled out of the tent. Alexei was no longer immobilized due to the wonderful gift from Josh's little pipe. With young Stein's help, he rose to his feet, a little wobbly. He couldn't stop grinning. He still felt something, a tingling in his side, but the pain was more theoretical than real. Once outside, they looked down the slope. Both were surprised to see that the vast majority of the concert-goers had vanished. The morning light revealed the cost of the concert. Trees, bushes, and grass along the entire side of the little hill were chewed up, leaving an array of trash.

Before heading down to the stage, Stein froze and scribbled something in his notebook. The youth tore the page out and left it just inside the floor of the tent. Alexei read: "WE'RE WATCHING HENDRIX! COME JOIN US!"

Stein slowly led Alexei down the muddy slope through the greatly diminished crowd. As they passed one garbage pile that included a tangle of discarded aluminum lawn chairs, Alexei snatched one that still worked and partially used it as a cane. The closer they got to the stage, the more dense the mob of youths became.

Ten minutes later, they finally nudged and inched their way through the crowd. Once they found a spot, seeing that the older guy was painfully limping, some of the kids pulled back, allowing Alexei to pry open the folding chair and plop down into it. From there, he cast his eyes upon the legendary minstrel. He was surprised to see he was a young, light-skinned African with scruffy facial hair. Hendrix was wearing a white leather jacket and had a red bandanna tied tightly around his springy hair. His band was still loading their equipment onto the stage.

"I can't believe Anna's missing this!" Stein groaned. "We came all the way up here just for him. It was all she spoke of! Him and Janis! And she slept through Janis."

"You're both young," Alexei replied. "You'll see them again."

As the band tested their instruments, Eric said he was going to dash up to the tent one last time and try to find Anna. While waiting for him, as the opium began to wear off, the pain in Alexei's belly began to gradually return. An ache gradually intensified like a dagger slowly being slipped into his gut. The pain only became manageable if he remained perfectly still.

While all eyes were fixed on Hendrix, Alexei kept staring the other way, up the slope for his young companion who he was now dependent upon. While glancing around, the Russian journalist started realizing how the contours of the slope really did look like the only battlefield he had ever fought on. He clearly remembered waiting all day for the German attack. Only now in direct contrast to this festival did he realize how utterly quiet his comrades were. Thousands of young untested troops held their collective breaths, as if hoping the lethal Nazi force would simply pass them by.

When Eric finally returned minutes later empty-handed, he could see that the older Russian journalist was pale, feverish, and muttering to himself in the heat.

"What are you saying?" he asked.

"I really did love her, but the reason I turned her in," he muttered, "was the fear. I just couldn't go back."

"Back?"

"I still don't know how I escaped that slaughter the first time, but I knew there was no way I would survive it a second time."

"Survive what?"

"The meat grinder," he said tiredly and grinned. "It took a lot of courage to be a coward."

Eric couldn't imagine being so terrified that he'd turn in someone he loved. Sensing he was scaring the young man, Haig smiled and said, "I'm okay."

In another minute, Hendrix was finally strumming his guitar and singing in his relaxed yet powerful voice. Young Stein shut his eyes and just rocked his head back and forth becoming part of the experience. Alexei closed his eyes as well, trying to collect his strength and not dwell on the sharp, steadily increasing stabbing sensation that seemed to spread throughout his body. After this final performance, this bizarre three-day test of human endurance, Sergei would load them all into his car and speed him non-stop to Aeroflot Flight 31B, window seat 4, where after a couple stiff drinks he'd be good as new. He closed his eyes and tried not to focus on the slow, sharp jabs he was experiencing. Although it had been only a week or so, it felt as though he had been away from home for years. After a couple songs, Hendrix took a brief intermission, at which time Eric said: "That Armenian writer and daughter who you mentioned before..."

"Morozov?"

"Yeah. If she really loved the guy she thought was her dad, why did she squeal on him?"

"Squeal on him?"

"I mean, why did she confess to you guys about him?"

"Confess to us?" Alexei asked absently.

"Didn't you say that she gave up the diamond and signed a statement claiming he was a spy? Did someone forge her signature?"

"Oh no, she signed it. That was real," Alexei realized what he was talking about.

386

"So why'd she turn on him?"

"After four days in solitary confinement, not being allowed to sleep or eat, interrogations interrupted by torture, it turns your brain into mush," Alexei explained. "Darya was a nineteen-year-old kid. She didn't have a chance. Then that old sadist Petrov took all the work that Ivan had already done, all the round-the-clock surveillance reports, and sculpted it into an elaborate accusation from the daughter against her father. A brilliant work of art."

"But you said he wasn't arrested."

"He wasn't."

"So I'd hardly call it brilliant," Eric said. "All this work, and he didn't even get arrested."

"That's just it," Alexei said. "We couldn't have arrested him anyway. So Petrov did one better."

"What?"

"A few days after being released, Morozov showed up at the Spring Faculty Luncheon and in front of Professor Alexandrovich and most of the senior faculty, he announced that his real reason for coming to Moscow was to shoot Comrade Stalin. He openly called him a homicidal maniac who had done far worse to Russia than the Nazis and all the tzars combined."

"He said that!"

"He sure did. Everyone knew he had cracked. Professor Alexandrovich tried to protect him, saying the poor man clearly suffered from a mental collapse and he immediately tried to get him packed up and put on a train back down to Yerevan. But the Armenian wouldn't budge. The next day word spread about his public betrayal. Petrov and his thugs went to his house where they found that he had killed himself."

"In his brief bio in the back of the book it only said he died," Eric remembered.

"Yeah, that's the official story. But he shot himself with some old pistol, a real relic. No one knew where he got it. What was amazing was that he left a note, reiterating his elaborate betrayal, everything he had said at the luncheon."

"Wow!" Eric said earnestly.

"His death was just the beginning," Alexei grinned. "The whole point of the investigation was to embarrass Commissar Zhdanov, so Petrov released a copy of the suicide note to the press. Everyone might've assumed it was a forgery, but Morozov stated the contents of the letter openly to a room full of professors who corroborated it. It was all over the newspapers. There was clearly no coercion. So immediately everyone denounced him. And soon, so did Zhdanov, who was greatly embarrassed, just as Malenkov had hoped."

"What happened to Zhdanov?" Eric asked.

"Officially, he died a few years later. Unofficially, let's just say it was very sudden."

"I guess when you're dead, it doesn't matter what happens afterwards."

"It does in the Soviet Union! And you need to understand that to realize *why* Morozov did what he did."

"Don't people kill themselves 'cause they hate their lives?"

"By all indications he hated life for years. And even then he could've quietly killed himself leaving his reputation fully intact. His suicide was designed to erase all traces of himself from this earth."

"How does one do that?"

"The day the news of his betrayal broke, all his books were pulled from all libraries and probably every private shelf in Russia. Within a week, it was like he never existed. No obituary, no memorial. They didn't even put a headstone on his grave."

"But how about that book that you gave me?" he asked.

"The final joke was on him," Alexei smirked. "Ten years pass and what do they do? They rehabilitate him. His book is back on the shelf. They even ignored his wishes and put his family name on it. He's now one of the more popular Soviet-Armenian writers. Supposedly a bust of him was erected somewhere in Yerevan."

"And what about the girl who wasn't his daughter?" Stein asked as Hendrix finally strutted back to the stage.

"I heard she got a stiff sentence, but I don't know what it was. In Russia they don't publish articles about this," he said. "She was only twenty-one and that was twenty-six years ago."

"So she'd be forty-seven now," Eric said.

Suddenly, a roar of applause went up, ending their conversation. Hendrix began strumming. They listened for about ten minutes before Alexei collapsed forward toppling out of his lawn chair. As the music blared, Stein tried lifting him, but was unable. He was breathing, in clear pain. Another lanky, long haired man about ten years older finally pushed through.

"Need help?" he yelled into Eric's ear.

"Yeah. He's got a stomach injury from World War Two," Eric yelled back. They could both see the profound agony in Alexei's contorted face.

The hippie touched Alexei's stomach and slowly felt downward until Alexei let out a shriek above the rock music.

"He looks septic. I think his appendix has burst." The educated hippie apparently had some medical training. "We need to get him out of here at once."

"Should we carry him?"

"No, moving him could spread the infection. He needs a wheelchair. We gotta stabilize him. You stay with him, I'll run up to the medical tent and get help." The hippie pushed his way through the rocking concert-goers.

"I'm with you, pal," Stein shouted into Alexei's ear, taking his hand.

Alexei breathed deeply until his pain grew bearable. He closed his eyes and listened as Hendrix played an odd yet familiar tune. As he slowly lapsed into unconsciousness, he realized it was a tense, twangy rendition of the American national anthem.

83

Eric, NYC, September 11, 2001

Most of those who tried to duck out were turned back at the Sky Lobby and told to go back to their offices until the North Tower was completely evacuated. His assistant, Mann, was among them.

"Caught trying to chicken out," one of the proofreaders said to him as Eric joined them.

"Yeah," he grinned. "They got cops in the Sky Lobby. "I should've sneaked down the stairs."

"Hey Eric, toast!" His assistant Ames had gotten three expensive bottles of chilled champagne from the caterers and was pouring it out to fellow workers.

Although he was operating on zero sleep, Eric was energized that the IPO was over and the worst was behind them. He knocked back a couple glasses of the bubbly before it went to his head. He had to use the bathroom.

"Mr. Stein!" the Vogue model secretary called out to him. "I got Mr. Oden on the line. He'd like to speak to you." She pointed to an extension. Apparently the ground lines were still working.

"I just heard that a plane crashed into one of the World Trade Centers. Are you okay?" Oden asked tensely. He could hear the news broadcasting in the background of Oden's office.

"Yeah, fortunately we're in the tower that wasn't hit."

"Thank god," Oden said. "Was it a Cessna?"

"No, I think it's a commericial airline," Eric said and added, "but, if the Empire State Building could withstand an air force bomber crashing into it, I'm sure the North Tower is going to be fine."

"Is the deal done?"

"Yeah, all parties have signed." Eric knocked back another cup of champagne. "But we can't leave the building 'til they empty the North Tower."

"It sounds like you're under attack," Oden half-kidded.

"Under attack by millions of dollars," Eric joked back.

"Well, congratulations, boy! You did it. This is a very important deal for all of us."

"I appreciate the call, but things are still hopping around here, so I should run." All the coffee and champagne was going right to his bladder. He had to piss something fierce.

"When you get back up here we're going to celebrate!"

"Soon as they let us out."

When Eric hung up, the sexy secretary said to him, "Mr. Lande is asking if you could join him in his office."

"Is it urgent?" he asked.

"I think he just wants to celebrate," she said with a smile.

"Could you direct me to the men's room first?" He rose.

She pointed to the door and as two co-workers were leaving, he went inside.

It was empty. Eric walked to the end of a long line of vacant marble urinals. As he unzipped, he sighed and thought, *Life from here on is going to get much easier.* While he peed, he thought about Oden's joke, *"It sounds like you're under attack."* From that came the thought, *Wouldn't it be amazing if this was an attack? The Twin Towers are two of the largest buildings in New York City. How the hell can the pilot not see them?* He further thought, *if someone deliberately flew a plane into the first tower.... No!* He reasoned if that was the case, this would be a big military operation. *If someone ordered someone else to fly a plane into the first tower, wouldn't they also have someone fly a second plane into the other tower? My tower.* Eric finished pissing but stood there slightly drunk, just holding himself. He remained frozen at the possibility that at any second another plane was going to strike his building. He thought about his wife Edna and his son Eriq and finally pulled up his zipper. As he washed his hands, he thought, *If I discreetly sneaked into the hallway, dashed down all those floors and out of the building and a second plane doesn't hit, I am going to be the laughing stock of the office for all time. But I could just say I felt nauseous. Simple as that. What are the odds that this wasn't really an accident and a second plane was actually on its way,* he thought. *On the other hand, if a plane does crash into this building, this many flights up, what are the chances of surviving. Play it safe,* his tired brain thought, *just walk out the door and down the stairs.* He closed his eyes and waited for the fear.

Made in the USA
Middletown, DE
23 December 2024